The Man I Think I Know

MIKE GAYLE

The Man I Think
I Know

HODDER &
STOUGHTON

First published in Great Britain in 2018 by Hodder & Stoughton
An Hachette UK company

1

Copyright © Mike Gayle 2018

A CIP catalogue record for this title is available from the British Library

Hardback ISBN 978 1 473 60898 6
eBook ISBN 978 1 473 60897 9
Trade Paperback ISBN 978 1 473 60900 6

Typeset in Plantin by Palimpsest Book Production Limited, Falkirk, Stirlingshire

Printed and bound in Great Britain by Clays Ltd, St Ives plc

Hodder & Stoughton policy is to use papers that are natural, renewable and recyclable products and made from wood grown in sustainable forests. The logging and manufacturing processes are expected to conform to the environmental regulations of the country of origin.

Hodder & Stoughton Ltd
Carmelite House
50 Victoria Embankment
London EC4Y 0DZ

www.hodder.co.uk

To Claire, for everything

PROLOGUE

Headmaster's Speech,
King's Scrivener Boys' School, Warwick
16 June 1997

'Thank you, Chairman of Governors, esteemed guests, governors, parents and last but by no means least, boys of King's Scrivener upper sixth. Today you will join a fraternity that from its inception in 1765 has been at the forefront of making our nation great. King's Scrivener old boys, young men like you, have gone on from this esteemed institution to become leading lights in the fields of science, the arts, law, medicine, finance, education and politics. King's Scrivener has produced countless medics, academics and scientists at the top of their chosen field of study, along with Booker and Turner prize winners for work in the arts. In the world of politics KS old boys can count among their number members of government past and present, ranging from foreign secretaries to Chancellors of the Exchequer, not to mention two prime ministers.

'This past month alone I have read of the pioneering work and achievements of King's Scrivener old boys in the fields of stem cell technology, Broadway theatre, literature and jurisprudence. To my albeit admittedly biased mind, it seems that wherever there is excellent work to be done, lives to be saved, history to be made and new frontiers to be explored, you will find a King's Scrivener old boy embodying the spirit of the school motto, "*Sic parvis magna*".

'In keeping with this tradition, you young men have produced the single best A-level results this school has ever seen, resulting in a record-breaking number of you heading off to some of the world's greatest educational institutions. To single out any individual feels unjust, but as you know, it has been a longstanding

King's Scrivener tradition to honour our founding father, Sir Thomas Carmody, by awarding a prize to a single pupil in recognition of greatness across the sporting and academic disciplines. Famous winners of the Carmody prize have included a former head of MI6, a world renowned sculptor and a prominent media proprietor, every Carmody prize winner – whether or not in the global spotlight – has gone on to some form of greatness. And so it is with no small amount of trepidation that I announce that the winner of the 1997 King's Scrivener Boys' School Carmody prize for outstanding achievement is . . .'

I

Danny

'You're stopping my dole money?'

The employment officer sitting at the desk across from me here at Coventry Job Centre Plus – mid-forties, blond-highlighted hair and a permanent air of 'This is hurting me more than it's hurting you' about her – nods.

'I'm afraid you've left us with no other choice, Mr Allen,' she says despondently. 'According to our records you've been given several warnings both written and verbal that action would be taken if we failed to receive evidence of you actively seeking employment. That evidence hasn't been forthcoming, therefore we have no choice but to—'

'—stop my money?'

'I know it's difficult to hear, Mr Allen, but you must appreciate we only ever take action of this kind as a last resort.'

A half smile rises briefly to my lips at the use of the phrase 'last resort'. It sounds like a holiday destination for people too broke to afford a real trip abroad, a Benidorm for the dejected, a Mallorca for the clinically depressed.

Maya is absolutely going to lose it when she finds out about this. She's going to go through the roof. She always said this would happen if I didn't sort myself out, and now it has. This could be the straw that breaks the camel's back, the end of everything, the end of Maya and me.

'What if I apply for a job right now?' I say, grasping at straws. 'I mean it, any job at all – I don't care what it is, cleaning toilets, sweeping the streets, you name it, I'll apply for it. Surely that's got to make a difference?'

She shakes her head sadly. 'I'm afraid in terms of today's

decision, Mr Allen, it won't make any difference at all. The sanction comes into effect the moment you fail to respond to your third warning and I'm afraid it can't be repealed under any circumstances.'

Brimming with rage, I shove my hands deep into the pockets of my jeans and scatter the contents one fistful at a time on to the desk in front of me: a fifty pence piece, a receipt for two jars of grilled peppers from Poundland, a bus ticket and a crumpled tissue. For her part my employment officer wordlessly evaluates the pocket detritus as if it's an avant-garde art installation but I can see she understands what I'm saying, she understands completely. With eyes fixed on the pocket debris, she opens a drawer to her left and pulls out two crisp white business cards.

I take them from her one at a time and read them carefully. The first has contact details for Coventry Citizens Advice Bureau emblazoned across it and the second is for a local food bank called Helping Hands.

I am truly screwed.

She straightens up in her chair as if to say, 'I think we both know that this is the end of the conversation.' I consider tearing the business cards up as a final act of defiance but in the end even that seems too much like hard work and so instead I tuck them into my jacket pocket, scrape the rubbish from the desk into my open hand and thank her for her time.

Taking a seat on the low brick wall outside the job centre, I roll myself a cigarette. While I smoke it I marvel at sights of the city I call home on a grey January Monday morning: huge grimey lorries loaded with goods from continental Europe, an assortment of cars carrying solitary passengers lost deep in thought, daredevil motorcyclists weaving in and out of the traffic. Across the road a group of young Muslim college girls wearing brightly patterned hijabs are laughing and joking, while on my side of the pavement two young men dressed in sharp suits and reeking of mid-priced aftershave stride purposely towards me, talking intensely about targets and sales figures, barely registering my existence.

I'm going to have to get a job.

I know this but at the same time it feels like I don't.

I'm going to have to get a job.

Maybe I should say it aloud instead of simply whispering it in my head?

'I'm going to have to get a job.'

No, it doesn't make any difference. I still don't want to work. I don't want to do anything at all. If I'm honest, all I really want is to be left alone.

There's no physical reason why at the age of thirty-six I can't work for a living.

I have two arms, two legs and the body that goes with them. Obviously with the fags, junk food and lack of exercise I'm not exactly what you might call a prime example of physical fitness but if I rocked up at my doctors' surgery and asked to be signed off work due to poor health, I'm pretty sure they'd laugh me right out of the consulting room.

Equally, it's not as though I couldn't find a job if I actually tried. Only last week I saw adverts for vacancies for work in an abattoir, on a building site, six retail 'opportunities', half a dozen telesales jobs and a position as a trainee embalmer. There are jobs aplenty if you're that way inclined. But I'm not interested in any of them and haven't been for a very long time.

It's not as if I haven't worked in the past. I've had plenty of jobs in my time: bar jobs, cleaning jobs, cooking jobs, warehouse jobs, labouring jobs, retail jobs, telesales jobs, call centre jobs and (and this was my least favourite) a job filling large metal drums with cooking oil day after day. While most of the jobs I've had I've hated, there have been a number I've enjoyed (I have particularly fond memories of a job I had once planting bulbs for the Council's Parks and Recreations Division) but the one thing they all have in common is that I never lasted more than a few months in any of them.

Employment and me do not work well together.

Employment and me do not get along.

The thing about work is that it's a habit. If you do it enough. it sort of sticks so that you feel wrong if you're not doing something. But when it doesn't stick, if for example something happens somewhere along the way so that you don't form that habit, and instead spend long periods of time barely going outside, let alone being part of the labour market, then work will inevitably always feel sort of alien. Like a thing that other people do. Like a foreign delicacy made of animal entrails that the locals love but you just can't seem to drum up the appetite for. Even thinking about working makes me feel queasy.

This I know makes me sound a lot like I have no ambition. It presents me as almost having given up on life. It suggests that I'm content to just exist like some corpulent bluebottle basking in the sunshine on the windowsill of life. The thing is, I just don't see the point in it all any more and haven't done for a very long time. I don't get it: why would you willingly spend a huge chunk of your finite time on earth doing stuff that ultimately amounts to nothing, spending day after day with people you can't stand, in order to earn money to buy things you'll never use? Wouldn't you much rather be sat at home in your favourite old tracksuit bottoms and hoodie watching a compilation edition of *Homes Under The Hammer* while some other mug pays your way? I know I would.

I leave it until after Maya returns home from work and we've eaten tea to break the news to her about my money being stopped. When she inevitably says, 'I told you this would happen,' I nod and look away because it's true. Her exact words to me a little over a week ago as we sat on this very sofa, watching this very same TV programme were, 'The dole are going to stop your money if you're not careful,' to which I'd replied, 'Think about it, babe, how many long-term unemployed people are there claiming dole? Do you really think they're going to bother with me? I'd have a better chance of winning the lottery.'

It could be you.

I can feel Maya's eyes on me, even though I'm not looking at her. I can tell she wants to know what I'm going to do about this. She wants to know that I have a plan. But the truth is I don't know what I'm going to do about anything and I don't have a plan. And so I keep quiet and she keeps quiet too, until we use up all the quiet in the room so that finally one of us has to say something.

'What are you going to do?' she asks. 'What's your plan?'

'I don't know.'

'Well, you should.'

'We'll be fine, I promise.'

'How exactly? Have you got a secret stash of money I don't know about? Isn't it enough that I already pay for everything around here? Isn't it enough that I've put up with this for so long?'

I turn my head towards Maya and our gaze meets awkwardly. While I'd been fully braced to see disappointment in my girlfriend's eyes, I'm taken aback by the depth of it. It's as if I'm looking into two vast tawny reservoirs of disillusion and regret. I think perhaps Maya is aware of how she's feeling, because she is the first to look away. She hates herself for being hard on me. She thinks that somehow she's letting the side down. She thinks that somehow she's letting down the version of her that first fell in love with me. The version who, two and a half years earlier, when I'd informed her that I wasn't really boyfriend material, had responded with the words, 'We'll see about that.'

She sighs and runs her fingers through her hair. 'I'm sorry, I shouldn't have said that, it was spiteful.'

'But that doesn't mean it isn't true.'

She looks tired and ground down by life. 'I think I'm going to have a bath and get an early night.' She makes her words sound deliberately half-hearted as if to take the sting out of the fact that we both know an early bath followed by bed is shorthand for, 'I can't be around you right now.'

As she picks up our empty plates, I smile to make it clear that I'm grateful she's even vaguely considering my feelings at this moment and she returns it in a perfunctory fashion before leaving the room. For a moment I wonder if I should follow her and reassure her that somehow things will be okay, that I'll work something out. Before I can get to my feet, however, she's back at the door, but only half enters the room, almost as if she's afraid of getting sucked into the vortex of despondency lurking within.

'Danny?'

'Yeah?'

'I know you might not want to see it this way but I've been thinking this could be exactly what you need. I hate that you're stuck is this pokey flat all day, every day. I hate seeing you wasting your life like this. There's so much that you could give the world if only you'd try, so much that you could do if only you wanted to.'

I thank her for being so kind because it is nice of her to try and see the world from my point of view, when it's probably the last thing she wants to do, but once she's gone from the room and I hear the bath running, I make a special effort to delete every word she's just said from my mind. I adore that woman, I really do, from the hairs on her head to the ends of her toes, but she's wrong about me having anything to offer the world. She's wrong about the difference trying hard would make to anything at all. What she doesn't understand is that even if I got a job tomorrow, one that paid well, engaged me on every level and handed me back my self respect, nothing about me is ever going to change, not now, not ever. Some people are simply beyond redemption or salvation or whatever, some of us are simply stuck being what we are.

2

James

'But I asked you not to do that.'

'Do what, darling?'

'Cut up my food.'

'Oh, I am sorry, have I done it the wrong way? Is that the problem?'

'I have asked you lots of times not to do it and you have just carried on. I am thirty-six years old. I am a grown man. I can cut up my own food.'

It was last Monday when I reminded my mum, Erica, not to cut up my food before she brings it to the table.

I know it was a Monday because my dad, Don, and my mum, Erica, and I were having lamb chops, potatoes and broccoli. We always have lamb chops, new potatoes and broccoli on a Monday. On Tuesdays we have baked salmon, new potatoes and broccoli. On Wednesdays we have chicken, mashed potatoes and broccoli. And I think that if I thought about it for long enough, I could probably remember what we are having for supper for the rest of the week too.

Anyway, last Monday my mum, Erica, put my food in front of me already cut into tiny pieces and I said, 'Mum, please don't cut my food up when you bring it to the table. I can cut it up myself.' And she said, 'Of course, next time I won't.' But when next time came around, she just did it again.

My dad, Don, says my mum, Erica, sometimes forgets things because she is a bit run down and needs an early night. And because I sometimes forget things too since The Incident, I try not to make it into a big deal because I know that she means well. So that is why I did not say anything all the other nights she carried on chopping up my food. But when she did it again just now, I felt as if I had just had enough. I felt like I did not want her chopping up my food any more. It was okay for her to do it when I was getting better but I am stronger now and can cut up my own food.

'Of course you can cut up your own food,' says my mum, Erica. 'I'm such a silly to forget like that. I promise it won't happen again.'

Everything goes back to normal after this. My dad asks my mum about her plans for the rest of the week and my mum asks my dad the same question, and they chat away to each other until I ask my mum to pass me the salt.

'I'm not sure you should be eating so much salt,' she says, 'it's not good for you.'

'But I like salt on my food.'

'I know you do, darling, but my GP is forever telling me to cut down on my salt intake because it's not good for my blood pressure, so he's bound to say the same about you. I'll get you the Lo-salt if you like. I haven't seen it for months on end but I'm sure it's in one of the cupboards somewhere.'

As she gets up from the table to get the Lo-salt, I say, 'Why?' and she turns around.

'Why what darling?'

'Why would your GP say the same about me? I have not got high blood pressure.'

My mum, Erica, and my dad, Don, look at each other then at me. Dad says, 'I think what your mother is trying to say, James, is that we all probably need to cut down on our salt intake. Isn't that right, darling? I mean my blood pressure is fine but then again, cutting down on my salt intake won't do me any harm.'

I push out my chair so that I can stand up. This is quite difficult for me to do because my right leg does not work as well as it used to.

'Where are you going?' asks Mum.

'To my room,' I say. 'I am not hungry any more.'

Dad says, 'James,' in a voice that sounds as if he is really tired, and Mum says, 'No, Don, it's all right. Let him go,' in a voice that sounds a lot like she might want to cry.

The next day after breakfast my dad and I go out in the car to Stratford-upon-Avon to run some errands while my mum has some quiet time. My parents and I live in their farmhouse in Stow-on-the-Wold. Before The Incident, when I was just about to become an MP, I lived with my girlfriend Zara in a penthouse apartment in the centre of Birmingham. The apartment was in one of my own developments from when I used to be a property developer. Now though, I live with my mum and dad and I am not an MP or a property developer, and Zara is no longer my girlfriend.

Today is a Thursday.

My dad, Don, used to work in finance but he does not now because he is retired. He used to work in The City and was almost always away from home even at the weekends. These days he is at home all the time and mostly mows the lawn and plays golf with friends and takes my mum to all the places she wants to go.

When I asked my mum, Erica, what she would do with her quiet time while dad and I were out, she smiled and said, 'I'm sure I'll find something to occupy me.'

In the car my dad listens to the radio. On the radio two women are talking. At first my dad, Don, seems fine listening to the two women talking but the more they say the more he sighs. When one woman on the radio asks the other woman on the radio how important the role of breastfeeding is to her as a young mother, my dad sighs and switches it off.

'I'm as much a man of the world as the next fellow,' he says, 'but I genuinely have no idea why they feel the need to talk about that sort of thing on the radio. Can't they just chat about books or tell us something interesting about history? Why does everything these days have to be about bodily functions?'

I am not sure if my dad wants an answer because it is not clear from his voice. I have not got anything to say anyway so I decide to keep quiet and look out of the window.

Where we live in Stow-on-the-Wold there are lots of trees and the roads are narrow and everything is very green. But soon all of that is left behind and there are lots of houses, shops and petrol stations and the roads are big and wide. When I lived in my penthouse apartment in Birmingham, I was so high up that I could see all across the city. It was a lovely view during the day but it was absolutely at its best at night because the city looked like it went on forever.

'You know you shouldn't have spoken to your mother like that,' says my dad as we sit at traffic lights. 'She was very upset by what you said.'

'All I said was that I did not want her to cut my food up any more.'

'I know, son, but your mother . . . she's . . . well . . . I suppose what I'm trying to say is that she tries her best, you know that, don't you? And well, I think perhaps we shouldn't have any more outbursts like that.'

'But I was just telling her that I did not want my food cut up.'

'I know you were, James, and I understand that completely but your mother's not like you and me, is she? She's well, you know, sensitive and so all I'm saying is whatever that was yesterday, let's try not to do it again, okay? It's just not worth the botheration.'

I say, 'Fine okay,' because I do not really want to talk about it any more and then he turns the radio on again. The first woman on the radio has stopped asking questions about breastfeeding and is now talking to a different woman on the radio about being a political activist in Iran. My dad grins at me and pretends to wipe sweat from his forehead. I think this might be a joke about breastfeeding, but then again I am not sure.

In Stratford-upon-Avon we run errands that my mum, Erica, has scribbled down on a sheet of paper for my dad, so that he does not forget them. Dad will be sixty-seven on his next birthday and is always saying his memory is not quite what it used to be. Whenever he says this, I always think to myself, 'Well, at least it is not as bad as mine.' I never say this out loud though, because I do not think he would find it funny. My parents never joke about The Incident. In fact, if they can help it, they never talk about it at all.

On my mum's list are things like picking up an Internet order from Waitrose, getting spare keys cut for the lock for one of our outbuildings, buying cards for some family members who have birthdays coming up, returning a cardigan that she bought from Laura Ashley which on second thoughts she decided made her look like 'mutton dressed as lamb', and picking up some broccoli from the Sainsbury's local for tonight's supper.

As we leave the supermarket with our broccoli, my dad, Don, tells me about the last item on the list.

'I need to pick up mum's necklace from the jeweller's,' he says. 'You know, the one I'm getting her as an anniversary present.'

My parents have been married for a long time. I cannot remember how long but it is long enough for them to be having a big party to celebrate. They are inviting lots of family and friends and it is being held at their favourite Italian restaurant in Broadway which is not very far from where we live.

I am not looking forward to it.

I do not like parties.

I do not like to be around too many people at once.

It makes thinking even harder.

Dr Acari, my neurologist, once tried to explain to my mum, Erica, what it is like to be me in a room crowded with people. He said, 'Imagine trying to say your thirteen times table while half a dozen people are shouting in your ear and you'll not be far off the mark.'

Dr Acari is right. It can be a lot like that. I think it is also a lot like trying to remember what you had for breakfast two weeks ago while a wasp buzzes in your ear.

Before The Incident I was the Labour MP for Birmingham South. Well, when I say that I was an MP, what I mean is that I was elected. Because of The Incident I never got to make my maiden speech in parliament. This makes me sad when I think about it because I think I would have been a good MP. And I think I would have made a good speech too.

Before I became an MP I was the managing director of DeWitt and Partners. It was a property development company.

My company used to turn old office blocks into residential apartments.

I do not work in property development or have ambitions to be in politics any more.

Mostly I just sit in my room watching DVDs.

My five favourite DVDs to watch are:

1. *Friends* (box set)
2. *Die Hard*
3. *The Matrix*
4. *The Bourne Ultimatum*
5. *Bad Boys II*

In the jeweller's Dad shows me Mum's necklace. I tell him she will love it because it is exactly the sort of thing she likes. Mum has lots of jewellery like it already and I tell Dad that he has chosen well. The lady in the jeweller's asks me if I think my mother will like it but because my speech is so slurred, she has to ask me to repeat what I say. Ashley, my speech therapist, says that even though my voice sometimes sounds fine in my head, it can come out slurred. I am a lot better than I used to be though. I used to be a lot worse and not even my mum, dad or my sister Martha could understand me.

In the car on the way home Dad tells me how he is going to present the necklace to Mum on Saturday at their wedding anniversary party and then tells me the story again of how they met.

It was at a summer ball.

My dad, Don, and my mum, Erica, were both at Oxford University.

My dad, Don, was studying Economics and my mum, Erica, was studying Art History. At the summer ball Dad asked Mum to dance with him, even though he could not dance. Dad stepped on Mum's toes a lot of times during that dance but Mum did not let on that he had hurt her feet until they were married four years later. 'And now here we are,' says my dad, and he laughs like he has made a joke.

I cannot help thinking that what my dad, Don, means is that because Mum did not tell him he was hurting her feet forty years ago, he is sitting in a car with me. If Mum had told him that he was hurting her feet, he could have got embarrassed and then I would not be here and my dad would be in a different car with a different son called possibly James or more likely something else.

That evening at dinner my mum, Erica, does not cut up my food and she does not do it the evening after either. But the evening after that, as Dad and I sit down at the table, she presents me with a meal of baked cod, potatoes and broccoli already chopped into little bits. I look at Dad and Dad looks at me, but neither of us says a word.

3

Danny

After my performance on my last visit, I had seriously considered donning a large hat, dark pair of sunglasses and fake beard for my tail-between-the-legs return to the Job Centre. But as I enter the building and walk past the fake potted palms, I quickly come to realise that not a soul cares that I am here. Instead there's just the usual queue of depressed-looking jobseekers waiting to sign on and a number of equally depressed-looking employment officers – stares set to a thousand yards – waiting to assist them.

The reason for my return is simple: I've come to terms with the fact that I need a job, any job, if I'm going to stop Maya leaving me. The truth is, I'm well aware that even her saint-like qualities can only be pushed so far before she breaks and as it is, I already feel as though she can barely look me in the eye any more, knowing that I'm no longer even contributing the little that I had to cover our joint expenses.

As I scan my surroundings, my eyes lock on the large touch screen to the right of me. I've lost count of the number of times that the existence of this computer has been pointed out to me by Job Centre staff, only for me to diligently ignore it. But today I don't disregard it, today I make it my sole destination, and as I stride purposefully towards it I feel strangely hopeful.

I wake the computer screen with a gentle tap and it's only the matter of a few more taps before I'm presented with my first potential job . . . for a full-time sheet metal worker/welder. It's in the south of the city so travelling wouldn't be a problem and the pay is pretty decent too. If I only knew what sheet metal working was or even had a rudimentary knowledge of welding, it would've been the perfect position for me but as it is, it's no use at all. As I scroll past vacancies for hairdressers, office managers, poultry unit supervisors, credit controllers and forklift truck drivers, it dawns on me that I'll be here all day unless I narrow down my search parameters. And sure enough the moment I do, a more suitable opening presents itself: 'Trainee care home assistant, Kenilworth, no experience necessary, training given, pay rate: minimum wage. Please quote ref: QF300BAFSD.'

Even though I'm not exactly sure what's involved in being a trainee care home assistant, I'm cheered by the fact that this job is reasonably local (Kenilworth is only about half an hour away from town) and, more importantly, doesn't require me to have any skills whatsoever and so, rather than skipping through to see if anything else catches my eye, I decide that this is it, and press the on-screen print button. Moments later a sheet of paper with the reference and contact details of the employer splutters out from a nearby printer and, after filling in my personal details with a barely working Biro, I take it over to the advice desk. Only when it's too late for me to turn back, however, do I realise that today the desk is being staffed by the same Job Centre employment officer who stopped my dole money.

'Can I help?' she says, thankfully choosing to pretend that we've never encountered one another before.

'I'm interested in this job,' I say, handing over my sheet of paper. 'Is it still available?'

'I can check if you like,' she replies. 'If it is, would you like me to call and book an interview for you?'

'That would be great if you wouldn't mind.'

'Of course,' she says, nodding coolly. 'I won't be a moment.'

As my nemesis disappears behind an office door marked 'Staff Only', it occurs to me that given our last encounter, she is highly likely to toss my information into the bin and make herself a cup of tea instead. True to her word, however, she re-emerges from behind the door in less than a minute and as she returns to her desk, she even smiles in my direction.

'You're in luck, Mr Allen. Not only is the position still vacant but I've managed to secure an interview for you for this afternoon at one o'clock.'

My stomach ties itself in a million knots at the very thought of it. Much as I desperately need a job, it's still something of a terrifying prospect now that it's close to becoming a reality. My every instinct tells me to run and hide, and only stops when I picture myself giving Maya the good news.

'Yes,' I say as my stomach continues to churn. 'One o'clock is fine by me.'

According to the blue and green sign beside the main doors, Four Oaks is a long-term respite and residential care home. The building itself looks exactly as I'd expected, a fairly modern two-storey block set in relatively attractive landscaped grounds. It looks just the sort of place where an anxious family member could leave a relative and not feel overly guilty as they watched their loved one waving goodbye to them in the rear-view mirror as they drove away.

After buzzing my way into the home, I explain at reception who I am and who I'm here to see, and the cheery receptionist picks up her phone and informs the person on the other end of my arrival. After a short wait a freakishly tall, acne-ridden man some ten years my junior appears in front of me. He's wearing an ill-fitting grey suit – too short on the arms, too long on the legs – and smells strongly of freshly sprayed deodorant.

'You must be Danny,' he says, shaking my hand. 'I'm Dean Tromans, trainee deputy manager here at Four Oaks. If you'd like to just follow me, I'll introduce you to my colleague, Pat.'

I'm led along a long corridor, the air of which reeks of pine-scented disinfectant, to a door marked General Manager. Sitting behind a desk near the window is a plump middle-aged lady with short dyed red hair.

'You must be Danny,' she says, shaking my hand. 'I'm Pat, General Manager of Four Oaks. Please take a seat and we'll get things started.'

Over the course of the interview, Pat and Dean ask me precisely two questions: do I have a UK passport and when can I start? Other than that all I do is respond to their request to tell them a bit about myself. I tell them what I always tell people. I tell them how I'm a local lad through and through and then move on to discuss my distinctly lacklustre education and extremely patchy work history. I'm also pretty frank about why I'm applying for the role ('I'm broke,' I explain, 'the dole cut off my money this week and if I don't bring in some cash soon, I'm pretty sure my girlfriend's going to leave me'), and equally blunt about my cluelessness with regard to what this job actually entails ('I'm guessing it's looking after old people'). It's almost as though nothing I say can take the shine off their enthusiasm for me. 'Sometimes, Danny,' says Pat as she idly picks at her nail polish, 'it can take people a while to discover their true vocation,' and then Dean adds, 'Sounds to me like someone's just found themselves the career they never knew they'd always wanted.'

There's an awkward pause before Dean glances at Pat and then leans forward, resting his chin on his hand, and his elbow on his knee. 'I hope I'm not speaking out of turn here,' he says with a smile, 'but I think it's safe to say that you, Danny, are absolutely one hundred per cent the right person for us. Wouldn't you, Pat?'

'He couldn't be more suited,' says Pat.

'In that case, Danny,' says Dean, sitting up straight in his chair, 'I have no hesitation in saying that we'd like to offer you the position of a grade two temporary trainee care assistant. So what do you say, Danny? Would you like to become a vital member of the Honeywell International stable of residential care homes?'

The fact that Pat and Dean aren't even remotely put off by anything I've said makes it abundantly clear that the interview process has been little more than a cursory check to make sure that I have the requisite number of arms and legs needed for the job while double-checking that I'm desperate enough to accept their exploitative working conditions (zero hours contract, two days of compulsory unpaid training, and unpaid lunch breaks), which of course I am. I also get the feeling that Pat and Dean have in recent times interviewed an awful lot of people for an awful lot of jobs, suggesting a regular turnover of staff because of appalling working conditions. I want so desperately to tell Dean and Pat what they can do with their job that it hurts, but I can't because this right here is my last chance, and no matter how awful it might turn out to be, I need this job badly.

'I'll take it,' I say, and I go to smile in Pat's direction but I can see behind her lifeless expression that she's already switched off, more than likely thinking about the next poor sucker she and Dean will have lined up to take my place when I leave.

When I reach home, I'm a little unsure about what to do with the rest of my day. Maya's on a late shift at the call centre and won't be home until after eleven, and so I have a good six hours or so to kill before she comes through the door. Even though part of me feels like celebrating, because for the time being at least I seem to have averted disaster, I'm oddly reluctant to text Maya. After all, it's not as though I've just scored the job of the century. We're not suddenly going to be rolling in cash just because I've got some low-paid job wiping strangers' arses. We're not going to morph overnight into one of those deliriously happy couples you see in magazine adverts just because I've managed to fix one item from a long list of things that are wrong with me. In fact, chances are things are more likely to get worse between us rather than better, especially once Maya realises that working hasn't changed me, that I'm still broken inside, that there really is no hope for me.

And yet despite all this, I do feel sort of good about myself, or at least enough to want to share my news with someone who might care. Helen was always great for times like these. Occasions when you want to celebrate something that isn't really much of a big deal to anyone but you. I remember the first time I took my driving test. I was eighteen and not particularly car minded and so it was no surprise that I failed. When I came home to break the news, however, the first thing I saw was a huge banner that Helen had made from an old bed sheet and then hung out of the bedroom window. On it she had painted the words, 'Well done, Danny!' for all to see and even though I'd failed, she never once stopped encouraging and assuring me I'd do better next time. When I returned home from my second failed driving test, that same banner was hanging in exactly the same position and when I broke the news of my failure, Helen gave me a hug and told me she reckoned I must only have failed because I'd had a really strict examiner. When I finally passed on my third attempt, I hurried home to tell everyone and sure enough that same banner was hanging from the upstairs window. I'll never forget the way she reacted to the news that I'd finally passed. She was happier than I was, laughing and crying at the same time as she hugged me out in the street. It's the best feeling in the world knowing there's someone in your corner. That no matter what and no matter how badly you mess up, they will always be on your side.

If Helen were here now she'd be happy for me, just like she was then. She might even have hung a little 'well done' banner from the window of the flat or perhaps, given that she'd be older, brought out a bottle of champagne. She would've told me this was the beginning of something special, that this was proof I could do anything I wanted if I just put my mind to it. I think if she'd said that, I might actually have believed her too.

But Helen isn't here. If she were, I would never have got myself into this mess in the first place. I would've been somewhere else, someone else, living the life I'd been meant to live, instead of the flimsy imitation I'd scraped together over the years since she'd gone.

I was never going to see Helen again. She was gone for good. There wasn't a day that went by when I didn't miss her. Without her there was no one I could share this tiny achievement with, no banners, no hugs and no smiles. Without Helen, there was no one in my corner at all.

4

James

I am watching *Friends*.

It is the episode where Chandler sees Rachel naked in the shower.

I am watching *Friends* on the TV in my bedroom at my parents' home. The TV is in the corner of the room next to the window. I am sitting in a worn leather armchair.

I have seen this episode of *Friends* a million times but it still makes me laugh.

It is very funny and it makes me laugh because I know what's going to happen. I know that Chandler will accidentally see Rachel naked. I know that Rachel will try and see Chandler naked but will end up seeing Joey instead. I know that Joey will try to get revenge on Rachel and will end up seeing Monica naked. I know that Monica will try and see Joey naked and will end up seeing Joey's dad in the shower instead. I know all this and yet it is still funny. I know all this and this is the way I like things. I like to know what will happen next. I know all this and yet I still cannot stop myself getting annoyed by the racket coming from downstairs. A racket of raised voices.

I need to find out what is going on.

I lean towards my good side and push myself up and out of my chair. It is a leather chair. The leather feels warm underneath my hand because the sun has been shining on it all morning and the chair is next to the window. This is my favourite spot. I feel calm watching *Friends*. It is a really good TV series and when I watch it, I feel like nothing can bother me. I like knowing what will happen next. I like that it is predictable.

I watched *Friends* all the time while I was recovering from The Incident. It made me feel better.

As I come down the stairs, I hold the banister tightly.

My mum, Erica, says my balance is getting better all the time but I am not so sure. I have fallen down the stairs in the past. I haven't hurt myself too badly. Just a few bruises, my mum said. No broken bones. I take my time coming down the stairs. I have to be careful. Sometimes I forget the bottom step. It is like I think I know where the ground is and then it turns out that I do not know at all. Sometimes I look down at my feet and check to see if the floor is still there, even if I am not going downstairs.

I think it pays to be safe sometimes. I think it is good to be careful.

The closer I get to the kitchen, the more I can work out who the raised voices belong to. The loudest is Martha's. Martha is my sister and she is younger than me but right now I cannot remember by how much. She works for the BBC. I am not sure what she does but I think it is pretty important. Martha is using her loud voice. She tells my parents that they are using James as an excuse. In a slightly less loud voice Dad tells Martha she is talking nonsense.

I am James.

My name is James.

They are either talking about me or possibly someone else called James.

I think they probably are talking about me though.

My mum uses her loud voice to tell Martha that she is being too hard on James. Martha tells my mum that she is not hard enough. She says, 'You keep treating him like he's a child but he's not. He's a grown man, Mum, and he can handle three weeks without you!' and then mum says sharply, 'Martha! That's enough!' Then it all goes quiet and I hear someone crying.

It is my mum who is crying.

I am definitely the James they are talking about. My mum, Erica, always cries when anyone says anything bad about me.

When I come into the kitchen, Martha and Mum are hugging. Dad is standing next to them with his arm around Mum's shoulders. When they realise I am in the room, they all stop what they are doing and pretend to be normal. Mum dries her eyes, Dad runs his hand over the silver-grey hair on his chin . . . his beard . . . he runs his hand over his beard.

It is mostly grey, his beard, and every other day he shaves near his neckline because if he does not, his neck gets itchy and my mum will tell him to stop scratching at the dinner table like a farmyard animal.

My family are pretending to be normal because I am in the room but I know they are not being normal.

Mum kisses my cheek and plucks a tissue from her sleeve. She dabs at my face with the tissue, wiping away any trace of her lipstick. Dad asks me if I would like a cup of tea and Martha kisses me on the cheek too, only she does not wipe away her lipstick afterwards. When she is not looking, I touch where she put her lips. It feels sticky but in a nice way. Like she has left part of her kiss behind for me to find later tonight, when I am in bed and dropping off to sleep.

Martha tells me that she had been on her way to see a friend in Leamington when she decided to pop in and say hello.

'Which friend?'

'What?'

'Which friend were you visiting?'

'Liza.'

'She's blonde and smokes.'

Martha nods. 'Yes, that's Liza.'

'I like Liza.'

'I know you do.'

'I do not like her smoking though.'

I want to ask Martha why she and my parents are talking so loudly that I cannot hear *Friends*. I do not ask this question though, because no one is talking loudly any more and because I think I know the answer anyway.

My guess is they were talking loudly because of yesterday – my parents' fortieth wedding anniversary – yesterday when Martha gave my parents a present that I did not like.

My mum, Erica, and dad, Don, didn't like it either.

In fact, the only person who liked it was Martha.

She thought it was a perfect present.

The party was at an Italian restaurant in Broadway. A lot of family and friends came. I am not very good with crowds. Too many people. Their talking makes me tired. A lot of people said I looked well. Much better than when they last saw me. They said that it was a good sign. That it showed I was a fighter. My uncle Terry told me I made him proud. I told my uncle Terry that I did not feel proud but I did feel tired. He did not laugh, even though it was a joke. I think sometimes people hear how I talk or see how I walk and think I cannot tell jokes.

I can tell jokes.

Rachel is my favourite one from *Friends*. She is beautiful. I would maybe like to be her boyfriend one day.

I was sitting at a table with Mum and Dad and Martha and my uncle Terry, and my great aunt who lives in an old people's home. The food was nice and there was lots of it. I did not used to eat very much but now I do. After The Incident I had to learn to chew. My mum, Erica, used to blitz my supper in a liquidiser and then I would drink it with a spoon. I can chew quite well now and I do not need anyone to cut my food up for me any more. I stay away from beef though, because it is hard to cut and it makes my head hurt to chew it.

I can't think of the name of the dessert I had. I remember it was made from meringue and cream and fruit. My mum, Erica, didn't have any dessert because she said she didn't want to get fat.

At the end of the meal there were speeches.

First Dad stood up and said a lot of nice things about Mum that made people smile and look fondly at Mum. Then Mum stood up and said that she did not like to speak in public and then spent a long time thanking everyone for coming. Then finally Martha stood up and said that she had some words to say too.

Martha thanked everyone for coming and said lots of nice things about my mum, Erica, and my dad, Don. She said something about the past few years having been especially difficult.

But the bit that really stuck in my head was when she said that she and I had got them a present.

She said, 'Mum, Dad, you are the best parents James and I could ever have hoped for and time and again you've gone above and beyond the call of duty to show us how deep your love is for us. It's with this in mind that James and I would like to give you a present to say thank you.'

She gave my dad an envelope and told him and everyone watching that it was a three-week cruise for two around the Caribbean.

When everyone finished clapping, my dad thanked me and Martha for our very kind gift but in the taxi home he said to my mum, 'But of course we can't possibly go,' and my mum said, 'Of course, that goes without saying,' and then my dad said, 'I'm telling you now, Erica, Martha won't like it one bit,' and my mum said, 'No, she definitely won't.'

After a while of watching my mum, dad and sister pretending that they have not just been arguing, I lose interest and return to my room. I start my *Friends* episode over again because I like to watch things from start to finish. It still makes me laugh when Chandler sees Rachel naked. I like knowing that it will happen next. It makes me feel calm.

When I get to the scene where Monica sees Joey's dad naked in the shower, there is a knock at the door. I pause the DVD as Martha comes into the room.

She glances at the TV. 'Oh, I like this episode.'

'It is really funny.'

'I think it's probably one of the best.'

'You were not really going to see Liza were you?'

Martha sits down on the edge of my bed. 'No, you're right. I told a lie, James. I came here to see Mum and Dad to try and change their minds about taking the cruise.'

'You said it was from both of us.'

'And it was.'

'But I did not give you any money.'

'You don't need to.'

'But if it is a present for Mum and Dad, I want to. I have got money. Plenty of it.'

Martha nods. 'Let's talk about it later.'

She gives me a strange look but I do not know what it means. I sometimes have trouble working out what people mean by looks. My dad says that I was not always bad at working out what people mean by looks. He said I used to be excellent at it. He said that was why I was so good at my job in property development and why I would have made a good MP, 'even if it was only for those bunch of bleeding-heart liberals you call the Labour Party.' The company I started used to redevelop old office buildings and turn them into luxury apartments. I had to be good at negotiating and dealing with people face to face.

Martha is talking. She may have been doing so for quite some time.

'James are you okay? I think I might have lost you for a minute there.'

I blink a few times.

Sometimes I can lose track of time. My mum calls it 'having a moment'. Sometimes I can be in the middle of a conversation and 'have a moment' and not even realise I have stopped talking.

Martha rubs my arm gently. 'I was talking to you about Mum and Dad, James. I was saying that I really think they need this holiday.'

Martha always thinks she knows what is best for everyone. I think she gets it from my mum.

'It has got nothing to do with me. They told me on the way home last night that they do not want to go. I did not make them.'

'That's the thing, James,' says Martha, 'I don't think that's true. I think they would like to go – who wouldn't want three weeks in the sun? – but they're worried about leaving you.'

'Well, if they are worried about that, I could just stay with you in Oxford.'

'I wish you could, I really do but I've got work and you can't be left on your own all day.' Martha takes my hand. 'I don't want you to get upset, James, but I've suggested to Mum and Dad that while they're away we find you a place to stay.'

'I do not want to find a place to stay. I want to stay here.'

Martha closes her eyes like people do when they are trying not to cry. 'You can't stay here on your own, James, you just can't. Remember we tried that once. Do you remember what happened?'

Bacon sandwiches.

She is talking about a while ago when my parents went out for the night and left me on my own. I got hungry and decided to make myself a bacon sandwich and I put some on to cook, but then I forgot all about what I was doing and went to watch a loud film upstairs in my room. I did not hear the smoke alarms because of the film and I only found out there was a problem when the fire brigade knocked down the front door.

'I do not even like bacon sandwiches any more,' I say, but Martha does not laugh, even though it is a joke and she knows I can tell jokes.

'You can't stay at home, my lovely,' she says, 'and you can't stay with me either. Mum and Dad really need this holiday, James, they need it a lot. The thing is, they're not as young as they used to be, they get tired easily and well, looking after you these past three years has really taken a lot out of them. I think they need a break and this holiday is it.'

'But I do not want to stay anywhere else.'

'It'll only be for a short while and I promise I'll visit you every weekend. It'll be fun, like going on a holiday yourself. The place I've chosen for you is amazing. I went to visit and have a look around just this morning. They do all sorts of great activities. I promise you, you'll love it so much the time will fly by.'

5

Danny

'Here's your breakfast, Harry.'

Harry, a bald-headed man of fifty-five, shakes his head while rocking gently back and forth, repeatedly growling something that sounds a lot like, 'Aaaadoooowaaaaannnnnn,' which I'm guessing means that he doesn't want breakfast.

If it was up to me I'd say, 'Fine, to be honest I'm not much of a breakfast person either,' but it's not, it's up to his patient notes which state, 'Patient prone to low blood sugar: must eat regularly.' So there it is in black and white. Harry has got to eat his breakfast and it's my job to encourage him.

Jean, one of the other care assistants here at Four Oaks, does an impressive line in bubbly that even the most truculent of residents finds difficult to resist. Mr Narwal in room G3, for instance, absolutely refuses to take his heart tablets. You should hear the fuss he kicks up over two blue ones and a white one, washed down with half a paper cup of water. Anyone would think we were trying to kill him the way he carries on. But the moment he kicks off, Jean starts singing 'Everybody Loves Somebody Sometime', and he's like putty in her hands. The funny thing is she's not even all that great at singing, she just sounds like someone's mum singing old timey songs in the shower.

Now I'm no singer but I can at least have a go at jolly. So that's what I do. 'You're havin' a laugh aintcha, Harry?' I say in my best cod-barrow boy accent. 'Breakfast is a top meal! It'll make you big and strong!' To add weight to my argument I flex my arms as if I'm a strongman at a circus, rather than an exasperated trainee care assistant. It's demeaning. Not just to Harry who, according to his medical records used to be a foreman at a local car parts manufacturer, but also to me because I've turned myself into a performing monkey. But it's all part of the job. He needs to eat his breakfast and playing the fool helps achieve that aim.

When I eventually stop flexing, I gently nudge the tray holding Harry's bowl of shredded wheat a little bit closer to him in the hope that he might take the hint. He doesn't. Instead he shakes his head again, meaning all my buffoonery was for nothing.

'Aaaadoooowaaaaannnnnn!'

'But you have to.'

'Aaaadoooowaaaaannnnnn!'

'Go on, just a spoonful for me.'

'Aaaadoooowaaaaannnnnn!'

'Please, mate.'

Reluctantly he reaches for his spoon and I allow myself to breathe a sigh of relief, but then he lets out one almighty, 'Aaaadoooowaaaaannnnnn!' and flings out his arms sending the bowl and its contents flying into the air, showering everything within a three-metre radius – the walls, his chair, a framed photo of his wife, and of course me, in a combination of semi-skimmed milk and mashed-up shredded wheat.

Despite this being only my third week in the job this incident is far from the worst thing to have happened to me. Here at Four Oaks food throwing is such a daily occurrence that along with the screaming, biting, punching, kicking and vomiting, it's barely worth commenting on. Cleaning up after leaking adult nappies, wiping up the contents of bedpans that have been deliberately tipped over by angry residents, and mopping copious amounts of blood from the floor following DIY removals of intravenous drips are all part of a day's work. And the worst thing to have happened to me since I started? That's easy. Last week a woman in D9 was prescribed some new diabetes medication that made her doubly incontinent and in the middle of cleaning her up, I ripped a hole in my glove. Colleen, my co-worker, had to yell into my ear for me to get a grip before I finally managed to tear my eyes away from the substance covering my index finger. For days afterwards I treated the offending digit as if it were no longer part of me, and it was over a week before I'd even let it come close to anything that I might eat.

It takes me a good half an hour to clean Harry, his room and myself, which means that I end up being behind on my duties for the morning. Strictly speaking, by ten o'clock I'm supposed to have all the residents under my care dressed and fed (either in their room or in the main dining hall), but it's more like eleven thirty by the time I've managed to locate the only shirt that Tom in 7B will wear, helped Margaret in 11A order a present for her grandson's sixth birthday, found where the new tubes of ointment for Veena in 17C's bed sores are kept, and given Iwan in 15D a shave in preparation for his daughter's visit.

As Iwan's daughter arrives, I leave the room and find myself wondering whether I've got the strength to make it to the end of the day. My shift started at six this morning and doesn't officially end until three o'clock this afternoon and even though it's only mid-morning, I feel dead on my feet and I know the day is only going to get worse. That's the thing about this place. There's always someone somewhere who needs cleaning, wiping, comforting, feeding or medicating. Always. I suppose if they could have done these things for themselves, then their families wouldn't have brought them here. That's the factor that links them together, the one detail they have in common despite the differences in age, race, gender and medical condition: they all need help. Some of their needs are obvious, like Vince in 22C, who shakes like a washing machine on maximum spin because of his Parkinson's. Others like Anjali in 3C are more subtle, she can laugh and joke with the best of them and will regale you with so many tales of life back in Mumbai that you wonder why she's here, and it's only when you ask her what year it is and she tells you it's 1964 that you realise something is up. Some of the residents, like Donna in 2D who suffers from spina bifida and whose mum is recovering from a hysterectomy operation, are only here for a matter of days while others, like Craig in 19B who, following a motorcycle accident two years ago, can't even feed himself, are here for the long haul.

If I were a nicer person, the stories of the residents here at Four Oaks would've moved me to tears. Honestly, some of their histories are downright heartbreaking. Couples looking forward to growing old together ripped apart by the most tragic of accidents; parents with young children turned into drooling wrecks, all because of heart-rending dumb luck; young people with their whole lives ahead of them struck down by a one-in-a-million disease in their prime. As it is, however, I'm still far too self-involved to give any of the residents more than a second thought. Though I see their pain and can even empathise with their troubles, no matter how sad the story, in the end nothing sticks. It's as though I'm Teflon coated. I suppose it makes sense to be like this when I know I'm not going to be here for long. Sooner or later I'll be sacked, of this I have no doubt, so at the end of the day there's really no point in me getting emotionally involved with any of these people. The fact of the matter is, I'm simply passing through.

As I check in with Margaret in 11A to see if she's changed her mind about going to the TV room, my phone buzzes with a text. Technically we're not meant to have our phones on when we're on duty but everyone – and I do mean everyone – ignores the rule, even though you'd think we'd know better after what we spend all our working days touching. But this is the world we live in: a world where we'd all sooner risk dysentery than be isolated from our Candy Crush scores for more than five minutes.

The text is from Maya. She's going out straight after work with friends and won't be back home until late. She signs off her message with three kisses, which is precisely three hundred per cent more than we've shared in real life since I started at Four Oaks. Far from saving us, I think my getting a job has made things worse. I think she feels like it's too little too late and every day that passes she drifts further away from me, and all I can do is stand by and watch.

Somehow despite an altercation between two residents, and a toilet blockage that I'm tasked to deal with along with all my other duties, I make it through to the end of my shift, catch the bus back into Coventry and not long after, I'm walking through town to catch the bus that will take me home to Coundon. As I zigzag my way through the crowds of shoppers, I begin to notice the shops they are emerging from, shops that I never venture into because I'm always broke. I watch a woman loaded down with multiple bags from Primark and then later see two men come out of Currys, sharing the load of a brand new computer. Normally I never notice this kind of thing, but I can only suppose that now that I'm just a week away from my first payday in three years, consumerism is getting the better of me.

I dip into a clothes shop but exit almost straight away because everything's way too expensive for my liking. More out of nostalgia than anything, I pop into HMV but as I walk around the racks of CDs and DVDs it feels as if I'm in a museum dedicated to preserving the recent past, rather than a shop selling things people in the twenty-first century might actually want to buy. As I leave the store, however, I glance at the window of a nearby jeweller's and a diamond necklace in the window catches my eye. On a whim I go in and find myself asking the young store assistant behind the counter if I can take a closer look at it.

'It really is a lovely piece,' she says, having retrieved the necklace from the window so that I can examine it. 'Is it for your partner?'

'No,' I reply, and I wonder if it's telling that the thought of getting Maya something hadn't even crossed my mind. 'It's for my daughter.'

'What a lucky girl she is. Are you thinking of it for a special occasion?'

'It's her fifteenth birthday soon. I've been out of work for a while but now I've got a job, I'm thinking I might just push the boat out.'

'Well, if you don't mind me saying, it's absolutely the right thing to do. Teenagers can be so picky, can't they? Still, I can't imagine she won't be wowed by this – I know I would be and I'm thirty-five!'

I nod and smile. 'Thanks.'

'It's such a special age, isn't it – fifteen? Your whole life in front of you and no idea just how truly beautiful you are. I bet she's a real daddy's girl, isn't she?'

'Just a bit.'

'Have you any photos?'

'Erm, no, my phone has been playing up and it lost a load.'

'Oh that is a shame. I bet she's gorgeous though.'

'She is, she's stunning.'

The young woman behind the counter smiles. 'A stunning piece for a stunning girl,' she says. 'So, would you like me to ring it up at the till for you?'

As much as I'd love to be buying this necklace for Leila, the truth is every last penny I'll get on payday, and every one that follows for the foreseeable future, will be eaten up paying back money I borrowed on the credit card, from payday loan companies and of course Maya. I'll be lucky if I can still afford bus fare, let alone flashy presents for a daughter I never see.

'I need to have a little think about it,' I tell the young woman, knowing full well that I won't be coming back. 'I'm sure she'll love it but it pays to be sure.'

I met Leila's mum during what I suppose were my darkest days. Living in a dingy shared house on the outskirts of town and still reeling from the shock of losing Helen, my days and nights passed by in a blur of drink and drugs in a bid to numb the pain. Simone had thought she could save me from myself and for a while I'd believed her. She made me happier than I ever thought I had the right to be but while it calmed down my excesses for a time, in the end the lure of oblivion proved too strong a force for me to resist. Time and again I promised to change, and time and again I broke those promises in two. But then she found out she was pregnant and her desire to protect our baby proved stronger than her desire to rescue me, and suddenly there were no more chances left.

Whilst I'd never given up trying to see Leila, at times I'd almost given up hope I ever would. Simone was adamant that she wouldn't let me be part of Leila's life. Not that I blamed her, after all before Leila was born she'd heard me promise to turn my life around countless times, only to fail within days if not hours of making my vow. Why would things be any different just because I was a father now? I tried to convince her that I could change but she mustn't have believed me because the next time I went round to the house, both she and all her belongings were gone, and I never saw her again.

About a year later I got a letter from her post-marked Dundee. She didn't say very much. It was really just a quick message to let me know that she and the baby were fine and that she'd named our daughter Leila. She wrote that she'd asked a friend of a friend to post the letter for her and that I shouldn't bother trying to find her in Dundee or anywhere else. Then she finished off by wishing me well and telling me that she hoped I'd get help dealing with my demons. The only other item in the envelope was a photograph of a baby girl, a baby girl that could've been Helen's double when she was a few months old. I stopped drinking that same day and the drugs too, and I haven't touched either since for nearly fourteen years. Once again it was a case of too little too late, but it really was the wake-up call I needed.

Despite not having met Leila in person, I've never forgotten a birthday yet, thanks to a ritual I've developed over the years: a week or two before the big day I buy her something special, something only her dad would think to get, and then I wrap it up and put it away for the day when I see her. That way she'll get the presents owed to her and there'll be proof that I was always thinking about her, even if I wasn't actually part of her life. Obviously it's not the greatest plan in the world – I can't begin to imagine what use a teenager will have for a set of second-hand Ladybird fairy-tale books – but it is, as they say, the thought that counts – and right now thoughts are all I've got to work with.

6

James

'We really ought to be getting off,' says my dad, Don. 'You know what the blasted traffic around Heathrow can be like. You almost wonder what it is the government actually do with all that road tax we pay them.'

'Of course, Don,' says my mum sadly. She puts her arms around me and hugs me. Even without being able to see her face I know that she is crying. 'You promise you will call us if you need anything at all, won't you, James?'

'No, he won't,' says Martha speaking for me, even though I am standing right here. 'Mum, if James needs anything at all, he'll call me not you because you'll be too busy enjoying your holiday with Dad. The home has got all of my contact details and those of my PA too, Mum. I promise, if James needs the slightest thing, I'll know about it straight away and whatever it is I'll get it sorted.'

Martha gives me a look. A look like she wants me to say something. A look like she wants me to tell my mum, Erica, that I will be okay so that she will not be sad about going on holiday.

'Martha is right,' I say, even though I do not think it is true. 'I will be fine, Mum. If I need anything, Martha will get it for me. You and Dad should go and have a nice time.'

My mum looks into my eyes almost as if she is looking for something inside my head. 'I love you,' she says after a long while and so I say I love you back, and she lets go of me so that my dad can give me a hug. 'We'll be back before you know it,' he says, 'and then you can tell us about all the amazing things you've done while we've been away.'

It was Martha who changed everybody's mind.

First she worked on me and said that Mum and Dad were not as young as they used to be. She said that they needed lots of rest and that although they loved looking after me, it was hard work for them. When she said this, I felt guilty because I knew it was probably true. My parents are not as young as they used to be and I am hard work. Most parents do not have sons or daughters my age living with them. And if they do, they can probably look after themselves and do not need caring for. But I do. I need caring for.

Then she worked on my parents but they were more difficult. Martha told my dad to take a look at the care home for himself, and so a week later he and Martha went for a visit. It must have gone well because when he came back he was smiling. 'Wouldn't mind staying there for a week myself,' he joked, when my mum asked what it was like. I think hearing my dad talk like that about the care home made Mum feel like it might actually be okay because the very next day she told Martha that she would not mind going on the holiday after all.

Martha and I wave our parents off and then, when we can no longer see their car, Martha says, 'I suppose we'd better go too,' and so we return to the house and collect my things.

I only have two bags.

One that my mum packed has clothes and toiletries in it and another that I packed has got the things in it that I will need.

My *Friends* box set.

My complete *Die Hard* box set.

Some sweets.

A bag of satsumas.

I cannot remember the rest but I am sure there is more in there.

I cannot help Martha with my big bag because I find it difficult to walk carrying heavy things. Martha does not seem to mind though, she makes a joke about it. In a funny voice like one Sasha Baron Cohen would make if he wanted to make you laugh she says, 'See, strong, like bull!' and puts the suitcase in the boot along with the bag I have carried. As she returns to the house to lock up, I take one last look at it. I will miss my home very much. I am not looking forward to living somewhere else, even if it is only for a few weeks.

I do not want to go.

On the way to the home Martha tries to talk to me about lots of different things but none of them have to do with where I am going. She asks me which season of *Friends* I am watching and how much weight she thinks Dad will have put on by the time he comes home or what sort of presents Mum will bring back for us. Finally I say to her, 'I would much prefer it if you did not ask me any more questions. I would like just to be taken home.' She does not take me home though. Instead she looks sad and says, 'You know I can't do that, Jamie. If I could, I would but I just can't.'

The man who shows Martha and me to my room at the care home is really tall, has lots of spots on his face and is wearing a grey suit that does not fit him very well. He is called Dean and he is the trainee deputy manager of the care home. My room is like a big box. There is a bed against one wall and a wardrobe next to it. Opposite the bed is a sink with a mirror above it and next to that a table with a lamp. Dean tells Martha there are jigsaw puzzles in the recreation room if I want to do one, and Martha laughs and tells Dean that I have always hated jigsaw puzzles even when we were young. Martha tells Dean that I will be fine as long as I have the TV and DVD player that she requested especially for me. Dean says, 'Of course, I'll just go and check where they are for you.'

When he has gone, Martha opens my suitcase on the bed and asks me if I want help putting my things away. Even though I know I will need help, I tell her that I will do it later on my own.

Martha sits down on the bed. She looks really sad. 'Please, please don't hate me, Jamie,' she says. 'I'm just trying to do what's best for everyone.'

I let Martha help me put away my things and afterwards we take a little tour of the home. We see the dining room and the main lounge and the recreation room and as we walk around, some of the residents wave at me but I do not wave at them. When we get back to my room, there is a TV and DVD player set up in the corner. I get a DVD from my bag so I can check that it is working properly but as I am getting it out of its case, Martha picks up her handbag from my bed and says, 'I think it's probably time for me to be getting off.'

I put down the DVD case and look at Martha.

'I am sorry,' I say, 'for being mean and saying that I did not want your help. I know you are trying your best.'

Martha gives me a big hug and I know even without looking at her face that she is crying. I hand her the box of tissues that my mum put in my suitcase and Martha dries her eyes and gives me another hug.

'Promise me you'll call if you need anything at all,' she says.

'I will,' I say, and then she gives me one last kiss goodbye and she is gone.

My first week at Four Oaks does not go very well.

I do not like anything about the home. The dining room is too noisy, the other residents are either quite strange or they do not say anything at all and it is always too warm. I miss my parents and Martha, and I miss my home too. Every night before I go to sleep I call Martha and ask her to take me home or to her house, and every night she tells me that I just need to hang on a little while longer.

At lunchtime on the one-week anniversary of my arrival, I go to the big dining hall to eat. There are lots of different things on offer but I choose fish, chips and peas. The food tastes nice but as usual the dining room is too noisy. There are too many people all talking at the same time and the dinner ladies keep clanging cutlery.

I sit next to a middle-aged man in a wheelchair who I have not met before. He tells me his name is Martin but that everyone calls him Smithy. He tells me he is only here to give his wife a rest from looking after him but he actually quite likes it because it is nice and busy. On the left of me is a smartly dressed elderly lady who has never spoken to me, even though I have sat next to her before. She makes quiet noises to herself as I eat but never once touches her plate of food. Opposite me are two sisters whose names I can't remember, even though I am sure they told me. They are about twenty years old and are quite funny sometimes. From the moment they sit down at the table with their food, they never once stop talking but still somehow manage to eat everything on their plates.

I try my very best to put up with the noise but halfway through a mouthful of fish and chips, I realise I cannot hear my own thoughts and so I ask one of the care assistants, an Indian lady with a nice smiley face, if I can take my plate to my room because the noise is making my head hurt. She smiles again and says, 'I know the feeling, love,' which makes me feel hopeful but then she tells me that I cannot take my food to my room because it's against the rules. Even when I tell her that Martha said I could eat in my room if I liked, it makes no difference. All she says is, 'Who's Martha, dear? Is she here with you now?' as if she thinks my sister is an invisible friend who I have made up. In the end I tell her it does not matter and I eat everything on my plate very quickly, take an apple from a bowl of fruit and leave the table.

On the way to my room I think about how long I have got left here. Fourteen days does not sound like a lot but when I imagine it in my head, it feels like forever. I tell myself that it will be okay. I tell myself that it will all be over soon and in my head I make a list of the things I will do when I get home.

I only get as far as adding, 'Have a nap on my bed,' and 'sit in my favourite chair,' when I have to stop because I have been concentrating so hard that I have bumped into an old man coming towards me, being pushed in a wheelchair by a carer. I try to apologise to the old man but he is fast asleep and so I apologise to the carer instead, and he says, 'No problem, mate.'

As I carry on to my room, I try thinking about my list again but I cannot because another thought is in my head and it will not go away.

The thought is this: I know the man. Not the old man in the

wheelchair but the younger man pushing the wheelchair: the care assistant. I know him. But I do not know where from. Because my head is not what it used to be, I tell myself that I have probably made a mistake. Maybe I just think I know him but I do not really know him. Perhaps he reminds me of someone I used to know.

My neurologist, Dr Acari, says that sometimes my memory is perfect and then sometimes it is not. He says that sometimes when I am trying to remember something, it's like being in a long corridor with a hundred different doors and you know the memory is behind one of them but you just do not know which, and so you have to try them all. When Dr Acari said this, he joked, 'And of course it is always behind the last door that you open,' which is funny not just because it is a joke but also because in my head I have just started opening doors, looking for the memory containing the man I think I know. I stand still while I am thinking. I close my eyes too because sometimes it helps, and then just like that I open the right door and I realise I know exactly who he is.

I walk back up the corridor after the man I think I know. I walk past reception, through the main lounge and back into the dining hall. I look around everywhere for him but he is nowhere to be seen. When the smiley Indian care assistant sees me, she asks me if it is pudding I am after but then I spot the old man in the wheelchair. He is sitting by the bay windows that look out on to the gardens. He is still fast asleep. I want to wake him up and ask him if he knows the name of the care assistant who has left him there, but then through the window I spot the man I am looking for outside. He is smoking a cigarette with two other care assistants, a man and a woman.

Standing in the bay window, I watch the man I think I know. He does not do anything interesting. He just smokes his cigarette and chats with the others. When they finish, he throws his cigarette on the floor, puts it out with his heel and follows the others to the main entrance.

I am not very good at walking quickly but I do it faster than

I have ever done before, and I reach reception as they are coming through the door. I stand in the middle of the corridor so that they will have to walk past me and when they reach me, the female care assistant says, 'Everything all right, love? You look a bit lost.' Looking at Danny Allen, I say in my clearest voice so that I can be sure he will understand me, '*Sic parvis magna*.'

7

Danny

'So what was it that new patient in G12 said to Danny then?'

'Sick Paris summat or other, I think. Made no bloody sense to me but it was hard to make out because his speech is a bit funny. It was dead spooky though. Like he was possessed and talking in a foreign language.'

'But you're saying he knew our Danny's name?'

'Well, that was the really scary thing. After he said that Sick Paris whatever, he looked at Danny and cool as you like said, "You're Danny Allen. We used to go to boarding school together."'

'What? The guy from G12 thought he used to go to boarding school with our Danny? But he didn't, did he?'

'Of course he didn't! Boarding school is where that David bloody Cameron and his cronies go when they're kids, isn't it? Do you think if our Danny went to boarding school he'd be here wiping arses?'

'When you put it like that, I don't suppose he would. So what did our Danny say to that then?'

'Well, he was like, "Never seen you before in my life, mate," and G12 was like, "Danny, it's me James DeWitt, we went to King's Scrivener together.'

'King's what?'

'That's what I said. Had to look it up on me phone didn't I? It's only like one of the poshest schools in the country. You know that fella on *Antiques Roadshow*, him what wears the funny hats and the loud shirts?'

'I know the one you mean – me Nan loves him. Any time he's on the TV she's like, "If only I was forty years younger," and we're like, "Nan, no thanks, we're trying to eat our tea."'

'Well, that guy Mr Loud Shirts went to this school that G12 was on about and so did loads of other famous types.'

'Go on then, who like?'

'I can't remember off the top of my head, can I? I just know there were loads of them on that Wiki-whatever-it's-called. Some of them I'd even heard of too.'

'And this guy in G12 thought *our* Danny had gone to *that* school?'

'Exactly! And Danny was like, "I've never seen you before in my life, mate," and G12 was like, "How can you say that? We were at boarding school together for seven years, you won" – now, what did he say? – the Charmoody . . . the Chimwilly . . . ah, it doesn't matter. He said Danny had won some school prize or other and then – get this – after school, he said Danny went to Cambridge University.'

'You mean that university like what that David Cameron and all his cronies went to?'

'The very same.'

'So what did Danny say to that?'

'Well, what could he say? He was like, "Mate, you've got the wrong guy," and then G12 started to get a bit worked up like he was gonna blow his top, so I told Danny to scoot and I'd deal with it. Even after Danny had gone, the lad was still like, "I'm honestly not making this up," and I was like, "Of course you're not, love," because you know how confused some of them are in here, so I said to him, "Maybe Danny's just got a really bad memory," and he said, "You don't believe me, I can tell," and I said, "Of course, I do, love," and he said, "Look, how do I know his name if I don't know who he is?"'

'That's a good point though, that is, isn't it? How did G12 know Danny's name if he didn't know him?'

In unison my co-workers, Brenda and Kath, turn to look over the break room table where I'm sipping a mug of coffee, wishing they'd just shut up about the whole thing. I wondered how long it might take for them to get round to asking me this question and thankfully, I have an answer at the ready which is vague enough to make it clear I'm not overly invested in their opinion, while at the same time gently directs the conversation away from me.

'I dunno, do I? Maybe he's psychic.'

Kath's eyes widen. 'Do you really think so?' she says. 'You know what? He did have that air about him.'

'I've heard of stranger things in my time,' says Brenda. 'For years we thought my next door neighbour's great aunt was loopy and then one day, when we'd gone to theirs for a barbecue, out of the blue she turns to me and says, "I've got a message for you from Auntie Margaret," and I said, "What is it?" because I actually did have an auntie Margaret and she said, "You've got to stop letting people walk over you." I tell you what, I felt a chill go through me when she said that because that was exactly the sort of advice my auntie Margaret used to give.'

If I believed in hell – which thankfully I don't – I think around about now Old Nick would be stoking up the heat in a special corner of his fiery kingdom in readiness of my arrival. To have told a barefaced lie that causes a disabled man to be dismissed as a delusional nutter is at best despicable and at worst outright appalling. But that's exactly what I've done. I nearly had a heart attack when I saw James DeWitt of all people standing in front of me. He was the last person on earth I ever expected to be a resident in a place like this. Bad things didn't happen to people like James DeWitt; his life was just too gilded. And yet here he was attempting to out me.

In my defence – and I use the term loosely – James's disability didn't factor in my decision to lie. When it came to refuting my past, I was an equal opportunities deceiver. He could've been as healthy as an Olympic athlete and possessed a mind as sharp as a chess grandmaster and I still would've peddled the same old 'Never seen you before in my life, mate', line. As far as anyone who asked about my past was concerned, I'd never been a pupil at King's Scrivener Boys' School, won a school prize which allegedly marked me out for greatness or for that matter, gone up to Cambridge University to study Economics. My CV was as uninspiring as they came. According to the story, I'd gone to an ordinary comprehensive, achieved half a dozen distinctly lack-lustre GCSEs, before launching myself into the world where I had achieved precisely zero. That was the way I told it (in the Nuneaton accent I was born with, rather than the received pronunciation I later adopted) in job interviews, dole office inter-rogations and even on my first date with Maya. To have told it any other way would've meant answering a question I had no interest in: what went so wrong that you ended up here?

These sorts of stories always begin with an inspirational teacher, and mine is no different. Mrs Ashworth, who taught me in year five at Waterman Street Primary in Nuneaton, was one of those teachers for whom nothing was ever too much trouble. She answered every question with patience, always knew the right thing to say to cheer you up and made every day in her classroom an adventure in which all the kids in the class, even the badly behaved ones, wanted to participate. Anyway, one wet autumnal parents' evening Mrs Ashworth told my parents something they hadn't been expecting to hear, news that for better or worse would change my life forever: she told them I was educationally gifted.

I suppose on some level, even before that day I'd been aware that I was a bright kid. I could read and write long before I arrived in reception and knew all of my times tables by heart. By the age of six I received special permission from my teacher to take editions of the school library's encyclopaedias home because I had devoured everything else I was given to read. And things that took other kids weeks to learn I'd pick up in a single afternoon. At the time, none of this seemed all that impressive to me because Waterman Street was a particularly average school, populated by particularly average kids from a particularly average housing estate and so if I thought about it at all, I put my success down to nothing more than being slightly better than average. But Mrs Ashworth didn't see it like that.

'I've been doing a lot of thinking about Danny's future lately,' she told my parents, 'and I firmly believe that a boy of his unique intellect needs to be in an environment where his talents are allowed to flourish, and I can think of no better institution where that might happen than King's Scrivener Boys' School.'

At this point I'd never even heard of the place, let alone been aware of its lofty status but I could tell from the way she said its name that it wasn't any ordinary school.

'It's a public school just outside Warwick,' she explained, 'and it's the best school in the county if not the country. I firmly believe that with preparation and lots of hard work, Danny could pass their entrance exam with flying colours. And given his academic aptitude, I'd expect him to receive a full academic scholarship so it shouldn't cost you a penny.'

'Cost us a penny?' repeated Dad. 'You mean it's not free?'

Mrs Ashworth apologised. 'I should've explained. King's Scrivener is a public boarding school with a very long and esteemed history, Mr Allen. Most of the parents whose sons attend have to pay many thousands of pounds per term for the privilege but, fingers crossed, Danny would get to go there for free.'

This last bit was especially important because if attending King's Scrivener had cost actual money there would've been no point in even talking to us about it. Dad had been laid off at the car parts factory he'd worked for three years earlier and barring a few odd jobs for friends and neighbours, had been out of work since.

'Boarding school?' said Mum. 'Isn't that where the children live at school full time?'

'I completely understand that this aspect of Danny's education will be of particular concern for you,' replied Mrs Ashworth. 'But for your son to get the most out of a school like King's Scrivener and not spend all of his time travelling to and fro, I think boarding would be the best option. Obviously he'd be home at Christmas, Easter, and the long summer holidays. And I'm sure you'd be able to visit him any weekend you liked.'

'I'm really not sure,' said Mum. 'What do you think, Roger?'

'Blowed if I know,' said Dad. 'Why not ask Danny what he thinks?'

Mum turned to me, her face the very picture of bewilderment. 'So what do you think, Danny? Do you like the sound of this new school?'

My ten-year-old brain fizzed with the possibilities. It felt like I was at the beginning of an exciting new adventure, on the verge of being handed a brand new life, one where I could be whoever I wanted to be. 'Very much,' I replied. 'I really want to go.'

Once Dad had checked and double-checked that it wasn't going to cost any money, a deal was struck whereby I would be tutored for the entrance exam by Mrs Ashworth. Every day after the end of school I'd wait until the other kids had left for home and she would give me lessons in verbal reasoning, Shakespeare, Latin, applied maths and anything else that came to mind. I loved every moment and soaked up everything I learned. When the day of the exam came the following September, Mrs Ashworth – worried that we might be late if we took public transport – drove Dad and me over to Warwick in her car. I remember as we passed through the huge cast-iron gates at the entrance and saw the school building for the first time, my jaw literally fell open. I'd never seen anything like it, at least nothing that was supposed to be a school. In the world I inhabited, schools were single-storey grey blocks surrounded by tarmac, and King's Scrivener was anything but. With its perfectly manicured lawns, water features and stately architecture it seemed more like a grand manor house or the home of a king or queen. I remember looking at Dad and thinking, 'What is this place?' only to see the same question written across his own face.

The three-hour exam was due to take place in the Great Hall and as my dad, Mrs Ashworth and I followed the other candidates along oak-panelled corridors, I gazed in awe at the walls lined with bronze busts of former headmasters, cabinets bursting with trophies and wooden plaques commemorating the sporting triumphs of scholars dating back to the late 1800s. It was like travelling back in time, walking back through history, and the more I saw of it the more desperately I wanted to pass the exam.

As we waited outside the Great Hall for the doors to open, I took the opportunity to get a better look at my rival candidates. Without exception they were in school uniform, even though it was a Saturday. I, meanwhile, was wearing the first clothes I'd picked up from the floor that morning: a pair of old jeans and a T-shirt. In addition to this it was hard not to notice how much taller and broader than my school friends these other boys were. If I'd passed them in the street, I would've guessed them to be at least a year or two older than I was, even though Mrs Ashworth had assured me we were the same age. Of all the boys I saw, however, one in particular stood out. He was a good four or five inches taller than I was, with a big mop of thick blond hair and the gait of a rugby player. I could tell he was the most popular boy at his school simply from the way he stood, shoulders back, spine straight as a rod, as if there wasn't a person or situation in the world that held any fear for him. When he spoke, the boys in his orbit hung on his every word and every now and then, boys in different school uniforms would go up and shake his hand firmly, in a way I'd only ever seen adults do. It was as if they imagined it was essential for them to pay their respects to him. As though he were a king, and everyone else mere subjects.

The doors to the Great Hall finally opened and as the first influx of pupils filed into the room, I felt an odd mix of dread and excitement. I felt sick at the idea that my entire future was riding on a single examination and yet, at the same time, I couldn't wait to show off everything Mrs Ashworth had taught me. As my turn to enter the room approached, my dad put his hand on my shoulder and told me he was proud of me no matter what happened, and then Mrs Ashworth patted me on the back and said, 'Now go and show them what we're capable of at Waterman Street.' Moments later, in the hall I sat down at a table not far from the centre of the hall and carefully set out my pens and pencils. Looking up at the stage in front of me, I noticed that painted on the wall in gold lettering, high above the red velvet curtains was the King's Scrivener school motto: '*Sic parvis magna*' which, using the Latin I'd learned from Mrs Ashworth, I translated as, 'Thus from small things comes greatness'.

8

James

'This is a bit of a change of tune isn't it, love? Last time I spoke to you, you didn't even want to leave your room and now look at you.'

I smile at the lady with the clipboard standing next to the coach that is going to take some of the residents to the Botanical Gardens in Birmingham. I hope my smile will be enough so that she will stop talking to me and let me just get on the bus.

'Well, whatever changed your mind, you really are in for a treat,' says the lady with the clipboard. 'The Botanical Gardens are an absolute delight. You're going to love them. Actually, if you're interested in plants, you might like to know that we've got a gardening club. It's every Wednesday morning in the rear gardens straight after breakfast. A lovely man called Nigel runs it – he works at the garden centre up the road – his uncle is a resident here. He's ever such an interesting chap. I can put your name down if you like.'

'Okay,' I say, even though I am not even a little bit interested in gardening, 'I will come to your gardening club. Can I get on the coach now?'

The lady with the clipboard laughs as if I have made a joke. 'Of course, love,' she says, 'be my guest.'

The reason I want to get on the coach quickly is because I want to get a seat next to Danny Allen.

If I get a seat next to Danny Allen, I can ask him why he is telling people that he does not know me when he does.

I know that since The Incident my memory does not always work like it should.

I know that sometimes I forget what I am saying or someone's name or what the right word for something is.

I know that in the past I have even forgotten to turn off the grill when I was cooking bacon for a sandwich and nearly burned down the house.

I suppose what I am trying to say is that I know that sometimes I make mistakes and get confused and muddled up. But I am not muddled up about Danny Allen.

The Danny Allen who works here at Four Oaks is the same one I went to school with. I told Martha this on the phone when she called on the night Danny Allen said he did not know me.

'Danny Allen from your year at school is at Four Oaks?' she asked, sounding very surprised. Even though Martha went to King's Scrivener Girls' School, she knew who Danny was because the girls' school and the boys' school used to do lots of activities together.

'Yes, Danny Allen from my school. And he is pretending not to know me.'

'Hold on, you're telling me that Danny Allen from your year at KS is a resident at Four Oaks?'

'No,' I said, wishing she were here with me so I could explain things properly.

'Is he a doctor?'

'No, he's one of the carers here.'

Martha laughed like I had just made a joke, even though I had not. 'Sweetie, you must be mistaken. You must have him mixed up with someone who looks like him. The Danny Allen we knew at school is most likely stuck in a lab somewhere creating a cure for cancer or writing speeches for the prime minister or doing whatever it is you do when you're someone like that. Come on, James, you remember what Danny was like, he was brilliant just like you. Chances are, this guy you're talking about is just someone who looks a lot like him.'

This made me really annoyed because I knew I had not made a mistake. I told her about how I had said, '*Sic parvis magna,*' to him and I felt sure that he had understood it but all she said was, 'Well, if he's there next time I visit, point him out so I can say hello because as I remember, he was quite the dish.' She said it in a way that meant she was joking, which made me feel like not talking any more. It also made me want to prove to her that she was the one that was wrong, not me. That is why when I saw Danny's name on the list as one of the carers going on the trip to the Botanical Gardens in Birmingham, I decided I would go too. I would go on the trip, sit next to Danny Allen on the coach and make him tell me why he was pretending not to know me. And then when he tells me, I will tell Martha and she will have to say sorry for making me feel like my head is not working.

Because the lady with the clipboard has talked to me for so long, lots of the other residents have been able to get on the coach before me. So when she finally lets me go, I push in front of a young man with a bald head and scramble up the steps on to the coach. The bald-headed man swears at me and tells me to wait my turn. I ignore him. Being in front of him means that at least he will not be sitting next to Danny Allen, so he can swear all he likes.

I spot Danny at the back of the coach, sitting in a window seat. It is good news. The space next to him is empty. But before I can get there, a man with a big ginger beard stands up and takes the seat next to Danny.

'You're all right, you are,' he says in a booming voice as he puts an arm around Danny's shoulders. 'I like you the best out of all of them.'

Because of the man with the big ginger beard, I have no choice but to sit down next to a young woman in a purple bobble hat. She smiles at me and holds out her hand. 'Hello,' she says, squinting her eyes as if she is really concentrating, 'my name is Vicky.'

I do not say anything to the young woman in the purple bobble hat. Instead I smile politely and then try and forget all about her while I keep an eye on Danny Allen.

The young woman in the purple bobble hat makes forgetting all about her very difficult because she keeps asking me questions.

She asks me what my name is, and how long I have been at Four Oaks, and if I have ever been to the Botanical Gardens

before. And because I am concentrating on spying on Danny
Allen, I keep my answers short. I say, 'James,' 'One and a half
weeks,' and, 'No.' I have a lot of problems with that last answer
because the truth is I cannot actually remember if I have been
there before – I might have because it sounds exactly like the
sort of place my parents would enjoy visiting – but since that
would need me to say more than a couple of words, I just say
no.

The young woman in the purple bobble hat stops talking to
me after I say, 'No.' Instead she takes out a pack of Polos from
her jacket pocket and pops one into her mouth without offering
me one. Soon I can smell her minty breath in the air and it makes
me wish I had some Polos of my own.

When we arrive at the Botanical Gardens, the lady with the
clipboard stands up and says, 'Right, ladies and gents, it's just
after eleven. If you're able, please make your way off the coach
and follow any staff member towards the reception.' The man
with the ginger beard who took my seat next to Danny has been
talking to him nonstop the entire journey. I cannot tell if Danny
Allen has been bored by what the man with the ginger beard has
been saying but I know I definitely have been because nothing
he says makes any sense. It is all . . . what is that word when
people do not make any sense? I cannot remember right now
but anyway, he is that.

We wait a long time in the reception at the Botanical Gardens
because some people need the loo. Danny and some of the other
carers have to go and help them. They are gone for quite a while.
In the end the lady with the clipboard has to send a carer with
blond hair to find out if they need help. When the carer with the
blond hair comes back with the others, she is really pink in the
face.

Next the lady with the clipboard says, 'It's eleven thirty now,
let's all try to stick together but if for any reason we do split up,
let's meet for lunch by the bandstand at one.' Danny is pushing
an elderly lady in a wheelchair while the man with the ginger
beard talks to him. The elderly lady is not saying anything. I'm

not sure she is even awake. We walk along the corridor to a set of double doors. There is a sign above the doors that says, 'Hot House'. The lady with the clipboard opens the door to let us all through. I feel a gust of warm, wet air on my face and that is when I remember that I have been here before.

I came here once with Zara.

Zara was my girlfriend and she was very beautiful.

It was a really hot day when Zara and I came here. We brought a picnic with us and ate it under the shade of a large oak tree. I think the day I am picturing was also the day that I first told her that I loved her. If it is not then at the very least it is very similar to that day.

After the hothouse we visit a greenhouse. It is full of cactuses. Afterwards we go outside to see all the different plants and trees. Vicky with the purple bobble hat tries to talk to me again. She says, 'It's nice here, do you like it too?' and I say, 'It is okay,' and then rush off so that I do not lose sight of Danny Allen.

Danny Allen is not doing anything interesting.

He and a plump carer are taking it in turns to push the elderly lady in the wheelchair. Every now and again they stop and sit down on a bench for a rest. The man with the ginger beard leaves them after a while. He booms, 'See you later, Danny,' and then goes off to bore some other poor carer instead.

A few times I try catching Danny's eye but he always looks away.

I wonder if maybe there is something wrong with Danny's brain, like there is with mine, and maybe that is why he cannot remember me.

I tell myself that I am not going to give up until I find out why Danny Allen is lying about knowing me. While I eat my sandwiches, I keep my eye on him at all times.

After a while I overhear Danny say to one of the other carers, 'I'm just going for a quick fag, won't be long,' and then he starts walking down the hill towards the children's playground.

This is it.

This is my chance to find out why Danny Allen is lying.

I put down my half-eaten sandwiches on the bench beside me where I'm sitting, stand up and follow Danny Allen.

I do not manage to get more than a few feet away before a voice calls out: 'And where might you be off to?'

I turn around to see the lady carer with the clipboard looking right at me with a frown on her face.

'I was just going to look at some plants.'

'Not without someone else being with you, I'm afraid. Health and safety.'

'But I am only going down the hill.'

She shakes her head. 'Not without a carer.'

I look down the hill at Danny Allen. If the lady with the clipboard had not stopped me, I could be talking to him right now and finding out why he lied about not knowing me. Defeated for now I turn around and head back to the bench where I left my lunch, but then suddenly there is a lot of shouting behind me. Two residents are arguing and look like they might hit each other and so the lady with the clipboard rushes over to break it up. The moment she turns her back on me I race down the hill as fast as I can manage before she sees that I have gone.

With my right leg being the way it is, it is difficult walking on any surface that is not flat and it really takes it out of me. I get down to the bottom of the hill though, and soon I find Danny Allen.

He is sitting on the edge of the koi pond, smoking a cigarette and playing on his phone. When he hears the sound of my feet on the crunchy gravel around the pond, he looks straight at me.

'All right, mate? You looking for something?'

'I want to know why you lied about knowing me.'

Danny Allen scrunches his face up like people do when they don't understand what I am saying. So I say it again only this time more slowly. 'I said I want to know why you lied about not knowing me.'

Danny throws his cigarette on the floor and crushes it underneath his shoe. I think he has understood me this time. 'Not this again,' he says. 'How many times have I got to tell you, mate? I don't know you.'

'But you do,' I say. 'I know you do. We went to boarding school together for seven years, we were in the same rugby team, we were in all the same top sets together and—'

'I've told you, mate, you've got the wrong person. Have you thought for a moment that maybe I just look like this guy you went to school with?'

'But you are him. I know it. And anyway, you have got the same name.'

Danny stands up and brushes down his trousers. 'Don't know what to tell you, mate. There are lots of people with the same name as me. Doesn't mean they all went to school with you though, does it?'

'No, of course not but—'

'So there you go. I'm not *your* Danny Allen, I'm just *a* Danny Allen. Sorry to let you down like this, mate, but I swear on my life we've never met before.'

For the first time since the day I saw him I begin to wonder if I might have got it wrong after all. Maybe he does just look like the Danny Allen I knew. Maybe my brain is playing tricks on me. I cannot think of any reason why the real Danny Allen would pretend not to know me. We might not have been best friends but we had always got along well.

'I think perhaps I have made a mistake,' I say. 'I am really sorry to have disturbed you like this and I promise I will never do it again.'

I feel sick with embarrassment as I begin making my way back up the hill. I tell myself that I am stupid and not to be trusted. But then from behind me I hear the man who I thought was Danny Allen swear loudly and I feel like I have to stop and turn around.

'Are you okay?'

The man I thought was Danny Allen looks unhappy. 'Ask me again if we went to school together.'

'But we did not. I know that now. I made a mistake.'

'Please, James. Just ask me one more time.'

I get a funny feeling in my stomach. I really wish someone else were here. 'I do not want to ask you again.'

'Please, James, just ask me and I promise I'll leave you alone.'

I rub my forehead with the back of my hand like I do some-times when I am scared or nervous. I do not like what is happening. I feel scared. I wish Martha were here. 'If I do it, do you promise to leave me alone?'

The man I thought was Danny Allen nods and puts two fingers up to his head like a salute. 'Scout's honour.'

I take a deep breath and say the words: 'Are you the Danny Allen who I went to school with?'

'Yes,' he says. 'Yes, I am.'

9

Danny

James DeWitt is staring at me open-mouthed as though waiting for me to deliver the punchline to a joke.

'It's me, James,' I say in case he hasn't fully understood. 'I'm Danny Allen. You were right when you said we were at King's Scrivener together. You were in Greville house and I was Beauchamp. We were both in the first XV rugby team and if I remember rightly, you played tight-head prop and I was on the wing. You've got a younger sister called Martha, who went to the girls' school . . . oh, and at the last awards day of our time at KS we were both up for the Carmody prize and it was me who won.'

'But . . . but . . . I don't understand,' says James in that same slurry voice that I'm only just about able to decipher. 'Why . . . why . . . would you lie about knowing me? Why would you let everyone think I was making things up?'

It's a good question and one that, considering everything I've put him through, he deserves to know the answer to, but right now I just can't summon the words or the strength required for such a mammoth task.

'It honestly doesn't matter. Whatever I say isn't going to justify the way I've behaved. You deserved better and I'm sorry I let you think you were wrong. I really am sorry. I know it's a long shot but is there anything at all I can do to make it up to you?'

'Make it up to me how?'

'How long have you got left here?'

'Two weeks. My parents are on a cruise. That is why I am here.'

'Okay then, name something you'd like to do in the next two weeks while you're here and I'll make it happen. It really is the least I can do.'

For a moment James just stares at me and I wonder if he's understood the question. The more I talk to him, the clearer it is that he's got some sort of mental impairment and finds interactions with people difficult. I decide to rephrase my offer in simpler terms but before I can say a word, something changes in his eyes as though an idea has just popped into his head.

'Anything at all?'

'Of course,' I reply, even though my natural sense of preservation wants to add caveats by the lorry load. 'You name it, I'll sort it.'

James doesn't speak for a long while. So long, in fact, that if it were not for the huge grin spreading across his face, I'd have thought he had forgotten my question.

'I would like to go to a pub,' he says, his grey-green eyes suddenly animated. 'I would like to go to a pub and have a proper drink. I think that is what I would like to do most of all.'

His request completely wrongfoots me. Of all the things I thought he might say, this hadn't even made the top ten. 'Are you absolutely sure about that?'

James nods eagerly. 'I want to go to the pub, have a proper drink and maybe even a packet of crisps.'

There are a whole host of reasons why James's request is problematic but for the sake of expediency here are the top three:

1. I can't take residents offsite without permission (and it's highly unlikely that I'll get permission for a trip like this).
2. I have no idea if or how his medication is affected by alcohol.
3. As a recovering alcoholic I haven't touched a drink or been inside a pub in nearly fourteen years.

'I'll tell you what,' I say, trying to salvage the situation. 'How about I bring you a nice couple of real ales from the off-licence instead and as many packs of crisps as you can eat?'

'That is very kind of you,' says James. 'But that is not what I want. What I want is to go to the pub and have a drink like normal people do. Like you said,' he adds grinning, 'it is the least you can do.'

'Fine, leave it with me,' I say, wondering how exactly I got myself into this situation, 'and I'll sort something out in the next few days.'

Seemingly satisfied by my response, James looks as though he might have more questions but then I hear one of my colleagues calling his name and not long after, she's joined by others.

'I think you'd best be going,' I say.

James holds out his hand for me to shake. 'It has been good to see you again, Danny Allen. It has been a long time. And do not worry, your secret is safe with me. I promise I will not tell anybody that you know me.'

His words hit me like a punch to the chest and I desperately want to explain that lying about knowing him had nothing to do with his disability but before I can say anything, he's heading back up the hill, leaving me alone to contemplate exactly what sort of person I am.

True to his word James doesn't tell anyone on the trip about our conversation; in fact, he doesn't do anything at all that might give the game away. Even when he's standing less than a few feet away from me, when we continue our tour of the gardens after lunch, he barely meets my eye, and while part of me is relieved that my lie hasn't been exposed, the rest of me feels guilty that the other carers still think he's completely deluded. I feel like I ought to do something, say something to make things right but in the end I decide the easiest thing to do is simply stop thinking.

The following afternoon, at the beginning of my shift, I start laying the groundwork for the mission I have planned to follow through with my promise. First off I swing by the office and let them know that James DeWitt has a hospital appointment later this afternoon and that Dean has asked me to accompany him. Next I get one of the qualified nursing staff to double check James's medical record to see whether he's actually allowed to drink alcohol. When she asks the reason for my question, I tell her it's because he's got a family party coming up and wants to know whether he's allowed a glass of champagne or two. After that I let the other carers know that I'll be out for a few hours this afternoon so will need them to cover my usual workload while I'm away and then finally I swing by James's room and deliver the good news directly to him: 'Be ready in half an hour because you and I are going to the pub.'

At three o'clock on the dot I return to James's room, pushing a wheelchair I'd picked up on a whim from the storeroom.

The moment James sees the wheelchair he pulls a face and mumbles something that sounds a lot like, 'What's that for?'

'For you. To help with the escape.'

'But I can walk. I do not need a wheelchair.'

'I know,' I say. 'I thought it might be more fun this way.'

James thinks for a moment and then smiles and climbs into the wheelchair. I grab a blanket from his bed and spread it over his legs to add a touch more authenticity to his invalided status. I catch a glimpse of us in the mirror of his wardrobe and can't help but think how insane this all is. I could lose my job for leaving the building without permission, let alone taking him to the pub. But it's too late for regrets. I owe him, and if a trip to the pub is what he wants to make things even, a trip to the pub is what he's going to get.

'Going anywhere nice?' ask Debs on reception as I push James past her desk.

'Mr DeWitt has got a hospital appointment and I'm taking him,' I reply.

'That's odd,' she says. 'Transport usually ring through when residents have hospital appointments. Do you want me to ring through for you and find out where they are?'

'Nah, don't bother,' I say casually. 'They're probably out in the car park having a fag. If I have any problems, I'll give you a shout.'

Even without being able to see James's face, I can tell he wants to laugh from the way his shoulders are hunched up and I just about manage to race through the automatic doors and halfway across the car park before he finally lets it all out.

'This is brilliant,' he says, after a small but nonetheless alarming coughing fit brought on by his laughing. 'It is like we are in a war film and escaping from the Germans.'

Once I've checked that the coast is clear, I help James out of the wheelchair. We hide it behind one of the huge bushes dotted along the main drive, then straighten our clothes and carry on towards the exit as if we are two ordinary members of the public taking an afternoon stroll.

As we trudge side by side through the long grass at the edge of the road on way to The White Horse — a fifteen-minute walk from Four Oaks — I try to make small talk with James.

'How come this is the thing you wanted to do?' I ask as a huge lorry passes by and almost blows us both off our feet. 'Does no one ever take you to the pub when you're at home?'

With his speech being the way it is and the noise of the traffic I struggle to understand his reply but I think he says, 'We do go sometimes but just for food not drink.'

'You never have a drink just to wind down at the end of the day?'

James shakes his head. 'My mum, Erica, and dad, Don, always say, 'Probably best not to, just to be on the safe side.''

'Doesn't sound like much fun.'

James shakes his head. 'Since The Incident I am always on the safe side of everything,' he says. 'Ever since The Incident the safe side is all I get to know.'

The Incident.

I'm guessing this is his way of talking about the accident or ailment that has left him like this. The James DeWitt I knew at school was nothing like the guy limping along next to me. The James DeWitt I knew at school was the boy everyone wanted to be. Athletic, sharp and boy-band handsome, he was the fourth generation of his family to have studied at the school and despite the presence of a number of actual European blue bloods within our ranks, James DeWitt really was the closest thing we had to royalty.

For reasons of circumstance James and I were never friends. Although popular, he tended to socialise with the boys he'd been at prep school with. I, meanwhile, preferred the company of other scholarship boys, if only because they were marginally less likely to mock me for being in possession of an identifiable regional accent.

I arrived at King's Scrivener determined to do my best and my hard work paid off. I ended up in the top set for every subject, as did James. We both excelled at sport too, playing for the school rugby team and the county and in the summer months, when we weren't busy playing cricket for the school team, we were hard at work winning silverware in athletics for the school trophy cabinets. Despite being thrown together at almost every opportunity, friendship eluded us. I think we both appreciated that for all our similarities in the ways that mattered most, in a school like King's Scrivener our differences counted for more.

The year before we were due to leave for university, our headmaster, Dr Fitzgerald, took us to one side and told us that 'barring an act of God' it was almost certain that one of us would win the Carmody prize. From our very first day at King's Scrivener, it was drummed into all of us that the Carmody prize was the highest honour the school could bestow. From its inception in the middle of the nineteenth century, we were told, Carmody prize winners had been destined for greatness. Despite Dr Fitzgerald's chat I was sure that the prize would go to James. After all he was a DeWitt, his great-grandfather, the famous philanthropist Charles Adolphus DeWitt, was a former Carmody prize winner, and it seemed only right that another DeWitt should win the day. But then on the final speech day of our school career, two months before I was due to arrive at Cambridge and James at Oxford, it was my name that was read out by Dr Fitzgerald, not James's.

I'll never forget that moment, the stunned silence in the Great Hall followed by an audible gasp from all corners as the shock of the announcement reverberated around the room. As I made my way to the stage, I was in such a daze that I failed to notice

James standing in my path until I almost walked into him. He shook my hand and without a shred of resentment said, 'Well done, Allen, the best man won.' It was like something from a different era, a time when things like honour, decency and scruples meant something. His response bewildered me to such an extent that the best I could offer in response was a hastily muttered, 'Thanks, DeWitt,' before collecting the award that would supposedly guarantee my success in the world.

As James and I walk along the edge of the road, side by side in silence, his reference to The Incident hangs heavy between us. As a carer I have full access to all residents' medical records but I had not even been slightly tempted to take a look and find out what had happened to him. I had no idea if he'd sustained his injuries while high on coke at the wheel of an overpriced sports car or undertaking humanitarian aid work in the Sudan. I suppose if I'm being honest, until now I don't think I really cared.

But when I think back to the grace and generosity of James's reaction to being pipped at the post by a kid from nowhere all those years ago, I realise that I owe him something. Maybe that was why I'd let my conscience get the better of me and confessed who I really was: because subconsciously I'd remembered that moment, and its impact on me.

I draw a deep breath as another lorry rushes by, blasting a gust of warm air in our direction. 'I know there's plenty in my own life I don't want to talk about,' I say, 'so I completely understand if you want to keep it to yourself but . . . I suppose what I'm trying to say is well . . . if you want to tell me about it . . . The Incident I mean … I'd be more than happy to listen.'

10

James

'Someone punched me.'

'What?' says Danny. 'You were in a fight?'

'No, not a fight, but I did get hit. I was out with friends because I had been elected to parliament.'

Danny looks confused like everyone does when they hear that I used to be an MP. 'You were in politics?'

'Yes I was,' I say. 'I was a Labour MP but I did not get to make my . . . to make my . . . thing in parliament though. I was in hospital. All my family thought I was going to die.'

I tell Danny how it all started. How on my night out a lad knocked into me on purpose, trying to cause trouble. I tell Danny that I told the lad that I did not want any trouble but he just would not listen. I tell Danny how he ran off when my friends came to help me and how we thought he had gone for good. Then I tell Danny that the lad came back and punched me from behind and ran away. I tell Danny that I hit my head when I fell and that is why I am like this now. I am like this because when I fell and hit my head I damaged my brain.

I tell Danny my injuries were so bad that for a while my family thought I was going to die. I tell Danny that because of what happened to my brain when I hit my head, I had to learn to do everything again. Like swallowing and chewing and how to talk and understand what people are saying. I tell Danny that it was like being a baby again and how three years on I still have problems thinking and remembering things. I tell Danny that I still cannot walk properly because my right leg and right arm do not work as they should, and how Dr Acari says rehabilitation is different for everyone who has a head injury. I tell Danny how some people get better straight away and it is almost like their injury never happened, and then others like me are never the same again. I tell Danny I do not think I will ever be like I used to be. I tell Danny that I can remember lots of things about my old life, like going to school and how it felt to drive a fast car and even what it was like to have a girlfriend, but that at the same time there are lots of things that I cannot remember. I tell Danny how Dr Acari says that sometimes I struggle to get the thoughts out of my head because they are stuck behind one another like cars in a traffic jam. I also tell him that sometimes I think of my head as being like a tube of toothpaste where my thoughts are like the toothpaste inside, and the words coming out of my mouth are like the toothpaste being squeezed out of a hole that is much too small.

'But you're getting better though, aren't you?' asks Danny. 'Or at least you're better than you were, surely?'

'I do not know,' I say. 'Dr Acari says most people with ABIs—'

'AB what?'

'Acquired brain injuries. That is what they call what I have got. Dr Acari says that most people with ABIs get better within a year, two at the very most. But for me it has been three years and I do not seem to be getting any better. I still get tired very easily. I still get confused sometimes. My speech is still slurred. I still have problems walking.'

We're silenced by the roar of two lorries passing by, after which a magpie makes a horrible noise in the tree above our heads. 'I'm so sorry,' says Danny when it is quiet again. 'It must have been a nightmare.'

'It was,' I say, 'but it is okay now.'

My legs are beginning to ache and I feel really tired but I do not want to say anything because I am enjoying being with Danny. I cannot remember the last time I had this much fun but I know that it has not been for a very long time. I feel as though I have gone from boring real life to being in a comedy action film where Danny and I are the stars.

I feel like I am alive.

When we reach the bottom of the hill, I ask Danny if we can sit down on a bench next to a bus stop and he asks me if I am okay and I say I am fine.

'I do not know why I said that,' I say, looking at Danny.

'Said what?'

'That I am okay after The Incident. I am not okay, Danny Allen. It was not fair what happened to me. It was not fair at all. I did not do anything to Kyle Baylis. I did not do anything and yet he ruined my life.'

'Is that his name then? The name of the guy who punched you?'

I nod. 'He is in prison now. He was twenty-one years old and had been in trouble with the police all his life. When The Incident happened, he had been drinking and taking drugs because he was angry, because he had been arguing with his girlfriend.' I smile. 'If he had just bought her a bunch of flowers and a box of chocolates like anyone else, I would be fine right now.'

Danny does not laugh.

'You can laugh, you know,' I tell him. 'It is okay to laugh sometimes. People think that because of the way I walk and the way I talk that I cannot make jokes but I can.'

'I'm just shocked that's all,' says Danny, 'not by you but by the situation. It seems like madness that this happened. Unreal. How long did he get in the end?'

'Five years. My barrister said that was good for a crime like this. But it does not seem like very much to me at all. One day he will be let out and he will get his life back. But I am never going to get my old life back. My old life is gone forever.'

I ask Danny how far we are from the pub and he tells me that we are only a few minutes away, and so I tell him that we should hurry up because we are wasting valuable drinking time.

'I can't believe how I treated you, when all you wanted to do was say hello,' says Danny when we have been walking for a while. 'You must think I'm a right scumbag.'

'I do not think you are a scumbag at all, Danny Allen,' I say, and it is true I do not because I am having so much fun. 'Anyway, a scumbag would not take me out to the pub for a drink, would they?'

It is not long until we reach the pub. It has whitewashed walls and ivy growing around the windows. It looks like the sort of place you might go to for Sunday lunch or a drink after you have been for a long walk in the countryside.

Danny and I cross the road and walk up to the entrance. I feel like we are two old friends going for a drink, something I have not done for a very long time. I am looking forward to going inside and remembering what it was like to go for a drink with a friend, but then something odd happens. Danny stops suddenly. He bends over, resting his hands above his knees as if he is out of breath from going on a long run.

I put a hand on the small of Danny's back like my mum, Erica, does if I am not feeling well.

'Are you okay, Danny Allen?'

'I just need a minute, I'll be fine.'

'Are you feeling ill? You do not look right.'

'I'm okay,' he says, straightening up, 'really I am,' and then without another word he walks inside.

What has just happened is odd. I have lots of questions I would like to ask about it. But I do not say anything because I do not want to spoil things.

There are lots of people in the pub.

Some are wearing suits and ties, and others have on normal clothes. I had forgotten how noisy pubs are. There is music and the sound of people talking and beeps from the fruit machine. I am finding it quite hard to think.

At the bar Danny asks me what I would like to drink.

My mind goes blank.

I know I would like a drink but I do not know what sort.

'I am not sure,' I say, 'maybe you should choose.'

'What kind of thing did you used to like?' asks Danny.

'I do not know,' I say. 'I know I should remember but I cannot.'

'I'll order a lager,' says Danny, 'and if you don't like that I'll get you something else.'

Danny orders a lager and an orange juice.

'Are you not having a lager too?' I ask.

Danny pats his stomach. 'Better not,' he says. 'I'm not exactly feeling great. Probably something I ate. Maybe next time though, eh?'

This feels odd.

Danny looks fine to me.

He does not look ill at all.

But then I remember his funny turn when we arrived and so I think that perhaps he might not be so well after all.

'If you are not feeling well enough to have a drink,' I say, 'maybe I should not have one either.'

I say this because part of me is a bit scared.

Part of me thinks it is probably best not to have a lager just to be on the safe side.

Part of me does not like the idea of being any worse than I am now.

'Rubbish,' says Danny. 'If there's anyone who deserves a drink more than you, I'd like to meet them. And before you ask, I've checked and you're perfectly fine to have a beer or two as long as you don't go overboard.'

I stop feeling scared.

I think I actually would like that drink after all.

I think this is going to be fun.

'I will have the lager after all, thank you, Danny,' I say. 'I would like it very much.

The barmaid pours our drinks and Danny hands me mine. It feels cold and heavy in my hands. Holding it reminds me of the nights out I used to have with friends.

Friends who I thought would be in my life forever.

'I don't want to sound like a broken record,' says Danny, 'but I just want to say again that I'm really sorry about . . . well . . . you know. It was out of order how I behaved and I just hope you can forgive me.'

'Forgive you for what?' I say, grinning.

Danny looks puzzled and so I explain. 'That was me making a joke . . . because . . . you know my brain does not work properly so I sometimes forget things and you know . . . you are asking me to forgive you, which is a bit like forgetting isn't it?'

'So it is,' says Danny. 'That was a good one.'

'The thing is,' I say, 'because of the way I talk and the way that I walk and because my brain does not always work properly, people think I cannot make jokes when I actually can.'

'I'll try to remember that,' says Danny and then he raises his glass in the air. 'What are we drinking to?'

'I do not mind. You say.'

Danny shakes his head. 'This is your treat. You decide.'

I think hard for a long while. Nothing springs to mind. I do not really care what we drink to. I just want us to have a good time.

'Come on, James,' says Danny. 'My arm's getting tired. What's it going to be?'

'How about old friends?'

'To old friends it is,' says Danny then we clink glasses and Danny says we should find somewhere to sit.

Danny and I find an empty table and he rips open the packets of crisps and lays them in the middle so we can share them. We talk about ordinary things. The ordinary things that people my age talk about when they go out with their friends.

It feels relaxed and easy.

No one is telling me to take my elbows off the table.

No one is cutting up my food.

I am just being me.

I cannot quite believe how happy I am.

We talk for a while longer. Danny tells me a funny story about one of the other residents at Four Oaks and I am about to ask him which one it is when something odd happens.

I see my parents.

They are in the pub and they are looking around all the tables as if they are searching for someone. Dean from the care home is with them too.

I tell myself that my brain must not be working properly.

My parents are on the other side of the world and are not coming home for another thirteen days.

I tell myself I must be seeing things.

But then Danny looks over his shoulder to see what I am staring at, and I can tell from his face that he is seeing the same thing as me.

11

Danny

Before I can ask James how it's possible for his parents to be both here in Kenilworth and some four thousand miles away in the Caribbean, Mr DeWitt launches himself at me with the ferocity and vigour of a much younger man. Such is his speed that I don't stand a chance of resisting his attack. He knocks me clean off my chair, sending me crashing onto the polished pine floorboards.

'What the blazes do you mean by absconding with my son like this?' demands Mr DeWitt, as Dean stands in between us while Mrs DeWitt shrieks wildly for her husband to leave me alone.

I can't believe it. He thinks I've kidnapped his son. 'I haven't *absconded* with anyone!' I protest as I scramble to my feet. 'James asked me to bring him here. Ask him yourself if you don't believe me!'

'Is this true, James?' demands Mr DeWitt, his voice brimming with indignation. 'Did you actually ask this man to bring you here?'

James nods reluctantly. 'I wanted to go for a drink in a pub and Danny Allen said he would take me,' he says. 'I did not mean to get anyone into trouble. Anyway . . . what are you and Mum doing here? I thought you were on holiday.'

'Daddy and I were missing you so much that we thought we would surprise you by coming home early,' says Mrs DeWitt tearfully. 'And then when we arrived at Four Oaks and couldn't find you, we panicked thinking the worst. Then someone said they'd spotted you being pushed in a wheelchair by this young man and another said they'd seen you walking towards this pub and we just thought . . . well I don't know what we thought . . . we were just so—'

Mrs DeWitt is silenced by the arrival of a tubby, red-faced man pushing urgently past her. He positions himself between Mr DeWitt and me like a referee in a boxing grudge match. 'I don't care what's going on here,' he says, splitting his attention between me and the DeWitts, 'but this is my pub and if you don't take this outside right now, I'm calling the police. Now clear off, the lot of you!'

Before we can object, we're surrounded by half a dozen of the pub's staff and roughly ushered through the lounge and straight out into the car park.

'This is an outrage!' bellows Mr DeWitt, as The White Horse's landlord informs us that we're banned from his establishment for good. 'I've never been treated in such an outrageous manner in my life!'

Dean puts a calming hand on Mr DeWitt's shoulder. 'On behalf of Honeywell International Care Homes, may I—'

A single glare from Mr DeWitt is all it takes to mute Dean's corporate apology and force him to meekly withdraw his hand. 'Not another word from you!' spits Mr DeWitt. 'From this moment onwards my next communication with you and your employers will be via my legal team. And trust me when I say that by the time they're done, both you and Honeywell International Care Homes will be finished in this industry for good!' Still fuming, Mr DeWitt barks, 'I am leaving,' to no one in particular and stomps angrily in the direction of a gleaming, brand new Range Rover. Mrs DeWitt jumps to attention and follows in her husband's wake, but then comes to a halt when she discovers that James isn't behind her.

'I'm not sure you quite heard me, James,' says Mr DeWitt after Mrs DeWitt brings James's inertia to his attention. 'I've said that we're leaving.'

'No you did not,' says James, his voice more unsteady than usual. 'You said, "*I'm leaving*," which means you are the one going, not me.'

I shift uncomfortably as I witness James's small act of rebellion. Much as I can completely understand the point he's trying to make, I'm not sure this is the time or the place.

'You're being ridiculous, James,' snaps Mr DeWitt. 'As you can see, your mother has quite clearly understood my meaning so there's no reason why you shouldn't have done. Let's hear no more of this, please. It's time for us to leave.'

'I do not want to go,' says James in a voice barely more than a whisper.

Mr DeWitt turns to his wife for clarification. 'What did he say? I couldn't quite make it out.'

'I don't want to go,' repeats James, a little louder this time as everyone, myself included, stares at him in shock. 'I want to stay where I am.'

In a bid to calm the situation down, a clearly emotionally drained Mrs DeWitt intervenes. 'Obviously today's events aside, darling, no one's more pleased than us that you've enjoyed your time away but, sweetheart, we're here now and we need to collect your things and go home. It's been an awfully long day for all of us so please, James, let's have no more of this.'

James casts a look in my direction as though he believes me capable of fixing this situation. I've got nothing.

'Look,' I say half-heartedly, 'we can keep in touch if you like and—'

'Over my dead body!' barks Mr DeWitt. 'If I discover that you've had any kind of contact with my son, young man, I will have you arrested.'

'Oh don't you worry, Mr DeWitt,' says Dean, seizing the opportunity to get on Mr DeWitt's good side. 'I can assure you that no employees of Honeywell International Care Homes will make contact with your son without your express—'

Mr DeWitt silences Dean with another glare before turning his attention to his son. 'James, I'm not going to tell you again: we are leaving with or without you. The choice is yours.'

Without looking back Mr DeWitt marches towards his car while his wife reluctantly trails after him. James looks at me, presumably hoping for some show of solidarity, but the best I can do is shrug and cast my gaze down to my feet. I'm in enough trouble as it is. I don't need any more.

'You do realise this is going to be a disciplinary issue,' says Dean as the DeWitts' Range Rover swings in a sharp arc across the car park, only narrowly missing us, before exiting on to the slip road of the dual carriageway. 'To be honest, I can't see how you're not going to be dismissed. It's a shame really. We had such high hopes for you, Danny, really we did. I actually said to Pat only the other day that I thought you showed a lot of potential. I'm not just blowing smoke up your arse either, I really did say that. And you know what, I think if you hadn't messed up today, six months down the line, with help from me, you could've secured a place on the trainee management programme. Not now, of course. Now you're just going to be tossed back on the dole heap where we found you, and for what? So you can treat some retard to an afternoon out?'

'Do you know what, Dean?' I say, only just managing to resist the urge to punch his lights out. 'In the time I've worked at Four Oaks I've met all sorts of people with all kinds of disabilities but the only retard among them was you. You can keep your job and your disciplinary procedures and shove them where the sun doesn't shine because, I quit.'

Despite getting to tell Dean exactly what I think of him, as I trudge back up the hill to the care home to collect my things my mood is far from celebratory. I have, after all, lost my only source of income and all hope of being able to sign on any time soon. Maya is going to completely detonate when she finds out everything that's happened. In an instant there will be such an intense release of energy that along with half of Coventry we will both be vaporised out of existence.

As I reach the entrance to the care home, it occurs to me that perhaps if I play it differently, things might not have to go the way I've imagined. This moment rather than heralding the end of my relationship could, for instance, be an opportunity for a new beginning. I could come clean with Maya once and for all, not just about getting sacked from Four Oaks, but about my entire life. I could confess all the secrets I've hidden from her over the years, from the fact that I was taught in the very same classrooms as the celebrities we sometimes watch on TV, right through to what happened with Helen and everything that followed in the wake of losing her. For the first time ever I could experience the sweet relief of sharing with another human being everything about me: the good, the bad, and the downright ugly. Finally someone else will understand that it was never part of the plan for me to be like this. I was never meant to be the self-centred and self-destructive creature that I now am. I was never meant to be like this at all. And then maybe, just maybe, once someone else understands everything, they can help me figure my way out of this mess so I can get back to being who I was always supposed to be.

Despite the danger involved in such a confession, by the time I reach home not only do I feel like it's still a good idea but that it's perhaps the greatest idea I've ever had. I really do feel like this could be the biggest change to happen to me in years. Perhaps having reached rock bottom, I'm about to bounce my way back up to the top.

The moment I step inside the flat I call out Maya's name and find her in the kitchen at the sink. She's still wearing her work clothes and when she turns to face me, her hands are dripping with soap suds. She picks up a novelty tea towel with the words, 'To dry or not to dry? That is the question,' on it next to a picture of William Shakespeare's face. It's one I bought for her as a joke present on a day out to Stratford-upon-Avon during our first few months together.

'I've got something I need to tell you.'

'Me too,' she counters. 'Can yours wait a minute? It's just that if I don't say it now, I've got a horrible feeling I'll never say it at all. I can't do this any more, Danny. I just can't. I feel terrible about it, really I do. I thought your getting a job would make a difference, I thought it would be the making of us but it hasn't been at all. The truth is I just don't love you any more, Danny, and I haven't done for a very long time. And I'm so glad that you're working now and I really hope that it helps you to sort out those demons of yours, and maybe some lucky girl will reap the rewards one day. But I'm afraid that girl won't be me. It's just too little, too late and it's time we call it quits. I'm going to stay with a friend from work for a few days. I've already packed some things, so I'll be out of your hair once I've finished up here. We can decide about the flat when you're ready to talk. I'm happy to take over the lease on my own but if you feel you'd like to take it yourself now you're working I'll be more than happy to let you have it. Just let me know what you decide.' She looks at me as if waiting for me to respond but I can't because it's taking all the strength I have to keep from collapsing right here on the spot.

'Aren't you going to say anything?' she asks.

I shake my head as all non-essential functions begin shutting down one after the other.

'Fine,' she says, 'but at least tell me what it was that you were going to say to me.'

There's absolutely no point in confessing anything to her now. In fact, if I've learned anything from this, it's that I was kidding myself when I thought things could be different. Even if I had told her everything, it's clear to me now that it wouldn't have changed anything. I'm alone in this, I get that now, and from here on in it's just me and my demons. Without saying a word to her, I grab my coat and my keys and head out of the flat with one intention: to get as drunk and wasted as is humanly possible.

12

James

'Is something wrong, James?'

As I lift my eyes from the plate of pork chops, potatoes and broccoli I imagine telling my mum, Erica, exactly what is wrong. I imagine telling her that I am angry because she has chopped up my food like I am a baby.

I imagine telling her that even though it has been a week since they brought me home from Four Oaks, I am just as embarrassed now as I was then.

I imagine telling her that I have not watched a single episode of *Friends* or a single action film or anything else because I feel so sad.

I imagine telling her that even though I pretend to like running errands with my dad, Don, the truth is I do not.

I imagine telling her that I hate all of the clothes that she buys me because they make me look like Dad.

I imagine telling her how sometimes I dream of having supper just once without a serving of broccoli.

I imagine.

I imagine.

I imagine.

'Nothing is wrong. I was just thinking about something.'

'Oh, that's nice,' she says. 'Was it anything interesting?'

'Not really,' I say. 'It was not very interesting at all.'

After supper I go to my room and think about when Danny Allen and I went to the pub.

Thinking about that day is my favourite thing to do now.

When I think about it I always smile because it was such good fun.

I still cannot believe I had a lager. Whenever I ask for a drink at home, my family always remind me about being 'on the safe side'. But when I was with Danny, I was not on the safe side and nothing bad happened to me.

I was okay.

Nothing went wrong.

And I learned something.

I learned that if someone tells you to be on the safe side lots of times then after a while they do not need to say it.

After a while you just say it to yourself in your head like, 'I had better not do that, just to be on the safe side.' I thought it when Danny gave me my lager. I thought to myself, 'Maybe I should not drink this, just to be on the safe side.'

Sometimes it feels like my family are all inside my head talking at once. They are all chat-chat-chatting so much that I cannot hear myself think. It is no wonder I get tired sometimes, if I am always thinking other people's thoughts as well as my own.

One day I would like to have a head full of thoughts that are just mine.

My favourite thing about being in the pub with Danny Allen was when we talked. Usually when I talk to people about The Incident I feel sad afterwards because I am remembering things that are not very nice. But when I was talking to Danny, I did not feel sad or happy.

I just felt lighter.

When Danny and I talked, it was like we were friends. I know that we were not really friends in the way that normal people are friends but it still felt nice.

Danny and I did not just talk about The Incident. We talked about normal things too. We talked about things that my mum and dad and sister would never talk about with me. We talked about football and TV programmes and science fiction films and films with explosions. It reminded me of when I had friends.

I used to have lots of friends.

I used to be popular.

I had friends from all over the place like school and university and the rugby club, and work and the local Labour Party.

My main friends were Sam, Miles and David. We were all at King's Scrivener together. Every weekend it used to be me, Sam, Miles and David, their girlfriends, Beatrice, Abbie and Annabelle, and my girlfriend, Zara. We were a bit like the friends in *Friends* for a while. Before Zara moved in with me, Miles and I used to live together like Joey and Chandler. We were like the friends in *Friends* because we used to spend all of our time together and have lots of fun.

These were the friends who were with me when The Incident happened.

I used to think that we would always be friends.

I used to think we would be friends forever.

My mum said that when I was in hospital, Sam, Miles and David came to see me every day but if they did I do not remember. I definitely remember them visiting after I came home from hospital though. One day after not hearing from them for a long time they turned up at the house. They kept saying things to me like, 'You are really looking better,' and 'I can't wait until we can all go out again.' They did not know then that I was not me any more. They thought that if they just gave it lots of time then one day I would be back to normal. They did not know that for me this was normal. They did not know this was the new me. After that visit they stopped visiting altogether. Instead I would get texts from them saying how busy they were and how they would call to make plans to see me soon. I never replied though, because I was not me any more and I was not ever going to be again. Anyway, by that time I had already split up with Zara, so I do not think I would have been much fun to be around.

As I am still very angry with my parents, at the weekend I ask Martha if I can stay with her. Martha lives in a nice house in Oxford. She used to live with her boyfriend Lucien but they split up at the beginning of the year and now she lives there alone. I did not like Lucien very much. He was not very nice. He would sometimes not talk to me even if it were just the two of us in a room. Other times he would speak to me slowly in a really loud voice as though I was a deaf person. When Martha split up with Lucien, I was sad but only because she was sad. Sometimes I like to joke that Martha is my favourite sister (when in fact she is my only sister) because it is my way of saying how lovely she is. If Martha had not been sad about Lucien, I would not have been sad at all. In fact, I think I might have cheered.

'I really am very sorry that I did not believe you about Danny,' says Martha as I help her clear away after we have eaten lunch. 'It was absolutely unforgivable of me. You said you'd seen him and I should've believed you.'

'It is okay that you did not believe me,' I say. 'Danny Allen made me think that he was not Danny Allen so I suppose I could not have been all that sure after all.'

'So do you think he lied to you because of his job?'

'How do you mean?'

'Well, you know, working in a care home. Maybe he was embarrassed.'

'Why would Danny Allen be embarrassed? There is nothing wrong with working in a care home.'

'Of course, I'm not saying there is,' says Martha. 'It's just that well . . . this is Danny Allen we're talking about. If anyone was going to make something of themselves after KS it was going to be him and now he's working as a carer. It's just odd, that's all.' She holds up her hand. 'I promise, I'm not just being a snob. It's just that it's a pretty weird thing for the Danny Allen we knew to end up doing.'

'Okay,' I say, even though I think she is being a little bit of a snob, 'I understand what you are saying.'

Martha clears the last of the dishes from the table and begins wiping down the surfaces. 'I'm really not a snob, you know,' she says.

I have been teasing her about being a snob ever since we were young. It is nice to have at least one joke to share with her that started life before The Incident. 'I know you are not a snob,' I say. 'I have seen you shopping in Tesco plenty of times.'

Martha throws the cloth in her hand at me. It misses and lands on the floor. 'So did Danny talk to you about what he's been up to since school?' she asks, picking up the cloth.

'A little bit,' I say but then I think about some of the things that Danny and I talked about and realise that unless I have forgotten, he did not say very much of anything at all. 'Actually, no,' I say to Martha. 'Danny Allen did not say anything about what he has been doing since school. I suppose he might tell me another time.'

'James, sweetie,' says Martha, 'you do realise you're not going to be able to see Danny again, don't you?'

'But I want to. We had such a good time.'

'I know you did but you must know Daddy will never allow it. Mum told me she'd never seen him quite so angry as she did that day. And then when she told me how Daddy had rugby tackled Danny to the ground, I couldn't believe it. Rightly or wrongly, after all that's gone on, James, there's simply no way he will ever let you see Danny again.'

'That is not fair,' I say. 'It is my life. I should be able to do what I want. I am a grown man!'

Martha dries her hands on a tea towel. 'Of course you are, sweetie,' she says, pulling me close for a hug. 'And there isn't a day that goes by that I don't wish you could have your freedom back. All I'm saying is that of all the battles that lie ahead for you, this isn't one worth fighting.'

Martha and I have a lovely weekend. We do lots of fun things like meeting up with her friends for a meal and going for a walk in the countryside. On Sunday morning after a late breakfast Martha brings me back home. She does not stay for long as she has got work to do at home. At lunch my parents try to talk to me about what Martha and I have been up to but I do not say a word. Instead I just stare at my plate of roast chicken with potatoes and broccoli that my mum has again cut up into tiny pieces.

'Is everything all right, James?' asks my mum.

'No it is not,' I say, still staring at my plate. 'I have had enough!'

'James!' says my dad in his angry voice.

'Whatever's wrong, darling?' asks my mum.

'I do not want to live here any more,' I say.

'He doesn't mean it, dear,' says my dad. 'I think he's just unhappy that you've cut up his food again.'

'Oh, I have, haven't I?' says my mum, Erica, staring at my plate. 'I'm so forgetful. You must think I need a new head.'

'It is not about my food,' I say, even though it is a little bit. 'I just do not want to live here any more. I want to move back into my old apartment in Birmingham, I think it is time.'

'I know you're frustrated, James,' says my dad. 'But you must know that's just not possible.'

'It's not safe for you to be on your own,' says my mum. 'You do remember the fire, don't you?'

'Of course I do!' I say. 'How could I forget, when you remind me of it every day?'

'But it was *a fire*, Jamie,' says my mum. 'A fire in our home! I dread to think of what might have happened if the neighbours hadn't heard the smoke alarm and called the fire brigade.'

'But I was okay,' I say. 'No one got hurt, did they?'

'But that's hardly the point, is it?' says my mum. 'The point is, you could've been hurt. And that means that without a shadow of doubt you can't live on your own.'

I want to cheer when my mum says this because she and Dad have fallen into my trap. 'But that is just the thing,' I say, 'I am not going to move back into my old apartment on my own. I am going to move back into my apartment with Danny Allen.'

13

Danny

'I'd just like to say thanks once again for all your contributions this week,' says the man in the checked shirt at the front of the room. 'And thanks for coming. Don't forget we'll be here again next week, same time and if over this coming week any of you feel like things are getting too much, as always just remember: we win this battle one day at a time.'

A few people clap in agreement and one or two even cheer but most are content to nod silently. Then, one by one the assembled crowd leave, picking up the hard plastic chairs we've been sitting on, adding them to the stack at the back of the room.

As I file out into the bright light of the midday sun I make plans to drop into the supermarket on the way home. I don't manage to get more than a few feet away from the church before I hear someone call after me. I turn around to see a woman looking straight at me. She's about my age, wearing a checked shirt and ripped jeans, and is carrying an old army surplus rucksack. Her dark brown hair is in dreadlocks tied back in a ponytail. It's a look that was probably quite cool when she started wearing it back in her twenties, but now it looks a little eccentric or at the very least as though her washing machine's broken and this outfit is made up of the only clean clothes she could find. There's something about her though that I'm immediately drawn to. Perhaps it's her deep brown eyes, or the slight scattering of reddish-brown freckles across the bridge of her nose, or maybe it's because she like me has just stepped out of an Alcoholics Anonymous meeting.

'I haven't seen you here before,' she says.

'And you probably won't again,' I reply.

'Not your thing?'

'I had a wobble recently. Didn't succumb but it was pretty close. Thought it might be a good idea to get a top up.'

She nods thoughtfully. 'How long?'

'Thirteen years. You?'

She theatrically doffs an invisible cap. 'I'm a veritable novice: eight years and counting. What started off your wobble if you don't mind me asking?'

'Addicts have always got a reason. That's why they're addicts.'

'But you're okay now?'

'Like I said, it was just a wobble.'

She reaches into her rucksack, takes out a pencil stub and a paperback, scribbles something on the inside cover, tears off the top half, and hands it to me. 'In case you have another wobble,' she says.

I look at what she has written. It's her name, Kaz, and her phone number, after which she's drawn a smiley face. I flip the torn book cover over. It's E. M. Forster's *A Room With a View*. I'm not sure which says more: her choice of reading material or her casual attitude to book vandalism.

'Thanks,' I say. 'But I promise you I won't need to call.'

'Let's hope not,' she says, and then she gives me a wink and disappears back inside the church.

On the bus on my way home I think about it, the moment I nearly started drinking again. When I'd left the flat after being dumped by Maya, it had been my full intention to drink and not stop until I was face down in the gutter. But as I reached the off-licence, instead of thinking about having a drink, all I could think about was Leila. How if I went through this door, I'd be giving up all hope of ever seeing her again; how if I start drinking again, I wouldn't just be letting myself down but her too. So that was that. The need to be a better man for my daughter was enough to turn me around, even when the odds of us ever meeting in reality are virtually nil. It didn't make sense. But then again, maybe it didn't need to. Maybe the most important thing was having a reason to stay sober and for better or worse Leila was mine.

Getting off the bus, I make my way across the estate towards the flat but as I approach my building's communal entrance, I notice two figures lurking nearby and brace myself for trouble. In recent weeks there have been a spate of muggings in the area but as I ball up my fist in preparation to defend myself, I spot their smart clothing and immediately relax. My first bet is that they're Jehovah's Witnesses come to convert the residents of Summerfield House but when they look in my direction I realise that they're not inner city missionaries at all. Standing on the left is James DeWitt and, though I haven't seen her in eighteen years, I'm pretty sure the person next to him is his sister, Martha.

Since that day at the pub, I'd thought of James DeWitt often and had even looked him up online. I'd hoped that googling him would fill in some of the gaps in my knowledge and answer some of the questions I hadn't felt able to ask.

From a mixture of social media, online newspaper articles and Labour Party newsletters I learned a lot about James DeWitt, most of which anyone who paid the slightest attention to current affairs would likely already know. I learned that having spent his post-university career working for a property development company in London, at the age of twenty-seven James had set up his own and started a company specialising in the redevelopment of old office buildings into residential accommodation in and around the Midlands. Within just five years his company was so successful that he was bought out by a major international developer leaving him free to finally pursue a lifelong interest in politics. Within a year James had gone from being a significant Labour Party donor and fundraiser to being selected by his local constituency to fight an unexpected by-election in the Conservative stronghold of Birmingham South. He campaigned hard and won the vote with such a sweeping majority that within hours of his victory James DeWitt was earmarked by political commentators in the national press as potential shadow cabinet material. It seemed like there was no stopping him. But then in an online newspaper article from three years ago, headlined, 'New MP fights for life following vicious assault', I read about the attack that changed his life.

In researching James, what I found most difficult to get my head around was the discrepancy between the man I'd met at Four Oaks, who liked action films and old episodes of *Friends*, and the business genius with political ambitions I'd read about online. It didn't make sense that a single event could have transformed someone so radically, that one day he was himself and then for no other reason than bad luck he woke up as someone else entirely. It seemed too much like the stuff of science fiction and horror movies, of *Revenge of the Bodysnatchers* or *Freaky Friday*, certainly not something that could occur in the real world. And yet James DeWitt was living proof that things like this could and did happen, that you could have the perfect life and have it wrestled from your grasp. As I read about James, I couldn't help wondering if he missed who he was, or could even recall his old life. And then, because all thoughts, no matter how altruistic, always end up being self-centred in some way if you give them long enough, I wondered how I'd feel if in a split-second I was stripped of the ability to be me.

'Danny Allen,' says James. 'I bet you never thought you would see me again. You remember my sister, Martha, don't you?'

Martha DeWitt. All the boys at KS adored her. Two years younger than her brother she was cool and clever and almost never single. She was the dictionary definition of unobtainable. I'd often wondered which minor member of royalty she would end up marrying.

I turn to Martha and smile. 'Good to see you. Keeping well?'

'Yes thanks,' she replies, 'how about you? Even at the girls' school you were a bit of a legend. The great Danny Allen.'

I don't think she'd meant it ironically. Most likely she was just trying to be nice. But given that we're standing in one of the grimmest council estates in Coventry and I've got takeaway curry stains on my jeans and a hole in my trainers, it sounds like the worst kind of sarcasm. I allow her compliment to fall on stony ground and attempt to usher us past the point of school reunion to the motive for their visit.

'So, what's this all about? I don't work at the home any more so I'm not exactly sure how I can help you.'

'Did they sack you?' asks James.

'Let's just say we had a difference of opinion.'

'I am sorry my dad tried to hit you,' says James. 'And I am sorry you lost your job.'

'I've got an interview for another care home job next week so I'll be fine. It was nice of you to drop by though.'

'Actually,' says Martha, 'we haven't just come to apologise. We're here because James has got a proposition for you.'

'I want to offer you a job,' says James.

'A job? Doing what exactly?'

'I want to move back into my apartment in Birmingham,' he says, 'and I would like to offer you the job of being my full-time live-in carer.'

My head throbs at how weird this day has been so far. How could it be that one moment I'm in an AA meeting because of a near relapse and the next I'm being offered a job looking after a brain-damaged guy with whom I used to go to school. Part of me is flattered because this is pretty much the only time I have ever been headhunted for a job, but mostly I'm thinking this is just too weird. I can't be James DeWitt's carer. I just can't, even if his job offer would be an answer to my two biggest problems right now: where am I going to live and what am I going to do for money?

'It's kind of you to think of me James, really it is but . . .'

'We should go,' says Martha coolly. 'Clearly we're wasting his time and our own. He doesn't want to do it, James.'

'But I do not understand,' says James, looking at me accusingly. 'Why don't you want to be my carer? Is it about the money because if it is, I have plenty.'

'It's not about the money,' I reply even though I'm partially curious about how much is on offer. 'It's just not something I want to do.'

'But . . . but . . . you haven't got a job,' stutters James, desperately trying to keep hold of his emotions. 'And I'm . . . I'm . . . I'm offering you one. Why don't you want my job?'

'He's worked so hard trying to sort this out, Danny,' says Martha. 'Coming up with the idea, begging me to track you down so we could come here. I think if you're going to turn him down then at least do the decent thing and give him a reason.'

She's right. James does deserve an answer but I'm not sure how much store he'll put by the only one I've got. 'I just think it would be weird.'

'Because you and James went to school together?' asks Martha.

There's no way I can answer this question without coming across as an even more self-centred jerk than I already do. 'Look, the only way I can even think about doing a job like being a carer is by not caring. When it comes to the people I look after I don't care about their hopes, dreams, or even their names. It's impersonal. And that's the way I like it. Anyway, I was never James's carer at Four Oaks. I don't even know what looking after him would entail. Does he need help showering, going to the toilet, getting dressed?'

'I can . . . I can . . . shower myself thank you very much,' says James with such indignation that I can only just about make out what he's saying. 'I do not need help going to the toilet either.'

'So what exactly *do* you need help with then?'

'All James wants is to move back into his old apartment in Birmingham,' says Martha. 'You'd be more of a live-in helper than anything.'

'But helping with what?'

James reaches into his jacket pocket, takes out a small notepad and reads from it. 'I'd need help with . . . cleaning . . . getting to my appointments . . . getting to and from places I need to go . . . oh, and . . . help not starting any fires.'

'It's a long story,' explains Martha seeing the look of surprise on my face, 'but suffice it to say he'll need help cooking too.'

I've only got to look at James to see how much he wants this to happen. It's that moment in the car park of The White Horse all over again. Him looking to me to save him from his parents, little knowing that I'm not capable of saving myself let alone anyone else.

'You need a proper carer, James,' I say finally. 'Not some waste of space who took the first job on offer after the dole cut off his money. I never wanted to be a carer. To be honest, all I wanted was to be left alone. I'm sorry, James, really I am. I wish you all the luck in the world because you deserve it but this idea of yours just isn't for me.'

14

James

'What do you think?'

Sometimes people ask me questions about what I think. And some of those times I know what I want to say but cannot think of the words to say it. Other times I do not know what I think but feel like I ought to. Then there are times when I have to ask people to repeat their question because even though I thought I knew what they were asking me and then what I want to say, when I try to say it, it is not there any more.

Sometimes – and this is quite rare – people can repeat their question lots of times in lots of different ways and raise their eyebrows as if to say, 'Now do you get it?' and I still will not have a clue what they are trying to get at.

This moment in the conservatory with my mum, Erica, and my dad, Don, looking at plans for the granny flat that they want to build for me is not like any of those.

I know exactly what I think about what I have been asked: I do not like it.

And I am not afraid to let them know that I do not like it either.

'What do you mean you don't like it?' asks my dad. His voice is sharp and stern like a teacher. 'This is the perfect compromise. It would be your own private space with it's own front door and you'd have all the independence you need with the added benefit of us being close enough to help out if the need arose.'

My mum puts a hand on dad's arm to calm him down. 'Now, now, Don,' she says, 'don't forget that we have rather sprung this on James. Perhaps what he's saying is he'd like to make a few modifications to the plans here and there like he used to do when he was a developer. You know, have some actual input into the project. I'm sure that's the case, isn't it, darling?'

They are not listening to me.

They never listen to me.

If they had we would not be having this conversation.

'No it is not the case,' I say. 'I do not want to live here with you, that is not what I want at all. What I want is to live in my old apartment with Danny Allen.'

My dad's eyes go all funny when I say Danny's name. 'There you go with that blasted man's name again! Really, James, what has he done to beguile you like this? He practically kidnaps you from respite care but you refuse to let me get the police involved! You conspire with your sister to offer him a job and he turns you down, and yet when I set wheels in motion for you to gain the independence that you allegedly crave, all you do is throw my efforts back in my face! This really is quite unacceptable behaviour, James, and it has to end now. This Danny Allen character has proved to be a far worse influence on you than I dared fear, and I rue the day we ever allowed you to stay at that damned care home. Well, enough is enough. While it's entirely up to you whether we go ahead with the plans for the annexe, this is still my house and as long as you live under this roof we still live by my rules! I want no further mention of that Danny – *bloody* – Allen under this roof. Do you hear me? Not another *bloody* word!'

Another word?

I feel so angry that I want to give him more than just the one.

'I am a . . . I am a . . . I am a grown man!' I snap. 'And . . . and . . . and . . . you cannot tell me what to do!'

My mum gasps when I say this. I am not sure where these words are coming from. They do not feel like they are mine. They feel like they belong to someone else. I am not really sure who I am any more but the one thing I am sure of is that I do not feel like who I was before I met Danny Allen.

At the weekend, because I am not talking to my dad, Martha comes over to the house and takes me out to lunch. She takes me to one of our favourite places, a 1940s-themed café in Stratford-upon-Avon. As we eat our usual Churchill club sandwiches, my argument with my dad is all Martha can talk about.

'What has got into you lately, James?' she asks. 'You're like a different person these days.'

At the table next to us there is a woman with a sleeping baby in a pram. The woman is reading a book and gently resting her hand on her baby's tiny legs. Even though she is sleeping, the baby has a smile on her face as if she knows exactly how much her mum loves her. I wonder if the baby is called Sarah or Suzie. I wonder if she will grow up to be a doctor or an artist. I wonder what she will name her own children or if she will ever have them.

I look at Martha. She is staring at me as if she is waiting for me to say something.

'What?'

'I think you were having a bit of a moment there,' she says.

'Was I?'

Martha nods. 'I was asking you what you think has got into you lately. Mum said your argument with Dad was really bad.'

'He was telling me what I can and cannot do,' I say. 'And I did not like it. I am an adult. I was a very good businessman and I was an MP too. Dad should not talk to me like I am a child just because of how I am now.'

'Of course,' says Martha. 'Dad was completely out of order. But—'

'—I want to go and see the apartment,' I say suddenly. All through lunch I have been wondering about the best way to bring this up. I never thought for a moment that the best way was to just say it.

Martha looks worried. 'Oh . . .' she says, 'you mean your place in Birmingham, don't you? Why would you want to do that? You do remember that Danny has turned down your offer don't you?'

'I know he did,' I say. 'But I still want to see it again.'

Martha puts down her tea. 'I'll be honest with you, James. I don't think it would be a very good idea. You haven't been there since . . . well you know . . . and I just worry that it will bring back too many old memories.'

'Well then, in that case I will be fine,' I say. 'Because you know as well as I do that my memory is not very good.'

Martha does not smile, even though that was a joke. 'You know what I'm saying, James,' she says. 'The apartment is where you lived with Zara. It was where you were happy. It's one thing for you to want to move back in there with a friend but it's an altogether different one to go waking the dead for no good reason.'

'But I do have a good reason,' I say.

I tell her about the idea I have had. My idea is this: if Danny Allen will not take the job as my carer then maybe I can still move back into my old apartment but pay for someone else to look after me.

I have seen people at the hospital who are looked after by people from care agencies. Sometimes the carers seem nice but mostly they look bored as if they would rather be somewhere else. Being looked after by a care agency worker would not be fun like it would be living with Danny Allen. It would take a lot of getting used to as well because I would have to get to know them and they would have to get to know me. But even if it was awful, even if they looked bored all the time and we had nothing to talk about, it could not be worse than my parents treating me like a child while I live in a flat above their garage.

I am not a child.

I am a grown man.

And they will not ever treat me like a grown man while I live with them.

'I don't think Mum and Dad would go for it in a million years,' says Martha after I've explained my plan to her.

'They do not need to,' I say, and then I tell her about Sangeeta.

Sangeeta is my social worker.

She has sleek black hair and is very pretty.

I do not know why I have a social worker.

I just do, in the same way that I have a physiotherapist and a speech therapist. Once in a while I see Sangeeta in her office at the hospital or sometimes she comes to my meetings with Dr Acari.

My parents do not like her.

My dad says that social workers are all 'scruffy leftie layabouts', which does not make any sense because Sangeeta is always dressed really smartly like an Indian Princess Diana.

Every time I see Sangeeta for a review she gives me her card and tells me to call her if I need anything.

I have never called her.

Until this week when I asked if she could help me move out of home, even though my parents might not like the idea. I cannot remember the word she used but she said that because she is this thing that I cannot remember she could help to make that happen.

'You've thought of everything, haven't you?' says Martha.

'Only because I have had to,' I reply.

Martha sighs and dips into her purse and tucks some money underneath the saucer of her empty cup. 'If we're going to do this, we'd better be quick because I told Mum I'd have you back by six at the latest.'

I remember the first time I saw the office block that I would one day have my home in. It was big and grey and so ugly that not very many people wanted to have an office in it. I knew straight away though that it would be a good place to make homes and I bought the whole thing the very same day. The development went so well that by the end of the first day they went on sale, they were all sold. People like footballers and actors and rich businesspeople bought them. I saved the biggest and best apartment in the building for me. This was where I was going to live.

The day I moved into my apartment with my friend Miles was a really happy day. I remember thinking to myself: 'I will be happy here.' But then I met Zara and after a while Miles moved out and she moved in and I realised that what I thought was happy did not compare to how happy I was after she moved in.

The apartment is not like I remember.

Then again, it could be because my memories sometimes get a bit jumbled. I do not let that worry me too much.

The apartment smells musty.

It is so big that even normal sounds, like Martha and I walking and talking as we go around it, feel like they have had the volume turned up.

The apartment has no furniture in it.

My dad had it put in storage after Zara moved out.

At one point my dad asked me if I minded if he rented out the apartment because it made 'sound financial sense'. I said it was fine because I could not imagine a time where I might ever go back. In the end though, my mum would not let my dad go through with it. She said it would be like giving up hope.

She said that one day I would be well enough to move back and pick up my life right where I left off.

She was wrong though, and so the apartment has sat empty all this time.

Martha does not say much as we wander around the empty rooms. I think it is because it is making her feel sad.

There are dead flies on the floor of the bedroom that Zara and I shared. Without all of our things in it, the room is just a big white box. I slide back one of the huge doors of the built-in wardrobe. It is the side that I think used to be Zara's. I think I half expected it to still be full of her long coats and colourful dresses – but of course it is empty apart from some dust balls and more dead flies.

I leave that bedroom and walk down the corridor to the room that would have been Danny Allen's. Even though it is only a second bedroom, it is still very big and the windows are on the same side as the ones in the living room. I think the views in this room are much better than in my room. You can see right out across the city.

I think Danny would have liked them.

When Martha and I return to the main space, she asks me how I am.

'I am fine.'

'So you're still determined to go through with your plan?'

I think about her question and then shake my head as I feel a tear roll down my cheek.

'It's just too big and empty, isn't it?' says Martha hugging me.

I nod, even though she is not quite right. It is not that it is too big and empty, it is that I cannot imagine myself being happy here without someone nice to share it.

Martha and I do not even bother taking a look out on the roof terrace, even though it used to be one of my favourite parts of the apartment. Instead we lock the front door and take the lift to the underground car park in silence. I think we are both feeling really sad. I think we both know this was my last chance to be happy.

When we reach the car, Martha's phone rings. She has an important job at the BBC and is always taking calls from important people so I do not think anything of it but then Martha screams, not in a horrible way but in a nice way like she has just had some good news.

'What is it? What is wrong?'

She hands me her phone. 'Find out for yourself.'

'Hello,' I say. 'Who is this?'

'It's me, Danny,' says the voice at the other end of the line. 'I've changed my mind. If you still want me to be your carer then I'm in.'

15

Danny

It's a clear and bright Sunday afternoon, the sort of afternoon that couples in matching sunglasses spend mooching through flea markets, looking for quirky items for their pad or sipping overpriced coffee on the shaded terraces of their favourite cafés. I, however, am in a silver sports car being driven by Martha DeWitt and our destination is her parents' farmhouse in Stow-on-the-Wold to meet with Mr DeWitt who, last time we met, pretty much threatened to kill me. It's funny how life can be sometimes, just when you think you know how everything is, it sneaks out a surprise that really tears the rug right out from beneath your feet.

It had been Martha DeWitt's dogged determination that had changed my mind. About a week after she and James had turned up at my flat she sought me out again. I'd been on my way home from my new job at Amber Lodge, an old people's home in Coventry. I got the job through a temp agency and was doing pretty much the same duties for the residents there as I had at Four Oaks: a mixture of feeding, wiping, cleaning, dressing, and undressing those who couldn't do these things for themselves. I wasn't in love with the job but I didn't necessarily hate it either. At any rate it kept me from thinking too much.

At the end of my shift that night, I'd changed into my normal clothes and had been about to head home when it started to rain. After a few minutes sheltering in the home's lobby, it dawned on me that of the two options – getting soaked to the bone or remaining one second longer at work than I needed to – I much preferred the former and so, zipping up my jacket, I stepped out into the pouring rain.

By the time I was halfway across the car park I was drenched
through to my underwear and just as I thought about turning
back, I heard a car door slam and a female voice call my name.
It belonged to Martha DeWitt. She was smartly dressed, holding
a large umbrella and was standing next to a sleek and expensive-
looking silver sports car.

'Fancy seeing you here,' she said mischievously. 'Any chance
of a quick word?'

There was nowhere for us to go except her car but its cream
leather interior looked so pristine that I insisted on sitting on the
copy of the *Daily Express* I'd taken from the staffroom to read
on my way home.

Martha explained how she'd tracked me down for a second
time. Having called round at the flat again without finding me
in, she'd bumped into my downstairs neighbour whose great
uncle happened to be a resident at Amber Lodge. Mrs Averman
told Martha that she'd seen me there and guessed that was probably where I was.

'You know,' says Martha. 'You don't look any different now to
how you were at school. You've hardly changed a bit.'

'That's kind of you to say,' I replied. 'But I think we can both
agree that there's a bit more of me than there used to be.'

Martha laughed. 'I think that's true of all of us. I can't believe
how much I used to worry about looking slim back then. There
was barely anything to me! I was as skinny as a rake. Sometimes
I wish I could go back in time and tell myself to stop worrying,
eat more cake and let my hair down a little because the day is
coming when the only way I'll be that skinny again is to chop
off a leg.' She laughed self-consciously and while it felt like a cue
to tell her that she looked good, I couldn't help thinking it would
be a bit odd given our close proximity in her car.

'Anyway,' she continued, 'you don't need me yabbering on as
if this is some sort of school reunion, when all you want to do
is go home. Has it been a long day?'

'Not too bad,' I reply. 'How about yours? I don't even know
what it is that you do exactly.'

'I'm head of local radio for the BBC in the south,' she said. 'And today has been like every other day, hectic.' On cue her phone buzzed from inside her bag. She took it out, examined it briefly and then tucked it away again. I sensed that someone somewhere in the busy world she inhabited needed her urgently and yet here she was, sitting in a nursing home car park talking to me.

'You won't be surprised to know that I'm here to discuss James,' she continued. 'I promise I'm not trying to emotionally blackmail you, Danny, but the truth is that since you turned him down he's been very low. He'd be furious with me if he knew I was telling you this but I think he . . . I think he really misses you. Honestly you should hear the way he talks about you, Danny. If I didn't know better I'd have said he was in love with you. I don't know what you did to make such an impression on him but he's simply not stopped raving about you.'

'I liked him too,' I replied, trying hard not to feel guilty, 'but you know my reason for turning the job down.'

'And that's why I'm here,' said Martha. 'To ask if there's any way you'd reconsider. Look, I don't know what happened to you after KS, but clearly something did. What I'm trying to say is that if you'd be willing to change your mind then financially speaking, I could definitely make it worth your while. You can name your price, I don't care about the money. All that matters to me is that James is happy.'

It occurred to me that if I was in possession of even a modicum of pride then right now would be the perfect time to feel insulted and not a little outraged that some well-to-do executive who didn't 'care' about money, but whose parents and parents' parents came from money, was trying to buy me like I was a piece of meat for sale. As it was, however, I didn't feel anything other than acute embarrassment that her assessment of the past sixteen years of my life was so accurate.

'I told you before, Martha, it's not about the money. It's about me not feeling comfortable looking after some guy I used to go to school with. Surely you must see that? How would you feel if I offered you a shed load of cash to give up your job and be Pippa Hamilton's carer?'

Pippa Hamilton was a girl we both knew from school who then, as now, was a grade-A bitch. The last time I'd seen her she'd been splattered across the front page of the *Daily Mail* celebrating her second divorce from a premier-league-level rock star.

'I can't answer that,' replied Martha, 'but what I can say is that you're the only person James has let back into his life since his own life changed so dramatically. He's pushed every single one of his old friends away and not let anyone else in until now.'

'But that's just the thing,' I told her, 'at KS we weren't even that close. I was a scholarship kid, he ran around with the money crowd. What does he want with me of all people?'

'I don't know,' said Martha. 'Maybe it's because you went to school together; maybe it's because instead of giving him a hard time like I do, or mollycoddling him like my parents, you just treat him like an ordinary bloke. Maybe it is because he's fallen in love with you after all. I really don't know and I really don't care. What I do know is that you've got a chance most of us never get, the chance to make a real difference to someone who has already been dealt a pretty awful hand by life.'

It was a good speech, hitting all the right notes in the right order. It was hard not to imagine her delivering something similar in some high-powered boardroom somewhere.

I felt myself wavering. 'I'm just not sure.'

'Fine,' said Martha. 'Being sure is overrated anyway. Just tell me that you'll give it a go.'

'And if I hate it, I can just walk?'

'If you hate it, you can do anything you like.'

'What about your father? I can't imagine he's on board with this.'

'He isn't yet but he will be,' said Martha. 'So is that a yes?'

'If you want an answer now it's a no,' I replied. 'But if you let me think about it then I suppose it's a maybe.'

For the next few days all I could think about was the decision I'd got to make. On some levels it seemed like madness that it was even a problem. Back of the fag packet calculations had long since confirmed that I couldn't afford the flat on my own. My debts from running the place were mounting, Maya was texting me almost daily asking me to make a decision and yet if I said yes to the DeWitts all my problems would disappear. In the end, however, it wasn't my accommodation or my financial worries that made me call Martha the following Sunday and agree to take the job. Part of the reason I changed my mind was my admiration for the lengths Martha was prepared to go to on behalf of her brother. I could see that she wouldn't rest until she got this problem sorted for James, which is exactly how it should be. Brothers and sisters looking out for one another. What she had said about being in a position to make a difference to someone in need also appealed to me. For far too long I've only ever been a drunk or a disappointment. I liked the sound of being a good guy for once even if I was out of practice. I liked the sound of helping someone for no other reason than it being the right thing to do.

When Martha and I reach her parents' farmhouse, she switches off the engine and turns to me. 'Just this last hurdle and it'll all be done,' she says. 'I can't thank you enough for changing your mind. James has been on cloud nine from the day you spoke to him. Just don't let my dad bully you and we'll be okay. He's used to getting his own way and it won't do him any harm to realise that the world doesn't always work like that.'

We get out of the car and walk up to the house. James flings open the front door to welcome us before we're even halfway across the gravel drive and the first thing he does is shake my hand.

'I cannot believe this is actually happening,' he says. 'I am so pleased that you changed your mind.'

'It's not all plain sailing,' warns Martha. 'We're nearly there but first dad and Danny have to talk.'

'I still do not understand why,' says James with annoyance. 'I used to have my own business. I was an MP. I do not need my dad's permission to do anything.'

'I know you don't,' says Martha calmly. 'But that doesn't mean we're not going to need Mum and Dad's help to get this off the ground. There's cover for Danny on his days off to consider, someone will have to take him through all your medication, all your medical appointments and set up a payroll. I'm not saying it will be impossible without Dad, but it will be a whole lot easier if he's on board.'

I'm only in the house a matter of seconds when the door to the kitchen at the end of the hallway opens and Mr and Mrs DeWitt come through. As I don't know him, it's hard for me to judge the expression Mr DeWitt is wearing but if I had to hazard a guess, I'd say it's one of fake cordiality.

'Mr Allen,' he says, when we're less than a foot apart. He extends his hand towards me and we shake hands. 'I think it's probably best if we speak alone. Would you mind joining me in my study?'

I look over to Martha almost as if I'm suspecting his invitation to be some sort of lethal trap but she gives me a small nod of encouragement and so I follow Mr DeWitt back along the corridor and through a doorway into an oak-panelled study. There's a large oak desk near the window with chairs positioned on either side. The walls are lined with bookshelves on which rest leather-bound tomes that must be worth a small fortune.

'Would you like a drink?' he asks, walking over to a drinks cabinet in the corner of the room.

'I'm fine thanks,' I reply quickly. 'Actually I'd much prefer it if we just got on with what needs to be done.'

Mr DeWitt nods thoughtfully and then gestures for me to take a seat, while he sits down at the other side of the desk.

'Well, now that we've established that you like to get straight to the point, Mr Allen,' says Mr DeWitt, 'might I get straight to mine? I'd like to know why a young man who has benefitted from a first-rate education has come to end up in employment as low paid as a carer? Before you answer, please be aware that I have at my disposal the means to discover the truth should you attempt to hide anything from me.'

'Are you really threatening to have me vetted by someone?'

'If I deem it necessary,' he replies matter-of-factly. 'I find that the only people who are alarmed by this sort of thing are those who have something to hide.'

I take a deep breath. He's clearly trying to bait me and I'm not going to let him. 'I've done plenty in my life that I'd like to hide from you, Mr DeWitt, but nothing that means you'd be putting James in harm's way if you left him in my charge. So while I'm more than happy to assure you that I've got James's best interests at heart, I am not the least bit interested in explaining my past to you. That will remain my own business. And if I have the faintest suspicion that my past is being looked into, I will pack my bags and inform James that you, and only you are the reason I am leaving.'

For a moment I wonder if I've gone too far. After all, Mr DeWitt is simply looking out for his son. But then after an awkward silence he says, 'Well, it doesn't look like I've got much choice in the matter,' and then stands up and leaves the room. 'I'll let you inform my son that he has my blessing.'

16

James

I do not remember anything about the day I arrived at my parents' house from the hospital.

I know I must have been well enough to be able to be discharged but I was not well like I am now.

Whenever I try to remember anything from those early days, it feels like when you take a picture on your phone and then you move it at the last moment and it comes out all blurry.

When I think about that time, days and nights and things people said and things people did are all blurry just like that.

Sometimes though, if I am feeling strong and I try really hard, I can get a little snapshot of those days.

One snapshot I get sometimes is a little flash of how the cotton sheets on my bed used to feel against my skin. Because I was in bed all the time, I used to sweat a lot and so the sheets would get damp. Every once in a while though, I would move a leg or an arm and find a cool patch of bed sheet that I had not made warm and it would feel like heaven.

Another snapshot I get is of the rainbow-pattern rug that used to be next to my bed. It was so bright and cheery that I used to turn my head so I could get a better look. Sometimes I would imagine I could see faces and places in its swirls of colour. It was almost like a work of art. The more you looked at it, the more there was to see.

The first memory I have of my room that does not feel blurry was one morning when my mum came to get me ready for the day. She was wearing a summer dress with flowers on it and the first thing she said to me was that it was a beautiful day and then she opened one of my windows. The air felt cold at first but I soon forgot all about that because of the birds singing in the tree underneath my window. It was the most beautiful noise I had ever heard.

My mum made me sit up in bed and then disappeared into my bathroom while I carried on listening to the birds. When she came back, she was carrying a white bowl half full with warm water, a white flannel and a pale blue towel.

She helped me out of my pyjamas and then washed my face and my armpits and down below. When she was washing me, it felt as if she had done it lots of times before, even though I could not remember her doing it. When I asked her if she had washed me before like this, she told me that she had done it every day since I had been home. I told her she was very kind and I said that from now on, I would try hard to remember her helping me to wash. When I said this, she just smiled and said, 'The only thing that matters is you getting better.'

Another memory.

My mum sitting next to my bed on an oak chair from the kitchen. She is holding my hand while I drift in and out of sleep.

I used to get tired a lot back then.

Sometimes I think I must have spent whole weeks asleep. I still get tired even now but not as much as I used to.

A final memory: I am in bed and my mum, Erica, is sitting next to me holding my hand. 'I am so sorry your room's not like it was when you lived here,' she says sadly. 'You hadn't lived at home in such a long time and I never imagined for a moment you'd ever be back with us.'

'It is okay, Mum,' I say, 'I did not think I would ever be back home either.'

The day of the move has come around quickly.

It feels like one moment I am in the hallway, cheering Danny as he gives me the thumbs up when he comes out of my dad's study, and the next my dad is calling up the stairs to let me know that the removal men are ready to go.

I am leaving home.

It is really happening.

Danny and I are going to be sharing my apartment.

I am getting my life back.

As I come downstairs, Danny, Martha and my mum cheer, as though I am a runner crossing the finish line of a marathon. When I reach the bottom, my mum gives me a hug and says, 'I can't tell you how proud I am of you,' and then Martha hugs me too and says, 'Can you believe it? It's really happening.' Danny pats me on the back and jokes, 'For a minute there I thought you had changed your mind. Are you always going to take this long to get ready because if you want to go out for a drink, you're going to have to start preparing at midday to make it in for last orders.' I look around for my dad but I cannot see him anywhere. 'Your father left for Birmingham about half an hour ago,' says my mum when she sees me looking for him. 'I think he just wanted to have some time alone to come to terms with today. You understand, don't you?'

I tell my mum, Erica, that I do, even though I do not. My dad has been funny with me ever since he agreed that Danny could be my carer. I do not mind though. Even he cannot take the shine off today. This is the first day of the rest of my life and he cannot stop me from enjoying it.

After the removal men leave, Martha says that we should probably get going too. My mum is going in Martha's car and Danny is going in the brand new Range Rover that my parents have bought for me so that Danny can drive me to the places I need to go. It is black and has tinted windows and has a personalised number plate that says, 'DW 1JD'. When Danny sat in the driver's seat for the first time earlier in the week, he said, 'This is nicer than any place I've ever lived.' I laughed because what Danny said was funny but my dad pulled a face as if he had understood the joke but wished that he had not.

There has been an accident on the motorway so it takes us over an hour and a half to get to Birmingham. And by the time we walk through the door of the apartment, the removal men have already begun bringing in the furniture that has been in storage. In the main space there is a large grey sofa and a coffee table and a pale grey armchair. On the wall is a very big TV.

When the removal men start to bring in other items for the apartment, they ask my mum where she wants them. I think the reason they do this is because she looks like she is in charge. When they ask, Mum makes a big show of telling them to ask me because it is my home. It is very nice of her to do this and it shows that she is trying hard to let me do things my way. But the thing is, I know she does not mean it. I know this because every time I tell them where to put something, she goes up to them and quietly whispers in their ear and they put it somewhere else. I do not mind though. She could ask them to stack up the furniture right up to the roof, for all I care. I am too happy to get upset about furniture. I am too happy to worry about things that do not matter.

About an hour later my dad arrives carrying a shopping bag. He does not say anything to me at all. Instead the first thing he does is talk to my mum, and then Mum goes and talks to Martha and then Martha goes and talks to Danny, while my mother goes to the kitchen area and washes out two mugs. Then something really odd happens. My mum gives Dad the mugs and says, 'I think there's a problem in your bedroom, James, could you and your father see to it please?' I have no idea what she is talking about because last time I went into the bedroom everything was fine. When I say this to my mum, Martha pulls a face and says, 'James, just do as she says!' and so I go to my bedroom and my dad follows after me, not saying anything.

'I'm sorry about that pantomime,' says Dad, still holding the shopping bag that he came in with along with the mugs that mum handed to him. 'I just . . . I don't know . . . I just wanted to have a quiet word with you, if that's okay.'

'I thought you were not talking to me,' I reply. 'You have hardly said a word to me all week.'

'I know,' he says and sits down on the bed, which has not got any sheets on it. I sit down too. 'And for that I owe you an apology. I have been very ill-mannered and I'd like to make it up to you. Would you like a drink?'

'I was in the mood for an orange juice earlier,' I say, 'but I am okay now.'

My dad smiles, 'I meant a proper drink,' he says, and he reaches into the shopping bag and takes out a brand new bottle of his favourite whisky. He opens the bottle and pours a little into each of the mugs.

'I'm sorry about the mugs,' he says, handing my drink to me, 'I don't think the removal men have brought up your glassware yet but these will do for now.' He raises his mug in the air and says, 'To your continued good health,' then we clink mugs and take a sip. To begin with, when I swallow the whisky, it feels like it is leaving a trail of fire behind all the way from my tongue to my stomach but then it fades to a warm glow. I had forgotten how much I like spirits. Before The Incident I used to drink them often.

My dad looks at me. 'How's that?'

'Nice.'

'Good,' he says, and then there is a long pause and he says, 'I really am very sorry, James. Neither I, nor your mother, ever set out to treat you like a child. We were just worried about you that's all, after the . . . well after The Incident . . . you were just so . . . so. . .' His voice goes funny like mine does sometimes when I get upset. 'I suppose what I'm trying to say is that all your mother and I have ever wanted is to do what's best for you. It was all we ever wanted when you were small and it's exactly the same now. But I can see now that in trying to do what we thought was best, we've stifled you, which isn't the best thing for you at all. So I wish you the best for this next chapter of your life, James. I'm sure you'll make a great success of it.'

I am feeling very tired when, just after seven in the evening, my family finally say that it is time for them to go home. It has been a long day and I feel as though I could fall asleep on my feet. At the front door my dad tells me that he will call first thing in the morning and then Martha and Mum hug me and make me promise to get a good night's sleep.

'So no partying for us on our first night,' says Danny, when we return to the living room and flop down on the sofa. 'You look shattered.'

'I am a bit,' I say, even though I can barely keep my eyes open. 'I would still like to go out for a drink, if that is okay, but I will need a nap first.'

'Of course,' says Danny. 'I could do with a bit of a power nap myself. How about this: I'll set my alarm for an hour, we'll both grab some shut-eye and then nip to the nearest pub for one drink and then back home? How does that sound?'

I lie on the bed fully clothed and fall asleep the moment my head hits the pillow but then, in what feels like the very next moment, I feel someone shaking me awake and when I open my eyes, Danny Allen is standing over me. He looks worried as though he has just seen a ghost.

He sits down on the bed next to me and I sit up and lean my back against the wall behind me. 'Are you okay?' he asks.

'Of course I am,' I reply, but the moment I say this I get a feeling like I am not at all okay and then I realise that my hands are sweaty and my chest is damp. 'What happened?'

'I think you must have been having a nightmare,' says Danny. 'You were literally screaming at the top of your voice. I couldn't make out a word you were saying but you seemed terrified. Do you remember what you were dreaming about?'

I shake my head, even though bits and pieces start to come back to me. 'I cannot remember,' I lie. 'It was probably nothing. I am sorry if I woke you.'

Danny does not seem convinced. 'Are you sure you are all right? That was really scary.'

'I am fine,' I say, 'really I am fine.'

Danny looks at his watch. 'Well, it's eight o'clock now anyway. Do you still want to go out?'

I shake my head. 'Can we do it another time?' I ask. 'It is just that I am really tired so I think I might stay here and get some rest.'

'Of course,' says Danny. 'I'll be in the living room tidying up, if you need anything.'

I wait until Danny has closed my door behind him before I dare to touch where I have been lying. Just as I expect, there is a damp patch on the duvet and another on my trousers.

I always wet myself when I have this nightmare. Whenever it happened at home, my mum would change the sheets on my bed the day after, even if they were clean on. She would not say anything to me about it. She would just put new sheets on and not say a word. It took me a long time to work out why this was happening but I got there in the end. I was wetting myself because I was having nightmares about Kyle Baylis, because I was dreaming that he had escaped from prison and was coming after me.

In the morning I will have to tell Danny that I spilled a drink on my bed and had to change my sheets. For now though, the only thing I can do is strip the bed by myself, leave the dirty sheets on the floor and go to sleep on the bare mattress.

As I fall asleep, I think how this was supposed to be my new beginning. My new start. But that will never happen because I will always be afraid of Kyle Baylis. I will always be afraid that one day he will come and find me and finish what he started.

17

Danny

'I've made a mistake.'

That's what I'm thinking as I wake up after my first night in the apartment sleeping in the most comfortable bed I've ever slept in. My next thought is similar, 'I really can't do this,' and is followed closely by a third as I warm to my theme, 'What have I done?'

While James's nightmare might not be the sole reason for my current anxiety, it certainly didn't help matters when I'd heard his screams and rushed to his room, genuinely fearing he was being attacked. I'd never heard anything like it before. He'd been absolutely terrified and even after he'd assured me that he was fine, I remained on high alert for the rest of the evening as I quietly unpacked boxes in the kitchen, wanting to be on hand in case it happened again.

Right now, however, my main concern is that my vastly over-rated abilities as a carer are about to be put to the test and will undoubtedly be found wanting. What was I thinking saying yes to a proposition like this when in terms of experience, all I have to my name is the two-day course I'd done at Four Oaks and less than six weeks of actual work experience? The number of things that could go wrong multiplied by the number of different ways I could be responsible for allowing harm to come to James makes my head spin.

I reach for my phone and scroll through the recently dialled numbers until I find Martha DeWitt's. As my thumb hovers over her name, I recall how she'd told me I could quit any time as long as I gave it a go. I know it will drop her right in it, that James will most likely never forgive me and it will all but crush my nascent plan to become a better person, but surely that is better than something awful happening to James because I've inevitably screwed things up? I lower my thumb and my phone dials Martha but she doesn't pick up. Instead it goes straight through to her voicemail but before I can say a word, there's a knock at my door. Reluctantly I end the call, pull on my jeans and go to the door to find James in the hallway. He's already dressed for the day, even though when I last checked my watch it wasn't even seven o'clock.

'Morning.'

'Everything okay?'

James nods. 'I wanted to tell you that I am sorry about last night. You looked really worried when you came to me when I was having my nightmare.'

'It wasn't your fault. It's one of those things. I was worried though.'

'Well, I am sorry. And I want to say something else too. I want to say that yesterday was one of the best days of my life. And it is all thanks to you.'

'I think you might be overstating things a bit there. All I did was turn up, mate.'

James shakes his head. 'None of this would have been possible without you, Danny Allen. You have changed my life.'

His eyes are filled with such genuine admiration that I don't know where to look. I want to tell him again that I haven't done anything special. That I am nobody special, that his belief in me is completely misplaced, but I know that even if I did it wouldn't make any difference.

'Are you hungry?' I ask.

'Starving.'

'How does a fry-up sound? Bacon, eggs, sausages, the works?'

'Brilliant,' says James.

'Good. Give me five minutes and I'll get cooking.'

Closing the door, I sit on the edge of my bed and pick up my phone. Martha's number is still on the screen, tempting me to follow through with my earlier decision. In the end, however, all

I do is toss my phone back on the bed and get ready for the day ahead. For better or worse, of the billions of people alive right now on planet earth, James has chosen me to accompany him on his journey to independence, so I suppose the very least I can do is see this thing through for a little while longer.

At James's request we breakfast out on the terrace, a fully landscaped rooftop garden that wouldn't have looked out of place in a glossy design magazine. Though the spring air around us is crisp enough for us to see our own breath, even as I sit shivering slightly in a coat and hoodie at the outdoor dining table, it's impossible not to be wowed by the unbroken views of the urban cityscape. I'm struck once again by how surreal my life is. One minute I'm living in an ex-council flat in Coventry scraping around for bus fare, and the next I'm living in a million-pound apartment with access to a brand new Range Rover. It feels like I've won the lottery.

As I'm loading the dishwasher after breakfast while James is brushing his teeth, the landline rings.

'Morning, Daniel, Mr DeWitt speaking,' says James's father with forced chirpiness. 'James's mother insisted I call first thing to see how he slept after his first night away. Motherly concern and all that, you know. Hope you don't mind.'

I don't mind at all. Especially as he'd told me last night before he left that he would be calling, and yet it's hard not to wonder why a) he's insisting on calling me Daniel when I've told him several times that I prefer Danny and b) he feels the need to pretend that Mrs DeWitt really has put him up to this call.

'Of course not,' I reply, keeping my tone professional. 'James went to bed a little after seven because he was feeling tired after the move and woke early, got himself dressed, then we had breakfast on the terrace and now he's brushing his teeth. Would you like me to call him so you can speak to him?'

'Thank you but no,' says Mr DeWitt. 'All we really needed to know was that he'd had a good night.' He pauses, and I imagine him examining the extensive list of questions he'd prepared in order to catch me out. 'Just one last thing,' he says. 'I was wondering, did James remember to take all of his medication both last night and first thing this morning?'

'I watched him do both,' I reply, 'but feel free to ask him yourself if you like. It won't take a second to put him on the line.'

Mr DeWitt graciously declines. 'Your word is good enough for me. Anyway, I'm sure we've taken up enough of your valuable time as it is. Have you any plans for the day ahead?'

'None as yet, but I'm sure that will change.'

'Hmm, right, yes, of course,' says Mr DeWitt, uncomfortably. 'Well, I'd be grateful if you'd let James know that we called and that we hope his day – whatever it is he decides to do – goes well. Please let him know that we'll be calling this evening after supper to speak to him.'

'Will do,' I reply and then I end the call.

'Was that my dad, Don?' asks James, emerging from his room with toothpaste showing in the corners of his mouth.

'He was just checking in on you,' I say, grabbing a tea towel and handing it to him. 'I think you missed a bit,' I say, pointing to his mouth.

'I always do that,' he says sheepishly.

'He also wanted to know what you were planning to do with your day,' I add.

'I have been thinking a lot about that,' says James, still holding the tea towel. 'And I think I know what I would like to do.'

'Go on then,' I reply, 'I'm all ears.'

'I want to go shopping for new clothes,' he says. 'I love my mum, Erica, a lot but look at me. I am dressed like one of my dad's friends. I just want clothes that are more me.'

Given our central location we could have easily walked to the nearest shopping centre but when I suggest it, to my delight, James shakes his head. 'I think we should go in the car,' he says and so that's what we do.

Much as I'd like to say that I'm conflicted about driving James's gas-guzzling, environment-wrecking, needlessly expensive Range

Rover, the fact remains that I loved every moment in it yesterday and can't wait to get behind the wheel again.

When I start up the engine, the dashboard lights up like something out of *Star Trek*, dazzling me with an overwhelming array of options which I can control with a single swipe of my finger or tap on the steering wheel. Donning our sunglasses as we pull out of the underground garage on to street level, past all manner of high-end sports cars, including two Ferraris, a Lamborghini and at least half a dozen other Range Rovers, I catch sight of our reflection in the mirrored glass of a nearby office block. Even though I say so myself, we look completely and utterly cool, like a couple of young guys at the top of our game. And for a moment it feels like we're glimpsing who we were meant to be before life went and got in the way.

In retrospect it doesn't surprise me that the first thing James wants to do with his new-found freedom is buy new clothes. Yesterday as I helped him unpack his things, I couldn't help noticing as I passed the open wardrobe how Mrs DeWitt had clearly divided the contents into two sections: clothes bought by James before his accident and those purchased by her afterwards. The clothes purchased by James revealed that he had been a sharp dresser with a taste for designer labels. But even just glancing at them as they dangled from their hangers, it was clear that James had lost a lot of weight since sustaining his injuries and they would now swamp his current considerably slighter frame. In contrast, the clothes purchased by James's mother were clearly the sorts of clothes a sixty-six-year-old woman might purchase for her retired company director husband. The one thing they weren't, however, were James's clothes: clothes that in any way at all represented his personality or how he wanted to present himself to the world, a task which is all the more difficult when you no longer know precisely who you are.

'Which one do you think?'

James and I are in a large high street menswear shop and he is holding up two shirts that it's taken him half an hour to whittle down from a selection of over a dozen. One is black with a loud leaf print and the other is checked navy blue and white. To be honest, neither is in a style I'd choose to wear myself but James seems to really like them.

'I think they're both fine,' I say. 'I don't think there's much in it.'

'But which one do you like most?' asks James.

'It doesn't matter which one I like. I'm not going to wear it. You need to decide for yourself. Isn't that the whole reason you wanted to move back to your apartment? So, you know, you could make your own decisions?'

James thinks for a while. 'But I do not know which one I like best,' he says eventually. 'That is why I am asking you.'

As much as I want this to be over, I can't help feeling that if I make this decision for James, I'm going to end up making lots of others for him too.

'This really needs to be your choice.'

Frustrated, James sighs heavily and I prepare myself for a third attempt at changing my mind but then he smiles and folds both shirts over his arm.

'Which one are you going for?' I ask.

'I still cannot make up my mind,' he says with a mischievous glint in his eye. 'So I think I will have them both.'

Reasoning that he's on to a winner, James applies the same logic to pretty much everything he wants so that two hours later, as we make our way back to the car, we're loaded down with shopping bags containing among other things three pairs of trainers, four pairs of jeans and over a dozen T-shirts.

That night, as I lie in the world's most comfortable bed, I go back over the day in my mind. I'm blown away by everything we managed to pack into it. After our epic shopping trip we had lunch at a Japanese restaurant, which we followed with a trip to the cinema, a second shopping trip (during which James bought three jackets), a fish-and-chip supper, and then finally a visit to the pub. This time I used the excuse of being too full as my reason for not drinking, but I know sooner or later I'm going to have to tell James about my problem. This aside however, it occurs to me that not only am I exhausted, but surprisingly I'm also happy. It's been good to have been distracted today of all days, and not simply because this is my first full day of being James's carer.

Today would have been Helen's thirty-third birthday. She would have been a grown woman, maybe with a young family of her own. Maybe she would've asked my parents to babysit my niece or nephew so that I could celebrate at a nice restaurant. It's amazing how many scenarios I manage to conjure up for my sister without even trying. There's one in which she becomes the kind and caring teacher I always thought she might be, another where she follows her natural analytical disposition to become an economist for a government think tank and on and on, everything from a travel journalist right through to an eco-warrior drop-out.

I turn over and plump up my pillows again but sleep will still not come. I can't get it all out of my head, tired though I am.

So many unlived lives.

So many choices left untaken.

I should have protected her.

Nothing bad should have ever happened to her on my watch.

18

James

It has been over a week since Danny and I moved into the apartment and we have had a lot of fun. So far we have been bowling, bought a new surround sound system, watched lots of films and been to the pub for a drink three times. I have also spent two nights back at my parents' house so that Danny could have his days off and although it was nice to see them, I really could not wait to get back to the apartment. This week is different from last week though, because we have got some hospital appointments booked. Dr Acari is first on the list.

If Dr Acari did not have a thick brown beard, light brown skin and glasses, he would look exactly like Tom Selleck when he was in *Friends*. When I said this to my mum on the way home from one of our appointments with him, she asked, 'Who's Tom Selleck?' and so when we got home, I showed her pictures of him on the Internet. 'Oh,' she said, sounding disappointed, 'he's that American actor, isn't he? Well, I'm afraid I don't see the resemblance.'

Dr Acari is my consultant at University Hospital Birmingham.

He is a clinical neuropsychologist.

That means that he is a doctor who studies brains.

He has been my consultant ever since The Incident and I stayed with him even after I left hospital because he is one of the best doctors in the country for people with brain injuries.

Dr Acari is the leader of my MDT.

MDT means Multi-Disciplinary Team.

This is a way of saying he is the boss of all the people I have to see here at the hospital's Acquired Brain Injury and Rehabilitation unit every month. As I have lots of things wrong with me, I have to see the following people:

1. Kay with the purple hair (she helps to get my arms and legs strong).
2. Really tall Ashley (she helps me with the way that I talk).
3. Fat Dr Davies (he keeps my epilepsy in check).
4. Owl-faced Dr Chalmer (she does something called Cognitive Behavioural Therapy with me which is supposed to help me manage my emotions).
5. There are other people from time to time, like the lady who does my cognitive tests and the nurses who take my blood pressure and check my weight, but it is mostly the people I have already mentioned.

Anyway, some of these people I like a lot. Others I do not like at all. But of all the medical people I have to see, Dr Acari is my favourite and now he will meet Danny Allen.

This appointment is different from all the others I have ever had with Dr Acari. It is the first time I have been to see him without my parents. My mum, Erica, was not very happy when I asked her not to come. She said, 'But we need to be kept up to date with your progress,' and I said, 'Do not worry I have already talked to Sangeeta my social worker about it. She says that she can ask Dr Acari to send you a letter saying everything that we talk about and anyway, Danny Allen will be there with me.' My mum still was not very happy but I told her that this was very important to me and so then she sighed and said, 'Okay, let's try it your way.'

I feel like this is a really important step for me.

This is my first time seeing Dr Acari without my parents. So when he asks me how I am, rather than my mum, Erica, telling him, I have to remember for myself all the times when I have felt dizzy or more tired than normal.

Dr Acari listens very carefully as I speak and sometimes he makes notes and then other times he just smiles. When I answer his questions, he does not speak straight away like a lot of people, instead he leaves a long gap, as if he is thinking.

'Well, James,' says Dr Acari, after spending some time looking at his computer screen. 'I've been studying your most recent rehabilitation reports and it's fairly positive news this month. Everything has come back more or less the same as usual but I can't help wondering if . . . I don't know . . . if there isn't something more we could be doing.' He leans back in his chair and looks at me as though I am a tiny creature under a microscope. 'The thing is, James, your rehabilitation as a whole isn't quite progressing as I'd hoped. It's been three years now and by now I would have liked to see greater improvement from you across the board, but especially in your cognitive tests.' Dr Acari picks up a black and gold fountain pen from his desk and rolls it between his fingers, saying nothing.

I know he is thinking something but I just do not know what. Whatever it is, I am afraid I might not like it.

'I'd like to ask you a question, James,' says Dr Acari, putting down his pen. 'How would you yourself say things have been going lately with regard to your rehabilitation?'

It feels like a trick question.

'I do not know. Okay, I suppose.'

'Do you perhaps feel there might be room for improvement?'

I think for a moment. 'Maybe.'

Dr Acari strokes his beard as if he is thinking again. It makes me feel nervous. 'Well, James,' he says after a while. 'I definitely think there is something we could be doing and I think our group therapy session for people with similar conditions to your own might be it. I know you've had reservations about it in the past but I wonder whether you might reconsider? I have a number of patients already attending who have benefitted tremendously from the experience and I believe you would too.'

I had been feeling really happy until Dr Acari brought up the ABI support group. I had been thinking to myself that it was really nice that two of my favourite people could get to know each other. But Dr Acari has spoiled everything.

Now I just wish I was somewhere else.

'I would still rather not go if that is okay,' I say, trying to sound casual as if Dr Acari has just asked me to taste a new type of food that I did not really like the look of. 'But thank you, anyway.'

'Not even a single session to see how you'd get on?' asks Dr Acari brightly.

'I would rather not, but thank you all the same.'

'Okay,' says Dr Acari. 'Maybe next time.'

'Yes,' I say, hoping he will never bring it up again. 'Maybe next time.'

Later when Danny and I leave Dr Acari's office and walk along the corridor to the lift, Danny does not say anything about the support group Dr Acari mentioned. Instead he asks me what I would like for lunch. Normally, this is one of my favourite things to talk about and I would make lots of suggestions but instead I shrug and tell him that I do not mind. The reason I say this is because I am still feeling upset because Dr Acari brought up the support group. I have told him many times in the past that I do not want to go to it and I do not see why he has to mention it again, especially in front of Danny. Now I feel as if Danny Allen is secretly thinking things about me.

Maybe Danny is thinking that I am scared of going, even though I am not. Maybe he thinks that I do not want to get well, even though I do.

Maybe he is thinking I am acting like a child and should just grow up.

Or maybe he is not thinking at all.

I do not like how I am feeling right now and I wish it would stop.

Danny and I reach the lift as the doors open. Because I am still thinking how much I do not want to go to the support group, I do not look at any of the people who come out of the lift. Instead I wait until the lift is empty, step inside and press the button for the ground floor. I turn to say something to Danny but he is not in the lift. Instead he is standing outside talking to an older lady and a younger woman. All three of them are looking at me.

'What is going on?' I ask, getting out of the lift.

'You must have been away with the fairies,' says Danny. 'This lady was trying to get your attention.'

Danny points to the younger of the two women. She has short dark brown hair, brown eyes and a small face. She is wearing a bright yellow dress. The older lady next to her has silvery hair, a kind face and is smartly dressed in a short navy-blue jacket and cream scarf.

'I was just saying to Mum that you and this man were both at Four Oaks,' says the younger woman. 'Your name is James and I was in the seat next to you when we went to the Botanical Gardens. And the man you are with, his name is Danny and he was one of the carers. My name is Vicky, Vicky Collins. Do you remember me?'

Even though the answer to her question is, 'Yes, you are the girl in the purple bobble hat who would not stop talking when I was trying to keep an eye on Danny Allen,' I do not say anything. The reason I do not say anything is because I know that if I say, 'Yes, I do remember you,' she will use it as a reason to carry on talking to me, even though I do not want her to.

Vicky looks at Danny and asks, 'What's the matter with him, can't he speak?'

Danny laughs. 'I don't know what's got into him. Come on, James, do you remember Vicky or not?'

Vicky has left me no choice. I am going to have to say something. 'I am sorry,' I say, 'but I do not remember you. I have tried to remember you but you are just not in my head.'

'Of course you remember me,' says Vicky. 'I was sitting next to you on the coach and was wearing a purple bobble hat. I had a pack of Polos with me but I didn't offer you one because you were being rude.'

'I was not being rude,' I say. 'I just wanted you to stop talking because I could not hear my own thoughts.'

'Aha!' says Vicky. 'So you do remember me then? I knew you did. I am very unforgettable. What are you doing here?'

I do not want to answer this question but I have a feeling she might keep asking it until I give her an answer.

'I have been to see my consultant.'

Vicky opens her eyes wide as if she is surprised. 'But we're in neurology. Does that mean that your brain isn't working like it should?'

'Vicky,' says her mum, 'what have I said about asking people personal questions like that?'

'But he's like me,' she says. 'I'm allowed to ask questions when people are like me, it's the law.' Danny and Vicky's mum do that thing when people know they should not laugh but do anyway. I do not laugh because if it was a joke then in my opinion it was not a very funny one.

Vicky wrinkles her nose as if she is thinking. 'Are you under Dr Moore or Dr Acari?'

'Dr Acari,' I reply.

'He's lovely, isn't he, Mum?' says Vicky giving her mum a wink. 'We call him Dr Dishy. He's like a Sri Lankan Tom Selleck. De-licious.' Vicky says the word delicious like it is two words and then licks her lips.

'I used to be under Dr Dishy's care,' she says, 'but now Dr Moore is my MDT leader. She's nice but she's no Dr Acari.' She looks at her mum and smiles. 'This is James, I know him from Four Oaks.'

'I know, darling,' she says. 'You've just told me.'

Vicky shrugs. 'Did I? Must not have been concentrating. Anyway, James has the same thing as me. He must have been in an accident but I don't know what kind because he hasn't told me.'

'And I am not going to,' I say quickly. I turn to Vicky's mum and say, 'It was nice to meet you, Vicky's mum, but Danny and I have got to get off because we are going to have lunch.'

'Of course,' says Vicky's mum. 'We'd better be going too, if we're not going to be late for our appointment. It was lovely to meet you both. Perhaps we'll bump into you again sometime.'

After the hospital Danny and I go for lunch at a nice burger place not far from the apartment. The food is very good and we talk about lots of different things and I stop feeling all wound up. When our waitress comes to clear our plates away, she asks us if we would like any more drinks and so I tell her that I would like a beer because I only had a Coke before, and then I ask Danny if he would like one too but he says no. 'I'm thinking about going to the supermarket later in the car so it's best not to,' he says. 'But don't let me stop you.'

Once the waitress has gone, I ask Danny a question that I have been meaning to ask him for a while. 'Why do you not drink alcohol, Danny Allen?'

'What do you mean,' says Danny quickly. 'Of course I do. I'm only not drinking today because, like I said, I'm going to the supermarket later in the car so I can't.'

'What about all the other times? We have been to the pub lots of times and not once have you had a beer.'

Danny does not say anything. Instead he taps his fingers on the table nervously like people do when they are thinking. 'I'm an alcoholic,' he says. 'I can't just have one drink and stop. If I have even one then I won't stop, I'll just drink until I'm wasted.'

I think about what Danny has said. It makes me feel sad that he is like this. 'I will stop drinking too,' I say. 'I do not want you to be on your own.'

'There's no need,' he says. 'I'm fine.'

Neither of us says anything for a while and then the waitress arrives with my lager and she puts it down on the table. Danny and I both stare at it, saying nothing.

'Can I ask you a question now?' says Danny after a while. 'Why don't you want to go to the support group Dr Acari was talking to you about? It sounds like it could really help.'

'Because I do not want to,' I reply.

'I know that,' says Danny. 'But what's the reason?'

I take a deep breath and look at Danny and feel ashamed because I know I am not supposed to think what I am about to say because it is not nice. 'I know The Incident changed everything about me,' I say. 'I know I am not like I used to be at all. I see it when I talk to people and as their face changes when they hear my voice. Even our waitress looked at me funny when I ordered my beer and I get fed up of it sometimes. Just because I talk funny and walk funny and my brain does not work like it should does not mean that I want to be around people who are like me. I do not want to be around people like me, Danny. I want to be around people like you, and Martha and my parents. I just want to be normal.'

19

Danny

It's early evening and I'm in the kitchen, watching James pouring over the recipe he's looking at on the iPad that's propped up in front of him on the counter.

'Are you sure you don't want any help?'

James doesn't look up but I can see how irritated he's becoming from the set of his shoulders. As if mustering all the patience he has left, he pauses before replying and then sighs almost inaudibly before saying, 'No thank you, Danny Allen, I will be fine.'

'Okay then, I'll leave you to it. But like I said earlier, keep an eye on the time because everyone will be here in an hour. Just give me a shout if you need anything.'

Not wanting to put James off his stride any more than I already have, I retreat to my room, closing the door behind me. I pick up the book from my bedside table that I'd started earlier in the week but after reading the same sentence half a dozen times, I realise that I'm obviously not in the right frame of mind for reading. I return the book to where I'd taken it from and instead just lie on my bed and look around the room.

I haven't exactly put my mark on this room. Despite James's insistence that I should treat it as if it were my own, I haven't put up a single picture or even a postcard. Virtually all of my stuff is tucked away in the built-in wardrobes, leaving my room a big white box with a bed in, and the only thing in my bedside drawer is some loose change and the name and number of the woman who I met at my one and only AA meeting. I'm not quite sure why I've kept it, but it seems wrong to throw it away somehow. Maybe I will one day, who knows. As for my room,

I like it this way. I feel free of all the clutter of my life, and it makes me feel peaceful.

It's strange to think how quickly this room has become the closest thing I have to a home. It's now a little over two months since I moved into James's apartment as his carer and in that time, much to my relief, I've grown considerably more comfortable in James's company and better still, the awkwardness I'd feared would make this situation impossible never materialised. I've sat in on hospital appointments where James has had to discuss his bowel movements, lifted his naked body up from the bathroom floor after he slipped coming out of the shower and on a couple of occasions, washed the urine-soaked bed sheets he'd tried to hide from me at the bottom of the washing basket, all without embarrassment or comment. And at the same time, James and I have had a lot of fun too. Whether it's been the lazy mornings we've spent playing video games, the late nights working through our latest Netflix addiction or the afternoons sitting around the apartment chatting, James has proved to be good company. It feels like we're flatmates, friends even: two young(ish) single guys with no ties, enjoying the freedom to fritter away hours of our lives guilt free.

Another thing I've noticed is that over these past few weeks James has gradually become more and more carefree and independent, discovering what it is he wants to do, rather than just slotting in with his parents and living a prematurely middle-aged existence. The longer we've been here in the apartment, the more James's confidence has grown and over the past couple of weeks I've noticed him taking more of an interest in cooking, starting with beans on toast but quickly graduating to more complicated dishes like curries and stir fries. Which is why I wasn't surprised when, a little over a week ago on our way back from a night out, he said, 'I would really like to cook a meal from scratch one day for my parents to thank them for everything they have done for me. It will also prove to them that I can cook a meal on my own without burning down the house.'

I agreed it was a good idea and encouraged him to make it

happen. Even with my own very limited cooking skills, I could help make a very simple curry and some rice to go with it. Later, however, James said that he couldn't have his parents over without inviting Martha too and the guest list gradually expanded from there, so that as well as the immediate family, two grandparents, an aunt, a couple of uncles and a cousin joined the list. At the same time, the menu had morphed from its humble origins to a three-course meal where the main attraction would be a repro-duction of a chicken laksa James once had at a business lunch at an upmarket Malaysian restaurant in Mayfair. 'It was the best food I have ever eaten,' he said, as if to justify its inclusion on the menu. 'And I think my family will really like it.'

So that was that, family members were invited, recipes were researched, difficult-to-find ingredients sourced, tableware purchased and rooms cleaned until we reached the point just over ten minutes ago where James announced that he felt confident enough to make the whole meal on his own, and banished me to my room with strict instructions to relax until his guests arrived.

Through a combination of messing about on my phone and picking up my book again, I manage to kill an hour before curiosity gets the better of me. Although we'd done a dry run only the night before, in which James had managed to reproduce the dish perfectly, the difference between then and now was that I'd been there with him the whole way through. And while I was confident that he could make this meal happen, I was also acutely aware of all the challenges he faces. I really want him to succeed tonight. This is his chance to show his family who he's become in the short time he's been away, to show them that there's more of the old James DeWitt left in him than they might have ever dared hope for.

Alarm bells start ringing the moment I emerge from my room and fail to smell cooking in the air. I know for a fact that the recipe calls for, amongst other things, onions, garlic, lemongrass and ginger, and that combination rising up from a hot wok should've been enough to have me salivating, but the strongest aroma I can smell is of the pine-fresh detergent I used to clean the floors late this afternoon. It's when I reach the kitchen that my worst fears are confirmed. James is still huddled over his iPad and the kitchen is exactly as it had been before I'd left an hour ago.

'James, mate, what are you doing? Why haven't you started cooking?'

'What do you mean started? I have plenty of time. I told you, no one is coming until eight o' clock and it is not even—' James looks at the clock on the wall above the fridge and as he does so his expression changes from one of self-righteous indignation to absolute horror. 'I do not understand. I was just looking up a few things on the Internet.'

An examination of the search history on his iPad explains everything. While he'd started off well at 18.31 with a search entitled, 'pictures chicken laksa', by 18.45 he's searching: 'What does laksa mean' and ten minutes later has abandoned all interest in cooking for, 'When is the next Bond film out' (18.55), 'Newest movie trailers' (19.01), 'Pictures Megan Fox' (19.15), 'Pictures Scarlett Johansson' (19.20) and 'funny videos people falling over' (19.26).

I hand the iPad back to James. 'Mate,' I reassure him as I reflect on the countless hours I myself have lost down the rabbit-hole of the world-wide-web over the past few years, 'if we're not careful the Internet will be the downfall of us all.'

'My whole family is going to be here in twenty minutes and I have nothing to give them,' says James, panic creeping into his voice. 'They will think they were right about me not being able to live on my own. What are we going to do?'

James gives me the same look he gave me that day in The White Horse when his parents wanted to take him home. It's the one where he thinks that I might have all the answers. I glance at the clock and do the calculations. If we cut a few corners and he lets me help with the preparation, James could get this meal cooked and still rightly claim to have done it himself.

'First,' I say, feeling strangely confident as I hand James an onion, 'we're not going to panic because that's not going to help anyone. And second,' I pause, open the drawer in front of me, take out a knife and hand it to him, 'you're going to have to start chopping right this very second.'

By the time the intercom buzzer sounds signalling the arrival of James's first guests, the scent of frying chicken, coconut milk and lemongrass are heavy in the air.

'Would you mind getting that?' asks James as the buzzer sounds again. 'I will be fine on my own for a while. I really want everyone to see me in the kitchen when they arrive.'

Much as I understand James's desire for his family to see him in action, by asking me to answer the door he has highlighted one of my main insecurities about this evening: my role here tonight. While I am happy to welcome James's immediate family as his friend and carer, I'm less keen to meet those I haven't met before in case they mistake me for his butler.

'Fine then, I'll go,' I say reluctantly when the buzzer sounds for a third time. 'Just make sure you keep an eye on everything until I get back.'

Thankfully I needn't have worried about James's wider family mistaking me for a bargain basement Jeeves, as aside from his uncle Oswald (a retired chief inspector of schools, who thrusts his coat into my hands without a word of thanks) they are a delightful bunch who are overflowing with praise for me and the work I do with James. With minutes to go before the food is ready to serve, the only person yet to arrive is Martha and so when the intercom buzzer sounds again, it's no surprise when I answer to see her smiling face beaming at me from the tiny black-and-white video screen.

As I wait at the front door to meet her at the lift, it occurs to me that I'm actually quite looking forward to seeing her after such a long time. Although my dealings with her of late have been minimal, I have to admit she's crossed my mind quite a bit. It had been good feeling like her hero even for a short while, when she'd approached me about working with James. And maybe it's because I feel fitter than I have done in years as I've started going for a run each day, or perhaps it's because I'm starting to get over losing Maya but recently I'd found myself wondering what it would feel like to be more to her than her brother's carer. Obviously I'm not deluded, Martha is clearly one hundred per cent out of my league but then again, Maya was too so anything is possible.

As the doors to the lift open, the first thing I notice is that Martha isn't alone. All hope that the smartly dressed guy with the strategically ruffled hair next to her is a downstairs neighbour here to borrow a cup of sugar evaporates the moment she introduces him.

'Danny,' she says, 'I'd like you to meet Lucien.'

The name rings a bell. I'm pretty sure that James had told me that Martha's ex, the guy she'd been living with at the beginning of the year, was called Lucien. Unfortunately, however, he must have failed to update me on the fact that they had apparently recently got back together, and that she had invited him to come along this evening.

'So you're the infamous Danny Allen,' says Lucien, sounding exactly as I had expected: clean-cut vowels, overly confident and condescending. 'Martha simply hasn't stopped singing your praises. On behalf of the family I want to thank you for all the work you're doing with James. By all accounts, you're doing a splendid job.'

I'm pretty sure he doesn't mean it. Most likely this is his way of saying he hasn't enjoyed hearing Martha talk about me in such glowing terms, and he wants to put me in my place. If it is, however, it backfires spectacularly because Martha plants another kiss on my cheek and says, 'This man is my absolute hero.'

As compensation for my current disappointment goes, it's considerably better than the nothing I'd been expecting and it's all the more valuable for the power it has to wipe Lucien's smug grin right off his face.

As luck would have it, Lucien ends up seated next to James's horrible uncle Oswald who monopolises his attention with a series of long and very boring monologues about his view on the state of the education system. The rest of the table, however, conduct the usual sorts of family conversations that are as amusing as they are revealing. For instance, I learn from Mr DeWitt's brother, Edward, that Mr DeWitt was nearly expelled from KS for streaking across the school rugby pitch for a bet. James's cousin Clara, meanwhile, tells me a funny story about when James and Martha were children and how they would regularly pretend that Martha was a relative from overseas who didn't speak any English, and James would 'interpret' for her whenever they met anyone new.

As I sit back from the table, listening to the chat and laughter as we plough our way through James's prawn fritter starter (perfectly edible if a little overdone), chicken laksa (spot on) and the back-up, shop-bought coconut-and-lime ice cream (the stuff James and I made earlier in the afternoon turned out to be inedible), I'm reminded of family gatherings from my youth. Christmases in my parents' tiny house, living-room furniture shifted to one side to allow for a couple of trestle tables to take centre stage, uncles, aunties and cousins telling the most inappropriate of stories in front me, Helen, and our cousins. It might have been a different family but the love we shared was just the same. And yet, as sweet as it is to revisit those memories, it's painful too, knowing that there'll never be a Christmas like that for me again. There will never be a time when my parents, Helen and I will sit around a table like this and share stories from our past.

'Are you okay, Danny?' asks Martha, seeing me lost in my thoughts. 'I hope we're not boring you with all this family nonsense. We DeWitts are normally quite a reserved bunch but put us all around a table, add wine and good food and I'm afraid we can get a little bit overwhelming.'

'It's fine,' I reply, 'I was just somewhere else for a minute.' And with that I'm back in the present, pouring wine for James's guests, keeping conversations going and generally trying to make things run smoothly.

It's after midnight by the time the last of James's family agree to leave, having been convinced by James and me that we can handle the clearing up on our own. Leaving James to say his goodbyes, I disappear to my room to find something a bit warmer to wear as now everyone has gone and the heating is off, it's a little chilly. As I search for a jumper, there's a gentle knock at my door and James pops his head into the room. He looks happy.

'Everyone said they had the best time, Danny. They all made jokes about how I had not set fire to anything, but they were the good kind of jokes, the kind where I can laugh too.'

'That's good. You've shown them what you can do. You must be proud.'

James nods. 'I am, but I could not have done it without you.'

A wave of tiredness hits me. I feel like if I closed my eyes right now, I could fall asleep standing up. But then I look at James and I notice that something isn't quite right. He's staring at me as if he's got something he wants to say, and is even opening his mouth to the same effect but no words are coming out. Then all at once, as though someone has flicked a switch inside him, he goes limp and crashes to the floor, convulsing as if there's a thousand volts of electricity running through his body.

20

James

My first words when I open my eyes are: 'Where is Danny Allen?'

I do not know why I ask this question.

It is as though it is just there on my lips when I wake up.

I feel like there might be people here with me but I cannot be sure because everything is blurry.

I cannot hear them either because my ears are all funny, like I am swimming underwater or hearing the world from inside a cardboard box.

I definitely know that I asked about Danny Allen though. I know because I felt my lips moving just like they are now when I ask the question again.

I feel someone touch my face.

Their hands are warm and soft.

They feel nice.

Every muscle in my body aches. As if I have just run a marathon or been in a boxing match. My arms, chest, face and legs all ache. Even my toes hurt.

I start to feel tired. I close my eyes for just a moment. The warm hands are gently holding mine.

I can hear voices in the room more clearly now.

One voice says: 'He's definitely awake,' and another, 'I'll go and get the nurse.' I think the first voice belongs to my mum, Erica. The second sounds a lot like my sister Martha but I could be wrong.

None of the voices sound like Danny Allen.

I open my eyes again.

I can see a lot better now.

I am not at home.

I am in a hospital room.

My mum is leaning over me, smiling.

'Can you hear me, darling?'

I nod and close my eyes. It is so difficult to keep them open.

'It's Mum here, how are you feeling, sweetie?'

I can smell her perfume. It is sweet and soft.

I hear myself say, 'I feel okay, Mum, but where is Danny Allen?'

'He just popped out to get coffee for us all.'

That was my dad, Don, speaking. I would know his voice anywhere. I open my eyes and smile.

'He shouldn't be too long,' says Dad. 'He'll be pleased to know you're awake.'

'But is he okay?'

'Of course he is, son. He was worried about you, as we all were. Do you know where you are?'

'Am I in a hospital?'

'That's right,' says Mum. 'You're in the emergency ward at UHB. The consultant thinks you might have had a seizure. Do you remember what happened?'

I think hard.

I remember cooking.

I remember my family coming to visit.

I remember thinking about how much I do not like Martha's boyfriend.

I remember laughing a lot because everyone was having a good time. I think I might even remember kissing my mum goodbye. But I do not remember anything about a seizure.

A woman who I have never seen before comes into the room, followed by Martha. Martha kisses my cheek.

'You had us worried there, big bro,' she says.

'I did not mean to,' I say. 'I think it must have been an accident.'

The woman next to Martha tells me her name. She is called Dr Carter and she is a neurologist.

'You're under Dr Acari, aren't you?'

'Yes,' I say. 'He looks like Tom Selleck.'

Dr Carter smiles. 'So he does, how very observant of you.'

'I do notice things,' I say.

'Well, I'll be sure to pass on your observation when I see him next but I'm afraid for now, you're stuck with me.'

Dr Carter tells me she has been looking after me since I came into hospital last night. She tells me there is no need to worry. She tells me everything is under control. She says I definitely had a seizure but at the moment she and her colleagues have no idea what brought it on. 'We might never know,' she says. 'It could just be one of those things.' What she does know is that it is under control and because she has changed the dosage of my medication, things should settle down soon.

I thank her for everything she has done. She jokes that it is all in a day's work. She sits on the bed and asks me if it is okay to do a quick examination. I tell her it is fine and my dad says, 'We'll give you some privacy,' and then he, Mum and Martha leave the room. The examination does not take long. Dr Carter shines a small light into my face and makes me follow it with my eyes. She listens to my heart with her stethoscope and asks lots of questions about how I am feeling. When she is finished, she says, 'Well, everything looks fine but I'd like to keep you in for another night just to be on the safe side.'

I do not want to be here overnight. I just want to go home. But I still smile at Dr Carter and say thank you anyway because I do not want to be rude.

Before Dr Carter leaves, I ask if she could do me a small favour.

'That depends on what it is,' she says in a voice that sounds like she is making a joke.

'Could you ask my family to send Danny Allen in now? I need to know that he is okay.'

Dr Carter smiles as though this time I have made a joke. 'I'd be delighted to,' she says. 'Is he a friend?'

That is a good question. I know Danny is my carer but is he my friend too? 'He is my . . . very, very, good friend, maybe even my best friend. Actually please do not tell him that I said that. He might get embarrassed.'

'Of course, James,' says Dr Carter with a wink. 'Your secret is safe with me.'

The moment Danny comes into the room I start feeling better.

'I hear you've been asking after me,' he says. 'What's the big emergency?' He is smiling as he says this so I know it is a joke. He pats my hand and moves a blue chair next to the bed so that he can sit close to me.

'I was worried about you. I wanted to know you were okay.'

'Shouldn't it be the other way round? You've just had a seizure.'

'I know, but I am okay and I needed to know you were okay too.'

'Well, if it helps, I'm more than happy to admit I could probably do with a good sleep but other than that, I'm fine. You really gave me quite a scare there. One moment you were standing at my door and the next . . . well . . . it wasn't nice. I knew I had to do everything I could to protect your head so I whipped off the shirt I was wearing to cushion it and then I called an ambulance.'

'So you saved me?'

Danny laughs. 'That makes it sound like I actually did something useful.'

'But you did, didn't you? You protected my head because you knew I had already been hurt there.'

'To be honest, James, I just did what I'd been trained to do. I thought I'd forgotten most of the stuff they taught me on my course at Four Oaks but when I saw what was happening to you, it all came flooding back. Anyway, I'm just glad I was able to help. Any idea when they're going to let you go home?'

I tell him exactly what Dr Carter said and then Danny says, when I come home, that we will celebrate. 'Whatever you want to do,' says Danny. 'We'll do it.'

'Anything?'

'Of course,' says Danny. 'A *Friends* box set marathon, the banquet menu at that Thai place you like, a day trip down to London, you name it.'

As Danny gets ready to leave when my parents and Martha come back into the room, I have one last thing to say to him. 'You did save me, Danny,' I say in a voice so quiet only he and I can hear it, 'and one day I am going to do the same for you too.'

Some of my test results are delayed so I do not get to go home until two days later. But while it could have been really boring just lying in bed in hospital, it was not because my parents, Martha and Danny Allen came to see me every day. And when Danny learned I was going to be staying in longer than we thought, he brought my laptop from home and some of my favourite DVDs so I always had something to watch.

So actually, even though having a seizure was not very nice, everything that happened after it was lovely, so it was sort of okay.

On the day I finally get to leave hospital, my dad and mum arrive early and tell me they have got something they would like to ask me.

'We'd really like it if you'd agree to come home with us,' says my dad. 'We know that your friend Danny has looked after you tremendously well, and that it was important for you to exercise your freedom but we'd really feel a lot happier if you came back home now. Your mother and I have talked about it a great deal and we're more than happy to agree to any living arrangement you'd like, so long as you return home with us.'

'That is really nice of you,' I say. 'Really it is, but I could not come home now even if I wanted to.'

'But why ever not?' asks my mum, Erica. 'I wouldn't even cook your meals for you if you didn't want me to.'

'I cannot,' I explain, 'because I have got Danny Allen to look after.'

Mum and Dad look at each other as though I am talking in a language they do not understand. 'Darling,' says my mum. 'I think you're confused. It's Danny who is your carer not the other way around.'

'That is what Danny said too,' I say, 'but if I do not look after Danny Allen, who will? I am lucky because I have you and Dad and Martha. But Danny does not have anyone. And he is really sad too. You would not see it if you did not live with him like I do, but Danny is sad through and through. So, you see, I really am his carer, and it really is a very kind offer you have made but I have got to go home and look after Danny because, well, he might not know it but he needs me.'

That evening, after my parents have dropped me home, Danny and I eat steak and kidney pie and chips and watch a movie. The film is *The Last Boy Scout*, a Bruce Willis film that we have both seen lots of times, even though we agree it is not very good. Anyway, just as we get to the best part of the film where Bruce says, 'Touch me again and I'll kill you,' I reach for the remote control and pause the TV.

'Danny?'

'Yeah.'

'You know how you said that when I got home we could do anything I wanted. Did you mean it?'

'I wouldn't have said it if I didn't. Why? Have you got an idea of what you'd like to do?'

'Yes,' I reply.

'Has it got anything to do with *The Last Boy Scout*?' asks Danny, making a joke. 'Is it that you want to join up with a down-and-out American football player and solve a murder case? Because if it is, I'm definitely up for it.'

'No,' I say grinning, 'it is not that. It is something else.'

'Well, come on then, don't keep me in suspense all night, tell me.'

'Well, it is like this: I want us to go back to school.'

Danny looks puzzled. 'You want us to do what?'

'Go back to school,' I reply. 'I want us to go back to King's Scrivener.'

21

Danny

Two things occur to me as I stare at my reflection in the hallway mirror, dressed as I am in a dinner jacket with satin lapels, white wing-collar shirt with silver cufflinks, black silk bow tie, and brand new shiny black Oxford lace-ups: first, that I barely recognise myself in this get up, and second, that there is only one person in the entire world who could get me to dress up like this. And right now that person is giving me the thumbs up behind my back.

'You look great,' says James, as I turn around. 'Really good.'

'Cheers,' I say and then realise from the look of expectation on James's face that he's waiting for me to return the compliment. 'Oh, and you look the business too,' I add, somewhat awkwardly. James is wearing exactly, and I do mean exactly, the same outfit as me. We look like bookends.

'I think I look good too,' he says as the intercom buzzer sounds. 'The King's Scrivener summer ball is not going to know what has hit it.'

When James explained that when he said he wanted us to go back to King's Scrivener, what he actually meant was for us to attend our old school's annual summer ball, my gut reaction, despite my promise to him, was to say no.

Not in a million years.

Not even on pain of death.

The thought of going back to that place, the idea of having to socialise with those sorts of people, was all too much. It was hard enough avoiding KS old boys in the real world, without going looking for them in their natural habitat. In the past month alone I'd seen one staring back at me from a magazine front cover in my dentist's waiting room, heard another voicing opinions on matters of global importance on the car radio and witnessed yet another bringing home gold for Great Britain on a foreign sporting field. Each and every one of these occasions was a reminder of the potential I'd squandered and the past I'd betrayed. And up until now, though James and I had arrived at our respective situations through very different routes, the one thing I'd been certain united us was a firm desire to leave the past in the past.

Given what I knew about James's life following his injuries, about how he'd pushed away both friends and acquaintances, it didn't make sense that something like the King's Scrivener summer ball would even be on his radar. Though I'd never been, I knew that the summer ball was little other than an annual opportunity for KS old boys and old girls to get drunk and pair off, or frantically network or seek out exclusive work-experience opportunities for their progeny, so what had made him want to go?

'You did,' said James, when I asked him the question. 'Before The Incident I had never missed a KS summer ball. But since I have been unwell, I have not wanted to go, even though my mum, dad and Martha have begged me to. But this year I feel stronger. This year I feel like I can do it and it is thanks to you. Will you go with me?'

What could I say? In the game of real-life Top Trumps the brain-damaged guy who overcomes his depression beats the able-bodied guy who squandered his opportunities and never made anything of his life hands down.

'Of course I will, mate,' I replied. 'If it's what you want to do, then it's what we'll do.'

First thing the following morning James asked me to take him over to his parents' to surprise them with the news. Their joy was plain to see. Mrs DeWitt had tears in her eyes and told me I was the best thing that had happened to her family in a long time. Even the normally undemonstrative Mr DeWitt shook my hand and informed me that I was doing a sterling job. That evening, after disappearing to his room for a few hours on our arrival home, James emerged and revealed that not only had he booked the services of a chauffeur but had even managed to negotiate a twenty per cent discount.

Of course now the time has finally arrived, I still don't want to go to the stupid ball and can't imagine that it won't be every bit as awful as I suspect it will be, but my enjoyment is hardly the point of the exercise. The point of the exercise is showing the world that after three years of hiding, James Charles DeWitt is finally ready to rejoin the land of the living, and I'd need to have a heart of stone not to get behind that.

On the way to Warwick James tells me we're going to need a cover story. 'I am thinking of you more than me,' he says. 'I do not mind telling everyone you are my carer because I think you are great but I was thinking that you might.'

The question of what I was going to say if anyone asked me (as I knew they would) what I did for a living had crossed my mind several times over the past few weeks and I had yet to come up with a satisfactory answer.

'I was thinking I might just come clean. You know, just to show them that the Carmody prize isn't the last word in greatness they all think it is.'

James looks surprised. 'Really?'

I shake my head and let out a heavy sigh. Much as I'd like to be, I don't think I'm quite that brave. 'So what do you think my cover story should be? Tell anyone who's interested that I'm working in the City or maybe go the more academic route and hand myself a fake professorship in Ornithology?'

'I think you should tell them that you made a lot of money in the dot com boom.'

I can't help but laugh. 'Either you've given this a lot of thought or that was some quick thinking right there.'

James shrugs guiltily. 'I just want you to have a good time.'

'In that case, I'll happily be a dot com millionaire. Sounds like it would be a lot more fun than studying birds. I do have one condition though: I want a supermodel girlfriend too. Those guys always have supermodel girlfriends.'

'It would be too easy to google and catch you out,' says James. 'How about a scientist girlfriend instead? No one will want to google a scientist because it sounds too real to be made up.'

'Fine,' I reply, 'she can be a scientist but a sexy one, okay? Maybe she could have started out as an underwear model before landing her PhD in nuclear fusion.'

James is quiet for a moment. 'What will we say if people ask why we have arrived at the ball together? People will know we were not friends at school.'

'How about this?' I say off the top of my head. 'We bumped into each other while on holiday at an exclusive island retreat in the Caribbean and now, even though I live in the States and you're in the UK, we've kept in touch. And then when you told me about the summer ball, I decided on a whim to fly over on my private jet.'

James laughs. 'This is going to be brilliant.'

For the rest of the journey we lose ourselves working out more details of my story. We decide which tech companies I'd invested in, exactly how much money I'd made in the dot com boom and how much I'd lost when the bubble finally burst. All the while we're talking, however, it occurs to me that James doesn't once mention inventing a story for himself and I wonder if that's because he doesn't need one. After all, unlike me he's got nothing to be embarrassed about, and certainly nothing to prove. He's started his own company and sold it for millions, been elected to parliament and despite suffering near-fatal injuries inflicted during an unprovoked assault, he's back after a three-year absence to show all the KS old boys what success really looks like. As odd as it sounds, in a way I feel a little envious of him.

As our car approaches the wrought-iron gates at the entrance to the school, James and I sit up to get a better view. By my calculations it's only eighteen years since I was last at King's Scrivener and yet, given everything that's happened during those years, it feels more like a hundred. The school still looks the same though, as magisterial as ever, and the grounds are beautifully picturesque. To think that for a while this place was my second home seems almost too ridiculous for words.

The ball's organisers have erected a huge white marquee to the right of the main school on the open field that was commonly known in my day as the lower lawn. From it the honeyed tones of a string quartet can just about be heard over the chatter of women in expensive cocktail dresses and men in evening suits lurking by its entrance. Our driver, Tony, is directed by a steward towards a temporary car parking area to the side of the school cricket pitch and as he follows the directions, we pass row after row of unfeasibly overpriced Italian-made penis substitutes but they all fade into the background once James spots an actual helicopter in the field behind the cricket pavilion.

'I bet it belongs to one of the Vlahakis brothers,' I say to James, referring to the infamous Greek siblings and KS old boys whose father made his billions in the cement business. 'They always were pretentious idiots.'

Once we've parked, our driver gives us his number and asks us to text him when we're ready to leave and he'll come and collect us. I think about telling him that he shouldn't go too far, as he'll be hearing from us in the next ten minutes but I don't because I don't want to dampen James's mood. He's more excited about being here than I've ever seen him about anything, and as we chat he's stumbling over every word he says in his desperation to get them out quickly.

As we continue to the marquee, I begin to spot a few faces I recognise so I keep my head down. Directly in front of us there is a guy from the year above whose parents are both distinguished actors, to our left is a bloke from our year who I'm pretty sure is now a famous novelist, and over to our right is another guy who, rumour had it, was twentieth in line to the throne. The idea that I might be able to hide from all, or indeed any of these people was idiotic in the extreme but that didn't stop me trying.

As a man who I'd last seen captaining a team on a TV panel game show catches my eye, I try to gently steer James in the opposite direction but then someone calls my name and I automatically turn around to see a tall yet oddly plump man holding the hand of a surgically enhanced blonde in a tight electric-blue dress.

'Danny bloody Allen!' he bellows. 'How the devil are you? How's that curing cancer going?'

I recognise him immediately. He's Lawrence Whittaker and back in our school days he was famous for two things: being a pretty good batsman and having a Tory MP father whose extra-marital affair was exposed by the tabloids. In recent times Whittaker himself is also most famous for two things: being the Conservative MP for East Jarrow and having his extra-marital affair with his secretary exposed by the tabloids. You really couldn't make it up.

'This fellow here was the bane of my existence,' says Whittaker, following an introduction to his blonde companion, Irena. 'He was brilliant at everything. Even won a special school prize that teachers believed meant that you were destined to change the world! So come on then, Danny boy, you've got to tell me what you're up to. I'm all ears.'

I open my mouth ready to regurgitate the story that James and I have concocted but before I can utter a syllable, James says: 'Danny Allen is a world famous Hollywood producer.'

I look at James and so does Whittaker. 'I'm sorry old boy,' says Whittaker to James. 'Didn't quite hear what you said there.'

James repeats himself in a crystal-clear voice and this time even Whittaker's companion is left in no doubt.

'He said he's a famous Hollywood producer,' she says in such an excitable Bristolian burr that I can only assume she has ambitions to be part of the film world.

I stare at James in astonishment. This wasn't the story we'd agreed on at all.

'And,' adds James as if he hasn't already said enough, 'Danny Allen is best friends with Bruce Willis too.'

22

James

Whittaker is looking at Danny with eyes wide like a frog. 'Is this true, Danny? Are you really friends with Bruce Willis?'

I am not quite sure what has come over me. Normally I am quite shy at parties and barely say a word. Normally I find the noise and all the people a bit too much because I cannot hear my thoughts properly. But tonight is different. The people and the noise are not bothering me. In fact, I think they are actually making things better. I do not think I would have dared tell someone like Whittaker that Danny was a Hollywood producer and is friends with Bruce Willis if we had bumped into him in the street. I feel like I can do anything tonight and that includes having a bit of fun.

'Er . . . yes, it's true,' says Danny, sounding like he needs to clear his throat. 'I am indeed a close friend and confidant of Bruce Willis and also a Hollywood film producer.'

'Outstanding!' says Whittaker. 'Always loved those *Die Hard* films. Jolly entertaining they were too. And you're friends with old Brucey, are you? Top stuff. Maybe you could introduce us sometime? I could show you both round the Houses of Parliament if you'd like. I'm sure Bruce would get a real kick out of something like that.'

'I'll run it by him next time I see him,' says Danny.

'That will probably be at Mel Gibson's birthday party, won't it, Danny?' I say because I think it is quite a funny thing to say.

'Yes, probably,' says Danny and Whittaker's eyes widen even more.

'So Danny,' says Whittaker. 'I'm quite the film fan. Would I have seen anything you've produced?'

'Have you heard of *Dawn of the Planet of the Apes*?' I say quickly, in case Danny messes things up by being too slow.

''Fraid not, old man,' says Whittaker. 'To be honest *The Lord of the Rings* trilogy is more my thing. Bloody fantastic films they are. So realistic.'

'Brilliant,' I reply. '*The Lord of the Rings* is also one of Danny's films.'

'You're joking?' says Whittaker. 'Are you saying that old KS boy Danny Allen is responsible for producing the most feted film trilogy ever?'

'Well . . . I . . .er . . . the thing is . . . Lawrence . . .' Danny Allen flaps for quite a while and I start to think that I might have to finish off his sentence but at the last minute he thinks of something. '. . . the thing is . . . big budget films like *Lord of the Rings* tend to have more than one producer because of the sheer scale of the task involved. But yes, *Rings* is definitely one of mine.'

'I don't know what to say,' splutters Whittaker. 'I'm absolutely stumped for words and as a Member of Parliament I can tell you that almost never happens! I adored *The Lord of the Rings* films, absolutely loved them. Saw each one literally the day it came out. And you were involved in making them?' He shakes Danny's hand again. 'Allen, you are a proper legend.'

'He worked on *The Hobbit* too,' I say, trying my best to keep a straight face. This is the best fun I have had in a long time.

Whittaker gasps. 'Did you really?'

'Yes, he did,' I say on Danny's behalf. 'But he does not like to mention it in case people think he has got a big head.'

'Fan-bloody-tastic,' says Whittaker.

'And do not forget he is friends with Bruce Willis,' I add as Danny tries to catch my eye. 'You and Bruce are like this, aren't you?' I cross my fingers and hold them in the air to show how close Danny is to Bruce Willis.

Whittaker pats Danny on the shoulder like they are old friends. 'Always knew you'd make it to the big leagues, Danny,' he says. 'Never imagined you'd make it right to the top! Well done, sir, well done indeed!'

Danny and I are soon joined by others from our year at school. They introduce themselves to Danny like this, 'Danny mate, Barnaby Thomas here, so good to see you again. I'm working in Telecoms myself,' as if anyone cares what they do now they know about Danny, who has produced amazing films and is friends with Bruce Willis.

Danny tells some very funny stories about his time in Hollywood. His best is about how he once went on a weekend fishing trip with Bruce Willis, Arnold Schwarzenegger, Tom Hanks and Steven Spielberg. It is such a good story and it makes every one laugh so much that for a moment I forget he is making it up and I want to know myself how it will end.

I am so glad that Danny is having a good time and that people think he has done well. It is all that I wanted. I know that he did not want to come tonight. I know that he was scared of what people would think of him if they found out that he is my carer. They might think he has wasted his life. But Danny Allen has not wasted his life. He is doing something good. Something that is more important than showing off how much money you have made. He is helping people who cannot help themselves. And that is not just a good thing to do with your life. It is the very best thing.

When Danny finishes his funny story, everyone pats him on the back and they give him their business cards and tell him that they should meet up for lunch some time. Danny tells them that he is really busy at the moment working on a new film so he might not be around for a while. Then he tells everybody his voice is getting hoarse from talking so much and so he is going to get a drink and catch up with me, his other best friend apart from Bruce Willis.

Danny waits until we have nearly reached the marquee before he tells me off. 'What was all that about, you loony?' he says, laughing. 'I thought we'd agreed I was going to be a dot com millionaire.'

'I know,' I say. 'But I thought it might be a bit boring.'

'Couldn't you at least have given me a warning before dropping me right in it? There I was thinking all I needed was a couple of made-up stories about my early days in silicon valley and suddenly I'm ad-libbing tall tales about me and the great and good of Hollywood!'

'But did you have fun?' I ask.

Danny thinks about it for a moment. 'You know what, once I got into it, I did.'

'Good,' I reply. 'Then that is all that matters.'

I think about telling Danny Allen that I think he is successful even if he is not really a Hollywood producer.

I also think about telling him how much he has helped me and how much of a difference he has made to my life, but I do not want to embarrass him and I do not want to embarrass myself either.

In the end all I say is, 'Let us go and get that glass of champagne you talked about.' And then I remember that Danny cannot drink alcohol. 'Sorry about that,' I say. 'We will get you a fizzy water or something instead.'

Inside, the marquee is just as busy as it is outside.

Some people are listening to the string quartet and others are at the bar on the opposite side waiting to be served.

Some of their faces look familiar and others I do not remember at all. But when people come and say hello, I smile and chat to everyone anyway.

Some people tell me that they have missed seeing me at the summer balls and that they have not been the same without me.

Others ask how I am doing and if I am better now.

I tell them all that I am doing really well but I am not fully better.

It makes me feel good to say these things to people and I think people feel good hearing me say them.

I do not think people like it when bad things happen to young people. I do not think people like the idea of people not living the lives they were supposed to live.

After a while Danny tells me that he is going to the bar to get us more drinks. For a time I stand on my own while people around me talk to each other, but then I wonder where my mum is because I know she is here somewhere. I take out my phone to call her, as a group of men squeeze past me trying to get to the bar. One of the men accidentally knocks into me and when he apologises, I realise that I know him and he calls the other two over.

'James,' says the tall one. 'Is it really you?'

'I never thought I'd see you here again,' says the short one.

'Still, it's great to see you're all better,' says the only one who has not spoken yet. 'For a while we thought you'd never be the same again.'

'Well, I am not and I never will be,' I say, and their faces change when they hear how my voice sounds now. I see that look all the time. It is a look that says, 'I did not know you were not normal.'

Samuel Hunter.

Miles Clifford.

David Goldacre.

They used to be my best friends.

They were with Zara and me on the night of The Incident.

But I have not seen them for a very long time.

They have changed a lot since I saw them. Miles has got a lot fatter. David has lost some of his hair. Samuel looks like he has not slept in a very long time.

They ask me a lot of questions about what I have been doing but I do not tell them very much. I say things like, 'I try and keep busy,' and, 'I still have a lot of hospital appointments to go to,' and then they tell me what they have been doing. Miles is a dad now. Samuel has just got married. And David has just bought a brand new Aston Martin. I feel odd hearing their stories. I do not know why at first but as Danny returns with our drinks, I realise it is because I am not in their stories any more. I used to be in them all but I am not any more. They have gone on making stories without me.

'Evening, gents,' says Danny, handing me a drink. 'Long time no see.'

It is fun watching their faces. They do not understand how Danny Allen and I are friends. I think it might have sent their brains funny.

Now they know how I feel sometimes.

'Have you guys just bumped into each other?' asks David.

Danny shakes his head. 'James and I have been back in touch for a few years now. I read about his accident while out in LA. I produce films out there. Anyway when I read his story, I reached out to him and thankfully he responded and sold me exclusive rights.'

My old friends all look at each other.

'You don't actually mean you're going to make a film about James?' asks Miles.

'That's absolutely what I mean,' says Danny. 'We're all very excited about it.'

'And it's actually going to get made?' asks Samuel.

'Put it this way,' says Danny. 'Leo signed his name on the dotted line late last week. And when he does that, that's a guarantee it's going to get made.'

My old friends all look at each other again. 'When you say "Leo",' asks Miles, 'do you mean as in—'

Danny shushes him before he can finish what he is saying. 'I know being old boys you'd never break a confidence but not even *Variety* knows yet. If word gets out before we're ready, it'll be my ass on the line. You understand surely?'

'Of course,' says Miles, and he and the others nod as though they know exactly what Danny is talking about. 'Mum's the word.'

'Thanks,' says Danny. 'Now if you wouldn't mind excusing us, James and I have quite a bit of business to discuss.'

I follow Danny to the other side of the marquee and when we are sure that we are safe, we burst out laughing.

'This Hollywood producer role is really growing on you, isn't it?' I say to Danny. 'My favourite bit was when you said it would be your "ass" on the line. I had to bite my tongue to stop from laughing.'

'What did you ever see in those guys anyway,' asks Danny.

'They were idiots at school and they don't seem to have improved much in the interim.'

'Maybe I was an idiot too, back then,' I reply. 'Maybe that is why I did not realise what they were like until now.'

With our drinks in our hands Danny and I go looking for my parents. After a while we find them in a corner of the marquee talking with some old family friends. When my mum sees me for the first time, she starts to cry.

'I can't help it,' she says, hugging me. 'You look so handsome.'

I think my dad must be feeling quite emotional too because when Mum is done he hugs me and says, 'I'm so proud of you, son.'

My parents' friends are all happy to see me too. They take their turns hugging me and say things like, 'You're such an example to us all,' and, 'You've been so brave,' and, 'You're an absolute hero.'

I do feel like a hero.

I feel as if I have saved lots of soldiers' lives from the enemy and now I am being awarded a medal for it.

I feel like I have been through the worst and now I am getting back to my best.

I want to feel like this forever.

But as I am thinking all of these good things and feeling all of these good feelings, I look across the marquee and see a face from my past.

And as I walk towards that face, I stop thinking all of these good things and feeling all of these good feelings. And instead as I walk towards that face from my past, I just feel sad.

23

Danny

James has pulled a disappearing act.

One moment he's right next to me, listening to his mum interrogate me on what it feels like to be back at King's Scrivener after all these years, and the next it's as if he's vanished into thin air.

'I didn't even see him leave,' remarks Mrs DeWitt, scanning the marquee. 'Do you think he's all right? Should I look for him or leave him be? It's so difficult to know what the right thing to do is these days.'

'He's probably gone to get himself a drink,' I reassure her, 'but to be on the safe side, I'll check. I've got your number so I'll ring you when I find him.'

Despite a thorough search of the scrum waiting at the bar to be served, I don't see any sign of James and so I send him a text and continue my search outside. My first stop is the posh Portaloos located out by the sports pavilion and, clutching my drink, I take up residence on a nearby bench, hoping to catch sight of him emerging from one. While waiting, I receive nods of acknowledgement from people I'm guessing have heard about my newfound Hollywood fame. But in the fifteen minutes I'm waiting, there's no sign of James and after another call to his mobile I begin to worry.

As much as James's confidence and ability have improved in recent weeks, I'm also aware of his limitations, particularly in the light of his recent seizure. It doesn't take much to imagine a scenario where he's got himself into difficulty. I try his number once again but it just rings out. When it goes to voicemail, this time I leave a message asking him to call me back urgently.

Much as I know it will embarrass James to hear his name announced over the PA system I start looking around for someone official who might be able to help find him. After a short search I spot Dr Baines, my old Biology teacher, looking very dapper if a trifle fragile in his evening suit. Though he was well on his way to being deaf even back when he taught me, I still consider him my best bet for finding out who is in charge of the ball but as I walk over to him, my phone vibrates with a text. It's from James: 'With an old friend. Do not worry. Will explain later. J.'

Relieved that he's okay but frustrated that he's chosen today of all days to be mysterious, I text back, 'No problem, see you later,' and then call Mrs DeWitt to let her know that James is safe.

Determined to give him space and yet unwilling to rejoin the DeWitts, I'm at a loss what to do for the rest of the evening and on a whim take a walk around the school grounds for old times' sake.

Heading away from the marquee, I walk towards to the main school entrance wondering if I might somehow be able to gain access to the building and have a poke around my old class-rooms. The huge heavy oak front doors, however, are firmly locked and so I continue on towards the clock tower, which was always the location of the school's outdoor Christmas carol service.

The first time my mum attended the service she cried the whole way through and told me it was the most beautiful thing she'd ever seen. I wonder briefly what she's doing right now, what she's thinking and feeling and even if she misses me. Thankfully, I'm prevented from following this train of thought any further by the sight of a lone woman on one of the benches opposite the school fountain. She's wearing a purple silk cocktail dress and smoking a cigarette. In spite of the dark sunglasses I know immediately that it's Martha DeWitt.

'Everything okay?'

Martha looks up, somewhat startled. 'Danny, I didn't hear you coming. You made me jump.'

'Sorry, didn't mean to. I just wanted to check you were okay.'

'Just taking a little break from all the noise. Where's James?'

'He's gone AWOL. Sent me a text saying he was with a friend and that he'd see me later.'

Martha immediately gets to her feet, throws her cigarette to the ground and stubs it out beneath the sole of her very expensive heeled sandals. 'Where did you last see him?' Her voice is urgent, as if she believes James might be in trouble.

'What's the problem? He sounded fine in his text.'

'Well, he won't be soon. I bet anything he's with Zara. I saw her here earlier.'

The name sounds familiar but it takes a moment before it finally hits me. 'Zara's his ex, isn't she?'

Martha nods. 'She was the love of his life. It was so awful when they split up. Absolutely horrible. Because of what happened, James basically drove her away but he was a complete wreck afterwards. I have to find him. I have to make sure he's okay.'

She starts off in the direction of the marquee and as I watch her walking away I'm torn about the right thing to do: get involved or mind my own business. I know her intentions are well meant, but I also know that James won't thank her for getting involved in his affairs. Then again she's his sister, so what do I know?

'Martha, wait.' She stops and turns around. 'I know this isn't what you want to hear but I think you've got to let James do this on his own.'

'He's my brother, he needs me.'

'And he always will. But what he needs more right now is your respect. He needs to know that you believe he can deal with life on his own.'

A flicker of doubt crosses Martha's face. She pushes her sunglasses on top of her head and I see for the first time that she has been crying. Rather awkwardly I place on her shoulder what I hope might be considered a comforting hand and to my surprise she takes a step towards me and rests her head against my chest.

'It's just so hard. I miss Jamie so much sometimes. The old

Jamie, the way he was before this nightmare started. He always knew what to do about everything.'

'He's still here, still your brother. He still loves you like he always did.'

'But he's not the brother I knew, the one I grew up with who used to tease me about my braces or throw spiders in my hair, the one I could always count on to protect me.'

'If I've learned anything it's that we're all paler versions of our past selves. But the people we used to be are still in there somewhere.'

Martha takes a step back, opens her handbag, fumbles inside and eventually pulls out a tissue. She dries her eyes and lowering her sunglasses again, returns to the bench.

'I'm sorry,' she says as I sit down beside her. 'You must think I'm so selfish talking like this.'

'No, not at all. It's easy to see how hard James's condition has been on all of you.'

'It's changed our family beyond all recognition,' she says, turning towards me. 'We used to be such a happy, active bunch. And we were all so proud of James and his achievements. Typical James, it wasn't enough for him to start a successful business from nothing and sit back and watch the money roll in. He really did want to make a difference. When he said he was going into politics, we all thought he was mad and Daddy especially tried to talk him out of it. But he was so committed to his beliefs, so determined to be part of the solution, so focused on doing the right thing that none of us were at all surprised when he got elected. I remember the first thing Daddy said to me when we heard the news, "Well, of course they voted for him . . . they know he won't stop until he gets the job done."'

'It's funny,' I say after a while, 'obviously, the only versions of James I really know are the one I live with and the one I went to school with – but those qualities you've described, I'm pretty sure I can see all of them in the person James is now.'

Martha nods. 'You're right, of course. Even now James is still an incredible person. If I'd been through just half of what he's been through, I'd be crushed. But I suppose what I'm getting at is how unfair it seems. All James ever wanted to do was make a difference. It feels unjust that he has to live a life like this when there are so many awful people doing terrible things day in, day out with all the energy and ability they need to carry on doing them.' From deep inside Martha's bag I hear her phone vibrate with a call but she dismisses it without investigation. I wonder where Lucien is, if it's him trying to contact her and whether he is the reason she was sitting here alone crying.

'It was so hard for us all when we got the news about James's accident,' she continues. 'For so long it was touch and go whether he would live or die and we were all so focused on willing him to pull through that it didn't occur to us how different things would be if he survived. We just assumed that if he did make it, then it would only be a matter of time before he was back to his old self. In some ways the day his consultant told us that James would never make a full recovery was worse than the day it all happened. With just a few words he destroyed all the hopes and dreams we'd had for Jamie – all the hopes and dreams Jamie had for himself – and left us devastated. I think that's when he first started to retreat from the world, when he decided to end things with Zara. I think he realised that if he couldn't be who he used to be, then he didn't want to be anybody at all.'

Martha and I sit in a companionable silence listening to the cascading water of the fountain and the distant sound of the string quartet coming from the marquee. It's funny to think now that I'd ever entertained thoughts of us getting together. It occurs to me that the relationship developing between us is worth more than that, being something closer to friendship. Other than James, right now I don't have that many friends and I like the idea that there might be another one in the world.

After a short while Martha's phone buzzes again. This time she takes it out of her bag and checks the screen.

'I'd better be getting back,' she says, standing up and rearranging her dress. 'You'll let me know when you hear from James won't you?'

'Of course,' I reply, getting to my feet too.

Martha smiles in my direction. 'James is so lucky to have someone like you looking out for him. I'm so glad you changed your mind, Danny. I really don't know where we'd be without you.'

As I watch Martha walk back across the lawns, my phone buzzes with a text. It's from James: 'Where are you?' I text back that I'll meet him by the main entrance to the school and head in that direction, only to walk straight into a stocky, balding man, roughly my own age.

'Danny Allen,' he says, shaking my hand. The smell of booze on his breath is so strong I can almost taste it. 'Well, I never! How are you, mate?'

I wrack my brains trying to recall a name. Or any memory of him but there's nothing. I'm going to have to bluff it.

'I'm fine thanks, mate, you?'

'Couldn't be better! Working for one of the big German banks in the city. Divorced. Two kids and a twenty-two-year-old Italian girlfriend. Could be a lot worse!' He laughs raucously at his own joke as if this is the first time he's made it, which it clearly isn't. 'And if the rumours are to be believed you're doing extremely well. Living it large in Hollywood, I hear.'

There's no point in denying it at this point in the proceedings, even though I have long since stopped caring what any of these people think of me.

'Guilty as charged,' I reply.

'That's amazing: you, Danny Allen, King of Hollywood! So glad to hear that you managed to get things back on track after that awful time you had at Cambridge. I'm not sure I'd have been able to pick myself up like you've done, if it happened to me. It was a real tragedy.' He looks at me, waiting for a response but when I don't give him one, he continues talking regardless. 'My brother, Toby was in the year above you at Queens,' he explains. 'He's the one who told me all about it. Must have been terrible for you. She was only eighteen, wasn't she?' He looks to me again for confirmation but I give him none and then finally he says apologetically: 'Me and my big mouth, of course you don't want to talk about it. All it takes is a couple of beers and I'm yapping away like I've got my own talk show. Please ignore me. I meant no offence.'

When I reach the main school entrance, James is waiting for me. While I'm sure that right now I'm no oil painting, he looks absolutely exhausted.

'You okay?'

'Not really.'

'Want to talk about it?'

'Not right now, thank you.'

'Shall we go then?'

'You do not have to. I thought you were having fun.'

'I was,' I reply. 'But things change.'

24

James

Danny always knocks on my door before coming in.

Always.

He does it so often that we sometimes make a joke about it.

Sometimes when he knocks on my door I do not say, 'Come in,' instead I knock back and then we both laugh.

Danny knocking on my door before coming into my room is just something he always does.

I think it is his way of saying that he respects me.

It is his way of saying that I deserve my privacy. I appreciate it a lot because my dad, Don, and mum, Erica, did not always knock when they came into my room. Neither did some of the other carers at Four Oaks.

But Danny has always knocked before coming into my room.

Always.

But today he does not.

Today without knocking, he walks straight into my room and finds me sitting on my bed doing something he has never seen me do before.

I am watching TV.

But it is not an episode of *Friends*.

Or even an action film.

It is not even a rude film.

It is video of me running in a race four years ago.

It was one of those army-type races where you have to crawl through mud and climb over obstacles.

I did it for charity.

For people less fortunate than me.

In the video I am covered in so much mud that you can hardly tell it is me. As I scramble over the rope wall you can hear my friends cheering me on – the same friends I saw a few days ago at the KS summer ball.

They are shouting words of encouragement. And the last scene on the video, as I reach for the remote, is me throwing myself over the top of a rope wall as a voice from behind the camera shouts: 'Come on, Jamie, you can do it! I love you so much!'

Pause.

Danny is holding armfuls of bedding.

I am holding the remote.

We both stare at each other, not knowing what to say.

'Mate,' says Danny, putting the bedding on the chair next to the wardrobe. 'I'm so, so, sorry . . . I just emptied the drier and I thought I'd put these away . . . my head was somewhere else . . . I wasn't thinking properly.'

I look over at the frozen screen again.

At the image of me climbing the rope wall.

At the image of me doing something that I cannot do any more.

At the image of the man I used to be.

I press the off button and the image disappears.

No trace left behind.

As if it had never existed.

That evening Danny and I go to the pub. So far neither of us have mentioned the video and I begin to wonder if we ever will. But when we sit down with our drinks, Danny brings it up.

'About earlier, you know . . . when I . . . well I could just kick myself for barging in like that. Really, I could, anyway, I just want to say that it won't happen again.'

'It is okay. It is not something I do a lot. Just every now and again.'

Danny shakes his head. 'Look, James you don't have to explain anything to me. It's your business. I'm just sorry I barged in like that.'

'Actually, I think I am sort of glad you know. I do not really like keeping secrets. They always make me feel like I have got too much going on in my head. Dr Acari says that ABI patients can sometimes feel that way.'

Danny does not say anything. I think he feels embarrassed. I also think he would probably like me to stop talking about it but I just cannot seem to.

'I think it was seeing Zara the other night that made me want to watch that video again. I have got others. Videos of me running in marathons. Videos of me speaking at hustings and local party debates. I even have videos of me being interviewed on TV. But the video you saw is my favourite because it reminds me of when I was at my best. When life was so easy that I had to look for hard things to do. I think that is why for a long while I never felt like doing anything much. My whole life feels like a challenge now so there is no need to go looking for more.' I stop and look at Danny and then at my beer and then at the torn corner of my beer mat. 'It really hurt seeing Zara the other day,' I continue. 'Even though it was me who ended things and not her, it hurt more than I ever thought it would.'

Even though she had changed the way she wore her hair, I knew it was Zara the moment I saw her.

You never forget a face you have loved.

Not even if you want to.

Not even if you have the best excuse in the world.

I did not know what I was going to say when I started walking towards her. When I lived with my parents, I used to spend hours thinking about what this moment would be like. What I would say to Zara if I ever got the chance. I would even practise the words I would say and if I got confused and forgot them, it never mattered because the meaning behind them was always the same: I was sorry.

But as I crossed the floor of the marquee towards her, past groups of people laughing and chatting, none of the words I had practised would come back to me. My mind was blank. As though someone had broken into my head and scrubbed them away. I was going to have to make this up as I went along – just like I had when I said Danny was a Hollywood film producer. But this time my brain did not feel sharp. This time thinking on my feet would not be fun.

The whole time I was walking towards her, she did not take her eyes off me. But it was only when I got closer to her that I saw she was crying.

'These aren't for you.'

Those were the first words she said to me.

'You took me by surprise, that's all,' she said wiping her eyes. 'I never expected to—' She got so upset that she could not get the words out. I always hated upsetting Zara. Always. I wanted her to be happy forever.

I asked if she wanted to go outside and get some fresh air. I led her out of the marquee towards the east lawn. Back in my school days the east lawn was where smaller functions happened. Like when parents came to look around the school in the summer months. My dad said it showed off the school in its best light and made parents feel like they were getting value for money.

'You look well,' she said as we sat down on one of the benches that looked out across the lawn towards the woods. 'Are you much better?'

I shrugged. 'I am better than I was but I will always have ABI.' I stopped and thought about all of the things I really wanted to say to her but then I suddenly remembered that I had not told her that she looked nice and so that is what I did. 'I know I should have said that first,' I explained, 'but I forgot because I am feeling nervous. But you do look nice. Very nice.'

After I said this, I felt awkward. I never used to be awkward around Zara. She always made me feel relaxed. I tell her about moving out of home and about living with Danny and how I go to the pub now and how the bar staff at one pub all know me and get my drink ready before I even ask for it.

'Sounds like you've come a long way since . . .' I think she did not finish her sentence because she did not need to. I think we both knew what it was she was going to say. She was going to say 'since we split up'.

Quietly, she started to cry again and I put my arm around her. 'I am sorry,' I said. 'I have wanted to say this to you for a very long time. I really am sorry. For everything.'

'Don't be,' she said and then she held up her hand and pointed to an engagement ring and a wedding ring. 'I've moved on, Jamie. I'm happy. I got married last summer . . . I don't know if you remember him, he's an old KS boy too, Seb Dyer. He says he was a few years above you at school.'

I felt like I should be happy for Zara and say things that people say when someone is telling you good news but the words would not come.

I felt hurt and angry.

Hurt that Zara had found happiness with someone else.

Angry about how my life had changed overnight through no fault of my own.

Angry about Kyle Baylis and what he did to me.

He took away everything I had, for no good reason.

He took away my life and left me like this.

I wished he was dead.

I think I must have forgotten where I was for a moment because the next thing I remember was Zara touching my arm.

'Are you okay? You weren't speaking.'

I shook my head and told myself to concentrate. 'I am fine. And I am pleased about you and Seb. He sounds nice.'

'I think you'd like him. I could introduce you to him if you like. In fact, he'll probably be wondering where I am. I'd only popped to the bar to get an orange juice.'

My head felt fuzzy.

I felt like I could not follow what she was saying.

'Who will be wondering what?' I asked.

Zara looked at me sadly. 'Seb,' she replied. 'My husband, I was just telling you about him.'

'I do not remember him. But I am glad that you are happy.'

Zara smiled. 'I've got some other exciting news too. I'm pregnant. It's early days yet but we're absolutely thrilled.' She looked at me as if she was trying to read my thoughts. 'Do you think you could be happy for me too?'

I nodded because I had never wanted anything for her other than for her to be happy.

Back to reality.

I take a sip of my pint and lean back in my chair.

I feel tired after talking for so long.

Tired of all this remembering.

Tired of all these feelings.

'I had no idea,' says Danny. 'I can't imagine how difficult it must have been for you.'

'I think that is why I wanted to watch that video,' I say and I look at Danny for a moment. Even now I still feel embarrassed about it. 'I think I was trying to remember who I used to be. Who I still would have been if things had been different.'

Danny takes a sip of his drink. 'We can't carry on like this. It feels like every step we take forward we both get dragged a couple of hundred further back.'

'I do not understand. What has happened to you?'

Danny shrugs. 'It's nothing really. Someone at the ball said something to me about something that happened a long time ago.'

'Was it to do with the girl in the silver picture frame in your wardrobe?'

Danny looks angry for a moment. 'You searched my room?'

I nod guiltily. It had been a few days after Danny told me that he was an alcoholic. I had wanted to ask him more questions about it but whenever I asked him, he just changed the subject. The thing is, I had other questions too. Questions about why he had pretended not to know me when we met at Four Oaks, and why he never spoke about his family, and why sometimes when he thought I was not looking, he seemed so sad. I felt like Danny knew everything about me and I did not know anything about him. And it did not seem fair somehow so one day when he went out for a run, I looked through the things in his room. He had lots of clothes, CDs and DVDs but there was nothing that could tell me what Danny was really like. Then I looked in his wardrobe and I found a silver-framed photo of a girl.

The girl looked pretty but she looked young too.

I was not sure how old. I am not very good at working out that sort of thing.

The photo reminded me of a picture on the wall of Dad's study that he took on Martha's last speech day at the girls' school. Martha has big hair in it and her clothes look funny now because it was taken a long time ago. This photo looked old like that too, although the girl did not have big hair like Martha, but I got the feeling it was an old photo, even though I could not really say why.

At first I thought it might be a picture of Danny's ex-girlfriend, but then I decided that it probably was not. If Danny was going to have a picture of his ex-girlfriend, it would more likely be one when she was older not younger. I then searched through the other bags in the wardrobe to try and find something that might help me understand who the girl was, but there was nothing else. Not even another photo.

I turned the photo frame over and took out the picture.

On the back someone had written: 'Helen on her sixteenth birthday, September 1997'.

'I was just worried about you,' I tell Danny. 'I have always known something was wrong with you, even back when you were at Four Oaks. I just did not know what it was, and I wanted to be able to help.'

'You had no right to do that, James,' says Danny sounding angry. 'It was none of your business.'

'I am sorry,' I say. 'Really I am. I promise I will never do it again. Please do not stop being my carer just because of this one mistake.'

Danny sighs. 'You're not going to get rid of me that easily. I probably should have told you about all this a long time ago anyway. The girl in the picture is my kid sister, Helen. She's dead now, died when she was seventeen. I'd rather not go into the details. But one way or another, everything that's happened to me since then: dropping out of Cambridge, falling out with my parents, not being able to see my daughter and pretty much giving up on life altogether, has been because of that.'

I wait for a minute for the words to stop spinning around in my head. 'You have a daughter?'

Danny nods. 'Her name's Leila, and she's fifteen. She lives with her mum, who won't let me see her.'

I feel sad for Danny.

I do not know what I would do if I did not have Martha.

And I know I have not got any children but it must be hard never seeing your own daughter.

I need to help Danny.

I need to help him right now.

I remember the time that he saved my life. I remember I said that one day I would return the favour.

Well, today is that day.

'I have got a plan,' I say to Danny. 'And if it works, it might just help both of us.'

25

Danny

I'm in the car outside my parents' house.

At least I think it's my parents' house. It's been over fifteen years since I last saw them, so who knows? Anything could have happened to them in the interim. They could've divorced, emigrated, downsized. They might even be dead.

Dead and buried.

It's sobering, contemplating the mortality of the people who gave you life while gazing at the house you grew up in and yet here I am, jazz hands at the ready, about to knock on their door and all because some guy with whom I used to go to school managed to talk me into it.

I'm still not exactly sure how it all happened. James is supposed to be suffering from the after-effects of an ABI. He's supposed to be so incapable of looking after himself that he can't be left on his own and needs a full-time carer to stop him from burning his home to the ground. And yet somehow he's talked me, the owner of an allegedly fully functioning brain, into using one of only two days a week I have off to do the one thing I've spent half a lifetime trying not to do.

James's plan was simple yet cunning. He promised to attend his ABI group if I, in return, promised to do . . . what exactly? His precise words were 'sort myself out' which I took to mean draw up a list of the things I've been meaning to do for the longest time. Things like trying harder to get in touch with my daughter, finally telling Maya the truth about me, even if she did not care, and of course getting in touch with my parents. None of these were things I remotely felt like doing. They were the painful, difficult things I had successfully avoided for years. But

James had put a metaphorical gun to my head so there was no way I could have said no. I knew how terrified he was at the idea of going to the support group, and had heard first hand from Dr Acari how valuable it could be to his rehabilitation. Knowing that he was prepared to face one of his worst fears just to help me was all the encouragement I needed. So this morning, after dropping James at his parents' house for the weekend, I promised myself that I would make a start. I tapped a postcode into the car's sat nav, put some early Bruce Springsteen on the stereo and headed for Nuneaton.

My parents' home has changed a lot since I was last here. The front door, which used to be dark green, has been painted royal blue and the old wooden windows have all been replaced with brand new double-glazing. The front garden, which back in my day had just been a small square of half-dead grass with a couple of spindly rose bushes dotted about it, is now an explosion of life and colour. The lawn is so perfectly green and neatly trimmed it almost looks artificial, while the borders are filled with all manner of flowers and not a dead head among them.

As I approach this new yet familiar front door, a trickle of sweat runs down my back and is quickly followed by others until the top of my underwear is soaking wet. I'm wearing completely the wrong clothes. When I'd peered through the blinds earlier this morning and seen the thick wall of cloud hiding the sun, the jacket, jeans and sweatshirt I'm now wearing seemed like the most appropriate outfit (if such a thing exists) for a family reunion. Now though, with the strong summer sun having virtually burned away all the cloud, leaving nothing but blue skies, I'm just a man wearing the wrong clothes, heavily perspiring in front of what might be a complete stranger's front door. I look down at my chest to see a dark patch of damp in the centre of my top and when I check, I find the same under each armpit. I look like I've come straight from a training session at the gym.

I can't do this.

I can't see my parents for the first time in over a decade, looking like I've just run a marathon. And anyway, chances are they've probably moved away.

Or died.

The moment I turn around and head back to the car I feel like a weight has been winched up off my chest, a load lifted from my shoulders. Like the contents of my skull are no longer in danger of boiling over. I switch on the engine and as the car's air-conditioning system springs to life, I breathe in the chilled air and rehearse what I'll tell James. I'll explain that I tried to speak to my parents but they weren't in. It won't even be a proper lie because statistically speaking, there's a good chance they might not even live there any more and even if it is their house, they could just as easily be taking their dog for a walk or visiting friends as be sitting in the living room awaiting the arrival of their only living child after so many years away.

It's a good plan, only undermined by the fact that I know I can't lie to James about this. I have to do something.

Even though I only have five names on the list of people to whom I need to make amends, I take out the folded sheet of paper from my back pocket and search it for inspiration as to what to do next:

1. Mum and Dad
2. Leila
3. Simone (Leila's mum)
4. Maya

Reaching across to the touch-screen panel on the dashboard, I dial Maya's number. The call goes straight to voicemail. I hear myself saying: 'Hey, Maya, it's me,' and realising it's too late to stop I carry on. 'I know this is going to sound weird but you know how in films when characters are in AA and they go around apologising to all the people they've hurt in the past? Well, I know this is not a film but I would really like the chance to apologise to you face to face. Hope that's okay. Let me know when is good for you.' Twenty minutes later as I'm returning to Birmingham on the M6 I get the following text: 'Hi Danny. I'm a bit tied up at the moment but can meet you later today around three if that's any use. Let me know and I'll sort something out. Maya.'

It had been four months since I'd last seen Maya as I'd handed over my keys to the flat. We hadn't spoken since and I hadn't allowed myself to think about her much. After all, hurting her was another one of my failures. Something else I had to make amends for. I was apprehensive about seeing her again. Her text had been fairly neutral but it was impossible to tell what she was really thinking about seeing me again.

Bread and Roses – a licensed café about five minutes' walk from our old flat – is an old haunt of mine and Maya's. When we first got together, we would come here for breakfast on a Saturday or Sunday morning. It hasn't changed much. In fact, I think some of the same staff are still working behind the counter. I spot Maya sitting at a table at the back and as I walk towards her, deluded though it sounds, I can't help wondering if she hasn't chosen this venue deliberately. After all, this is where it all began. Where we spent so many lazy mornings talking and laughing. Was it really so far fetched to think that she wanted to give us a second chance? I'm not the man I used to be, not even close. And wasn't that really what her leaving me had been about? Wanting me to change and stop wasting my life? Well, here I am, four months on, a new creation, ready for a new chapter.

Hi,' she says, greeting me with the most gentle of kisses on the cheek. 'How have you been? You look really well. Have you lost weight?'

'A bit,' I say, trying to hide my desperation for her to know that my external metamorphosis is matched by an equally dramatic internal one. 'I joined a gym, took up jogging, you know, the usual stuff.'

'Good for you, I'm glad.'

'You look well too.'

'Sadly I haven't lost as much weight as you but that's fine. I'm actually feeling pretty good.' She stops and picks up two menus from the centre of the table and hands one to me. 'Shall we get some drinks? I could murder a coffee.'

'Absolutely,' I reply. 'And I insist, my treat.'

I order my filter coffee and Maya's cappuccino at the counter, along with a slice of cake. When I return to the table she asks me what I've been up to, and so I tell her all my news. About how I left Four Oaks only to end up with an even better job that pays more money than I've ever earned, doing something I feel good about. I tell her a little about James but don't explain how I know him because I still haven't made up my mind whether to tell her that part of my story yet. But even with the little I share, she seems impressed and tells me how pleased she is that I'm doing so well.

In return, I ask Maya about her news and she tells me about a recent promotion, her dad's hernia operation and her sister's wedding. While she's certainly chatty enough, I get the sense that she, like me, is holding something back. What it is I can't guess but before I can ask she gets to the point, something I seem to have a great deal of trouble doing myself.

'So what's this all about? You've not found religion, have you?'

'Me? No. Why? Have you?'

'As it happens, yes.'

'Really?' This doesn't sound like Maya at all but in the end my gullibility proves too entertaining for her to keep up her pretence any longer.

'What are you like?' she says, laughing. 'Anyone would think you've never met me before. So go on then, what *is* going on?'

This is it. Showtime. 'I'm trying to sort myself out. I'm trying to draw a line under the past so I can move on. And well, I decided that the best way to do this would be to apologise to all the people I've hurt over the years and so well . . . here I am and . . . I'm sorry.'

I tell Maya all the things I think she deserves an apology for and somehow my list ends up being far longer than I'd intended. It covers everything from all the money I borrowed from her over the years, right through to the way I treated her. I even end up apologising for a whole bunch of stuff that I can tell from the look of surprise in her eyes she hadn't been aware of and probably hadn't wanted to know.

'You weren't joking about this whole confession thing, were you?' she says, with such disbelief that I wonder if I've gone too far.

'I couldn't be more serious.' I reach into my jacket pocket, take out an envelope and hand it to her. She carefully opens the envelope and the moment she sees what's written on the cheque inside she covers her mouth with her hand.

'Is this real?'

'Well, if by that you mean have I got enough money in the bank to cover it then yes, I have. This should more than repay everything I borrowed from you over the years. If it doesn't, just say and I'll write another one.'

Maya stares at me momentarily speechless. 'Who are you and what have you done with my ex? Of course it's enough. It's more than enough. I can't take this much from you.'

'You deserve it,' I reply, 'all of it. To be honest I should've paid you back a lot earlier but . . . I don't know . . . I didn't feel like I could just get in touch.'

'I don't know what to say. You really have changed, haven't you?'

'More than you could imagine.'

'And what brought it on? This change of yours?'

I draw a deep breath. It's time for me to tell her the truth, the whole truth and nothing but.

'So, you know this guy I work for? Well, the thing is we're not exactly strangers. I knew him before . . . before he was unwell. We went to the same boarding school.'

Maya is quiet for a minute.

'Boarding school? What are you talking about? You didn't go to boarding school. You said your school was a dump and that was why you left with barely any exam results. What kind of school was it? Like a remand centre type of thing?'

'The complete opposite. I never told you the truth. I didn't go to a state school . . . I attended a private one . . . and not just any old private school, but one of the top five public schools in the country.'

Maya's face is the picture of confusion. 'I don't understand. How did your parents afford that? Didn't you tell me they were quite poor?'

'They were. I only got to go because I passed an exam and got a full scholarship.'

'So you're saying you were clever?'

'Put it this way: by the time I left to go to Cambridge my IQ was—'

'You went to Cambridge?' Maya's disbelief is palpable. 'As in Cambridge University? As in the place where all the toffs go?'

'Actually it's not just toffs. Quite a number of—'

She cuts me short again. 'Danny, you know that's not the point I'm making. The point I'm making is that I lived with you for two years and I never knew any of this. The point I'm making is that you had what sounds like an amazing education . . . the kind most people dream of and yet for virtually all the time we lived together you seemed absolutely determined to make nothing of your life . . . of our life . . .' She stops and sighs as though she is as disappointed in herself as she is with me. 'I'll tell you what, Danny. This makes my own confession a lot easier. The last six months we were together I was sleeping with somebody from work. I felt terrible for doing it, as if I was the worst person in the world. But thanks to you now I don't feel so bad any more so I suppose every cloud has a silver lining.' She picks up her bag from the chair beside her and stands up. 'For a moment there, you really had me thinking, "He's turned himself around, maybe we could give it another go." But do you know what? I'm done with you, Danny Allen, I'm done with you for good. I don't care if there's a reason why you gave up on life like you did, you could have had the best excuse in the world and it still wouldn't change a thing. I don't know who you are any more. I don't know anything about you. You and I are done. I never want to see or hear from you again.'

26

James

'Today, everybody, we have a friendly new face come to join us.'

A pretty lady in a polka-dot dress (whose name I think might be Trudy) nods at me and smiles as though she is waiting for me to do something special. I am not sure what she is expecting. It takes me a while to work it out but I think she is probably waiting for me to tell everyone in the room my name.

I do not want to.

In fact, I think I would much rather not say anything at all and so I pretend not to have heard her and stare at my feet.

'I think everybody here would love to know your name and a bit more about you,' says the polka-dot dress lady in what my mum, Erica, would call 'an outdoor voice'.

I still do not want to say anything but because she has used her 'outdoor voice' I cannot pretend I have not heard her.

So I shake my head.

Then I shake it again.

And then I shake it once more just to make it really clear that I have heard her but do not want to talk.

'I think our new friend might be feeling a bit shy so I'll do the introductions, shall I?' says polka-dot dress lady. 'Everyone, this is James. James, this is everyone from the St David's ABI Support Group.'

I did not want to come here this morning.

I know I made an agreement with Danny. And I really did want to help him to stop being sad. But I still did not want to go through with it.

I have always hated the idea of coming to the support group.

I never liked it from the moment Dr Acari first suggested it.

He said something about it being somewhere I could meet other people with ABI and talk about how it feels. I do not remember my exact reply when he made his suggestion. I think it was probably, 'No thank you,' because that was what I said every other time he brought it up. It was what I said when my parents brought it up too. And when Martha brought it up as well. Again and again they brought it up and again and again I told them I did not want to go.

And then Danny Allen told me about his dead sister and it made me feel sad.

That is when I knew I had to help him.

That is why I made our pact. I would do something difficult for him and he would do something difficult for me.

When I got back from my parents', Danny told me that he had done one of his difficult things. He told me he went to see his ex-girlfriend. I asked him how it went and he shrugged and said, 'About as well as I could have expected.'

I asked him, 'Do you feel any happier?'

He shook his head. 'Not really, but I'm glad I did it.'

I did not sleep very well last night.

Actually I do not think I slept at all.

I had felt brave when I made my pact with Danny.

Like I could do anything as long as it would help my friend. But the closer it came to us having to come here, the more I did not want to go. I still wanted to help Danny, of course, but I just did not feel strong enough. This morning I did not want to go so much that I was sick in my bathroom. I missed the toilet completely and it went all over the floor. I did not want Danny to know I had been sick. I did not want him to worry. So I just mopped it up with a towel and hid the towel underneath a dirty pair of jeans and a T-shirt that was already in the washing basket.

On the way to the meeting Danny talked to me about what he was going to do next. He told me how he had found going to see his parents too difficult and that was why he had decided to go and see his ex-girlfriend instead. He told me that the next thing on his list was to try and get in touch with Simone but he did not have any contact details for her. I had to ask Danny who Simone was because I had forgotten. He reminded me that Simone is the mother of his daughter, Leila. I told him that Facebook would be a good place to start because nearly everyone is there, and Danny laughed and said, 'I'm not,' but then he also agreed that it was a good idea.

When Danny reached the hospital car park, he said, 'Do you want me to come in with you?' I said no, because my plan was to pretend that I was going to my meeting but actually go somewhere else and hide. But when I got out of the car someone called my name and I looked up to see Vicky from Four Oaks who used to wear the purple bobble hat. She came running up to me and gave me a hug. 'I knew you'd come and join us sooner or later,' she said, and then she took my hand and made me go in with her.

Now because of her I am here. And I hate it.

The lady in the polka-dot dress tells everyone in the group to introduce themselves. Going around the circle it is like this:

Fat man with grey beard who looks like a music teacher: 'Hi, James, I'm Andrew.'

Lady with punk hair and a pink T-shirt: 'Hi, James, I'm Joolz.'

Plump lady in the sari: 'Hi, James, I'm Jasvinder.'

Young man with spotty face and scruffy trainers: 'Hi, James, I'm Jake.'

Muscular man wearing shorts that show off leg tattoos of dragons: 'Hi, James, I'm Everton.'

Smartly dressed older lady with grey hair: 'Hello, James, I'm Alice.'

Young woman about my age, whose name I already know: 'Hi, James, I'm Vicky . . .ha . . . but you already know that.'

On the outside none of them look like me.

But when they talk some of them sound like me.

I still do not want to talk but I hate it a little less, now I know everyone's names. I suppose that now I am here, there is no harm in listening.

The room we are in is quite small.

It is a bit like a classroom. There are windows on one side but they all have that criss-cross pattern going through them.

I think the term for it is safety glass.

There are a few posters on the wall. One says, 'Please take your rubbish with you'. Another says, 'Get the flu jab, get safe!' and another says, 'Stop Family Violence'.

'Has anyone got anything they'd like to share with the group this week?'

All the people who are supposed to be like me stare at the lady in the polka-dot dress (who I think might be called Trudy).

'I'd like to say something,' says the man with the dragon tattoos on his legs. He raises his hand in the air like he is at school. 'I'd like to say something very much.'

He tells us all a very long story that is very hard to follow, mainly because I do not think he knows what his story is actually about. He mentions a shopping trip to Matalan to buy some shorts. Then a meal from a Chinese takeaway that he had two nights ago that he did not like. Then he finishes with a description of the woman who sat next to him on the bus on the way to support group. 'She was really fat,' he says. 'Much fatter than Andrew and her hair smelled of chips.'

A number of the group shake their heads and tut their disapproval. I think it is because he has used the word 'fat'.

(I used the word 'fat' to describe Andrew too but I only used it in my head so that is okay.)

The lady in the polka-dot dress (who I think might be called Trudy) says, 'Now, Everton, that is not the sort of word we use to talk about each other is it?'

Everton shrugs his shoulders.

Once.

Twice.

Three times.

The lady with the punk-style hair and pink T-shirt puts her hand up.

'You know you don't have to do that, Joolz,' says the lady in the polka-dot dress and puts her hand in the air like Joolz. 'As long as we're not interrupting each other, we can all feel free to just speak.'

Joolz tells us a story about the night before last. She had gone out to a local pub with some friends she had not seen for a long time. As she waited at the bar to be served, a man started chatting her up. 'He were dead fit an' all,' she says in a voice that sounds like she ought to be on *Coronation Street*.

Joolz tells us that she had not been chatted up since before her accident.

I want to know what sort of accident she had. I want to know if it really was an accident or more like my own Incident. I cannot ask those questions though, because I have made up my mind that I am not going to speak.

Joolz says that when she got chatted up, she did not know what to do and she was worried because often people do not realise straight away that she has a brain injury.

She says she did not know whether to tell the man or not.

She says she worried that if she did not tell him, he would wonder why she took so long to answer his questions.

She says she worried that if she did tell him, that he might not like her any more.

Then she laughs and says that in the end she decided not to tell him but that it did not matter anyway because he did not ask her any questions. All he did all night was talk about himself.

When she says this, most of the group laugh but then some others wait for a minute as if they do not get the joke but they laugh anyway because they do not want to feel left out.

While everyone is laughing, I think about how if I was talking, I would tell everyone how, because of the way I talk and the way I walk and because my brain does not work properly, people usually think I cannot tell jokes, even though I can.

I think if I said this, they might find it interesting.

Anyway, by the time I have finished thinking about what I would have said if I was talking, they have already started talking about something else.

I decide that if I come again, I might bring a pencil and a notepad with me for moments like this.

The hour goes much more quickly than I thought it would.

It feels like one minute, everyone is talking in angry voices about a story that the young man with the spotty face and scruffy trainers tells us about how his parents will not let him go on holiday with his friends, even though his friends have all promised to look after him. And the next, the lady in the polka-dot dress (who I think might be called Trudy) tells us that we have to finish because a single mums ante-natal class has the room after us and they need to rearrange the chairs.

As everyone starts leaving, the lady in the polka-dot dress comes over to me.

'So how was that for you, James? Did you find it helpful?'

'I do not know.'

'Well, whenever I glanced in your direction, you seemed to be enjoying it.'

This time I do not reply. Instead I just look at my shoes.

'Well,' says the lady in the polka-dot dress, 'if you think you might like to come back again next week, we'd love to see you.'

When I get outside, Danny Allen is leaning against the car reading a newspaper. When he sees me, he folds the paper up and tucks it underneath his arm.

'How was it, mate?'

'I think it was okay.'

'What were the other people like?'

'They were okay.'

'What sort of things did you talk about?'

'Lots of different things.'

'But did you enjoy it though?'

I spend a moment remembering everyone's stories. Most of

them I have already forgotten but there are some like Joolz's which have stuck in my head and make me smile.

'Yes,' I say. 'It was okay.'

We get in the car and Danny starts the engine. I think about how when I get home, I might like to watch a DVD with Danny. Before I can tell Danny my idea, he nudges me with his elbow and points across the car park.

'I think someone wants to talk to you.'

I follow the direction of Danny's finger to see Vicky waving at me trying to get my attention.

'What do you think she wants?' I ask Danny.

Danny shrugs and winds down the window on my side of the car. 'Let's find out.'

'Some of us are going to the Old Crown for lunch,' says Vicky poking her head into the car. 'Do you want to come? You can bring your friend, if you like.'

I do not reply.

I do not even look at her.

Instead I keep my eyes fixed forwards.

'James, mate,' says Danny, 'the lady's speaking to you.'

I turn towards Danny as Vicky looks on. 'But she is asking me if I want to go to the pub with her and her friends and I do not want to go.'

'Why not? It'll be fine.'

'I just do not want to.'

'It might be fun. I could stay here in the car and wait for you. It wouldn't be a problem.'

I tell Danny that I do not think I will enjoy myself, which is why I do not want to go.

'Fine,' says Danny, even though he makes it sound like he does not believe me, 'but if you're not going with them you at least need to tell Vicky.'

I can feel Vicky's eyes staring at the side of my face. She has not said anything since she asked me the question.

'Thank you very much for the invitation,' I say, keeping my

eyes fixed ahead of me. 'But I would rather not go, if that is okay. Maybe next time.'

'Are you sure?' asks Vicky. 'We always have a good time when we all go out together.'

'I am absolutely sure,' I say. 'No thank you.'

Out of the corner of my eye I see Vicky shrug. 'Oh well,' she says. 'Maybe I'll see you again next week?'

'I do not know,' I say to the windscreen. 'You might but then again you might not. I have not quite made up my mind yet.'

27

Danny

'I'd always wondered when you would turn up again,' says Simone, cradling a mug of tea. 'I imagined that if it ever did happen, it would be because you had six months to live or something.' Freeing her right hand from the mug, she uses it to cover her mouth in horror at what she's just said and how casually she's said it. 'That isn't why you've asked to see me, is it? You're not dying, are you?'

'Not that I'm aware,' I reply. 'Although I suppose anything's possible.'

Simone smiles. 'You always did have a good sense of humour, even when things got tough.'

'I'd agree with you,' I reply. 'But to be honest, I don't remember much about those days.'

'No,' she says, looking down at the child sitting at her feet on a patchwork blanket surrounded by large multicoloured building bricks. 'I don't suppose you do.'

Fifteen years ago, it would have been virtually impossible for me to have found Simone without some form of professional help but, with the modern world being what it is, it took me less than half an hour. It's not that I hadn't tried to find Simone using social media before. I'd tried lots of times without success. I don't know whether it was because I had been doing it wrong or more likely she was a recent convert, but it seems that James was right: everyone in the free world was on Facebook. I'd typed 'Simone Kavanagh' into the search bar, crossed my fingers, hoping that she hadn't changed her name, and searched through all the results until I found the one I was looking for. A quick friend request later, followed closely by the message: 'Can we meet and talk?'

led me here: to the rear reception room of a three-bed terrace on the outskirts of Tamworth, in the middle of the afternoon, with the mother of my fifteen-year-old daughter Leila.

Simone sets down her tea in order to pick up her son, who has begun to grizzle. She holds him up to her face, covers him with kisses until he's all smiles again and then sets him down on her lap. Back when we were together, I'd thought Simone the most perfect woman I'd ever laid eyes on. She was cool, smart, funny and always looked amazing. Despite the years that have passed she's just as attractive as I remember and though she is in her early thirties, she could easily pass for mid-twenties. She wore her hair quite long when I knew her but now it's cut in a curly bob; the row of piercings going all the way up to the top of her right ear have gone and now the only jewellery she wears is a small silver stud through one nostril.

'He gets like that sometimes, when he thinks I'm not paying him enough attention,' she says bouncing the child on her knee. 'Just like his dad.'

'How old is he?' I ask, and then add quickly, 'The baby, not his dad.'

Simone laughs. 'Fourteen months, which is probably about his dad's mental age.'

'You're not together?'

'He left just before Kieran was born. Someone he met at work. To be honest, if it wasn't for the boys, I wouldn't give him a second thought. He was useless even when we were together.'

'The boys?'

'Kieran's brother, Max. My ex is his dad too. He's at school at the moment. Year three. He loves his dad to the moon and back but my ex just isn't interested. He hasn't seen either Max or Kieran in at least six months.'

'I'm sorry to hear that.'

'Don't be. I've learned the hard way that it's better for them to find out what people are like sooner rather than later. Saves heartache in the long run.' With the child in her arms, she stands up and tells me she's going to put him down for a nap. Before

I can say anything, she's gone, leaving me to contemplate exactly what she may or may not have told our daughter about me.

I look around the room as I wait for her to return and spot a couple of photos on the ledge above the fireplace. I pick one up. It's a classic official school photograph: a smiling girl with her hair in pigtails, wearing a maroon school jumper. She must be about nine or ten in the photo and while there's no doubting she's Simone's daughter – the shape of her face and her lips and nose are exactly like her mum's – her eyes are just like my sister's. In an instant I miss Helen and Leila so much I feel like I can't breathe.

Thankfully the sound of Simone coming down the stairs breaks my concentration. I quickly return the photo to its rightful spot and resume my seat, as she begins tidying away the toys on the floor. 'So when did you finally stop drinking?' she asks, dropping the bricks into a zip-up bag. Both the question and the casual manner in which she asks it take me by surprise to the extent that I'm temporarily rendered mute. It's only when she pauses, a handful of toy bricks in each hand, and looks me straight in the eye that I finally speak.

'It was the day you sent me the baby photo of Leila!'

'And you've not drunk since?'

'Not a drop.'

'That's some going . . . if it's true.'

I briefly recall the dozens of times I've come close to relapse over the years. 'It wasn't easy, in fact at times it felt like it was impossible. But yes, it's one hundred per cent true.'

'So what kept you on the straight and narrow, if you don't mind me asking?'

Again the question takes me by surprise. It's not something I'd allowed myself to think too much about over the years, despite on some level always being aware of the answer.

'Do you really want to know?' I'm not sure how she'll take what I say if I tell her the truth. The last thing I need is to scupper things this close to making amends.

Simone nods but says nothing.

'It was Leila,' I reply, thinking about all the times I used to talk to the picture I've got of her as a baby whenever I felt like life was getting too tough. 'It was her who kept me going, and the idea that one day you just might let me see her.'

'You do know I only ever wanted what was best for Leila,' she says. 'I couldn't risk letting you into her life the way you were.'

'But what about when I did try to get in touch?' I say, thinking about all the times I called her parents' house, sent letters and cards containing what little money I had when I had it. 'I always let you know where I was. I never tried to hide from my responsibilities.'

Simone shrugs. 'I know you might have wanted to see her. But were you ready to see her, ready to be a father to her?'

My gaze falls to the floor. In my heart of hearts I know she's right. I hadn't been ready back then. I hadn't been ready at all.

Simone fills in the gaps in my knowledge of the past fifteen years. A few months after she kicked me out of the flat we shared, she moved back in with her parents so that they could help out with childcare while she looked for work. What followed was a series of jobs working in clothes shops – Simone had always loved fashion – and a string of failed relationships but when Leila was seven, Simone's mum died of pancreatic cancer, and three years later her dad died of a heart attack. By this time she was going out with Nick, a graphic designer who was the elder brother of her best friend. They had only been together a few weeks when she found out she was pregnant with Max; Nick moved in the same day and they tried their best to be a family. Max was born the following summer, Kieran a few years later, by which time, as she'd already explained, Nick had left her for someone else.

In return, I try to cover the past decade and a half as best as I can manage. For a moment as I'm speaking, I think I see a look of horror in her eyes as she asks herself the question, 'Why is he telling me this?' Finally, however, I get to the point. I tell her how things have changed. I tell her about my job working with James, about how for the first time in my life I'm financially solvent. How I've started looking forward to the future and at the same time made up my mind to deal with my past.

'And now you've revamped your life, you think you're ready to be part of Leila's?' she asks, when I finally finish. 'Is that it?'

'Pretty much,' I reply, painfully aware of how pathetic it would sound to the person who had single-handedly raised the daughter that was half my responsibility. 'I know it's not much but it's all I've got.'

I ask her what Leila's like and she smiles and tells me she's amazing. She tells me she's doing really well at school, and how she loves sport and art and wants to be a physiotherapist. 'I can show you her room, if you like,' she says. 'I don't think she'd mind. It's her pride and joy and she shows it off to pretty much anyone who comes through the door.'

Leila's room is exactly how she'd described it. The walls, furniture and bedding – all in white – are very tasteful in their understatement. On the opposite wall to her bed is a long desk and everything on it is perfectly organised: pencils and pens in rows, notepads and textbooks stacked neatly. Positioned above the desk is her timetable and just to the left of it are some wooden letters that spell out the word 'love'. Underneath the window is a small, white bookcase. I quickly scan some of the titles hoping to find one I'd read at her age. Among the *Harry Potters*, *Twilights* and *Hunger Games* is a *Complete Works of Shakespeare* and a copy of *The Catcher in the Rye*, both of which I owned in my mid-teens. It's a tenuous link but right now it's all I've got, and for a moment I let myself daydream that the reason she has those books is because in some way yet to be revealed she is a little bit like me.

I'm desperate to ask Simone what Leila knows about me and if she ever asks where I am or has even seen a photo of me but when we go back downstairs, she tells me that she has a few errands to run before she has to pick up Max. It's clear that this is her polite way of saying that she wants me to leave, perhaps she's tired of indulging me and my excuses. I feel as though there's still so much I need to ask, so much I want to know but the last thing I need right now is to get on Simone's bad side.

Aware of the limited time I have, I decide that of all the questions I'm desperate to ask there is one that matters most of all. 'I know it's early days,' I say as I stand on the doorstep. 'I know you don't owe me anything but do you think . . . is there any way . . .?'

'That I'd let you see Leila?'

I nod.

'There might be,' she says. 'I might not always have been the best judge of character but I can see that you're a long way from who you used to be. So yeah, I'd be more than happy to ask the question. But it'll be Leila's decision if she wants to see you, Danny, not mine. She's fifteen now. She knows what she wants and doesn't want, and I can't tell her any different.'

'But you'll ask?'

Simone nods. 'I'll talk to her tonight after her brothers have gone to bed,' she says, 'but I can't say when or if she'll get back to you. Leila can be a funny one. Sometimes it takes her a while to get her head around an idea. I know it's probably not what you want to hear but it's just the way it has to be.'

28

James

'And I'm afraid that once again we seem to have run out of time.'

I am at St David's ABI Support Group again. This is my second time. The person speaking is Tanya. Last time I saw her, she was wearing a polka-dot dress and I did not know her name. This time she is wearing a stripy top and leggings and I have learned that her name is not Trudy, it is Tanya. Tanya (not Trudy) is the group facilitator. Which means she helps us with our discussions.

Because Tanya has said that we have got to finish, everyone is talking to the person next to them or putting on their jackets or doing things with their bags. I am the only one who stays in my seat and puts my hand in the air. It takes longer than I would have hoped for Tanya to notice me. In the end I have to wave my hand around and call her name a few times before she stops what she is doing.

'Is everything okay, James?'

My eyes dart down to the piece of paper in my hand, on which I have written: 'Tell them about jokes', and then back to Tanya.

'I had something I wanted to say.'

'To me?'

'No,' I reply. 'To everyone in the group.'

'Oh,' says Tanya. 'And is it that you didn't get chance to say it?'

'It was to do with the story Joolz told last week,' I say, talking over her because I know she is going to tell me to save my comment until next week. 'You know the one about the man she met and how he did not know that she had a brain injury. Everyone laughed because she got worried over nothing because he did not ask her any questions.' Tanya nods. 'Well, I wanted to tell everyone that because I walk funny and sound funny and my brain does not work properly, people think I cannot tell a joke, when I actually can.'

'That's an excellent observation,' says Tanya. 'You're absolutely right, people certainly do make all sorts of assumptions about people with ABIs.'

'They do,' I say, 'so are you going to tell the others so they know too?'

Tanya makes her eyes go small and the corners of her mouth go up a bit as if she is trying to smile but has forgotten how to.

'I think perhaps it'll have to wait until next time. But I really am glad to hear you're enjoying participating. That's what support group is all about.'

'So you are not going to tell them all now?'

'I can't,' says Tanya. 'You know the drill. We have to be out by midday or the scary nurses running the ante-natal class in this room next will have our guts for garters!'

I nod as though I understand what she is saying but I cannot help feeling that in the time she has spent telling me all this, she could have told everyone to stop what they were doing so that they could listen to my really interesting point.

Tanya holds out her hand. 'I'll tell you what, why don't I keep your piece of paper safe, then I'll give it back to you next week and make sure you get to speak first. How does that sound?'

I only mean to think about Tanya's question for a moment because it is a pretty easy question to answer but then Vicky suddenly pops up behind Tanya and waves at me. She waves at me so much that I keep getting distracted from what I am doing and my thinking ends up taking much, much, longer than I want it to. In the end I have to squeeze my eyes shut just so I can make my decision. Now when I open my eyes, Vicky is still waving at me but at least I am able to hand my paper to Tanya and say, 'Yes, I think I would like that.'

'Are you sure you're feeling okay?' asks Tanya.

'Yes,' I reply. 'I am feeling fine.' I look over her shoulder and give Vicky, who is still waving at me, a really hard stare. 'I just do not like being distracted that is all.'

When Tanya leaves, Vicky comes and sits down next to me.

'I was trying to get your attention.'

'I was talking to Tanya about something important. What do you want?'

'To know if you are going to come to the pub with us.'

'I do not know,' I reply. (This is not the truth. The truth is I have already decided that if Vicky asks me if I want to go to the pub, I will say yes.) 'I will have to think about it.'

Vicky puts her face close to mine. So close in fact that I can see all the tiny little blond hairs on her face and she stares at me, not saying anything. It is very hard to ignore her, so hard that I soon give up.

'What are you doing, Vicky?'

'Waiting for you.'

'Waiting for me to do what?'

'To make up your mind.'

Because it is my first time going to the Old Crown, even people who Vicky says usually go straight home after support group (like Jasvinder and Jake) decide to come for lunch too. When we get there, we are shown to a big table in the conservatory at the back, overlooking the beer garden. Although the weather has been nice all week, it is not today. Today it is raining and a crow the size of a cat is pecking at an ashtray on one of the tables outside.

Vicky sits next to me, on my right. On the way to the Old Crown she kept trying to hold my hand and I kept having to snatch it away.

Next to Vicky is Fat Andrew; next to Andrew is Joolz with the punk hair; next to Joolz is big Everton; next to Everton is plump Jasvinder; next to Jasvinder is elderly Alice; next to Alice is young Jake; and then next to Jake is me.

When the waitress comes to take our order, Vicky tells her that I want a red wine just like her. I look at Vicky crossly and have to tell the waitress that I do not want a red wine like Vicky. I would like a lager instead.

I feel quite special, knowing that everyone from support group has come to the pub because of me. I feel like it is my birthday (even though that is not until December) and that they have all come to help me blow out my candles.

While everyone looks at menus and talks about what they would like to eat, I text Danny. Before I left today, I promised I would let him know how I am getting on at the pub.

Danny has not been his usual self this week. He has been waiting for a message from his daughter to say that he can go and see her but so far he has not heard from her. I told him he should not worry because teenagers often take a long time to do things. Danny agreed but I do not think it has made him any happier.

My text to Danny goes like this: 'Everything OK here. Hope you are too. I will text when I need a lift home.'

After we order our food (which takes a long time because Vicky tries to make me order the lasagne like her, when I want a chilli chicken pizza), our drinks arrive. Joolz raises her glass of wine and says that we should all say cheers and then Andrew says, 'We should raise our glasses to James because he's new.'

Jake says, 'And to me because it's my birthday the day after tomorrow.'

So they all raise their glasses and say, 'To James because he's new and to Jake because it's nearly his birthday,' and Jake and I both smile because it feels nice to be celebrated.

'So come on then, Jamie,' says Everton as we are all drinking and chatting, 'What's your story?'

I do not understand.

'My story?'

'He means, how did you get your brain injury?' explains Vicky, leaning in very close to me. 'What happened to you? Some of us have had accidents. Other people have hurt their heads in a different way. But we've all hurt our brains somehow. How did you hurt yours?'

I suddenly do not want to talk. I think about shaking my head and saying nothing but because we are in a pub and not at the centre, and because Tanya is not here and everybody else is, I feel like I have to say something.

I decide I will talk but only very quietly.

'I was punched.'

'What's he saying?' shouts Jasvinder. 'He'll have to speak up.' She turns to Alice beside her, 'Can you hear what he's saying? I can't hear a word.' Alice shakes her head and Jasvinder says loudly, 'He needs to speak up then, doesn't he?'

'I was punched by a stranger,' I say, this time a lot louder than before. 'I was out with friends and a man called Kyle Baylis, who was very drunk and angry, attacked me when I was not looking. He is in prison now. He hit me when I was not looking and then ran away.'

'How old were you?' asks Everton. 'I was thirty-one when I had my accident. Bloke in the warehouse where I worked knocked into a pallet-load of oil drums with a forklift. The lot came down on top of me. I was out cold. Don't remember a thing.'

'I was thirty-three,' I tell Everton. 'I was about to become a member of parliament. I do not do politics any more. I have not done it for a long time.'

'Well, I was a deputy head teacher of a really big secondary school,' says Vicky. 'And I was one of the best rock climbers in the country. I went climbing in India with my boyfriend during a school holiday. The weather changed very quickly and we got into trouble and we both fell. My boyfriend died and I could have died too but I didn't. I think I might have been thirty-one when it happened and I'm thirty-four now. I used to be a deputy head teacher of a really big secondary school but I'm not now. Now I'm just Vicky.'

After this everyone tells me their story, the story of how they hit their heads.

Fat Andrew's story goes like this: 'I was out doing some DIY on our house. A tile had come loose and I thought I could fix it myself. But when I was on the roof, I lost my footing and fell to the ground. The surgeon said that I was lucky to be alive. I was fifty-four when it happened. I used to be a new account manager for a high-street bank but now I just help my wife with her dog-grooming business.'

Joolz's story goes like this: 'I used to get depression and it was bad sometimes. I'd taken an overdose a couple of times but had always been okay. Then I broke up with my boyfriend and my depression got really bad. I must have been about forty-one around this time. One day I got very drunk and started playing silly buggers on the balcony of our third-floor flat. I didn't mean to fall, I just lost my balance and that was that. I was in hospital for six months and my boyfriend never once visited me. I'm fifty-five now. On a positive note though, I don't get depressed any more.'

Jasvinder's story goes like this: 'It was late, and my family and I were travelling home on the motorway from a wedding in Manchester. We were all in good spirits and everyone was very happy. The last thing I remember is my eldest daughter Jamilla asking me if I had a spare tissue because her nose was running. Two weeks later I woke up in hospital to hear that my husband and youngest daughter were dead. A Portuguese lorry driver had fallen asleep at the wheel. My husband had tried to avoid him and we'd crashed into the central reservation. I was twenty-nine when it happened and next year it will be twenty years. There is not a day that goes by when I don't wish that Pally and Anjali had survived instead of me.'

Alice's story goes like this: 'I slipped and fell in the bath. It sounds ridiculous but that's what happened. I'd thrown my old rubber bath mat away because it was mouldy and I'd meant to get a new one but hadn't got around to it. It was the one and only time I've ever taken a shower without the bath mat being in. I must have slipped and fallen and hit my head on the side of the bath. Now I tell people to always use bath mats. I was forty-five and worked in an estate agent's on my local high street. Haven't done that for a long time now though.'

Jake's story goes like this: 'I was showing off in a PE lesson at school. I was fifteen and wanted to be a professional footballer. All the gymnastics equipment was set up and when the teacher was out of the room, one of my friends dared me to hang upside from the bar above the ropes. I did it three times and didn't have a problem but the fourth time my mates started wobbling the equipment and I lost my grip and fell. It was a year before I could walk. My friends all got expelled from school. And I never got to be a professional footballer.'

When Jake finishes telling his story, everyone looks at me as though I ought to say something, like it is still my birthday and I need to make a speech. I cannot think of anything to say though, because mostly I am still thinking. I am thinking about Fat Andrew and Joolz and Alice and Jasvinder and Jake and Everton and even Vicky. And I want say how sorry I feel for Jasvinder and Vicky especially because they have lost people they have loved. But I also want to say how sorry I feel for everyone else too. And I want to say so many things that I can feel my head beginning to clog up with words, but then Vicky leans into me again and whispers, 'See, James, everyone has bad luck, not just you.' I feel annoyed by what she has said and I want to tell her how annoying she is being, but instead I find myself saying, 'Yes, I suppose you are right.'

29

Danny

I'm in the car on my way back to the apartment, having dropped James at his parents' for the weekend, when my phone vibrates with a text. I flick my eyes towards the screen on the dashboard where, by means of some sort of technological dark arts, a message appears informing me that the text is from Simone. It's been over a fortnight since she promised to ask Leila if she would see me and until now I'd heard nothing. Most of me had assumed that no news was bad news. That Leila simply wasn't interested and this was her way of letting me know how little she thought of me. A small part of me, however, hoped that Leila's silence was at the very least evidence of an internal struggle taking place in her heart, proof that she hadn't written off my request without a second thought, rather that she was struggling to reach a decision. I told myself that people don't struggle with decisions unless they care about the outcome and deluded as it was, I found it impossible not to infer that there must be at least a small part of her that cared about me too.

I slow down for a set of traffic lights and tap the steering-wheel control that makes the full message from Simone appear: 'So sorry Danny. Tried best to talk Leila round but she won't budge. Doesn't want to meet and isn't going to change her mind. I know this must be hard for you but please respect her wishes. S x.'

It takes every last bit of self-control I've got not to ignore that final sentence. I feel like maybe I hadn't conveyed strongly enough how much I had changed, and should have said more about how much I'd missed Leila and how desperate I was to be part of her life. Maybe I could've done more or explained things better to make it absolutely clear to both Leila and her mum that I wasn't going to drift in and out of their lives as the mood took me. I should've let them know that I wanted to be part of their lives for good.

As the lights change, I pull away a little too sharply and almost hit a car coming out of a side road on my left. For a short while we exchange abusive gestures and furious bursts of car horn but while his are full of self-righteous indignation, mine are little more than pantomime because I know the fault is all mine.

Though I'd always known it would be a long shot, it still feels like the biggest kick in the teeth to hear that my own daughter, my own flesh and blood doesn't want to see me. I don't want to believe it. I'm her dad after all, and whatever mistakes I've made in the past, surely this fact alone has to count for something. I wonder if she knows how much her decision has hurt me. Maybe she does and that's the whole point of the exercise, to share around some of the feelings of pain and rejection she's endured over these past fifteen years. The hurt of a child growing up without one of its parents, the rejection that comes from a lifetime of wondering if you're the real reason they are not around.

Seeing things from her point of view for a moment gives me pause for thought, but it is only brief. All too soon I'm back to my own feelings of hurt, outrage and rejection, and I've got a horrible feeling that it isn't going to end well. I call Simone's number up on to the car's dashboard screen and get ready to . . . what exactly? Give her a piece of my mind? Talk her round? Beg for her mercy? I'm not sure what I'm going to say. All I'm certain of is that I have to do something, say something, anything at all. I can't just sit and let things happen.

I lift my thumb to tap the button that will dial Simone. But as I lower it, the phone rings taking me by surprise. A glance at the screen tells me it's James.

'Now's not a good time, mate. Any chance you could call back later?'

'I was calling to see how you are. You did not seem yourself this morning.'

He's right. I wasn't. I was frustrated because I still hadn't heard from Leila. And now of course, I'm even worse. I tell him about Simone's text.

'I was about to give her a piece of my mind when you called,' I say, concluding the story. 'Not that it will make any difference of course, it's not like it's actually her fault.'

James is quiet at the other end of the line. So quiet that I wonder if we have been cut off or that perhaps he's having one of his moments.

'Are you okay, James? You're not saying anything.'

'I was thinking about what you said.'

'Which bit?'

'All of it.'

'And what exactly were you thinking?' There's an edge of impatience in my voice that shouldn't be there. I know he's only trying to help. 'I'm sorry to snap, mate, it's just that I'm feeling a bit stressed. Maybe we should talk later when I'm less wound up.'

'Okay,' he says, 'but do you want to know what I was thinking about what you said? Because what I was thinking was, how you and your daughter must be very similar.'

I haven't a clue where he's going with this. 'Why's that then?'

'I was thinking you and your daughter must be very similar because, you know . . . you both find it difficult to talk to your parents. You wanted to see your parents a few weeks ago, didn't you, but it did not work out and I was thinking that maybe it is the same for Leila. Maybe she would like to see you but she is finding it difficult too.' There's a long pause and then James says, 'It was just a thought.'

This time around it's me who is completely silent. I'm utterly speechless. He's right about Leila, about my parents, about the whole situation.

James coughs politely. 'Did I say the wrong thing?'

'Completely the opposite. Look, I'd better go. But I'll call you later, okay?'

'Okay.'

'Oh and James?'

'Yeah.'

I feel like I should thank him. Reel off the long list of things he's done to help me. But the words won't come. They just get stuck inside my head. 'Nothing,' I reply, as I do a three-point turn and then head in the direction of my parents' house. 'I'll catch up with you later.'

The good news is that despite my worst fears, my mum is very much alive. The bad news is that the very sight of me on her doorstep has her in floods of tears. She throws her arms around me and refuses to let go in case I somehow slip back to the netherworld from which I emerged, while she's not looking. In the end it's only when one of her next-door neighbours pops her head over the privet hedge and asks if she's all right that she finally breaks her hold on me. Releasing her grip, she reassures her neighbour that everything's fine and without another word ushers me inside the house and then closes the door firmly behind her.

Fifteen years is a long time. When you see someone every day, you don't tend to notice them changing as the greying hair, wrinkles and thickening waistlines happen so gradually. But here I am being presented with all her changes at once. It's quite a shock. She's just as I remember her only older, almost as if she's been flung forward into the future while I have remained in the present. As she sorts out mugs and teabags in the kitchen, she tells me that my dad has gone into town for an eye test but should be back soon. I ask how he is and she says, 'He'll be all the better for seeing you.'

'We thought we'd never see you again,' she says as we sit down at the kitchen table with a steaming mug of tea in front of each of us. 'We really did think you were gone forever. We've been worried sick about you. Where have you been all this time, Danny?'

Right now she probably doesn't need to hear a blow-by-blow account of the last fifteen years. 'It doesn't matter, Mum. What matters is that I'm here now.'

She quickly corrects herself, presumably for fear of offending me. 'Of course, of course, I don't mean to overwhelm you, I've missed you so much. This has been such a shock. Look at me, I'm shaking.' She lifts her hands to illustrate her point and sure enough she can barely keep them still. 'At least tell me where you're living. Are you local?'

'I live in an apartment in the middle of Birmingham. It's not my place exactly. I work as a live-in carer for a guy who has got a brain injury and can't look after himself.'

Mum seems relieved. 'I'm so glad to hear you've got a roof over your head and regular work. So many people these days don't seem to have either, it's shocking really. And this man you work for, is he completely disabled? How old is he? I do hope he's not young. It's such a shame when things like that happen to young people.'

'He's my age,' I explain. 'And no, he's not completely disabled. He has problems with thinking, communication and some of his motor skills but he can walk and get about and do most things for himself.'

'So why does he need you then?'

It's a good question. One that of late I've been asking myself quite a lot. There's so much that James can do now that he couldn't when I first met him, or rather so much more that he's realised he's capable of doing.

'I'm not sure he does need me any more,' I say. 'He seems to be getting better all the time.'

'Aren't you worried that he won't need you soon and you'll have to find a new job and somewhere to live?'

'If that happens, Mum, and I hope it will,' I reply, 'it'll be because I've done my job well. I want James to get better. I want him to be able to live life on his own.' I pause and think about James's advice that encouraged me to come here today.

'He deserves happiness, he's quite an amazing bloke really.'

Mum asks me lots more questions about James and about me too. She asks if I've been looking after myself and then tells me I'm looking thin, but makes sure to enquire whether it's because that's just how I like to be rather than because I've been forgetting to eat. She asks if I'm seeing anyone, and my response is truthful if a little vague. 'I was,' I explain, 'but it didn't work out,' to which she responds with a question about whether I think it's possible for me to fix the problem. 'No, Mum,' I sigh, thinking about Maya's last words to me, 'I think that door is well and truly closed.' The interesting thing about this exchange with my mother is that between all the questions and the comments, she never once takes her eyes off me. She's like a scientist forensically studying my movements or a sketch artist trying to commit every last detail to memory. It's exactly how I imagine I would've been if Leila had let me see her. I'd want to drink her in and never stop.

For a moment I imagine myself blurting it out: just coming out with it and telling her she's a grandmother. But before I can turn thought into action, I'm brought to a halt by the sound of keys in the front door. Moments later a male voice calls from the hallway: 'Val, it's me, love, I'm home. You'll never believe it . . . some idiot's parked one of those bloody great Range Rover things right in front of the house . . . it's an eyesore!'

Dad's reaction on seeing me is pretty much the same as Mum's. He's confused and scared in equal measure, wondering if he's seeing things while at the same time convinced he's not. He hugs me fiercely, repeating the words, 'Oh, son, oh, son,' and it's only when we finally part and he's forced to dry his eyes on the sleeve of his jacket that I realise he's been crying.

He slumps down on one of the kitchen chairs and sits with his head in his hands. He's a shadow of the man I remember, he's lost weight and seems smaller somehow and frailer. Mum comes over and rests her hands on his shoulders and finally he looks up at me.

'How long have you been here?'

'About half an hour.'

'And you're well?'

'He's absolutely fine,' says Mum. 'He's working as a carer.'

'A carer? In hospitals and the like?'

'He works for a young man who was in some sort of accident

and can't look after himself,' says Mum. 'That's his car outside. Danny gets to drive it whenever he wants.'

Dad stares at me, eyes wide, still unsure this isn't part of some elaborate dream. Finally he sits up straight, draws a deep breath and speaks. 'You should never have left us like that, Danny,' he says. 'Never. What you've put us through over the years . . . what you've put your mother through. She had cancer, you know – I thought I was going to lose her, I thought I was going to lose her and be all on my own . . . Why ever did you go, Danny? Why would you put us through years of not knowing where you were, of not knowing if you were alive or dead?'

I feel awful seeing him so upset and even worse knowing I am the cause. I owe him an explanation. I owe them both the truth, even though I know they already know the answer.

'I left because even though you never said it out loud, I knew exactly what you were thinking. I left because even though you said the opposite, every time I looked in your eyes I saw it was a lie. The fact is you were right: I killed Helen. She is dead because of me.'

30

James

'So you'll text me and let me know when to pick you up?' asks my dad, Don.

'I will definitely text you,' I repeat back to him.

'And you'll give me plenty of notice?' he asks.

'Yes,' I say, 'I will give you plenty of notice.'

'And you'll call if you need anything?' he asks.

'I will definitely call you if I need anything,' I say.

'Right then, well, have a good time, son. Just remind me what it is you're going to see again?'

'*Jurassic World*,' I say. 'It is sort of a *Jurassic Park* reboot and I am very excited about it because all the reviews I have read have been very good.'

'Well,' he says. 'I'm looking forward to hearing all about it later.'

The reason why my dad is dropping me off at the cinema is because Danny has had a family emergency and has had to have some time off work. I do not know what his family emergency is or what part of his family is involved because he has not told me. I have texted him to make sure he is okay and he has told me that he is fine but just needs a little time to sort things out.

In the meantime my parents have been staying with me at the apartment and it has actually been quite good fun. Last night we went out for a Chinese meal that was lovely and the night before my mum, Erica, cooked fish and chips and there was no broccoli at all. My parents have also been taking me to my appointments this week and it was at this week's ABI support group meeting that I came up with the idea for the cinema trip.

I told everyone at support group that I was looking forward

to seeing the new Jurassic Park film with my friend Danny, and some of them said they would like to see it too. So I texted Danny to see whether he minded if I saw the new Jurassic Park film with some of my ABI friends and when he said it was fine, I started making plans for us all to see it together. To begin with it was only going to be a few of us but then some others who had not been interested in the film said that they wanted to see it too and before I knew it, we were all going.

The only problem was that it was quite hard to organise everybody. We needed to choose the right time and place, or at least that is what Vicky said. She made everyone be quiet and then said that she would make all the arrangements and let everyone know the plan by text. I personally thought this was a bad idea and could not see why we could not just make all the arrangements while we were all in the same room together. Then Vicky said something like, 'Typical man! Just leave me to do the organising, will you?' and so I did, because it seemed a lot easier than arguing with her about it all day.

As I carefully cross the road, I spot Vicky outside the front of the cinema and she waves to me and I wave back. She is on her own and is dressed like she is going to something like a wedding. Instead of wearing jeans and trainers like she usually does, she has on a blue dress and white shoes with heels. She is also wearing jewellery and make-up. She tries to give me a kiss on my cheek, even though I do not want her to. And when I ask her why she is dressed like she is going to a wedding, she shrugs and says, 'I like to dress like this sometimes.'

While we wait for the others to turn up, Vicky and I talk about the sorts of things we have been doing all day. She tells me that she has been helping her parents in the garden, while I have been mainly practising some new exercises that my physiotherapist gave me to do. All this talking takes exactly five minutes (I know this because I looked at my watch before we started talking and straight after we finished) and when I stop looking at my watch, I say, 'Why is nobody else here yet, Vicky? Did you tell them the right time? Six o'clock?'

'Of course I did.'

'Well, it is now five minutes past six and nobody is here.'

'They're probably stuck in traffic or something, so why don't you just stop moaning and tell me about what other interesting things you've been up to instead.'

I try to do as Vicky asks but I find it very difficult because I do not like being late to the cinema.

I do not like missing the trailers.

Sometimes the trailers are the best bit.

And now because the rest of the group are late, I am probably going to have to miss them.

'This is ridiculous,' I say, getting tired of waiting. 'Where is everyone?'

Vicky shrugs. 'How should I know?'

'You could text them and find out.'

'Can't. Haven't got their numbers.'

I think long and hard about what Vicky has just said. And then I think about it again, just to make sure I have got it right. 'But,' I say finally, 'when we were making plans to come here today, you said you were going to text everyone and let them know what time to meet.'

Vicky nods. 'Yes, now I think about it, I did say that.'

'So you have got their numbers?'

Vicky shakes her head. 'I've left my phone at home.'

This does not sound right. Vicky is always playing with her phone. How could she possibly forget it?

'I do not believe you.'

Vicky sighs impatiently. 'Why would I lie about leaving my phone at home? That would be crazy.'

It occurs to me that maybe she has made a good point. After all, if she is always playing with her phone then she might, for instance, have played with it so much that she needed to charge it, and then forgotten to take it out with her because that happens to me all the time.

'Okay, I believe you,' I say, 'and I am sorry for accusing you of not telling the truth. But if the others are not here soon, then

I think we should get our tickets and see the film without them. Is that okay with you?'

Vicky smiles a huge smile. 'Yes,' she says, 'that is definitely fine with me.'

After another five minutes the rest of the group have still not turned up and so we go inside. The ticket queue is really long and by the time we get to the till not only has our film started, but it is also sold out. The lady at the till asks us if we want tickets for the next screening in an hour and I am about to say, 'Yes, please, that would be lovely,' when instead Vicky says, 'I can't wait that long because Mum is picking me up after the film at eight thirty and this next one doesn't finish until nine thirty.'

I am not sure what to do because I really want to see *Jurassic World*. It has had really good reviews, but I feel bad because Vicky is the only person from group who has bothered to turn up.

'We could go and see another film,' suggests Vicky. 'For instance we could go and see . . . I don't know . . . that one!' She points to a poster with eight young women on it, all standing in a row. One of them is very pretty and is wearing a tartan skirt and has her arms folded, and the others are all standing side on. I think I have seen the tartan skirt woman in other films before but I cannot remember which ones. Above the women's heads it says, 'This time the world gets pitch slapped.' I think it is meant to be a joke but if it is, I do not get it. It does not look like a film that has a single car chase, explosion or dinosaur in it.

'I do not think that one will be very good.'

Vicky disagrees. 'Well, I've heard it's brilliant. Didn't you see the first one? It was really funny.'

'I did not even realise this one was a sequel,' I say, now noticing the number two in the title. It being a sequel makes me want to see it even less than I did before. 'Are you really sure you cannot just wait another hour? It is not like your mum will leave without you is it?'

'Come on,' says Vicky, 'I promise you, you'll like it,' and then, without checking with me again, she asks the lady at the till for two tickets.

Things that happen during the film:

1. People sing.
2. A chubby blonde lady falls over quite a lot.
3. Vicky keeps trying to hold my hand (and I do not let her).

'So what did you think?' asks Vicky when the film is over.

'I thought it was okay for a film that was about a group of ladies singing.'

'Did you really like it?' asks Vicky excitedly. 'Or are you just saying that because you like me?'

'No,' I say, feeling baffled by her question. Vicky really does say some of the strangest things sometimes. 'I do not like it – I just thought it was okay. The chubby blonde lady was funny and the lady with the red hair was nice to look at, but I do not think I would want it for my collection or anything like that. Was it as good as the first one?' Vicky wrinkles her nose. 'I did not think so,' I reply, 'I could just tell.'

'Do you want to go for a drink at the bar next door?' asks Vicky once we are in the lobby. I pull a face because I did say to my dad, Don, that I would text him when the film was over. 'It would only be a quick drink,' says Vicky, and she tilts her head slightly. 'I'll make sure you're not too late.'

I actually would not mind a quick drink. Normally Danny and I go for a drink a few times a week but because he has been away, I have not been out for a drink for a while. 'Okay,' I say to Vicky. 'I will go for a drink with you.' We carry on towards the exit and then I stop as something occurs to me, 'But what about your mum? You said she was picking you up from here after the film?'

'Yes,' says Vicky, looping her arm through mine. 'I did say that, didn't I? But she'll be fine waiting. She always takes a book with her wherever she goes.'

As we walk to the bar next door, I think how if I was Vicky's mum, I would not be very pleased if my daughter went off with her friend instead of coming out to meet me after the film like she had promised. It is not very thoughtful behaviour. At the same time I think I might secretly be quite pleased about it. Tonight I have discovered that Vicky is actually quite a lot of fun to be around. Lots of the things she says make me smile and she is really good at talking, so I usually do not have to search around for things to say. I do not tell her any of this though, because she will make it into a big deal when it is not.

Vicky has a gin and tonic and I have a lager. We talk about lots of things like family and what we like to watch on TV and where we would like to go on holiday. After a while though, I find myself wondering again why no one else from the group turned up. It feels like a mystery. I decide to bring it up with Vicky again.

'I was just thinking. Don't you think it is very odd that no one else from group turned up?'

Vicky shakes her head. 'Not really. We've all got ABIs so it's a wonder that *we're* even here, let alone everyone else.'

We both laugh because it is a good joke that she has made but when we stop, the question is still bothering me.

'But it is strange. Do you think they are all okay? What if they all caught the same bus in together and there was an accident and we are here having a fun time and right now they are all lying in—'

'There wasn't any accident,' says Vicky.

'How do you know? Anything is possible—'

'No, it's not,' she says quite loudly. 'I know they weren't in an accident because I didn't invite them.'

Now I really am confused. 'But you took everyone's number and said that you would text them.'

Vicky sighs. 'I did text them. But I texted them to say that the cinema trip was next week and not this week.'

'Why would you do that? That makes no sense.'

'Oh, come on, James,' says Vicky. 'Do I have to spell it out?'

When she says this, I think about the game hangman. 'Okay,' I say, 'give me a few clues and I will work out the rest.'

'Fine,' says Vicky. 'But I'm only going to give you one clue and you're going to have to close your eyes to get it.'

'But why do I have to—'

'Do you want the clue or not?' snaps Vicky.

I close my eyes. I can hear the chatter of people talking around us; the songs coming from the speakers in the bar; the clatter of plates and crockery in the bar's kitchen. Then all at once I cannot hear anything but my own heartbeat as a pair of soft lips press against my own.

I open one eye a little bit just to check: Vicky is kissing me.

It feels good to be kissed by Vicky.

She has nice soft lips.

I think she might have planned this all along.

She has been quite sneaky really.

I am not sure I approve.

But I like being kissed by Vicky.

I like being kissed by her a lot.

31

Danny

There's a knock on the door of the bedroom I'm sleeping in. I call out it's fine to come in, and moments later Mum timidly pokes her head around the door.

'I'm so sorry to disturb you, Danny,' she says, peering into the darkness of the room. 'The thing is, your dad and I are just popping to the shops and I didn't want you to wake up and worry when there was nobody here. We shouldn't be too long – we're just getting a few bits and bobs to tide us over – although I can stay if you'd like me to. Your father will be fine on his own.'

I tell her several times that I'll be okay but because three days earlier she'd witnessed her husband cradling her thirty-six-year-old, fourteen-stone son as he sobbed like a child, she takes a lot of convincing. I promise to call them if I need anything and eventually she agrees to leave. 'We won't be any longer than an hour,' she promises before closing the door. 'And if you need anything . . . anything at all, just call and we'll come straight home.'

Resting back on my pillow, I overhear my parents have a 'whispered' discussion on the landing. Despite my protestations Mum still thinks it's a bad idea to leave me alone when I'm clearly still 'fragile'; Dad, however, reckons I'll be all right. 'But what if he does something silly while we're out?' counters Mum. 'You read about it all the time in the papers. Young men like our Danny, lost souls taking their own lives.'

'That's not our Danny,' replies Dad. 'That's not what this is about. He's just having a rest, that's all. He's been carrying this load on his shoulders for the past fifteen years. I think the poor lad's just shattered. All he needs is a bit of a rest and a lot of love.'

Rest and love.

They're not wrong about that. From the moment I broke down in front of my parents, that's pretty much all I've received. I hadn't realised just how exhausted I was, how wound up, until I let everything I'd been holding on to all this time come spilling out. And since then I've been allowed to rest and been fed love by the bucketload and feel a million times better for it.

I leave it a good while before I finally get out of bed – long enough for my parents to have returned if they'd forgotten something, but not quite so long that they might be home any time soon. I pull on my jeans and – because it's been three days since I arrived here without a change of clothes – an old T-shirt that my dad has loaned me. It is a size too small and has a picture of a beach on the front, over which are emblazoned the words: 'Paignton: The English Riviera'.

Once dressed, I cross the hallway and take a deep breath before gently pushing open the door to what used to be Helen's room. Even though Mum told me the first night I stayed here that they'd long since packed away all of Helen's stuff and redecorated, I've not been able to stop thinking that I should take a look at it, make a pilgrimage, see what's changed.

As I survey the room, it's clear that there's no trace of Helen left at all. Her walls used to be plastered with tour posters of her favourite bands and films, but now they are just painted cream, with a couple of framed prints depicting woodland scenes dotted about. The floor of Helen's room used to be dominated by a multicoloured rag rug that she'd brought home with her the first time she went to Glastonbury when she was sixteen, but now there's only cream carpet. It's the same story wherever I look, a second-hand 1930s' wardrobe swapped for a modern white IKEA unit, a second-hand school desk and chair replaced with a clean modern dressing table and stool. It's as though she was never here. As if she'd never inhabited this room. As if she'd only ever existed in my head.

I was twenty when Helen came to stay with me during my final year at Cambridge, and on course for a first-class degree in Economics. Although the previous two years had been challenging, they would have been considerably more troublesome had I not been to King's Scrivener beforehand. My time at the school had not only prepared me for the demanding nature of my course and the heaviness of my weekly workload, but also enabled me to cope far better than most with the eccentricities of tutors, the boorishness of some fellow students and the bizarre, antiquated, nonsensical traditions of my particular college.

Having spent the previous two summers interning at the headquarters of two separate financial houses and with no desire to stay on for another year to get my masters, I'd given a lot of thought to my post-university career. Full of the optimism of youth and more ideas of how to revolutionise the banking industry than I knew what to do with, I'd even drafted a tongue-in-cheek ten-year plan that I kept pinned to the wall above my desk, next to a black-and-white postcard of a young Sophia Loren. By the time I was twenty-three I intended to have founded my first company; by twenty-four to have floated that company on the stock market and made my first million; by twenty-six to have turned that first million into six; and by thirty to have turned my six million into thirty-six million and be looking forward to a semi-retired future living in a big pile in Kent with my Danish model girlfriend.

Of course it was a joke. Or at least that's what I told anyone who ever asked about it. But at the same time, it was no joke when it came to the scale of my ambitions. I was going to conquer the world. I was going to make a fortune doing so. And at the end of my life I didn't doubt for a moment that I would have left my mark on this world. That was the kind of unshakeable self-confidence that a school like King's Scrivener had instilled in me during the seven years I was there. A self-confidence that not even the most demanding of Cambridge tutors nor the precociousness of my peers could shake. I never once questioned whether my future would turn out the way I envisioned it. I never once thought that I didn't deserve the success that awaited me. The prospect of failure simply never occurred to me. Irrespective of circumstance, life would always go my way because King's Scrivener scholars never failed. Life would always go my way because King's Scrivener scholars were winners. Life would always go my way because I was a King's Scrivener old boy.

Helen wasn't a King's Scrivener scholar, but not for want of trying. When it came to her time to think about secondary school, I convinced her that she could make it to the girls' school, even though my old primary school teacher, Mrs Ashworth, had insisted that it would be a gamble. I did all I could to help her revise for the exam but when the day came around, I think her nerves got the better of her. When she received her rejection letter, she came to my room crying. 'I've let you down,' she said, and no matter what I said to the contrary, she refused to be comforted. Disappointed not to be following in my footsteps and disillusioned by the exam process as a whole, Helen didn't even bother sitting the test for our local grammar school and opted instead for the nearby Langley Comprehensive.

But not even being at an underperforming school like Langley could stop my sister. By the end of her first term she was earmarked as a star pupil and the new head teacher, desperate to change the narrative attached to her school, seized on Helen as the answer. A gifted-student programme was put in place, one-to-one teaching time set aside and funds found for Helen to attend extra-curricular courses at the weekends and during summer breaks. Helen's GCSE results for the eleven subjects she studied were so spectacular that she featured on the front page of the local newspaper. So when later she applied to Cambridge to study Maths, no one, least of all me, was at all surprised that she was granted an interview, a first for any Langley Comprehensive student. I remember Mum said to me at the time, when she called to let me know the good news, 'This was always going to happen. That girl idolises you. Even when she was a baby, all she ever wanted was to be like her big brother, Danny.'

I should have sensed trouble when I turned up to meet Helen after her interview to discover that she wasn't alone. She was with a tall, curly-haired kid in a sixties-style suit, pointy shoes and sunglasses. She'd introduced him as 'Alistair' from Wokingham but the moment I heard his cut-glass accent I knew exactly who he was. I'd met plenty of 'Alistair's in my time at KS and never one I liked. They were the ones to whom everything came easily, whether it was exam results or girls, and whose only currency was a desire to be seen as cool.

Alistair, like Helen, was at Cambridge for his interview. He was staying over with his older brother, who just happened to be throwing a party to which he had cordially invited Helen. 'Of course,' he'd said to me, 'it goes without saying you're invited too,' but the thunderous look Helen threw in my direction made it clear that I wasn't to accept. I'd already made plans for us, a meal out with friends followed by a night out at the pub: something to give her a taste of the student life, while keeping her under my watchful eye. But she wanted to go to Alistair's party and after everything she'd achieved, I felt like she'd earned the right to let her hair down, and I gave her new plans my blessing.

It was one in the morning when I got the call. A police officer at the end of the line informed me that Helen was dead. They suspected she was the victim of a bad batch of ecstasy tablets the police had been trying to get off the streets for the past few months.

My parents tried to tell me that they didn't blame me for what happened, but I was too busy listening to the voice in my head, the one that said I could have done things differently, to hear a single word they said. The voice in my head shouted louder than anyone. It told me that I should have known something was wrong. It told me that Helen had only come to harm because she'd wanted to be like me. It told me that if I'd never gone to King's Scrivener, if I'd never let them instil their confidence in me, if I'd simply lived the ordinary life I was always meant to lead, Helen would still be alive.

My parents, true to their word, are home after exactly an hour, by which time I have returned to my room and climbed back into bed.

'Just wanted to let you know we're back,' says Mum. 'They had some of that nice soup in the cartons on sale. I'll make you some for lunch. Everything okay here?'

I think about Helen's room across the hallway. I think about how, if she hadn't died, she'd be thirty-three now, maybe happily married with kids or happily single or even working on that elusive cure for cancer. That was the thing about Helen. She had so much potential. There were so many things she could have done, lives she could have lived and people she could have been.

'Everything's fine,' I say, relieved that the curtains are closed, so she can't see the tears falling on to my pillow. 'Soup sounds lovely.'

32

James

It is midday, I am in the back of a cab parked outside Vicky's parents' house in Sutton Coldfield and am on the phone to Martha.

'But I will not know what to say to him,' I tell her.

'Of course you will,' says Martha. 'Just be yourself.'

'But that is just it. I do not want to be myself. I want to be someone who makes a good first impression. And I do not think I am very good at making a good first impression.'

'You're worrying over nothing,' she says. 'Vicky's dad will love you because everyone loves you. You're very loveable. Now look, I've got to go – I'm supposed to be in a meeting in twenty minutes and I haven't even read through my notes – but remember I love you, and they'll love you too, okay?'

There is a reason I am asking Martha for advice while sitting in a taxi parked outside Vicky's parents' house. The reason is because yesterday at support group Vicky invited me for lunch. She asked me while she was waiting for her mum to pick her up. She said, 'You should come to my house for lunch tomorrow and then you can meet my dad.' I agreed because at the time it sounded like a good idea, but now I am not so sure. I do not know anything about Vicky's dad but I have met other girlfriend's dads in the past. And while some of them can be nice, others are not so nice and it has been a long time since I have had to meet one, so I am out of practice. I have tried to speak to Danny about this, because he would know what to do, but he has not been returning my calls and so the only other person I could think of who might be helpful was Martha.

If you had asked me last week what the next seven days would look like, I do not think I would have guessed the right answer. I would have guessed something sensible like, 'I bet I watch some DVDs, go to all my usual hospital appointments and have dinner with my parents.' Not, 'I will spend every day with my brand new girlfriend,' which is what I have actually been doing.

On the night of our first kiss, Vicky and I ended up staying at the bar until late. In fact, we had such a good time that I forgot to text my dad to pick me up. By the time I remembered, just after midnight, he had already called the police because he thought I must have been kidnapped. When my dad found out that I had not been kidnapped, I thought he might explode. 'You were in a bar with a lady friend,' he snapped. 'I can't believe how selfish you've been!' Normally I would get quite upset if he shouted at me like this, but instead I just could not stop smiling. The reason I was smiling was because Vicky had agreed to be my girlfriend and had made me the happiest man in the world. That night I went to sleep smiling and then the next day I woke up smiling too. And I have done the same every day since.

I cannot believe that I used to find Vicky annoying, because she is really amazing. Some of the things she says make me laugh and sometimes the things I say make her laugh too. This is my favourite thing to do – to make her laugh – because I love the sound of her voice when she does it. It sounds like she is really happy inside and it makes me feel happy too.

And now all I want to do is be with her all the time and be as happy as I am right now. That is another reason why I agreed to meet her dad. I told myself that if I am going to spend a lot of time with Vicky, I want her dad to like me and not mind me liking his daughter.

I pay the taxi driver and ask for a receipt, just like my dad said I should. He offered to give me a lift but I said, 'Thank you that is very kind but I am thirty-six years old and I am going to meet my girlfriend's dad for the first time. It would not look very good to be dropped off by my dad, would it?' I said it like it was a joke. My dad laughed and said he understood. He very kindly called the taxi firm for me and said that I should give him a ring if I needed anything and I said, 'Thanks, Dad, but I will be fine.'

As the taxi pulls away, I look up at Vicky's house. It is a terraced house with a light-blue front door. There are purple flowers growing around the doorframe. It looks like a nice house to live in. When I ring the doorbell, I start to feel sick. My head feels fuzzy and I feel like I might faint. When this happens, I put my hand on the door to steady myself, only then the door opens and I lose my balance and nearly fall over. I manage to steady myself at the last moment but I think if you were looking at me, you might think I am dancing.

'You must be James.'

I straighten up to see a balding man with grey hair and bright smiling eyes.

'Yes, I am,' I say nervously. 'Pleased to meet you, Mr Collins.'

'Mr Collins is my dad,' says Vicky's dad. 'And he's dead so you can call me Brian. Oh and in this house we like to say hello like this,' and then he gives me a huge bear hug until I hear Vicky's voice say, 'Dad, put him down, will you?'

Brian laughs. 'I was only welcoming him to the family, love,' he says and then lets me go. I try my best not to look like I am struggling to breathe and smile at Vicky. She is wearing a bright yellow dress and has a big smile on her face just like mine.

'I've missed you,' she says, even though we saw each other last night.

'I have missed you too,' I reply. 'I was so excited about seeing you today that I could not sleep last night. I had to keep checking my watch to see if it was morning yet.'

Vicky gives me another kiss, not a peck though, but a proper kiss on the lips. Her dad is still standing next to us the whole time. It makes me feel very uncomfortable indeed.

'I think I'd better make myself scarce,' says Brian.

Vicky takes a break from kissing me. 'I think that's a good idea, Dad,' she says. 'We might be some time.'

Afterwards Vicky takes me to the kitchen where her mum is making lunch with Brian's help. Vicky's mum gives me a big hug and says, 'Are you any good at chopping? Because if you are, I've got some work for you.' She shows me how she wants the carrots cut into batons, hands me a knife and tells me to get on with it.

It is fun making lunch with Vicky's family.

They laugh and joke with each other all the time.

Brian is especially funny. Before he retired, he used to be a policeman and he tells me lots of funny stories about the things he has seen.

'So, James,' says Vicky's dad, Brian, as he cuts a large pork pie into slices. 'What did you do before . . .?'

I don't know what he means but as soon as he says it, Vicky's mum nudges him with her elbow and says his name sharply, as though he's done something wrong.

'It was just a question!' says Brian.

'Well, it's rude,' says Vicky's mum.

'I do not mind being asked questions,' I say, wanting things to be normal again. 'I just do not know what he meant.'

'I think he was wondering what you did for a living before you got your ABI,' says Vicky.

'Oh, I see,' I reply. 'I can answer that easily. I was the elected MP for Birmingham South.'

'You mean like in parliament?' asks Brian.

Vicky's mum tuts at Brian. 'Of course that's what he means.'

'I don't know, do I?' says Brian. 'I've never met an MP before.' He smiles and turns to me. 'There's me going on like there's no tomorrow, when you must have some stories of your own. So, what was it like?'

'I do not know,' I say. 'I had my . . . the thing that happened to me happened before I could take office.'

After a long silence Vicky's dad apologises. 'Oh, James, I'm so sorry,' he says. 'I'm always putting my foot in it.'

'It is okay,' I say, and I look at Vicky, who is standing near the door to the garden. I give her a wink and a smile and she smiles back. 'I would have liked to have known what I would have been like as an MP too. I like to think I would have been a good one.

I like to think I would have helped lots of people. But I think I am okay with not knowing what might have been now . . . I think I am okay not knowing because there are so many things that I still get to find out.'

We eat lunch at the table in Vicky's parents' kitchen. Because it is such a lovely day, they have their French doors open and a nice breeze comes in. Over lunch Vicky's mum tells me stories about what Vicky was like when she was young. She says she was very studious and quiet and very, very shy. Vicky says that she was still a bit like that sometimes before her accident, unless she was standing up in front of a class teaching. She makes a joke that if her old self met her new self, they probably would not get along. 'I think my old self would find me annoying,' she says. 'And I think who I am now would find her really boring.'

'We always like to joke that it's been like having two daughters,' says Brian. 'Trouble and more Trouble.'

Vicky turns to her dad. 'Do you ever miss the old me?' she asks.

'Sometimes,' says Brian. 'Is that the wrong thing to say?'

Vicky shakes her head. 'I miss her too, sometimes. I miss how she always knew the right thing to do and the right thing to say.'

'I used to miss the old me a lot,' I say, keeping my eyes fixed to my plate. 'I would miss the old me so much that I used to dream sometimes that I was back to being the old me and living my old life.'

'And how did you feel when you woke up and found that nothing had changed?' asks Vicky.

'Not good,' I reply.

'Oh, that's a sad story,' says Vicky's mum. 'How do you cope with feelings like that?'

'I have taught myself not to dream,' I say. 'Life is a lot easier that way.'

After lunch I try to help clear the table, but Vicky's parents insist that I sit in the garden and they will bring me a drink. I do as I am told and I sit on a picnic bench at the bottom of their garden.

The bench is in the shade under a tree and there are lots of things going on, like bees popping in and out of flowers and birds chasing one another.

I am not sure how long I am there before Vicky joins me, but it is long enough for a robin to dare to sit right at the end of the bench next to me. But the moment Vicky sits down, he flies away.

'Here you go,' says Vicky, and she hands me a photo album. The cover of it is soft and purple and sort of glittery. 'These are pictures of me before my accident.'

'Oh,' I reply. 'Why are you showing them to me?'

'I thought it was only fair because I've seen pictures of you before your ABI on the Internet,' she says. 'My dad just looked you up on the computer because he thinks you were famous.'

'And what did you think? You know, of the picture of me before my accident? Do I look different?'

Vicky nods. 'A bit,' she says, and then she opens the photo album. On the first page is a photo of Vicky standing next to a group of children in school uniform. The children look young, like they are at primary school, and they are all smiling. Vicky has shorter hair and is wearing a navy top, leggings and black ballet shoes. She looks young too.

'This is 3VS. They were the last class I taught.'

'They look like nice kids.'

'They were, very.' She stops and looks at me. 'Can I ask you a question. If I hadn't had my accident and what happened to you hadn't happened, do you think you'd still want to be my boyfriend?'

I am confused. 'Why are you asking me that?'

'Because I saw a picture of you with your old girlfriend,' she says. 'She is very pretty.'

I think I probably know the picture she is talking about. It is a picture of me standing next to Zara, taken on the day after I won my election. 'Yes, she is very pretty,' I say, 'but even if I had not had my accident, I still think I would want to be your boyfriend.'

'But why would you?' asks Vicky. 'She is so much prettier than me.'

'Because even though she was pretty, I did not tell her I loved her until we had been together for a whole year,' I say. 'And the thing is, I have only been with you less than a week and I already feel like saying it all the time.'

33

Danny

I can feel my parents watching my every move from their doorstep as I load the few bits I've got with me on to the back seat of the car. It's been good being here with them. We've probably achieved more in the past six days than we have in the past sixteen years, just by listening to all of our separate viewpoints. I feel relieved and rejuvenated, ready to take on the world, even though there's been no change of heart from Leila. That's why I haven't told my parents about her yet. I don't want to build their hopes up and end up just adding to their heartache.

'You know you don't have to go,' says Mum. Her voice is full of emotion, although she's trying her utmost to put on a brave face.

'I know, Mum, and thank you, but I can't afford to lose this job and anyway I don't want to outstay my welcome.'

'Nonsense,' says Dad. 'There's no such thing when it comes to family. You can stay as long as you like.'

'Your dad's right,' says Mum. 'This is your home, son. And it always will be.'

I hug them both and even my dad, who was never exactly renowned for his public displays of affection, returns it warmly.

'Are you sure we can't talk you into staying a little bit longer, even just until lunch?' asks Mum.

'I'd love to but I've really got to go. I'll give you a call next week to see how you are.'

'But you will be coming to see us again at some point?' asks Dad, and the apprehension in his eyes makes me feel ashamed.

'Of course I will,' I say, even though I hadn't got any further in my thinking than the next ten minutes. 'Maybe I can come for tea next week on my day off.'

Before leaving, I apologise for having stayed away for so long, but all this does is make Mum cry. 'You don't have to apologise,' she says. 'We're just glad you're back, that's all that matters.' She holds on to me with one hand and dabs her eyes with a tissue with the other. 'You do know we love you, Danny, don't you? We've always loved you and we always will.'

James is over at his parents' for the weekend so I head straight from Nuneaton to Stow-on-the-Wold to pick him up. As reunions go, it's one of the most heartfelt I've ever experienced. The moment he spots me in his parents' hallway he rushes over, and declares how much he's missed me. 'It has not been the same without you, Danny Allen,' he says. 'It has not been the same at all.'

To celebrate my return to work, James suggests that we stop off on the way to Birmingham for something to eat. So we make a detour to a riverside pub near Stratford-upon-Avon for a late breakfast.

'I have got some news to tell you,' says James as I return to our outdoor table, having ordered the food. 'It has been very hard not to tell you until now because it is very exciting news: I have got a girlfriend.'

Though I hadn't seen that one coming, I try my best not to sound too surprised. 'A girlfriend? I've been away a less than a week. When did all this happen?'

'Saturday night. Vicky and I—'

'Your new girlfriend is Vicky?' I can't believe what I'm hearing. 'As in Vicky with the bobble hat?'

'She does not always wear a bobble hat. In fact I do not think I have seen her wear a bobble hat once since we were at Four Oaks. Normally she does not wear any kind of hat at all.'

My head is still reeling from James's news. 'I don't understand. How did this happen? I thought you didn't like her. In fact, nearly every time I've seen you with her, you've been categorically rude to her.'

'That was when I thought she was annoying. I do not think that now. Now I think she is lovely.'

I shake James's hand. 'Mate, that's amazing, I'm really chuffed for you.'

'I am pretty chuffed myself. She is beautiful, Danny. She is the most beautiful girl in the world and I cannot believe how lucky I am to have met her.'

James tells me the story of how they got together, a story that involves Vicky conning James into going to see a chick-flick, him getting drunk and Mr DeWitt calling the police because he thinks James has been kidnapped. Despite the madness of the story there's no doubting how happy James is. He can't stop smiling any time he mentions her name.

'Maybe I should go away more often,' I say.

James looks horrified at the thought. 'No,' he says. 'It has been very hard not having you around. It has been hard not having someone to talk things over with. I do not know what I would do without you. I do not know at all.'

As our breakfasts arrive, I take my turn to tell James about everything that has been going on in my life since we last saw each other and the full story of everything that happened to Helen too. He listens carefully to everything I say and when I eventually finish, he doesn't say anything at all for a while.

'You okay?' I ask.

James nods. 'I was just thinking of the best way to tell you that what happened to your sister was not your fault.' He stops and looks at me. 'It was not your fault, Danny Allen. You did not know what she was going to do. You thought you were doing the right thing. Just like I thought I was doing the right thing going out on the night of The Incident. Things happen all the time that we cannot control. Sometimes they are bad and sometimes they are good. It is just the way life is.'

When James and I finally reach home, the first thing we do is have a proper clean-up because he's invited Vicky over and this will be her first time seeing the place. I put James on vacuuming duty while I tidy but we've barely made any inroads when Vicky and her mum buzz up from the ground floor to let us know they've arrived.

The moment Vicky comes through the door with her mum in tow, she wraps me in a hug. 'Is your family problem sorted out now?' she asks.

I glance over at James and he shrugs embarrassed. I tell her everything is fine.

'We were really worried about you,' says Vicky, and glances over at James but he looks at the floor.

It's Vicky's mum who breaks the awkward silence. 'Well, I'm off now,' she says. 'Vicky, text me when you want picking up, okay?'

'I might do,' Vicky shrugs. 'But then again I might not. I've got a boyfriend now so it will depend on what he wants as well.'

Vicky's mum and I exchange pained glances.

'It's really good to see you again,' I say to Vicky as we return to the apartment, having waved her mum off the premises.

'And you too. I'm James's girlfriend now, you know.'

'I know. James told me this morning.'

She leans a little too close to my face. 'Did he say anything else about me?'

'Actually, come to think of it,' I reply, grinning in James's direction. 'I think he might have. I think he said something about you being the prettiest girl he's ever seen.'

She laughs, delighted. 'Did he really or are you just pulling my leg?'

'I wish I was. No man needs to hear his best mate being mushy over some girl . . . especially while he's eating breakfast.'

Vicky turns to James with the biggest smile on her face. 'I think you're the most handsome man I've ever seen,' she says. 'There isn't a single thing I'd change about you.'

Over freshly brewed mugs of tea we all chat for a while in the living room. Vicky and I make a couple of good-humoured jokes at James's expense that he joins in with, but mostly I just listen to the pair of them talking. Though it's been less than a week,

James already clearly adores Vicky and she obviously dotes on him. I find it impossible not to think that this is a happiness they both more than deserve. They've each had horrible things happen in their lives, things that would make most of us want to give up altogether, and yet here they are, somehow finding their way through it all to happiness.

I make lunch – nothing special, just soup and crusty bread – and then afterwards, at Vicky's request, we watch a film together. Reading between the lines, I get the impression that Vicky knows watching films is mine and James's thing, and this is her way of saying she'd like to be part of it too. However, when James goes over to the cabinet where we keep the DVDs and returns clutching *Die Hard*, assuring Vicky she will love it, I catch a look on her face that makes me think she might already be regretting her suggestion.

In the middle of the opening credits my phone rings. I check the screen. It's Martha. I haven't spoken to her since the night at the King's Scrivener summer ball and can't imagine why she's calling me instead of James. I wonder briefly if she wants my opinion on his budding relationship with Vicky but the moment I hear her voice, I can tell by its urgent tone that this isn't that sort of call at all.

'Are you with James?'

'He's right next to me. Do you want me to put him on?'

'Actually it's you I need to talk to . . . about something to do with James. Something important. Would you mind going some-where out of earshot for a moment? It won't take too long. I just need to be able to talk to you properly.'

I signal to the happy couple to carry on with the film without me, then head to my room.

'What's wrong? Is everything okay?'

'I've just heard some news that I think James is going to take badly,' says Martha. 'A solicitor friend of mine has just told me that the man who attacked James, Kyle Baylis, has applied for parole.'

'Oh, right. I wasn't expecting that. Still, there's probably no need to tell James, is there? I mean chances are a scumbag like that isn't going to get it, is he?'

'Well, that's just the thing: from what I can gather, Baylis has been a model prisoner and it's less a question of if he'll get early parole than when.'

I feel myself getting angry. 'After what he did to James? After everything he took from him? James is only just starting to rebuild his life. You should see him right now, Martha, he's so happy. If that creep gets out before he's served his time, I don't know what it will do to him.'

'That's what I'm afraid of. You know he still has dreams about Baylis? Really horrible ones where he even wakes up screaming.'

I think back to the first month after we moved into the apartment and James's nightmare that had woken me. James had told me that he couldn't remember what it had been about, but now I'm not so sure.

'What do you need me to do? Name it and I'll do it.'

'Well, you might think twice after you've heard what I've called to ask. The thing is, I've been going over it in my head pretty much constantly since I heard the news. Part of me doesn't want to tell him at all in case it comes to nothing but then if he hears about it some other way, we might not be there to support him.'

'So you want me to tell him.'

'Yes, if you don't mind. I've talked it over with Mum and Dad and I've persuaded them that you'd be the best person to break the news. My parents and I are too emotionally involved, and the last thing he needs is to have to deal with us getting upset. I think you're less likely to make a mess of it than we are. I know it's asking a lot, but if you'd at least think about it, I'd be really grateful.'

I think about James in the next room, so completely unaware of the bomb about to blow his fragile new life apart. I don't relish the idea of having this conversation with him but Martha was right: he didn't need to hear this sort of news from family, he needed to hear it from someone more detached but who at the same time still cared for him. He needed to hear it from a friend.

'I don't need time to think, don't worry, I'll do it. Just leave it to me.'

I wait until the film has finished and Vicky's mum has come to collect her before telling James that we need to talk.

James looks uncomfortably at me across the dining table where we're sitting. 'You are not going to try and talk to me about sex, are you? Because you do not need to, I have already had that conversation with my dad when he dropped me off at Vicky's last week. I know that everyone is only trying to help me but I am a grown man and I have not completely forgotten everything!'

'I really wish it was something like that but I'm afraid it's not.' I stop and draw a deep breath. 'It's about Kyle Baylis. I'm sorry to say this but it looks likely that he's going to be granted early parole.'

James blinks a number of times in quick succession, as though trying to establish whether he's heard me correctly.

'But that cannot be right. He has at least two years left to serve.'

'Well, nothing's definite yet, but Martha's heard about this on the grapevine and thought you should know.'

James starts to get upset. 'But that is not fair. Why does he get a second chance when I do not?'

'I don't know,' I reply. 'But what I do know is this: you've got me and you've got your family. And I promise you, we're going to do everything in our power to make sure it doesn't happen.'

34

James

'So are you going to tell me what's in the box file?' asks Danny.

It is midday and Danny and I are parked at the rear of Fitzwilliam and Partners, a barristers' chambers in Solihull, waiting for my parents and Martha to arrive. We are here because we are going to see my uncle Charlie who is a barrister. He is going to help us stop Kyle Baylis from getting parole.

I hand Danny the box file that has been on my lap the entire journey. 'It is everything that was written about The Incident in national and local newspapers. I thought Uncle Charlie might find it useful. I thought he might find some information in it that will help us win our fight.'

Because I was in hospital trying to learn how to walk and talk again, I do not remember anything about Kyle Baylis being sent to prison. My mum, Erica, kept cuttings of all the mentions of my case in newspapers so that when I got better, I could read all about what had happened for myself. I think she also did it because she believed that one day I would get better and go back to being an MP. She did it because she thought that there would be a day when life would get back to normal. That I might want to see all the things that had been written about me while I was recovering. But life never did get back to normal. Instead we had a new kind of normal: one where I could not think properly or walk properly, or talk properly. One where I had to leave the home I had made for myself and live with my parents instead. And so one day, after over a year of living at home, my mum, Erica, came to my room while I was watching *Friends* and told me that she had something for me. She gave me the box file with the newspaper cuttings in it and said, 'This is for you,' and she never mentioned it again.

I had been an MP and a successful businessman so my case attracted a lot of attention in the press. Lots of it was good and some nice things were said about me, and the things I had done. But some of it was not so nice. One newspaper wrote a story saying I had taken 'recreational drugs' on the night of The Incident, which was a lie. Another one wrote that a few years before The Incident I had slept with the wife of one of my colleagues and that was not true either. They also wrote stories about my family. Things that were true but which my mum, Erica, and dad, Don, would never have wanted people to know about. They wrote about how my dad had been made bankrupt twice. And they wrote about how when I was a teenager, my parents split up for a while. It was not fair of the newspapers to print those articles. My parents had not asked to be in the news like that. When I first read those things, I knew I could not ask my parents about them and so I asked Martha instead. I asked her what it had been like for our parents to read about themselves in the papers and she told me they had been heart-broken and my mum, Erica, had cried for days. I asked Martha why the newspapers would print articles like that about us and she said they had probably got the stories from Kyle Baylis's defence team. 'It's a tactic,' she explained. 'You leak stories about the other side to the media and that way your client seems less guilty.'

The only thing I liked about the box file was that it felt like it told a story.

A story where The Incident was the beginning and the court case was the middle and Kyle Baylis being put in prison was the end. Or at least that was how it was supposed to be.

Danny looks sad when he finishes looking through the cuttings. 'I knew some of what happened but not all this,' he says. 'It must have been a nightmare.'

'It was fine for me because I do not remember any of it,' I say as I spot my dad's car pulling into the car park. 'But it was horrible for my family. Kyle Baylis does not deserve to be free, Danny Allen. He does not deserve to be free at all.'

'So good to see you again, James,' says Uncle Charlie. 'Just wish it was under nicer circumstances.' He leads us through to a room that has a long table in the middle, with lots of chairs around the edge. Uncle Charlie is not really my uncle. He is an old family friend who I have known since I was a child. His children, Thomas and Sabina, are the same age as Martha and me and when we were young, we would visit each other's houses all the time. I think my mum said that Thomas works in the city now and Sabina in advertising. I have not seen them for a very long while, but I remember them being nice when I knew them.

'Much as I'd love to be telling you some good news, I'm afraid the outlook isn't great,' says Uncle Charlie once we are seated. 'The facts are that with the time spent on remand and time served to date, Baylis is already over two-thirds of his way through his custodial tariff. Add to this written reports of impeccable behaviour while incarcerated and confirmation of an offer of full-time employment as a trainee mechanic at his uncle's garage on his release and I'm afraid to say that as galling as it no doubt is to hear, there's actually very little we can do to stop this.'

'That can't be right,' says Martha. 'There has to be something. We can't just stand by and let that bastard walk free.'

Uncle Charlie gives my dad a funny look and Dad gives him a funny look back. 'Do you want to take this one, Don?' he says.

We look at my dad, wondering what he is going to say. 'When I was arranging this meeting, Charlie did outline one thing we could do but I've already ruled it out.'

'What was it?' asks Martha. 'Surely if there's even the slightest chance it will make a difference, then we should do it.'

This time Dad gives Mum a funny look.

'Martha, I'm afraid your father and I have already ruled it out,' says Mum.

'On what grounds?' asks Martha. 'Surely this is a family

decision. Whatever it is, James and I should have a say. We're not children, so stop treating us like—'

'All of us except James would need to submit impact statements to the parole board,' says Dad. He looks very tired.

'Why except James?' asks Martha. 'Why can't he do it too? He's the injured party.'

'I'll take this shall I, Don?' says Uncle Charlie. 'The law says that where a victim has been rendered mentally incapacitated by injuries sustained as a result of the actions of a plaintiff, family members may submit victim impact statements on behalf of the injured party.' My mum gives Uncle Charlie another funny look and then he turns to face me. 'Basically, James,' he says, 'what it would mean is that your family – rather than you – would need to write letters to the parole board explaining all the different ways life has been difficult for them these past three years because of the injuries you sustained.'

'But my life has not been difficult,' I say. 'Okay, it might have been at the beginning but it has not been for a long time.'

Everyone apart from Danny looks away as if they know something I do not. No one says anything. And then slowly, very slowly, I realise that the reason they are not talking is because I have made their life difficult but they do not want to say so in case they hurt my feelings.

I look at Danny to see if he knows what I should do, but he shrugs as though he does not know what to do for the best either. This is a decision I am going to have to make on my own.

I stop and think about how scared I am of hearing what my family really think of me.

But then I think about all of the nightmares I have had about Kyle Baylis.

I think about how scared I am that he might be set free.

And then finally I think about the newspaper cuttings in my box file and the way he hurt my family.

'I want you all to do it,' I say, trying my best not to get upset. 'I want you to tell the parole people what it is like to live with me. I am giving you my . . . permission. You do not have to worry about my feelings. All you need to do is tell them the truth.'

For the next few days I try hard to be positive, even though I do not feel positive. I tell myself that I am not going to let Kyle Baylis spoil things. I decide that I will do things to cheer myself up. And so I see Vicky and go out for nice meals, and even buy myself some new clothes because the July weather is really warm. For a while I feel okay. But then one night Danny and I go for a curry and when we return home, there is an envelope propped up on the kitchen counter. The envelope is addressed to me.

'Who do you think it's from?' asks Danny.

'Martha,' I reply. 'I would know her handwriting anywhere.'

I tear open the envelope. Inside it are two sheets of paper. On the top sheet it says this:

Dear James,

This is a copy of the victim impact statement I sent to the parole board. I agonised for hours over whether I should show it to you because I would sooner die than hurt your feelings. But I also hate the idea of keeping secrets from you, and I hate the idea of sharing such personal thoughts with a complete stranger about my brother who I love more than life, when I've not even told you myself. I would love it if you chose not to read it but I also believe that you deserve to make that choice for yourself.

Love always,
Martha.

I show the letter to Danny.

'What do you think I should do?'

Danny shrugs. 'This isn't my decision to make but if it was me, I'd leave well alone. Then again, what do I know?'

I decide that Danny's made a good point and I leave the letter unread and go to bed. But then I cannot get to sleep. I just keep thinking about it and so after an hour I get up out of bed, go to the kitchen and read it.

To whom it may concern,

Although my mother only gave birth to one son, as her only other child I have known two brothers. The first was the most wonderful and charming man I have ever met. He was a man full of passion, energy and drive who dedicated his life to making this world a better place.

The second came into the world on the evening of 26 February 2012 as a result of the actions of Kyle Baylis. Though this new brother came into being an adult, in truth he was little more than a baby to begin with. Unable to speak, move or eat, unable to control any of his most basic bodily functions, my parents and I spent many sleepless nights wondering desperately if we could cope with this new addition to our family for yet another day, all the while hoping beyond hope that he would still be there tomorrow. We took nothing for granted. We had to take each day as it came.

Three years on, my brother has moved into an apartment albeit with the support of a full-time carer. He has recently joined a support group for people who have sustained injuries like his own and as a result of joining that group has embarked upon his first romance.

I am thrilled that my second brother is showing all the determination and drive of the first. I am humbled by his achievements, the everyday battles he undertakes that, because of the health I take for granted, I don't even consider worthy of a second thought. I love my second brother dearly, I would give my life for him a thousand times over without pause for thought. Despite this there isn't a day that goes by when I don't wish I could have my first brother back. There isn't a single day when I don't mourn for the memories that have been lost forever or for the in-jokes we shared as children to which now only I know the punchlines. I miss my brother so much that some days it's all I can do not to scream with rage. I miss my brother so much that I have to work constantly to keep myself from considering the gaping hole in my heart where he belongs. I miss my brother so much that I've lost relation-

ships, hopes and dreams for the future because I can't get over the fact that the brother I knew will never be again. It is for these reasons and more, which would take me a lifetime to document, that I strongly object to early parole being granted to Kyle Baylis, the man responsible for changing all of our lives forever.

Yours sincerely,
Martha Esme DeWitt

35

Danny

'You promise you will let me know if you hear anything, won't you, Danny? Even if support group has not finished?'

'Of course I will. I've already spoken to Tanya and filled her in so if I do hear anything, she'll be fine with me coming to get you early. I promise everything's sorted.'

James doesn't look convinced. 'It is going to be okay, isn't it, Danny? The parole board will not let Kyle Baylis free after they have read my family's letters to them, will they?'

'You know I can't say for sure, James, but I'm hopeful.'

'But we have got a good chance though, haven't we? You said that my mum and dad and Martha's letters were very moving.'

'They were.'

'So you think the parole people will find them moving too?'

'I can't say for sure but I'd be surprised if they didn't.'

'And if they do, they will not let Kyle Baylis go free, will they?'

'If the letters do the trick then no, they won't grant parole and he'll definitely have to stay in prison a little while longer.'

I glance at the clock on the dashboard and so does James. 'I think you'd better be getting off if you don't want to be late.'

James doesn't move. 'Maybe I should not go this week.'

'It's up to you but perhaps it will help take your mind off things.'

James thinks for a moment. 'Okay, Danny. I think I will go after all.'

He gets out of the car but only manages a few steps before he stops and turns as if he's just remembered something important. I lower the car window.

'Did you forget something?'

'You do promise you will let me know if you hear anything at all, won't you?'

I nod. 'Yes, James, scout's honour.'

James smiles. 'Were you ever a boy scout?'

'No,' I reply. 'But I don't think it matters. I promise, as soon as I hear anything, I'll come and get you.'

It's been over a month since we first learned that Kyle Baylis might be released from prison early but the wait is finally over. The parole board are meeting today and although I am aware it could go either way, I feel hopeful that they will make the right decision. I can't imagine anyone reading the letters that James's family had written to the parole board and not being deeply affected. They are such raw testaments of grief and loss that I could barely read them myself. Mrs DeWitt's letter mentioned how she used to love the sound of James playing the piano and how since the accident he hadn't gone anywhere near it. Mr DeWitt talked about his need to protect his son and how frightened he was at the prospect of a future where he wouldn't be there to keep him safe. And then there was Martha's letter in which she talked about missing her 'other' brother. They are all so moving, so heartfelt, so unrelentingly honest that I can't imagine them not having an impact on the parole board's decision.

As I start up the engine and watch as James disappears inside the building, I'm struck by how difficult these past few weeks have been for him. His nightmares have become more frequent and Baylis seems to be the only thing on his mind. He's been uncharacteristically quiet and hasn't wanted to go out much, as though expecting to find Baylis lurking around every corner. He even asked if I thought Baylis talked about him or made jokes about him to his friends in prison. I'd said no and tried to reassure him, but my words felt hollow. I didn't know what kind of a monster Baylis was or whether he felt any remorse for what he had done. All I knew for certain was that he alone was responsible for where James was today, and as such deserved at the very least to serve the remainder of the paltry sentence he'd been given.

With the big decision looming I, like James, felt I could do with something to take my mind off things so rather than go back to the apartment, I decide instead to get a food shop in, and drive to a nearby supermarket.

As I'm pushing my trolley along the fruit and vegetable aisle, I become aware of a large group of small children wearing high-vis jackets, rummaging through the produce in front of me. A young woman, also wearing a hi-vis jacket, claps her hands together briskly and the children immediately gather around her. She holds aloft a sweet potato and asks if anyone knows what it is called. Several small hands shoot up into the air and she rewards one tiny boy with a warm encouraging smile as he shyly volunteers the right answer.

Though these children are considerably younger than Leila, I can't help wondering whether she ever went on a trip like this when she was younger, maybe even to this very supermarket. I think of her eagerly answering questions and soaking up knowledge, much as I had at school, and feel a pang, not for the first time, about all the things I'd already missed out on as she'd been growing up. Now she was a year away from finishing secondary school and I didn't even know if she was considering sixth-form college or thinking about university.

Since Helen died, I'd tried my best to forget about my own route through the education system, as in my mind it was inextricably linked with losing my sister. But with the perspective I gained after seeing my parents, my opinion has gradually shifted. The truth is that I had been lucky to have a teacher like Mrs Ashworth, who was so patient and kind and had seen something in me that no one else had. And for all my regrets about the direction my life has taken, none of this was ever Mrs Ashworth's fault. I'd come to realise that what had happened could still have happened had I left school at sixteen to work in a factory or building site like the rest of the kids I grew up with. Bad luck isn't the preserve of an educated life, any more than good luck. Time and chance happen to us all.

As I make my way past the children and their teacher, who is making them laugh as she waves around a courgette as though it were a magic wand, I smile to myself and hope that Leila, like me, has had the benefit of knowing what it's like to have a good teacher in your life.

I carry on with the rest of my shopping, even making a detour along the entertainment aisle in order to pick up a couple of films that I know James hasn't seen, and as I arrive at the checkout, I feel quite optimistic about what's left of the day. Joining the queue behind a young woman and her toddler, I begin unloading my shopping on to the conveyor belt when my phone rings. It's Mr DeWitt.

I listened carefully to everything he told me. How the parole board had remarked on the particularly 'moving and heartfelt' letters written by the DeWitt family. How they had studied the reports submitted by prison officers too. And how ultimately, given the time that Baylis had served on remand and his exemplary behaviour whilst in prison, it meant that they felt they had no choice but to release him on parole. I listened to everything and yet I still couldn't quite believe what I was hearing. It simply refused to sink in.

'But they're not actually going to release him, are they?'

'I'm afraid they have no choice.'

I feel myself getting angry. 'Of course they have got a choice. Everyone's got a choice. Why do people keep hiding behind that kind of excuse?'

'Are you all right, Danny? If you're feeling upset, perhaps I should be the one to break the news to James.'

'No, I promised James that I would tell him the moment anything happened, and I'm not about to let him down now.'

As I end the call, the cashier looks up at me and I realise for the first time that the young woman with the toddler is nowhere to be seen, and I am now at the front of the queue. 'Do you need any bags for your shopping today?'

For a moment I stare at her, not even managing to verbalise a reply, but then as I come to my senses, I offer a simple shake of my head and then, leaving my shopping on the conveyor belt, I run towards the exit as though my very life depends on it.

It's a quarter to twelve as I reach the room where James's support group session is taking place. And yet, despite having driven like a maniac in my desperation to get there as quickly as possible, I find myself unable to go in. Partly it's because I know this is perhaps the last moment that James will have the true peace of mind he deserves, but mostly it's because the door to the room is open slightly and I can see a young man I don't recognise talking to the rest of the group.

'I'll be twenty . . . twenty . . . twenty-nine in ten years' time,' he says. 'Right now I live with my parents even though lots . . . lots . . . of my old friends from school have gone off to uni . . . but when I'm twenty-nine, I don't want to be still living with my parents. We don't like to watch the same things on TV or eat the same food although Mum's Sunday . . . dinners are amazing and so even if I did move out, I'd still come back home on a Sunday because I like the dinners – chicken and gravy, and lots of veg, and stuffing balls, and sometimes if we're lucky, those tiny sausages too.'

The young man stops talking and smiles as though he's imagining one of his mum's dinners is right in front of him. I look over at James, who is sitting next to Vicky, and they are both smiling too.

'Your mum's dinners sound amazing,' says Tanya, the group's leader, attempting to get the discussion back on track. 'But you were telling us about where you'd like to be ten years from now.'

The young man sits up with a jolt, looks around him wide-eyed and then apologises. He tells the rest of the group how even though his parents are pretty cool, in ten years' time he doesn't want to still be living with them. He tells them that in ten years' time he wants to be living with his girlfriend and their Staffordshire bull terrier. He then explains that he doesn't have a girlfriend right now or a dog but thinks he will have both in the future. He tells them all that his girlfriend in the future will be really nice and will like doing the same things as him and she won't mind that sometimes it takes him a while to say what he's thinking because she will be kind.

When he says that last bit, James looks over at Vicky, not knowing that she is already looking over at him. It is a look of complete and utter adoration.

'That sounds lovely,' says Tanya to the young man. 'And ten years from now when you're living with your girlfriend and your staffie, do you think you will be working?'

'Definitely,' says the young man. 'I really like video games and I'm quite good at them, and I have ideas for new games all the time so I think I will be doing that.'

'That's a really hard job to get into,' says a larger man wearing shorts that reveal a tattoo of a dragon on his leg. 'I've got a cousin who wants to work in computer games and he's been trying for three years and he hasn't got anywhere, Miss.'

'Miss,' says the young man. 'Everton isn't allowed to interrupt me like that, is he?'

'No you're right, he isn't, is he?' says Tanya. 'We wait for each other to finish speaking before we—'

'I don't know what video games are,' says an elderly lady. 'Do you need a dice to play them? When I was a girl, I used to love playing card games. Patience was always my favourite.'

'While I'm grateful for your lovely contribution, Alice,' says Tanya. 'It's Jake's turn to speak and so I think we ought to be listening to him.'

'But I interrupted you, not Jake,' says the elderly lady. 'I'd never interrupt Jake, that would be rude.'

Tanya rubs her temples as if she's got the beginnings of a headache coming on. 'Come on, troops,' she says, 'please, let's all listen to Jake.'

'I don't know what else to say, Miss,' says the young man. 'I just know that ten years from now I'm going to be really happy, and my life is going to be completely different than it is now. I probably won't be coming to group any more because I will have learned all the things you're trying to teach us, but I might come along every now and again just to say hello.'

Everyone claps when the young man says he'll come and see the rest of the group in ten years' time. Then James raises his hand as if he would like to take his turn speaking and, noticing him, Tanya gives him the nod.

'Ten years from now I would—'

James stops speaking as a woman roughly my age with bright pink hair points at me. 'I think there's somebody at the door,' she says, and everyone in the room looks in my direction. I have no choice but to go in.

'Sorry to interrupt,' I say to Tanya, 'I spoke to you earlier. I'm Danny, James's friend.'

'Oh yes, of course,' she replies. 'I take it there's news then? Well, of course, James, you can leave group early.'

I look over at James but he doesn't move. 'Come on then,' I say, 'let's go and I'll fill you in on what's happened.'

James shakes his head. 'I have changed my mind. I do not want you to tell me outside. I want you to tell me now while I am with my friends.'

This sounds like a terrible idea. 'Are you sure?'

I watch as Vicky squeezes his hand, and then he looks at me and I can see from the tears in his eyes that he already knows what I'm going to say. 'Yes,' he says, 'I am sure.'

36

James

Danny and I are in the car. We are looking at my parents' house through the windscreen. In the boot of the car is a suitcase. Inside the suitcase are enough clothes, toiletries and DVDs to last a week, maybe two.

'Are you sure this is what you want?'

I turn to Danny and nod. 'I . . . I just want to be somewhere else for a while.'

'Of course you do. I get it completely but I can't help thinking that if you let this affect you so much that you leave your own home, then doesn't it mean that Baylis wins?'

I try to see Danny's point of view but it just will not come. 'But he has already won, hasn't he? He is free now. He can do what he wants and go where he wants.'

'But you're forgetting he's still on probation. If he messes up, then he'll be right back where he started.'

'But he will not mess up, will he? He did not mess up in prison so why would he now?'

'But you've worked so hard to get where you are today, I just think it's wrong to give up now. Why not stay? Why not fight? Why not see if we can get through this together?'

I close my eyes. I feel like a phone with only a little bit of battery left. I could switch off completely at any minute. 'What if I was out with Vicky and he walked past us in the street? What if I was out with you and he sat down right next to us? What would I do if he said something to me? Or made fun of me? Or laughed right in my face?' I reach down for the handle and open the car door. 'I just want to be somewhere else for a while,'

I say again as I get out of the car. 'I just want to be somewhere I know I will not have to see him.'

When Danny told me that the parole people had said Baylis could go free, I did not understand how such a thing could happen. I still do not understand. It made no sense. Why did him hurting me not count for anything? Why did my life not matter to the parole board? No one could answer my questions, no matter how often I asked them. I spent a long time in my room thinking about it. Danny tried to cheer me up by making me nice food and coming up with plans for things to do. But I did not feel hungry and I did not feel like going out.

Then yesterday my parents came to visit. I think they came because Danny had asked them to. He told them he was worried about me and did not know what to do. I was in my room when they came. They knocked on my door and asked to come in, and the first thing I said to them was, 'I want to go home.'

'But you already are home, darling,' my mum said. 'Don't you know where you are?'

I think she thought that I was confused. But I was not confused. Danny understood though.

'I don't think he means here,' he said. 'I think James means home to your house.'

'Is that right?' asked my dad. 'Do you want to come home with us?'

'Yes,' I replied. 'Yes, I do.'

My parents wanted me to leave with them straight away, but I asked them if it would be okay if Danny dropped me over in the morning. 'I just want one last night here,' I said.

Danny helps me unload my things from the back of the car and as we walk to the house, my parents open the front door. They are all happy and jolly to have me home but when I look at Danny, he seems really sad. I feel worried that he does not think I care about him. I feel worried about leaving him on his own. But after everything that has happened, I am so very tired. I do not feel strong enough to look after anyone, not even myself.

My parents show me up to my old room. 'Look,' says Dad, 'we've even got a new TV for you.' He points to a very big TV in the corner of the room. 'The man in John Lewis said it was top of the range.'

I try to smile but cannot quite manage it. Instead I say thank you, and then I stand at the window and stare out into the garden and watch some magpies pecking at moss on the roof.

'I'm sure you'll be putting it through its paces and showing us all what it can do later,' says my dad, but I do not say anything. I just carry on watching the magpies.

Everyone is quiet for a moment and then Danny says, 'I think it's time for me to go.'

While my parents unpack my things, I go downstairs with Danny and walk him to the door. 'Are you disappointed in me?' I ask quietly.

'Of course not,' says Danny. 'You just take it easy for a bit and when the time's right, you'll come back.'

I nod and look down at my feet. 'I will, won't I?'

'Of course you will,' says Danny in a voice that makes me think that he knows I am never coming back. 'Take care of yourself,' says Danny, and he pats me on the back. 'And any time you fancy going out for a drink, just give me a call.'

That night, after we have eaten, I ask my parents what they are going to do for the evening. When they tell me that they will probably be in the living room watching TV, they ask if I am asking because I want to join them. 'You don't have to ask, you know,' says Mum. 'You can join us any time. This is your home.' I tell them that I am feeling tired and that I might watch TV with them another night. Then I sit on the stairs, wait until I hear them turn on the TV, then go to my room. Once I am sure that it is safe, I close the door, walk over to the wardrobe and start pushing it away from the wall. It is very old and quite heavy and it takes me a long time but eventually I push it far enough so that I can properly reach the wall. Then I ball up my fist and I punch the wall, and when I feel like that is not enough, I start kicking it too. I pretend the wall is Kyle Baylis. I pretend that every blow is hurting him and not me, and I only stop punching and kicking when my hands and feet get so sore that I cannot feel them any more. Out of breath, I stand for a moment looking at the patches of blood on the wallpaper, then push the wardrobe back in place and crawl into bed.

A few days later, while I am sitting in my room waiting for Martha to come and visit me, there is a knock at my door. Because I think it is Martha, I call for her to come in, but the person who comes in is not Martha. It is Vicky.

I have not seen Vicky since the day I got the news about Baylis's release. We have texted a lot though. In my texts I have tried my best to explain to her that right now I do not really want to be around people, but she has not listened. Instead she has called me every day and left messages and sent me cards and flowers. It is very sweet of her but at the same time it is all a bit too much. This morning for instance, she sent me a text telling me she was going to get her mum to drive over to my parents' house so she could come and see me. I texted her back at least half a dozen times telling her not to. And now here she is, wearing another one of her posh dresses – this one is blue and gold with diamond patterns – standing in the middle of my room, holding a bunch of flowers and a box of chocolates.

'These are for you,' she says, handing the gifts to me. 'And this is for you too,' she says, and then she presses her lips against mine so hard that afterwards I can feel her lipstick on me.

I put the flowers and the chocolates on the table. 'I thought we agreed you would not come.'

'No,' says Vicky. 'You asked me not to come but I didn't agree to anything. People who are down shouldn't be on their own because it only makes things worse. People who are down should be with people who love them and care for them and want to cheer them up. And that's what I'm here to do. Make you happy.'

I hear my mum, Erica, coughing nervously and it is only then that I realise she is in the room too, hidden by the door, and that she has heard everything Vicky and I have just said.

'I'll just leave your lunch here on the floor,' she says. 'Let me know if Vicky would like anything to eat.'

After Mum leaves, Vicky and I both stare at each other not saying anything.

'I have missed you,' she says after a while.

'I have missed you too.'

'It doesn't much feel like it,' she says as we sit down on the sofa. 'It almost feels like you don't want me around.'

'Of course I want you around,' I say, and I place my hand on hers. 'It is just . . . well . . . things are difficult for me right now.'

Vicky frowns. 'But why are they difficult? Nothing's really changed, has it? So what if the guy who hurt you is free? It's not like he's going to hurt you again, is it?'

'You do not understand,' I say, feeling myself getting annoyed.

'Then explain it to me,' says Vicky. 'Tell me why it is you feel the way you do.'

'It would not make a difference even if I did,' I say without thinking.

'What do you mean by that?' asks Vicky.

'Nothing,' I say, wishing I had kept my mouth shut. 'I did not mean anything at all. Let's talk about something else.'

'I don't want to talk about something else,' says Vicky, taking me by surprise with her anger. I have never heard her raise her voice before now. 'I want to talk about what you meant,' she continues, 'and I want to talk about it now!'

'I just got confused,' I say. 'I honestly did not mean anything by it.'

Vicky will not let it go. 'What did you mean? When you said I wouldn't understand. What was it you were trying to say?'

'I just meant . . . what I was going to say was, you would not understand because the way we got our ABIs is different. But I did not mean it, Vicky, honestly. I just—'

Vicky slaps me hard across the face. 'How dare you!' she yells. 'How dare you suggest that your ABI is worse than mine because I got mine rock climbing! I was doing an activity that I loved, I did all the things I was supposed to do and wore all the protection

I was supposed to wear, and I still lost someone I loved very much, and my ABI still happened to me. I didn't ask for this, James! I didn't deserve it either. My ABI happened to me just like yours happened to you and it's not fair that you think yours is worse than mine. It's just not fair!'

I try to calm her down. I try to explain that I did not mean what I had said. But everything I do and say only seems to make her angrier, until finally she gets so angry that she stands up and runs out of the room. I call after her to stop but she ignores me. By the time I reach the top of the stairs, she has already opened the front door and run outside. I struggle down the stairs as quickly as I can and when I reach the door, the first thing I see is Vicky's mum hugging her daughter. With all the noise it is not long before my parents come outside too, wanting to know what is going on.

I feel like the worst person in the world.

I am the worst person in the world.

I hate seeing Vicky like this.

I hate knowing I am the person responsible for making her miserable.

I take a few steps towards her. 'Vicky, I am sorry. Please do not cry.'

'Go away and leave me alone!' she yells. 'Just go!'

My head feels all fuzzy.

I do not know what to do. I look to my parents, hoping they might help me sort things out.

'Why don't we all come inside for a cup of tea?' says Mum. 'I've got some lovely fresh ginger cake we could all have while we talk things over.'

'I don't want any ginger cake,' says Vicky to her mum. 'I just want to go home.'

'Darling, don't you even want to try and patch things up?' asks Vicky's mum. 'I really do think James is sorry for upsetting you.'

'I don't care if he's sorry,' says Vicky. 'I just want to go.'

'But I am really sorry,' I tell her. 'Really I am. I did not mean it. What I said was stupid. I just got confused that is all. Please stay, Vicky. Please stay and sort things out.'

She does not stay.

She does not try and sort it out.

Instead she gets into her mum's car, then her mum gives me a sort of sad shrug and she gets into the car too. I watch as the car disappears down the drive. Inside my chest, my heart feels like it has just broken into a million tiny pieces.

37

Danny

It's three o'clock in the morning and I am alone in the apartment frantically trying to get hold of a complete stranger on the phone. On the kitchen counter there's a scrap of paper with a phone number written on it, and to the left of it an open bottle of whisky and a tumbler. As I am only a matter of moments away from using up my last reserves of willpower, I have given myself permission to pour a drink into the tumbler unless the person I am calling picks up within the next thirty seconds. I am well aware that if I then drink from this tumbler, I will not only drain the glass, but the bottle too and then every drop of alcohol in the apartment. And because that won't be enough (to an addict like me there is no such thing as enough), I will then probably drive to the nearest all-night shop and since I now have more money than I know what to do with, the amount of booze I buy will only be limited by my ability to carry it.

This is what will happen if the stranger I am calling doesn't answer their phone in . . .

Ten.

Nine.

Eight.

Seven.

Six.

Five.

Four.

'Hello? Who is this?' Her voice sounds groggy as mine would've done if I'd been woken in the middle of the night.

'Hi, is that . . .' I glance over at the scrap of paper in front of me, on which she'd written her name and number. What novel had she torn it from again? Thomas Hardy? George Eliot? Something like that. I read the phone number and the name underneath. Kaz. Her name is Kaz.

I decide to start over. 'Hi, is that Kaz?'

'Who is this?'

'You won't remember me. I came along to an AA meeting at George Street maybe four or five months ago. I'd never been before and I haven't been since, but you were there and we spoke and—'

'—I gave you my number.'

'You wrote it on the back cover of the book you were reading along with your name, tore it off and gave it to me.'

'You were the guy that came to AA that week because you'd had a wobble and needed . . . what was it you called it? That's it . . . a top up. I remember you. I was reading . . . what was it? Oh, yes it was . . . *A Room With a View*. I think I've still got it somewhere . . . but what am I doing going on about books? You haven't called for a catch up. You're calling because you're in trouble aren't you? You're about to relapse?'

I glance at the tumbler again. Maybe I was exaggerating. One drink couldn't do that much harm, could it? Catching myself before I reach for the glass, I take a step back to put myself out of harm's way.

There's no point in lying to her. 'I really want a drink. I want a drink more than anything.'

'So I'm guessing it's been a tough day. Why don't you tell me about it?'

'But you don't even know me. Why would you want to listen to me rambling on about my problems?'

'Because people have done the same for me. And because maybe one day you'll do the same for someone else. Now stop stalling and start talking. What started this all off?'

Do moments like this have a beginning? Aren't they always bubbling away just under the surface? For a moment I think about replying the same to Kaz, but then the longer I think, the more I begin to realise that yes, moments like this do have a beginning, and for me that moment was a week and a half ago when I left James at his parents' and realised that he was probably never coming back.

It had been hard leaving him behind. After nearly six months together I felt like we were a team, and taking him back to his parents' house, even though it had been what he'd wanted, felt like I'd let him down. As though I was betraying all the faith he had in me. Wasn't I supposed to step up when he couldn't? Wasn't I supposed to be the one who was always in his corner? I'd said as much to his parents and Martha before I left but I don't think they really understood what his return meant.

'I think James just needs a rest,' Mr DeWitt had said. 'Erica and I have discussed it at great length and we fully expect him to return to the apartment when the time is right. And of course when he does return, we fully appreciate that he'll only be happy if you're there too.'

'That's very kind of you to say,' I replied, wondering why they still weren't getting it. 'And I'm more than happy to hang on for as long as you think is appropriate but I'm telling you now, I don't believe that James is coming back to the apartment. He's simply too scared. If we could've convinced him to not come back here, we might have been in with a chance but as it is, I just feel like he's given up.'

As I returned to the car, wondering what I was going to do next, Martha followed me out of the house.

'I think you're right about James,' she said. 'And although my parents wouldn't admit it in a million years, I think they know you're right too. I think they'd like to believe that keeping him safe is the best thing for him but the truth is he's only ever going to be safe if he believes he can look after himself. And you were so close to giving him that, Danny. I just wish . . .' Her voice faltered and I put my arms around her. This is the end of the road for us all, it seems. 'I don't know what we would have done without you,' said Martha, drying her eyes. 'You gave us hope.'

For the next few days I tried to convince myself that I was wrong, that James would return, and that everything would get back to normal. But then those few days became a week and that week became two, until tonight when it finally dawned on me that I needed to start making plans. Kind as they were, the DeWitts weren't going to bankroll me indefinitely, nor should they. While my bank account was currently the healthiest it had ever been, the fact remained that in a matter of weeks I could be without either a job or a place to live.

A quick search online threw up endless results for care worker jobs, most of which were appallingly paid, and as I scanned through some of the better ones, I wondered if I'd even got it in me to do this kind of job again with someone who wasn't James. It wasn't long before I gave up the search and, feeling hungry, rummaged around in the cupboard for something to eat, and that's when I'd come across the half-drunk bottle of single malt whisky that Mr DeWitt had bought James as a moving-in present. The internal argument I had about pouring myself a drink had been an interesting one, because it didn't go at all the way I had expected. I told myself I didn't want a drink because I felt particularly sad and wanted to change my mood, nor even that I thought I deserved one after all my years of abstinence. No, the reason I decided to pour myself a drink was that right there and then I couldn't think of a single reason not to. My ex-girlfriend had cheated on me and thought I was a fraud, my own daughter didn't want to see me, and James, who had been the focus of so much of my attention for so long, had given up and no longer needed me. 'And so really,' I'd reasoned, 'who is there to stay sober for?' and before I could reply, I'd grabbed the bottle, found a tumbler and stood contemplating both.

Back in my drinking days my poison of choice had been cheap vodka or lager. Never whisky, and certainly not an outrageously expensive single malt, but as I'd carefully removed the lid from the bottle and inhaled the peaty aroma of the contents, it occurred to me that I had never wanted anything in my life quite as much as I wanted this drink right now.

Standing there, staring at the bottle, I'd recalled in edited form all the times in the past I'd rejected a drink and added another day to my abstinence record. I did a rough calculation in my head. Fourteen years multiplied by three hundred and sixty-five days (give or take the odd leap year and an inability to recall the exact date I stopped drinking) worked out to be five thousand one hundred and ten days sober. It was a big old number and yet part of the appeal of succumbing to the temptation in front of me was the idea of wiping out my record once and for all. Yes, it would take a long time to get that record back, but part of me couldn't wait to feel the sweet relief of having no record to contend with at all.

Picking up the bottle, I'd tipped it gently towards the glass when I recalled my encounter with Kaz on the day I'd left that AA meeting. I remembered how she'd insisted on giving me her number despite me telling her I was fine. I'd carried that scrap of paper around in my wallet for weeks, nearly emptied it into the bin twice and eventually dumped it in a drawer, but I'd never once thought of throwing it away. It felt like a talisman, warding off evil spirits that would lure me back to drinking. As long as I had the piece of paper, I was reassured whenever I came across it that I would never need to make that call.

As I sought out that scrap of paper, bent and faded now, it occurred to me that it wasn't so much a talisman as a hand reaching out to me in the darkness, offering me hope where it seemed there was none, offering a connection when I felt most alone.

Kaz and I talk through the night. I make myself comfortable on the sofa and she tells me the story of her life from beginning to end, and I tell her mine. And somehow, by the time we stop talking at around a quarter to five as the sun begins to rise, not only do I not want to drink any more but I also don't even want it in the apartment.

'And I bet it was the really good stuff too,' says Kaz, as she listens to me drain the contents of the bottle down the sink. 'Why do relapses never happen when you've only got access to the cheap stuff?'

Returning to the living room, I sit down and rub my eyes. I feel exhausted, like I could sleep forever.

'I should probably let you go,' says Kaz, when I yawn for the third time in a row. 'You sound like you're dead on your feet. Take care of yourself, Danny, and if you ever get like this again, just remember you can call any time.'

'Wait!' I say, fearing she might already be gone. 'I feel like I should . . . I don't know . . . take you out for dinner or buy you a present or something.'

'No need,' she replies. 'It's like I said at the very beginning, someone did it for me, and today I get to pay them back by helping you. If you really want to repay me, find someone who needs help and give it to them. It's that simple.'

When I finally make it to bed a few minutes later, I sleep like a dead man and only wake when my phone rings,

I don't recognise the number. And I'm tempted to switch it off and go back to sleep because I know it'll be someone in a call centre somewhere asking whether I've been in an accident recently. At the last moment, however, I wonder if it might be Kaz ringing to check that I'm okay and so I take the call.

'Hi,' says the young, female voice at the other end of the line. 'Am I speaking to Danny Allen?'

'Whatever it is you're selling, I'm not interested, okay?' I reply, unimpressed that she knows my name. Given that at least ninety-nine point nine per cent of the modern world features on a digital database somewhere it's not that impressive.

'I'm . . . I'm not selling anything,' says the voice. 'My name's Leila and if you're Danny Allen, then I'm pretty sure you're my dad.'

38

James

'Would you like a cooked breakfast or something else?' asks my mum, Erica.

'I do not mind,' I say, pulling the sleeves of my jumper down over my bruised and battered knuckles so that she cannot see them.

'Okay then, I'll make you a cooked breakfast. Any preferences as to what sorts of eggs you might like with it? I can do scrambled, poached or fried. And I think there are mushrooms too, that is if your father hasn't eaten them all.'

'Mum, I do not mind. I will eat whatever you give me.'

'Okay then, I'll make you a nice fried egg to go with your cooked breakfast because even though it's not the healthiest option, I think it's the best flavour combination, don't you?'

'I will eat it no matter what sort of eggs you put with it.'

'Okay, then cooked breakfast with a fried egg it is, and mushrooms if there are any. Would you like any condiments? We've got tomato ketchup or I think there's a touch of Worcestershire sauce left from when your father had a small obsession with it a while ago. Which would you like?'

'They both sound lovely,' I say, trying my best to stay calm. 'Either of them will do.'

'Right then,' says Mum, 'that's a cooked breakfast with a fried egg and bacon with mushrooms if there are any and condiments on the side. Would you like a cup of tea with it or some decaffeinated coffee or even a hot chocolate?'

'Tea sounds lovely.'

'Or I think there might also be a tiny bit of . . .' Her voice goes quiet as she sees the angry look on my face. 'I'll just bring the tea,' she says, and then leaves the room, closing the door behind her.

Now I am home, my mum, Erica, does not cut up my food like she used to.

She does not feed me broccoli at every meal either.

What she does do, though, is ask me questions: lots of them.

Sometimes I think she is never going to stop. She asks me how I am, if I slept well, if I am hungry, if I am comfortable, if there is anything she can get me, if I would like more, if I would like less, or if she has done something right, and even if she should turn the light out. She asks so many questions all day everyday that I do not know what I think about anything any more. She asks so many questions and I do not care about the answers. All I care about is Vicky and how I can get her to stop hating me.

Since Vicky split up with me I have rung her over and over again, trying to speak to her. But whenever I call, I only ever get her voicemail. I send her lots of texts too. Texts telling her how much I love her. Texts telling her how sorry I am. Texts begging her to forgive me. Until this morning she never replied to any of my calls or messages. But today when I was in bed with the curtains closed, wondering what I had done that was so bad that I was not allowed to be happy, I got a text from Vicky. I was so excited when I saw her name. I thought, 'This is it, she has finally forgiven me,' but it turned out not to be that kind of text at all. 'I used to think that everything in life happened for a reason,' it said, 'but you have made me wish I'd never had my accident because then I'd never have met you. Please stop contacting me because I never want to see you again.'

It was a mistake coming back here. I know I should have been stronger. I know I should not have cared that Baylis is free. But it was just so hard to let go of the idea of him being out in the world. It was just so hard to stop thinking about how he might hurt me again.

More than anything, I wish I could be the kind of person who is not scared of life. I wish I did not feel like running away. I have only been home a few days but I already feel like I am shrinking. I am becoming like the person I used to be. The person I was before I met Danny. I hate that person. And I hate that person's life.

It was Danny who made me believe that I could live my own life again. He made me think that anything was possible. He was disappointed in me when I came home. I know he was. Even though he did not say it I know that he felt like I was letting him down.

I feel so angry.

Angry and helpless.

I am a thirty-six-year-old man who cannot look after himself or the people he loves.

This is no way to live.

This is not a life worth living.

I look at the flowers on the windowsill that Vicky brought for me when she visited. They are so bright and cheering and pretty, like her.

I make a decision.

I am not going to let Kyle Baylis hurt me any more.

I am not going to let him take Vicky away from me.

I am going to get my life back.

There is a knock at the door.

Mum comes in with my breakfast and sets it down on the table next to the wardrobe. 'Here you go,' she says. 'There weren't any mushrooms, I'm afraid. Is there anything else I can get for you?'

I look at my breakfast, then at the flowers on the windowsill and then at Mum. 'Yes, there is something,' I say. 'I would like a lift to Birmingham please. I need to see Danny. It is urgent.'

Mum does not say yes straight away. Instead she asks me lots of questions which I refuse to answer. In the end I tell her that if she does not want to give me a lift, then I will get a taxi instead. When I say this she says, 'Fine, James, just let me get my shoes on and I'll take you.'

On the way to Birmingham Mum tries to get me to tell her what is so important that I need to see Danny instead of just talking to him on the phone, but I tell her that it is between me and Danny, and that she does not need to know. I know that she is annoyed by this but I know that if I tell her what I am doing, she will try and stop me, and I do not want to be stopped. I know that she loves me and is only trying to be kind, but this is my life I am fighting for. I am not going to let myself be talked out of what I need to do.

'How long do you think you're going to be?' asks Mum when we reach the apartment building. 'I only ask because I've got a few errands I need to run later today.'

'I do not know how long I will be, Mum, but you do not need to wait. I will be fine making my own way back, thank you.'

'But what if Danny's not there? I don't want you to be left stranded.'

'I will not be stranded,' I say as I get out of the car. 'I will be home. Do not worry, everything is going to be fine.'

Danny cannot believe his eyes when he sees me. 'James! What are you doing here? Is everything okay?'

'I need your help.'

'Help? To do what exactly?'

'Find Kyle Baylis.'

Danny looks surprised. 'And . . . when you do find him, what exactly are you going to do?'

'I am going to tell him what I think of him because then I will never have to be scared of him again.'

Danny shakes his head as though he thinks this is a bad idea. 'What's brought this on?'

I tell Danny about splitting up with Vicky. 'It was my fault. I said something stupid. Something I did not really mean. Something I only said because I wanted her to understand how scared I am of Baylis. I think Vicky is the most amazing person I have ever met. I do not want to split up with her, Danny. I want us to be together.'

'So your plan is, what? Confront Baylis, give him what for and hope that it somehow solves all your problems with Vicky?'

I feel like Danny is teasing me. 'I thought you were on my side. That is why I am here.'

Danny apologises. 'Of course I'm on your side, mate, it's just that I don't think you're really thinking things through. Say we do find him – and I'm not saying we will – how would it work? Would we wait for him outside his parents' house? What if he's living somewhere else? What if he's already started work and is out all day? And even if we do get the right house at the right time of day, what then? You say your piece, he says his, then what? Is it really going to make a difference? Is it really going to help get Vicky back? Maybe you'd be better off talking to her, rather than facing up to Baylis. It's certainly going to be a lot easier.'

'You do not understand,' I say. 'Of course I want Vicky back. But this is not just about her, it is about me too. I need to do this so I am not scared of him any more.' I look Danny in the eye. 'So are you going to help me or not?'

'You're going to do this no matter what I say, aren't you?'

I do not even have to think about my reply. 'Yes.'

'Looks like I've got no choice, then,' says Danny, looking at his watch. 'But if you want me to help you do your thing, then you're going to have to come and give me some moral support while I do my thing first.'

I do not know what Danny is talking about. Although now that he has said this, I can see that he is dressed smartly in a suit jacket and brand new jeans. 'What is your thing?'

'My daughter,' replies Danny. 'She called. She's changed her mind about meeting me. And today's the day. I can't keep her waiting, James, I'm already fifteen years late as it is.'

On the way over to Leila's house in Tamworth, Danny tells me all about his first conversation with his daughter. He tells me they talked about music and his parents and lots of other things too. I can see how happy this is making him because even when he is talking, it is as though he has got a great big grin on his face.

I look at Danny and smile. 'And now you are going to meet her. You must be excited.'

'You'd think so, wouldn't you?' says Danny. 'But to be honest I'm sick with nerves. I just want her to like me.'

It is odd seeing Danny like this. It is a side of him I have never seen before. 'Of course she will like you. You are a very likeable person.'

'But what if she's angry with me for not trying harder to get in touch with her all these years? She's every right to be and I've got no defence.'

'You will not need one. I think your daughter is meeting you because she wants to get to know you, not shout at you. I think she wants to find out who you are.'

'And what if she doesn't like who I am? I'm a thirty-six-year-old man who until this year had never had a steady job. I'm not exactly superdad material, am I?'

I think for a moment. 'You could tell her about me. You could tell her how when you first met me I was not very good at being around people and did not like going to places . . . and then you can tell her how you helped me become someone different. Someone who was not always scared, someone who was not always hiding. I think if you tell her all that, she will be impressed.'

Danny shakes his head. 'Who you are now is down to your own hard work, not mine. I just happened to be around when you were ready. What I did was no big deal.'

'Well, it was to me. Lots of people tried to help me be independent, but you were the only one who treated me like I was just the same as you.' I want to say more. To tell Danny more about how much he has changed my life, but I cannot seem to find the words and even if I could, I am not sure I am brave enough to say them out loud.

'So this is it,' says Danny as he slows down in front of a small terraced house. 'Any last words of advice?'

I think for a moment and a good joke comes to mind. 'Just be yourself: everyone else is taken. I read it on a mug at Vicky's house. It is meant to be a joke but I think it is very true.'

Danny laughs and unfastens his seatbelt. 'Because this is our first meeting, I can't imagine I'll be more than an hour – I don't want to overwhelm the poor kid – and when I'm done, we'll go and do your thing, okay? Any problems just give me a shout.'

'Do not worry about me, Danny Allen. I will be fine.'

Danny nods. 'Okay then, I suppose this is it,' he says. 'See you on the other side.'

39

Danny

As I get out of the car and walk towards Leila's house, my heart starts thumping so fast that I feel like I might pass out right here in the middle of the road. Even if I don't, I'm pretty sure I'll throw up before I reach her front door. I just hope she's not looking out of the window.

The closer I get to my destination, the more I think about what her first impression of me will be. Ever since she agreed to meet up with me, I've found myself unable to walk past men with their children – in parks, in the supermarket, in cafes, streaming in and out of the local school gates when I'm out for my morning run – without studying their look. When I meet Leila, I want to look just like them, like a regular dad with a regular life, even if I'm not exactly either of those things. I don't want to look cool or down with the kids; I want to look like someone she can trust, someone she won't have to be ashamed of, someone she'll want to get to know.

I ring the doorbell and after a short wait Simone answers the door, dressed in a white blouse, skinny jeans and trainers. Somehow she manages to look infinitely cool and effortlessly elegant, and I immediately feel overdressed. I look down at my jacket and wonder what I was thinking, wearing clothes that make me look like I'm going on a first date.

'Looking sharp, Mr Allen,' says Simone. She's got a mischievous twinkle in her eye, as if she knows exactly what it is I was trying to achieve and just how far I am from getting there. 'Leila said she'll be down in a minute. I think she's just getting her head together.'

I follow her into the kitchen. While she puts on the kettle, I sit down at the dining table. Without asking if I'd like a drink, she takes out three mugs from the cupboard in front of her and puts a teabag in each. When she notices me looking at the mugs, she laughs. 'We're all out of coffee and I figure even if you're not much of a tea drinker, you won't say no to having something to do with your hands.' When the kettle boils, she makes the teas, hands one to me and then offers me a biscuit to go with it, which I refuse. 'So how are you feeling? Nervous?'

'Like I could throw up at any second. You?'

Simone laughs. 'You'll be fine. I've packed the boys off to their gran's for a few hours so you won't be interrupted. I think Leila's really looking forward to finding out more about you. Ever since you came to see me, she's been bombarding me with questions. In the end she was asking so many that I had to say, "If you're that curious why don't you ask him yourself?" I don't know whether it was what I said or whether she came round on her own – who knows with teenagers – but a little while later she came to me and said that she wanted to call you. And here we are. I bet you never thought this day would come.'

'Did you?' I ask, and I look at Simone. It feels like a lifetime since we were together.

Before she can answer, Leila comes into the room. She looks beautiful. Stunning, even. She's wearing a navy hooded top and navy leggings and under her arm she is carrying what looks like a photo album. She looks so much like Helen that for a moment I almost stop breathing. Leila's just a kid. It's enough that she's meeting me for the first time, she doesn't need to be burdened with the knowledge that she's a carbon copy of her dead aunt too.

'Sorry to be late,' she says. 'My hair wasn't doing what I wanted it to.'

'I have that problem all the time,' I say, and both Leila and Simone stare at my shaven scalp and smile. 'Maybe you can give me a few pointers later.'

'Maybe,' she replies. She picks up the mug of tea that her mum made, takes a sip and then stops suddenly. 'This is mine, isn't it?'

Simone laughs. 'Who else would it be for? The invisible man?'

There's a brief lull in the conversation. I feel like I'm in danger of coming across as a bit of a dud. I search my brain for a suitable topic for discussion but my mind's gone blank. Suddenly a picture of her room pops up in my head and in the absence of any other ideas, I go with the first question that occurs to me.

'How's netball?'

Leila and Simone both look at me as if I'm mad.

'Netball?' says Leila. 'Er . . . I don't play netball.'

'Oh, I'm sorry, I thought I remembered seeing some trophies when your mum showed me your room, when I came to visit the other day.'

Leila and Simone both laugh.

'Those aren't mine,' says Leila. 'They're mum's. We were clearing out the loft the other day and I found them in a box. She wanted to throw them away but I wouldn't let her. I'm hopeless at sport, I hate all that running around. I'm more of a yoga type. Mum and I go every Monday to a class at the gym round the corner. Mum always falls asleep in the relaxation bit at the end. I don't normally mind but last week she woke herself up snoring. It was so embarrassing. Everyone was looking at us like we were a right pair of freaks.'

'Watch it, you,' says Simone. 'Or I'll nick your phone and start WhatsApping your friends telling them how much I love you.'

'You wouldn't dare!' scoffs Leila.

Simone laughs. 'Just try me, kid.'

There's something really lovely about the warmth between them. They're more like sisters than mother and daughter. Much as I'm aware that I've only just met her, and how mad it is to even be asking myself this question, I can't help wondering if a day will ever come when Leila and I will be like this. If there will ever be a time when we'll have in-jokes and anecdotes of our own.

'Sorry about that,' says Simone, suddenly conscious of my presence. 'We get a bit giggly sometimes.'

Leila laughs. 'You more than me.'

'That's debatable,' says Simone. She looks from me to Leila and back again, as though checking we're both ready. 'Right, I'm going to leave you two on your own for a bit, if that's okay. Are you going to stay in here or move to the living room?'

'Here's good,' says Leila. She picks up a biscuit and sits down at the table opposite me. 'Then once we've worked our way through these chocolate digestives we won't have to go far to get more.'

Simone tells us that she'll be in the living room if we need her and just like that, she leaves, instantly halving the energy in the room. Panicking at the thought that an awkward silence might in some way be an indicator that our relationship is doomed, I throw out an icebreaker, the first thing that pops into my head. 'So . . . how are you?' The moment the words leave my mouth I realise how hopelessly inadequate my question is, given we have a whole lifetime to catch up on. 'Don't answer that. It's a ridiculous question. How are you supposed to answer something like that?'

'Pretty easily. I'm okay, thanks, I got the results back for a Spanish test yesterday and I was top of the class. First time ever.'

'Fantastic. You must be really pleased.'

'I am actually. My Spanish teacher doesn't like me. So I studied really hard for it just to spite her.'

I can't help but laugh. 'Ah, spite, the great motivator. When I was at school, I had a Latin teacher who could not stand the sight of me. I won a regional competition for Latin translation once just to spite him, so I hear where you're coming from.'

'Wow, you did Latin? Did you go to school in the eighteen hundreds then?'

'Not exactly, although it was a pretty long time ago.'

'Did you like school?'

'Yeah, I suppose I did. Do you?'

'Yeah, it's okay. I can't wait until I get to college though. I hate wearing school uniform. It's really ugly. What was your uniform like in your day?'

'I think it was a black blazer with red piping on the collars, which doesn't sound that bad, but then twice a year on what they called King's Day we all had to wear a sort of weird red robe thing. I think it was supposed to represent something important from history, but I don't think any of us really knew what. We only put up with it because in the evening there was always a big banquet and the puddings were amazing.'

'Latin and weird ceremonies? What school did you got to? Hogwarts?'

'Pretty much. Minus the broomsticks. It was a boarding school.' I feel funny telling her this. I don't want her thinking I'm anything special, but the very least I owe her is honesty.

'Boarding school? You mean like in Enid Blyton books, with a trunk for tuck and stuff like that?'

I nod guiltily.

'So are you posh then?'

'No, far from it. I won a scholarship.'

Leila smiles knowingly. 'So you're not posh but you are brainy. That's it then, next time I get stuck on trigonometry, I'm calling you.'

We chat a while longer about school and teachers but then her phone buzzes with a text. As she reads it, she fills me in on some drama that's going on between her friends. I love hearing her talk like this. I could sit and listen for hours. She's so funny and warm and clever and like Helen in so many ways. If only she was here to meet her, I'm sure that they would get on like a house on fire.

I suddenly realise that I haven't spoken in ages as, it seems, does Leila, who stops mid-sentence. 'Sorry, I'm going on a bit, aren't I?'

'No, not at all, I was just thinking how lovely it is hearing you talk.'

She laughs. 'Mum says I could chat for England.' She picks up the photo album that she brought in with her. 'I thought you might like to see some photos of me when I was a baby and stuff.'

'Great idea, I'd love to.'

As we flick through the album, Leila chats about the photos. She tells me all about the birthdays, Christmases, family celebrations and holidays depicted in these captured moments, times that I have never been, and never can be, part of. I've missed so much of her life, all the while wasting mine. Time suddenly seems like the most precious commodity, more valuable than gold or silver. I tell myself I'm going to spend it more wisely from now on. I tell myself that I'm going to make each moment count.

'That's me and my half-brothers at the pool at our hotel in Alicante last year,' says Leila, pointing to a photo in which she's grinning with her arms around a young boy and a baby. 'It was the best holiday ever because they had a really good kids' pool we could all go in together.' She considers me carefully for a moment. 'Have you got brothers or sisters?'

The question takes me by surprise. I'm answering before I know what I'm going to say. 'I have . . . I mean I had a sister. She died when she was seventeen.'

Leila's hands go up to her mouth. 'I'm sorry. I didn't know, Mum didn't tell me. Was she sick?'

What exactly to say? I don't want to lie but the truth might be a little too much, even at fifteen. 'It was . . . it was an accident. A terrible accident. We were all very sad about it for a very long time. But it wasn't anyone's fault. It was just one of those things.'

'What was her name?'

'Helen.'

'Did you get on well together? I love my brothers to bits but sometimes they really wind me up.'

'She was the best sister in the world. And I miss her every single day.'

I sense Leila wants to ask more questions, but she's stopped by a knock on the door followed by her mum coming in.

'Sorry to disturb you,' says Simone. 'But something weird just happened. I was coming through the hallway on my way upstairs, when I heard a noise and noticed these lying on the mat by the front door. They're not yours, are they?' She holds up a set of keys that look a lot like my own, even down to the Blackpool tower key fob that Maya bought for me as a joke present.

Taking the keys from Simone, I go outside to see what James is playing at. But while the car is exactly where I'd left it, James is nowhere to be seen. I look up and down the street to see if he's stepped out for a breath of fresh air but there's no sign of him. Crossing the road I check the car doors but they're firmly locked. I reach for my phone to call him. It rings out for a moment and then finally, much to my relief, James picks up.

'James, mate, where are you? Is everything okay? I've just found the car keys. I didn't know where you were. What are you doing?'

'I have found him, Danny.'

'Found who?'

'Kyle Baylis.'

My stomach flips over. This makes no sense. I should never have left him alone with all this going through his head. I try to keep my voice calm. 'James, just tell me where you are and I'll come and get you.'

'No thank you, Danny, please do not worry. I will be okay. I do not need help. I hope you will understand, but I need to do this on my own.'

'Do what on your own?'

'It is okay, Danny, really it is. But I have got to go now.'

And before I can say anything else, the line goes dead.

40

James

I should have looked at my watch.

Or my phone.

When Danny got out of the car to go to see his daughter I should have looked at my watch or my phone because then I would know how long I had been waiting for him to come out. But because I did not look at my watch when Danny got out of the car, I do not know how long he has been away or what time he might be back.

It feels like he has been gone for hours already.

Dr Acari says that people with ABIs sometimes find it hard to keep track of time. If I had been thinking properly, I could have set an alarm on my phone and waited until it went off. But I think I must have been distracted because I did not.

Because I am thinking about time and setting alarms, I take out my phone and the first thing I see is the photo of Vicky that I use as my screensaver. It is my favourite picture of her. I took it the very first time I went to her house. She looked so pretty. I wish I could have known then how things would have turned out because I would have taken more photos of her. Details are important when a day is special to you. But the difficult thing is that quite often you do not know a day is special until long after it is over.

Vicky.

I decide that it is probably not a good idea to keep looking at photos of Vicky. She does not want to see me any more and looking at photos of her is only going to make me feel sadder. Instead I decide that I could pass the time looking up a few things online. I start by looking up release dates for new films on DVD that I might want to buy. There are quite a few good ones coming out soon and so I pre-order them. Doing this makes me feel a lot better than I did when I was staring at Vicky's photo. Now, at least I have something to look forward to.

I start another search: 'Good films coming out this year'. I look through the results, but all they do is remind me that Vicky and I had our first date at the cinema and then I feel sad all over again.

I decide that I am not going to look up anything else online in case I get reminded of Vicky again. It works for a while but then I start thinking about how unfair it is that Vicky and I have split up. I really miss her. I wish she were here right now. But she is not, and she never will be now, and it is all Kyle Baylis's fault. Without thinking, I type, 'I hate Kyle Baylis' into the search box on my browser.

There are 409,000 results. Most of them are news reports about my court case. None of them are about hating Kyle Baylis.

Next I type, 'Kyle Baylis address Birmingham'. I am hoping that the Internet might tell me where Baylis lives so that I can show Danny the address when he comes out. It would be good if I could do that, because I do not think Danny believes I am serious about confronting Baylis. I think he thinks I am just angry. But I am not just angry. I am going to find him and tell him what I think of him.

When I press return, there are 1,899,087 results. The top one is for a dentist called Kyle Baylis, who lives in Birmingham, Alabama. There are just too many results to go through.

I get another idea.

In the search bar I type: 'Baylis garage Birmingham UK'. I do this because I remember that someone in Baylis's family has given him a job as a mechanic. That means that they must have a garage. And if the person who owns the garage is Kyle Baylis's uncle or cousin on his dad's side, then there is a very good chance that they might have the same surname too.

I cannot believe my eyes when I see the top result: 'Baylis Auto Services, Endicott Street, Nechells.'

I tell myself that just because this garage has got the name Baylis in it, does not actually mean that Kyle Baylis is definitely working there.

I tell myself that Kyle Baylis's family might just as easily own a garage called 'Cooper's' which they bought from a man called Cooper.

I tell myself that all the while I am thinking Kyle Baylis is at Baylis Auto Services he could just as easily be at Cooper Car Services.

This is what I tell myself but I am having a very hard time believing me.

I think this is definitely the garage where Kyle Baylis is working. It is the only garage I can find in the city with the name Baylis in it. I do not think it is a coincidence. Vicky once told me that she did not believe in coincidences. She said that she believed in destiny. When she said this, I thought to myself: 'I do not believe in destiny because coincidences happen all the time.' But now I am beginning to wonder if she might not have been right after all.

Maybe destiny does exist.

Maybe destiny is trying to tell me that Kyle Baylis is at Baylis Auto Services.

Maybe destiny is telling me that even if I do not believe in it, then I should at least find out, one way or the other.

I decide I will text Danny so he can tell me how long he thinks he is going to be. But then I think: What if Danny and Leila are having a lovely time together? The last thing he will want is to get a text from me asking him how long he is going to be.

I do not know what to do.

I think for a while and then I have an idea.

My idea is this: I will set the timer on my phone for one minute and if Danny has come out by the time it goes off, I will stay. But if he has not come out, I will go and find out if Baylis Auto Services is where Kyle Baylis is working.

Danny is nowhere to be seen when the timer goes off and so I call a taxi. The lady at the end of the line asks me where I want to go and because she finds it difficult to understand my voice, I have to tell her four times. Then she asks me where I want to be picked up from. I have to tell her another four times that I do not know but will find out for her. When I find out where I am on my phone, I have to tell her another four times where I am before she understands what I have said. It is exhausting. 'Your car will be with you in five to ten minutes,' she says, and then I set the timer on my phone for ten minutes and wait.

When the taxi turns up with two minutes and twenty seconds to spare, there is still no sign of Danny. I decide that this is destiny's way of saying that it is okay for me to go to Baylis Auto Services. As I get out of the car though, I realise that Danny has left the keys in the ignition. I am not sure what to do for the best. If I leave them in the car, someone could steal it. But if I take them with me, then Danny will not have any way of getting home. In the end I ask the taxi driver if he would mind waiting, and then I cross the road and post the car keys through Leila's mum's letterbox.

'Where to, mate?' asks the taxi driver when have finally got my seatbelt on.

'Baylis Auto Services on Endicott Street, Nechells in Birmingham please.'

He looks over his shoulder at me. 'I'm sorry, didn't quite get that, mate.' I tell him again and this time he understands. 'Got a bit of car trouble, have you?' he asks as we pull away.

'No, I am not allowed to drive because I have some problems with one side of my body not working very well.'

'I think you must have a similar thing to a cousin of mine. He talks a little like you. Good bloke though, and I'll tell you what, even after his accident he can still beat me at poker.'

For a moment I think he might have stopped talking but then he asks me another question.

'So why are you going to the garage then? Picking someone up?'

'I am going to find out if someone works there and if they do, I am going to tell them what I think of them and then I am going to leave.'

'Okay,' says the taxi driver with a smile, as if I have made a joke. 'I suppose we'd better get a move on then.'

I time the journey with my phone. It takes twenty-five minutes to get to Baylis Auto Services. This is roughly the same amount of time it takes me and Abdul to exchange names and for me to tell him about everything: Kyle Baylis, splitting up with Vicky and moving back in with my parents.

'You see,' I tell him as we pull up on the opposite side of the road to the garage. 'If I do not confront Kyle Baylis, I am going to spend the rest of my life hiding from him and people like him. I do not want to do that.'

'I completely get what you're saying,' says Abdul as I pay him. 'If this had happened to me, I'd be just the same. But do you really think this is a good idea, my friend? It's not too late to change your mind.'

I shake my head. 'No thank you, Abdul, I really need to do this now.'

'Then at least take my card and call me when you want picking up. Be careful. He is obviously a very bad man and I would hate for anything bad to happen to you, my friend.'

'I would hate that too,' I say, taking Abdul's card, 'but I have thought about it a lot. And I think I hate being scared of him far more than anything else he could do to me.'

When Abdul's taxi pulls away, I stand and stare across the road at Baylis Auto Services. The area is not very nice. There are no houses of any kind. Just lots of factories and warehouses and boarded-up shops. Further down the road a big lorry making a delivery is belching black fumes into the air. Even just standing here I feel like I need a wash. There are no benches or even a wall for me to sit on while I wait. Instead I have to lean against the outside of an empty industrial unit. The metal grille on the front of the building is broken and there are lots of posters on the wall either side. Most are advertising nightclubs or concerts, but there is a group of them in the middle about a demonstration at the weekend organised by the Socialist Worker's Party.

Baylis Auto Services seems to be made up of two parts. On

the left there is a workshop. There are long strips of plastic sheeting hanging down over the entrance so I cannot see inside. On the right there is a sign saying 'Reception'. Behind the counter in reception there is an older man with a thick grey beard. He is leaning on the counter and talking on a phone.

The man with the thick grey beard is not Kyle Baylis. In fact, he does not even look a little bit like Kyle Baylis.

I begin to think that I might have made a mistake.

I check my phone. No message from Danny. I check again a little while later. Still no message. I wish Danny were here because he would know what to do. I think about crossing the road and asking the man with the thick grey beard if he knows Kyle Baylis, but I feel a bit too scared. I decide instead that the best thing I can do is just wait. It is nearly midday and if Kyle Baylis does work at Baylis Auto Services, then maybe he will go for lunch soon. Then I will see him and I will know for sure I am in the right place.

After ten minutes a group of men push their way through the long plastic sheeting in front of the workshop and begin walking down the street.

There are five of them.

They are all wearing blue overalls covered in grease and big black boots, and they are laughing and joking.

I feel like I want to be sick.

I stare very hard at the men. None of them is Kyle Baylis. They are not even close. I have looked at Kyle Baylis's photo online a lot and I know exactly what he looks like, and these men are not him.

I feel sad and relieved.

I have got it wrong.

Kyle Baylis does not work here.

Abdul said he would try to pick me up if he was free. I make up my mind to ask for him directly because it has been nice talking to him. I take out my phone to call for a taxi, but then I spot another man leaving the garage workshop through the plastic sheeting. He is wearing blue overalls and big black boots like the other men. He is Kyle Baylis. I would recognise him anywhere.

I feel sick and my head feels all fuzzy.

I think: 'What if he sees me? What if he knows that I am here?'

He does not go the same way as the other mechanics.

Kyle Baylis walks in the opposite direction.

He is holding a plastic bag that looks like it might have his lunch in it.

My phone rings. I am so nervous that I nearly jump out of my skin. I check the screen. It is Danny.

'James, mate, where are you? Is everything okay? I've just found the keys. I didn't know where you were. What are you doing?'

'I have found him, Danny.'

'Found who?'

'Kyle Baylis.'

'James, just tell me where you are and I'll come and get you.'

Kyle Baylis is walking further away from me. If I do not do this now, I might never do it. But I cannot wait for Danny Allen to get here or it will be too late. Maybe this is destiny telling me I have to do this on my own. 'No thank you, Danny, please do not worry. I will be okay. I do not need your help. I hope you will understand, but I need to do this on my own.'

'Do what on your own?'

'It is okay, Danny, really it is. But I have got to go now.'

I switch my phone to silent and put it into my pocket.

I take a deep breath and then, like someone out of a spy film, I start to follow Kyle Baylis.

41

Danny

Standing next to the car I frantically redial James's number, but it just goes to voicemail. Simone and Leila cross the road to join me.

'Is everything okay?' asks Simone.

'Not really. My friend James, the guy I look after, he was supposed to be waiting for me in the car. I've just spoken to him, but he cut me off without telling me where he is. I'm worried that he's going to end up hurt.'

'But who would hurt him?'

'The thug who attacked him and left him brain damaged,' I tell Simone. 'His name is Kyle Baylis, and he was released early from prison a few weeks ago. This morning James came to me with some half-baked plan to find this guy and confront him. I told him I'd help him do it. I didn't mean it of course, I thought I'd be able to talk him out of it. But somehow while I was with you guys, he's actually managed to track him down and get himself over to where he works.'

'And you think this Baylis person will actually hurt your friend, even if he just talks to him?'

'I don't know, but I wouldn't like to take the chance. The thing is I've no idea how James even managed to track him down, so I haven't got a clue where he is.'

'What sort of phone has your friend got?' asks Leila, looking at my phone. 'Is it the same make as yours?'

'I think so,' I reply. 'His is a newer model though.'

'And do you know his password and everything?'

I nod. The amount of times James had locked himself out of his phone was unreal. In the end we decided that it would just be easier if I had access to all his passwords so that we didn't have to wait in line for a million years at the shop where we bought it, in order to get them to sort it out.

'In that case,' says Leila, taking my phone from me. 'I think we can find him.'

I give Leila James's email and password. She taps them into my phone. and seconds later I'm staring at a map of the city with a tiny red flashing dot in the centre of the screen.

'That's your friend,' says Leila, pointing to the dot. She makes the map bigger so we can see his exact location. Right now James is on Endicott Street in Nechells, in Birmingham, which according to the phone is about a half an hour drive away.

I now have a hunch how James found Baylis. He only knows four things about Baylis: his name, the city he lives in, his trade and the fact that he's been offered a job by a relative. I type all four facts into my browser. The top hit is for Baylis Auto Services, Endicott Street, Nechells. He really has found him.

I look at Leila. This is not at all how I hoped our first meeting would be. 'I'm really sorry but I'm going to have to go. You do understand, don't you?'

She nods. 'You've got to help your friend. I'll see you another day. I hope he'll be okay.'

As I head back towards Birmingham, breaking all manner of speed limits, I wonder if I should call someone and let them know what's happening. I think about the police but I'm not even sure what I'd say to them. After all, although James is vulnerable, it isn't like he's been kidnapped and while Kyle Baylis is an ex-con, as far as I know he hasn't actually done anything to James yet and might not do so at all. If not the police, maybe I should contact the DeWitts, but I don't want to worry them if there's a chance I can stop James before he does anything dangerous.

Not for the first time I berate myself for not paying better attention when James was talking about his plan to tackle Baylis. I should have tried harder to get across to James what a bad idea confronting him was. Men like him were hardly going to respond to reason. More likely he would become angry or defensive, and the risk of the situation getting out of hand was high. Even if Baylis had learned his lesson, for James the stress of confronting him alone might be enough to bring on another seizure.

I try James's phone again. It continues to ring out. Worse still a check on his location reveals that he is on the move. He's now two streets on from Baylis's garage and getting further away by the minute. What's he doing? Where's he going? I call again but there is still no answer. A thought crosses my mind. What if James has been mugged and the dot I'm following is some scumbag who has stolen his phone? I tell myself there's no point in speculating about worst-case scenarios. I'll have to deal with whatever I find when I get there, but for now the most important thing is getting to where I need to be as quickly as possible and to this end I make a decision to ignore the speed cameras and press down harder on the accelerator.

Thanks to a combination of a few green lights in my favour and driving like a maniac, I manage to get to the outskirts of Nechells way ahead of my phone's projected arrival time. James's red dot has for the past five minutes been stationary, leading me to believe he has either paused to rest somewhere or has come face to face with Baylis.

At speed I pull into the road where James should be and nearly crash into the back of a refuse lorry blocking the road. The more I sound my horn, the slower the binmen seem to do their job and when I look in my rear-view mirror, all I see a queue of traffic snaking out behind me, making it impossible to turn around and try another route. I'm stuck. There's nothing else for it: I abandon the car and start running.

The faster I get, the closer my own blue dot comes to James's red dot and when they're almost one, I look up to see him sheltering next to a bus stop, staring intently across the road at a row of shops.

'What were you thinking, coming all the way out here?' I say, when I finally reach him. 'Do you realise how dangerous this is?'

James shrugs. 'I am following Baylis,' he says. 'I found him,

Danny, I found him all on my own.' He points across the road to a seedy-looking betting shop sandwiched between a pound store and a fried chicken takeaway. 'He is in there right now, Danny, and when he comes out, I am going to tell him what I think of him.'

'James, you can't do that, mate. I know you think it's going to help matters, I know you think it's the answer to everything, but I'm telling you now it isn't. I'd never forgive myself if anything bad happened to you. Look, let's forget about this and go home.'

'You can go if you like,' says James, his voice clear and firm. 'I am not going anywhere.'

I think about calling James's parents or maybe even Martha in the hope that they can convince him to change his mind, but I can tell from the determination on his face that there's not a living soul who could talk him out of this now.

'You're going to do this no matter what I say, aren't you?'

James nods. 'I do not want to be scared for the rest of my life.'

'In that case, we'll talk to him together. Maybe that way things won't get out of hand.'

James shakes his head. 'Thank you, Danny, but no. I want to do this on my own. I want to stand up to him on my own.'

'But what if things get physical?'

James shrugs. 'He cannot hurt me any more than he already has.'

There's no getting through to him. 'You really think putting yourself in a position where you might get hit again is going to help matters?'

'It has to,' says James. 'It is my only hope.'

It feels like there's nothing more to say. Instead in silence we stand, eyes fixed to the entrance of the betting shop, barely daring to breathe. We don't have to wait long. An elderly man carrying a small white dog comes out first, closely followed by a young man in blue overalls, the top half of which are tied around his waist. Even if James hadn't shown me the newspaper cuttings, I would've known it was Baylis. He's got a thug's gait and holds himself like he isn't scared of anything or anyone. Even I'd think twice before tackling him.

I open my mouth to make one last ditch attempt to talk my friend round but he's already crossing the road. Baylis, meanwhile, is killing time. Leaning against the betting-shop window, he tears opens a new pack of cigarettes and casually tosses the cellophane to the ground. My every muscle is braced for the sprint I know I'm going to have to make and with each step James takes, the more convinced I am that this is going to end badly. I decide I can't afford to let him take the risk. Dodging oncoming cars, I manage to make it halfway across the road before I'm forced to a standstill by a steady stream of oncoming traffic and have no choice but to look on as James fearlessly approaches Baylis. When a break in the traffic finally comes I seize the opportunity but my timing's all wrong and I'm forced back once again narrowly avoiding getting flattened by an articulated lorry. Across the road through brief gaps in the traffic, I spy James and Baylis. James is doing all the talking and Baylis is listening, motionless. I'd give anything to be able to see Baylis's face but the angle's all wrong and I can't see a thing.

Eventually there's another break in the traffic and this time I make it all the way to the other side. Despite my desperation to come to James's aid, something holds me back. So far he appears to be handling the situation and I feel like I owe it to him to at least wait a while.

With the noise of the traffic however I still can't make out anything that's being said although Baylis appears to be talking now. Their back and forth goes on for what feels like an age and then suddenly it's over. Turning his back on James, Baylis walks quickly towards me and for a moment I wonder if he knows I'm with James but he doesn't even acknowledge my presence. He simply keeps his head down, eyes to the ground and walks away.

42

James

'That'll be six pounds eighty,' says the barman to Danny, even though I was the one who ordered the drinks.

'You're talking to the wrong bloke,' says Danny, pointing at me. 'He's the guy with the money.'

'Oh, sorry . . . I thought . . .' the barman fumbles for the right words and realising that there are none, lets his sentence fade away.

'I would like to know,' I say, pulling a twenty-pound note out of my wallet, 'what exactly was it that you thought?'

'It . . . er . . . doesn't matter,' says the barman quickly.

'I really hope that you did not think that just because I talk a bit funny and walk a bit funny that this guy,' I gesture to Danny with my thumb but give him a wink to let him know I am joking, 'is in some way in charge of me?'

'No . . . of course not,' stammers the barman. 'I just got mixed up, that's all. Happens all the time, mate.'

'Glad to hear it,' I reply and hand him the note in my hand and because I am feeling generous, tell him to have one himself.

Danny and I take a seat near the frosted-glass windows that overlook the busy street. The Bull's Head is not the sort of pub Danny and I would normally have chosen to go for a drink: the tables are sticky, the curtains are faded and the bar staff are not very friendly. The one good thing though, is that it is a short walk from the betting shop where I spoke to Kyle Baylis. Talking to Baylis was the hardest thing I have ever done and after it was all over, the one thing I needed was a drink. Even thinking about it now, sitting here in the pub with Danny, makes my hands start shaking all over again.

That is how nervous I feel.

I feel like I am full of energy.

Like I could pick up a car.

Or punch my way through a brick wall.

Or even tell off a stupid barman for making assumptions.

'So come on then,' says Danny, once we are settled in our seats and I have calmed down a bit. 'You can't keep me in suspense all day. Tell me what happened with Baylis.'

When I crossed the road over to where Baylis was standing, I was going to tell him exactly what I thought of him.

That was the only plan I had.

Tell him what I thought of him and then walk away.

I was scared how he might react.

I knew that if he tried to hit me, then there would not be very much I could do but I knew I had to go through with it anyway. But when I called out his name, something really odd happened: I found that I was not angry or scared any more. This was odd because I felt angry and scared when I first saw Baylis coming out of the garage. And I still felt the same when I was following him from the garage, all the way to the betting shop, and again as I crossed the road to talk to him. But the moment I opened my mouth and spoke to him, those feelings were not there any more. Instead I just felt sad for him. Up close he seemed a lot younger than I remembered. When I looked in his eyes, I could see that he knew exactly who I was. The funny thing is that he did not look angry or like he wanted to laugh at me. He looked afraid. As though he did not know what was happening. As though all he wanted in the world was to be safe again. It had never occurred to me that Kyle Baylis might sometimes be scared just like I am. I always thought he was the one who did the scaring.

'What are you doing here?' he asked. 'I know who you are.'

'I followed you from your work,' I said. 'I looked for garages with your family's name in them and guessed that this might be the one. I wanted to tell you what I thought of you. I wanted to tell you how you ruined my life.'

'So why don't you then?'

'I do not know,' I said. 'I do not want to now.'

We stood staring at each other for a long time, saying nothing, and then finally he said something that surprised me.

'I'm sorry,' he said. 'I know it's only words but I really am sorry. If I could go back in time to that day, I never would have gone out that night, I'd never have got in the state I got myself in. I'd never have hurt you. I'm sorry.'

That was the last thing he said to me. We stood for a while longer, saying nothing, and then he turned around and walked away and I could not think of a reason to try and make him stay.

'So that was it?' asks Danny. 'He told you he was sorry and that was enough? I'm surprised.'

'Me too. To be honest I am not sure I cared all that much about the apology. I . . . I think the important thing for me was that even though I had not said what I thought I wanted to say, I had at least done what I had wanted to do.' I stop and look at Danny. 'I do not have to be scared any more. I do not have to be scared of anyone or anything any more. From now on I can just be me.'

'Sounds like a good plan,' says Danny. Then I remember that today had been a big day for him too.

'I nearly forgot, how did it go with Leila? I hope I did not spoil things for you.'

'Of course not,' says Danny. 'It was brilliant. She was just as amazing as I knew she'd be. I could've talked to her all day.'

'I am really happy for you,' I tell Danny. 'And I am sorry if I nearly ruined things and I am sorry for making you worry about where I was.'

'It all came good in the end,' says Danny. 'Question is, what's next?'

'Next? What do you mean?'

'Well, Vicky, for example.'

'She does not want to see me any more.'

'And you're just going to leave it at that?'

'What else can I do?'

'Well, for starters,' says Danny, 'you can try not giving up. So you made a mistake, we've made enough of those between us. The question is what you do next: sit around feeling sorry for yourself or prove to Vicky that you've learned from your mistake?'

'I want to prove to Vicky that I have learned from my mistake,' I reply. 'That is what I want more than anything.'

'Good,' says Danny. 'Then finish up your drink and let's go. You've got some serious grovelling to do.'

On the way to Vicky's Danny tells me more about Leila and even mentions how much Leila looks like his sister Helen.

'It was the oddest thing,' he says, 'I kept thinking to myself if only my parents could see her. This would completely blow them away.'

'You should introduce them,' I say. 'It will be nice for them to meet their granddaughter.'

'It had crossed my mind,' says Danny. 'But it's still such early days. Leila's only just getting her head around me popping up from nowhere. The last thing she needs is a couple of brand new grandparents too.'

'Maybe you should just ask her,' I say, thinking about how all too often I keep things in my head without saying them. 'Maybe you should ask her and see what she says.'

For the rest of the journey we do not talk about Baylis or Leila or any of the other things in our lives. Instead we talk about favourite films and TV series for a very long time and then Danny goes quiet and says to me: 'Can I ask you a question?'

'Of course you can,' I say.

'Before your accident did you used to watch films and TV like you do now?'

'No. My mum says that before my accident I could not sit still long enough to watch a programme from beginning to end, let alone a whole film.'

'So where did it come from?'

'I do not know. I cannot remember a time before the TV arrived. I just know that when I was able to sit up and everything, it was there and I just started watching it.'

'And what about the whole thing with the *Friends* DVDs?' asks

Danny. 'I never really understood it. You used to watch them all the time when I first met you and now I can't think of the last time you got them out.'

'I do not know,' I say. 'They used to make me happy, like I was part of the world and not just hiding in my bedroom. I suppose, now that I have got different things to think about, I just do not need them so much any more.'

Danny's question stirs up so many thoughts in my head – things to do with The Incident, and things to do with what happened afterwards – that I only realise we are at Vicky's after he gives me a nudge and tells me that we have arrived.

'Are you sure this is a good idea?' I ask Danny. 'Vicky was very clear when I saw her last time that she does not want to see me again.'

'I think it's the best idea,' says Danny. 'I don't think I've ever seen you quite as happy as when you were with Vicky, and I think you made her happy too. If there's even a glimmer of hope that you two might get back together, I think you ought to give it a shot.'

Danny's words of advice are still going round in my head as I ring the doorbell. I tell myself that Vicky and I make each other happy. I tell myself that if there is a glimmer of hope, then we should give it a shot, but then through the glass I see someone coming to the door and seconds later it opens. It is Vicky's mum. My mind goes completely blank.

'Hello, James,' says Vicky's mum. 'Are you here to try and see Vicky?'

'I do not know,' I say. 'I think I am . . . yes, I definitely am . . . I am here to see Vicky. Is she here?'

'She is,' says Vicky's mum, 'but I'm not sure she'll see you. She's still very cross with you.'

'I know what I said was wrong,' I say. 'And . . . and . . . and that is why I am here. I need to tell her . . . I need to tell her—'

'You need to tell her what?'

Vicky's mum opens the door a little wider. Vicky is standing by her side.

'Hi, Vicky,' I say. 'I have really missed you. And I know that you are probably still angry with me but . . . but . . .' I am trying to think of Danny's advice to me, to remember exactly how he put it but it will not seem to come.

'What is it that you want, James?' asks Vicky. 'Just say whatever it is, say what's on your mind.'

'You are on my mind,' I say. 'You are always on my mind. I go to sleep thinking about you and wake up thinking about you and in between all I do is think about you. Sometimes I wish it was not like that because I actually quite like thinking about other things, like my phone and really good films and nice things to eat . . .' I stop and check Vicky's face just to make sure that she knows I am joking. She has got a big smile on her face so I know that she gets it. 'You see,' I say, 'because of the way I walk and the way I talk, some people think I cannot tell jokes but you know I can, and I know that because you have got a smile on your face. From now on that is all I ever want to do: put one smile on your face after another. I want you always to be happy.'

Vicky puts her arms around me. 'And I want you to be happy too,' she says. 'I've hated being angry with you. I don't want to fall out with you ever again.'

'And we will not,' I say. 'I promise.'

'And what about Kyle Baylis?'

'It is a long story but I am not scared of him now,' I say. 'I am not scared of anything any more. Especially now I have got you back again. Do you forgive me?'

'That depends,' says Vicky. 'How would you feel about going on holiday with me?'

'I would love it,' I say without thinking.

Vicky smiles. 'That's the right answer,' she says, and then she gives me a kiss, the kind of kiss I know I will dream about, the kind that no matter what happens in the future, I know I will never forget.

43

Danny

The luggage for James' ten-night holiday in Capri has been checked in and as we stand at passport control, all that's left for me to do is say goodbye.

'I really wish you were coming with us,' says James.

'Right,' I say, waving to Vicky and her parents, who are gesturing for James to hurry up. 'That wouldn't be at all weird, would it?'

He laughs. 'You know what I mean, Danny Allen. I wish you were coming because I know we would have a laugh.'

'I think you'll have a laugh anyway. Vicky's dad's jokes on the drive here were so awful, I'm beginning to think they might actually be genius.'

'If you think that is true maybe you are the one who needs a holiday,' says James grinning. 'He stops for a moment and looks at me. 'What will you do with your time off?'

'I haven't given it much thought,' I reply. 'Hopefully I'll see Leila, visit my folks, catch up with all of the things I've been meaning to do since forever and haven't gotten around to yet.'

'You won't have too much fun without me, will you?'

'I'll probably have no fun at all,' I reply, and then Vicky calls to James to hurry up and so I give him a quick hug and remind him to send me a postcard.

Despite his initial keenness, as the date of his holiday with Vicky got closer James had begun to have doubts.

'What if I do not like it?' he'd asked me at the pub a week before they were due to go.

'It's the Italian coast,' I reassured him. 'There's no way you won't like it.'

'Okay, then what if I do like the place but do not like being away from home for so long?' he countered.

'You're going to be with Vicky,' I said finally. 'The girl you faced up to your worst fears just to be with. I don't think you'll get homesick. I think you'll get to the end of your holiday and wonder where all the time went.'

The morning after James made his decision to go, the first thing he did was call his parents to let them know and the second thing he did was inform me that he was going to get a taxi and go shopping on his own for holiday clothes.

'You don't want me to drive you?' I asked.

'I like taxis,' replied James.

'And you're definitely sure about me not coming with you? I won't give you my opinion about anything if you don't want me to, if that's what you're worried about.'

'I just want to do it on my own,' said James. 'Well, as on my own as I can be when Vicky is making me text her photos of everything that I buy. She says it is so our holiday wardrobes do not clash but I am not so sure. I can text them to you too if you like.'

So that's what James did. He went shopping on his own, texted me over two dozen photos of clothes he'd purchased, then over the next few days he drew up a list of all the things he needed to take on holiday, gathered them together and packed them in his suitcase without forgetting a single item. Bright and early this morning I drove him, Vicky and her parents to the airport for James's first holiday abroad in three years.

As I return to the car I work through a mental list of things that I need to do. There is the small matter of telling my parents about the existence of their granddaughter, and the arrangement of their first meeting should they take the news well, and I also have an endless list of tasks to do around the apartment before James's return. I imagine the next few days will fly by and in truth, I am glad to be busy.

As I hit the motorway, my phone rings. My first thought is that it's one of the DeWitts calling to find out if James has departed safely, but when I check the dashboard, the number on the screen isn't one I recognise. As ever I'm tempted to ignore it but then curiosity gets the better of me.

'Can I speak to Mr Daniel Allen? It's Carole Pettier from university admissions. Am I right in thinking you left a message on my voicemail the other day? About undergraduate degrees in education?'

'I did, yes. I'd assumed you'd forgotten about me.'

'It's that time of year, I'm afraid. But better late than never, eh? Is now a good time to talk?'

I look at the queue of traffic up ahead. 'As good a time as any.'

It had been on a complete whim that I'd left the message a week and a half earlier. I'd been for my first meal out with Leila and we'd been talking about what she wanted to do after her GCSEs. She told me she wanted to do A levels but only in things she was interested in, like drama, psychology and art, and then after that while she knew she wanted to go to university, she had no idea what she might study.

Afterwards, on my way home I found myself thinking about her future and about my own too. I'm not sure whether it was all of our talk, or perhaps it had always been on my mind on some level, but I wondered if now wasn't a good time for me to return to education. James needed me less and less, and I didn't want to go back and do just any care work, so perhaps getting a degree might be a good idea. For the rest of the journey home I tossed the idea around and by the time I reached the empty apartment – James was out for the night with Vicky and her family – I'd made up my mind to put wheels in motion. Teaching seemed like a good fit for me, and looking up half a dozen courses online, I decided on one and gave them a call. When I didn't hear anything, I assumed that it wasn't meant to be, a sign that it wasn't the right path to follow. So what does it mean now that she's returned my call? Is it a sign that fate, or the universe or whatever, might actually have an idea of what I should be doing with my life, or is that more a case of wishful thinking?

My chat with Carole from university admissions lasts the entire journey home and ends up being more like a professional therapy session than a quick review of my CV. She has such a kind and easy-going manner that despite my efforts to keep the conversation short, she ends up coaxing my full life story out of me. I tell her about my parents, about KS, my time at Cambridge, my sister, my alcoholism and wilderness years, right up to and including my dropping James off at the airport. The moment I finish talking, I feel a heavy weight come down on my shoulders because I know that I've blown any chances I had of getting on the course by laying all my flaws out for her to see.

'Do you know what, Danny?' she says, after what feels like an extended awkward silence. 'I think you're exactly the sort of person who should be on this course. You're funny and clever but most of all you've got life experience, which, on a course that's ninety-nine per cent filled with kids fresh from their A levels and who – if you'll pardon my French – don't know their arses from their elbows, is going to give you a huge advantage. I've been doing this job for a long time and you're just the sort of person who has the potential to become a fantastic teacher. You're still going to have to formally apply to join the course but if you come in and see me tomorrow, I can help you with that. There will be a few other forms and tests you'll need to pass too but I'm not worried about those, from what you've told me. As far as I'm concerned, you've just bagged yourself the last place on our degree course. Congratulations!'

I don't know what to say. It all sounds so unreal. 'Are you actually talking about me being on a course starting in September?'

'Of course,' she replies. 'Weren't you?'

'Yes,' I reply. 'I was . . . it's just . . . it's full time, isn't it?'

'We do have a part-time course but it's fully booked, I'm afraid. Is that going to be a problem?'

'Absolutely not, I'll sort it out.'

It's hard to know exactly how I feel. Obviously I'm worried about the future, how much this course is going to cost and whether I have enough money saved up to last me while I take it, but the biggest concern I have, of course, is James. I have no idea how I'm going to break the news to him that I'll be leaving. It was fine when it was theoretical but now it feels like my timing couldn't be worse. He's only just got his life back on track and here I am throwing a spanner in the works. I'm not sure he'll forgive me if he has to get someone else to be his carer. This news could really mess our friendship up for good and yet . . . I can't help it, I feel excited about getting on the course, about securing my future, about being able to contribute to Leila's upkeep, and about making her proud of me too. It's the oddest feeling for me; I've often thought that the word taciturn came into being just to describe me and yet here I am driving along the motorway, feeling like I'm going to explode unless I tell someone about my good news right this very second. I mentally sort through a list of potentials, ranging from Leila through to my parents, but even as I discount them all, I know exactly who it is I want to speak to. Without giving myself time to change my mind, I dial the number.

'Kaz speaking.'

It is good to hear her voice. Since the night I nearly started drinking again, Kaz and I have been in touch quite a bit. What started as an occasional exchange of texts has over the past few weeks grown into regular chats on the phone. Thanks to those chats I've discovered we have more in common than our past addictions. In spite of all we've both been through, we share a similar sense of humour and I find her incredibly easy to talk to. Now a drug charity outreach worker, Kaz had also spent many years in the wilderness before figuring out her path in life and if anyone would appreciate the significance of my news, it was her.

'Kaz, it's me, Danny. Have you got a minute?'

'Sure, what's up?'

'Well, I'm sort of calling for two reasons. The first is to share with you what I hope you'll think is good news: I've been accepted on to a degree course in education and if everything goes well, I'll end up being a maths teacher.'

'That's fantastic,' says Kaz. 'I'm so pleased for you. We should go out and celebrate some time. It feels like forever since I've had some good news to let loose about.'

'Well, what about tonight?' I ask tentatively. I've been wanting to pose this question ever since the night of our first heart-to-heart. I'd felt a real connection with her but wasn't sure she felt the same. Maybe to her I was just the guy she helped that one time. Maybe she had a rule about the kinds of men she went out with.

'Tonight sounds great. In fact, why don't you let me take you out, my treat?'

We chat for a while longer about possible venues before one of her colleagues interrupts her. When she comes back on the line, it's to apologise for the fact that she's going to have to go.

Later, as I'm parking the car at the apartment, I get a text. 'Just wanted to apologise for having to rush off like that. Looking forward to tonight, K x.' I begin tapping out a reply but then my phone vibrates with another text. 'PS, If your second reason for calling was what I think it was then I'm sorry I pre-empted you but just for the record my answer would have been yes and what took you so long? ;-) See you tonight. Xxx.'

44

James

According to the timer on my phone, we have been waiting in line at passport control for nearly half an hour. Vicky, her parents and I are nearly at the front of the very long queue. There is only one family ahead of us, which means that soon we will be able to collect our luggage and then after that I will get to see Danny. I have not seen Danny for over ten days now, and that feels like a very long time. We did share a couple of texts at the beginning and end of the holiday. The first was from me saying that we had arrived at the hotel safely and the second was Danny letting me know that he was still okay to pick us up from the airport. I am very excited about seeing Danny because I want to tell him all about my holiday, but at the same time I am nervous too because I have some news I need to tell him. I am not sure how he will take it.

The man sitting at the checking desk has got grey hair and is very smiley. When our turn comes Vicky's mum hands all of our passports over to him.

'Been anywhere nice?'

'Capri,' says Vicky's mum. 'First time in Italy for me. It's so gorgeous.'

'You'd recommend it then?'

'In a heartbeat,' says Vicky's mum.

'And how about you, madam?' he asks, looking at Vicky. 'Did you enjoy your holiday?'

'It was the best holiday I've ever had,' she says.

'Well, that's saying something,' says the man. 'What was so special about it, if you don't mind me asking?'

'My boyfriend proposed to me,' she says proudly as she squeezes my hand. 'And I said yes.'

It is true.

I did propose to Vicky and she did say yes and I think that it might possibly have been the best moment of my life.

It happened about a week into the holiday. Vicky and I had gone for dinner on our own, without her parents, to a rooftop restaurant overlooking the sea. The food was very nice but it was the scenery that really made the evening special. The sun looked beautiful as it set and the sea so calm and lovely that I kept telling Vicky to look at it. In the end the waiter very kindly moved her place setting so that we could both face the same way and admire the view. After a while Vicky said to me, 'I don't think life gets any better than this,' and then I turned to her and said, 'I want to marry you.' At first Vicky thought that I was joking, and I was not at all sure what I thought because before I said the words, I had not planned to say them and so I had to think about them afterwards. And the more I thought about them, the more I realised that this really was what I wanted. I did love Vicky and I did want to be with her for the rest of my life.

'I am not joking,' I said eventually. 'I really would like to marry you, if you will have me.'

'Of course I'll have you,' she said, grinning. 'You're my favourite person in the whole world.'

To celebrate we ordered a bottle of champagne and that night when we got back to the hotel, we woke Vicky's parents up to tell them the good news. And they were happy for us. Not just pretend happy but properly happy, and they said that they could not wait to welcome me into their family. They ordered another bottle of champagne to celebrate but I only had a little bit of it because I was already quite tipsy.

For the rest of the holiday Vicky and I made plans for our future, when and where we were going to get married and things like that. It was fun and I felt excited about them, but every time I thought about Danny Allen I felt funny. I knew he would be happy for me, because that is just what Danny is like. But Danny and I had been through so much together and we had come so far, and I felt like I was being a bad friend for thinking about moving on without him. So while in one way I could not wait to tell him about Vicky and me, in another I was not looking forward to it at all.

The chatty, smiley man at border control congratulates Vicky and me on our engagement and he wishes us good luck for the future.

At the arrivals gate I spot Danny straight away, even though there are lots of people waiting. I give him a big wave and when he sees that it is me, he smiles and waves back.

'Good to have you home,' he says. 'You look well.'

'I feel well,' I say. 'That was the best holiday I have ever had.'

'We've got lots to tell you,' says Vicky, and she gives me a funny look because she knows that I am feeling nervous about telling Danny our news.

'Yes, we have,' I reply, 'but I think we ought to hear about what Danny has been up to first.'

'I doubt I've done anything anywhere near as interesting as you guys,' says Danny. 'It's been weird not having you around. The apartment seems much too big for one person.'

'It has been strange not having you around too,' I say. 'I am really glad to be back.'

We are going to drop off Vicky first and on the way I call my parents, just to let them know that I am home safely. They tell me they cannot wait to hear all about what Vicky and I have been up to. I do not tell them about our engagement because that is the sort of thing you do in person and anyway, I am not really worried about how they will take it, like I am with Danny. Even if they think I am making a mistake, it will not make any difference to me. I love Vicky and she is all I want, so I already know that I am making the right decision. I just hope that Danny can be happy like I am and that my good news does not have to be bad news for him.

When we reach Vicky's parents' house, Danny and I help them in with their luggage and afterwards they ask us if we would like a cup of tea. I tell them that we are fine, and so Danny says goodbye and goes back to the car while I say goodbye to Vicky on the doorstep.

'Do you think you're going to be okay telling Danny about us?' asks Vicky. 'I can come with you, if you like. Sort of moral support.'

'I think I will be fine on my own,' I say. 'It is just hard.'

Vicky nods. 'Danny's your friend and you want to do what's best for him. I know whatever you say to him will be the right thing. Danny will understand.'

I look at Vicky and wonder what I did to deserve having her in my life. 'If I had not already proposed to you,' I tell her, 'I would do it again right now.'

'And if I hadn't already said yes,' says Vicky, 'I'd say yes all over again.'

On the way home Danny tells me what he has been up to. Last week he introduced Leila to his mum and dad for the very first time.

'That must have been amazing,' I say.

'It was,' says Danny. 'They got on so well that they are even seeing each other again this week without me.'

'And did you give Leila all the presents you have bought for her over the years?'

Danny laughs. 'She said she thought it was weird and sweet and crazy all at the same time. I think she appreciated the sentiment though. I think she liked knowing that I'd been thinking about her all this time. But anyway, enough about me, tell me about your holiday.'

I tell Danny about the holiday, leaving out the part about where I proposed to Vicky. I tell him about how nice the view was from our room, that he would have really liked the breakfasts and how one day we did not go outside for the whole day because it was just too hot. I tell him about our trip to Pompeii where we saw all the people who looked like they had been frozen in lava. I tell him story after story, until I run out of stories and the only thing I have got left to tell him is about Vicky and me.

'Danny, I have got something I need to tell you.'

'Sounds serious. Is it?'

I think the question over. 'Yes,' I say, 'I think it might be.'

'Funnily enough,' says Danny, 'I've got something I need to tell you too.'

I think for a moment that it would be funny if we both had the same news. But then I remember that Danny has not got a girlfriend, let alone a girlfriend he wants to marry.

'Which one of us do you think should go first?' I ask.

'Let's toss for it,' says Danny. 'I call heads.'

I toss the coin but it is too difficult to catch and ends up on the floor.

'It is tails,' I say, picking up the coin. 'I win.'

Danny smiles. 'Then the choice is yours: first or second?'

I want to say second because I think that would be easier, but in the end I say first because I remember that I am not supposed to be scared of anything any more.

'Vicky and I are getting married,' I say. 'I asked her on holiday and she said yes.'

'That's fantastic!' says Danny. 'I'm really happy for you both.'

'Thank you,' I say. 'I was worried that you might think we were rushing things.'

'I think you're really good for each other,' says Danny, 'and no, I don't think you're rushing things. I think you're going at exactly the right speed for who you both are.'

'I am glad you think it is a good idea. I would still have done it if you thought it was a bad idea, but it feels better to know that you think it is a good one.'

'I do,' says Danny.

'Thanks,' I say, 'but it is also going to mean that things are going to change.'

'You don't need to say any more,' says Danny. 'Of course, I'll move out.'

'Are you sure? You will not have to go straight away it is just—'

'Actually,' says Danny. 'That's sort of what I wanted to talk to you about. The thing is, I've been accepted on a degree course in education – in a few years and with a bit of luck I might even end up being a teacher – and well . . . because it's full-time I wouldn't be able to be your carer any more. To be honest, even if I hadn't got on the course, I probably would've handed in my notice. You don't need me any more, James, in fact I don't think you've needed me for a long time now. I've seen you cook, clean and get yourself to where you need to be. You don't need a carer, I think you're pretty much ready to take on the world, so honestly I couldn't be more pleased to know that you're moving on. It's been a long time coming but I really think you've got there.'

'Really?'

'Yes,' says Danny. 'Really. This calls for a celebration. How about we drop in at the pub on the way home? Pint of lager for you, Coke for me and all the crisps we can eat?'

'That sounds perfect,' I say, resting back in my seat, and then I turn up the volume on the car stereo and fix my eyes on the road ahead, feeling tired but very happy.

One year later

Mr Daniel Allen's first teaching placement
Redhall Academy Trust School, Coventry
Year 9 'D' set Maths group
September 2016

'Morning, class. I'm Mr Allen, and I'll be teaching maths until the half-term break. You'll be pleased to know that my summer reading over the school holidays has been your end-of-term test results for the last few years, along with your most recent school reports. From these I gather that not only has this school written you off, but so too have the endless supply teachers you've endured over the years and also you yourselves. Your work is careless, mistake-ridden and messy, and illustrates not only your total lack of mathematical ability, but also your sheer indifference to your own futures. Well, I'm here to tell you, this stops now. I'm drawing a line under everything that's happened in the past, and from today we're starting afresh. From today you will care about maths, you will care about how you present your work, but most of all you will care about your future.

'I can see a lot of you rolling your eyes and wondering why things should be different this time. And for those of you with a Netflix account and a passion for old films, I guess you're wondering when I'm going to get you to stand on your desks and ask that you, "Seize the day". But I'm not here to make myself look good, or live out some fantasy of winning Britain's Top Maths Teacher. I'm here to show you that there is another way. That you don't have to be defined by your past mistakes or anybody else's, for that matter. You can choose, right here and now, a different path, one that ends with you feeling proud of what you've achieved and the difficulties you've overcome.

'Thanks to a wonderful teacher who saw something special in

me I had the privilege of attending a school that expected great things of all its pupils, but over time I came to learn that this only has the power to make a difference to your life if you too expect greatness from yourself. For a lot of us this is a new experience, one that can be at times both daunting and challenging. We may never have been required to expect anything of ourselves, or we may have made mistakes in our pasts that seemingly prove that we have nothing good to give. Let me tell you that I know for a fact that it doesn't have to be this way.

'The truth is that we all fail sometimes, we all do things or have things done to us that will throw us off course, but you always have a choice: give in or get up. From this moment, with my help, you are all going to get up and fight to be the best versions of yourselves you can be. I will expect great things of you, but they will be nothing compared to the greatness you will come to expect of yourselves.

'I'm not saying change will come quickly, or easily. I'm not saying that there won't be times when you will feel like giving up. But what I am saying is this: the small changes we make today sow the seeds of the greatness that is to come. We've all got to start somewhere and for you guys, that place is right here.'